LOCKER 32

By
Gregory Leonard Baltad

ACKNOWLEDGMENTS

I'm not sure why I sat down and began writing *Locker 32* and I really never expected to see it in print. On a whim I sent the manuscript to my friend Adam Bercovici, who himself is an author and was one hell of a cop. I was delighted when he phoned me and said, "This is great. Would you mind if I showed it to my agent?" I doubt you would be reading this were it not for him. Thanks, Adam.

Before going any further with this book I knew I needed the skills of a master of copy. Enter Mark Mullinax, who gave my manuscript a sound geeking. I still owe you that trip to watch the Cubs play the Dodgers, Mark.

Soon thereafter I found myself in cahoots with big-city editor and author Jane Cavolina. During the hours of phone calls and rewrites something remarkable occurred: we became friends. Her incredible skill and experience were only exceeded by her patient schooling of this author. Thanks, Buckaroo!

A big hug and back scratch goes to my long-suffering wife, Meg. The life of a cop's spouse is at best arduous and I really piled it on. Thanks for hanging in there, Meggie!

After months of being read and then reread, my creation was ready for fresh eyes and opinions. Greet my beta readers, who provided frank and much appreciated opinions. My gratitude goes to those who risked friendship to tell me the truth: former magazine editor and painter extraordinaire, Elaine Cuesta; fire chief and childhood buddy, Vince Williams; cop book connoisseur, Ester Williams; and English teacher and force of nature, Sandra Ludwig. My heartfelt appreciation goes to David J. Sensenig, Esquire, Officer Andrew Taylor, John, Paul, Chris, Gregory, Haley, Paulette, and my former agent Stu Miller.

Finally, I send my thanks to the Godfather of the modern police novel and former LAPD detective, Joseph Wambaugh. He kindled the flame within me that lit my path to a career in law enforcement and a passion for a good *police story*. Semper Cop Joe.

This book is dedicated to my "partner man" Paul Clements whose company I never tired of and advice I never took lightly. I love you Pablo.

PREMONITION

The old man's deformed fists seemed too large for his emaciated frame. Every few seconds his head jerked to the side, while drool that collected in the corners of his mouth ran to his chin. He looked at Brian O'Callahan and blinked his bright blue eyes. A moment of recognition caused the creases in his face to turn up into a smile.

"How'd ya do tonight, lad?" the old man asked.

Brian dabbed the spittle from the man's chin.

"We won, da."

Brian felt his father's time was approaching and wondered about life afterward. He was sure of one thing; he would not continue to make his living as a fighter. Their train stopped at the subway station and they exited the car. Brian slipped his arm under his father's and led him up to the street. Standing at the top of the stairs under a flickering streetlight was a large man dressed in blue. He nodded at Brian and smiled at the old man.

"How you doing, Mr. O'Callahan?" he quizzed.

Seamus O'Callahan looked at him vacantly.

"He's off and on these days, Paddy," Brian commented.

Officer Patrick Reilly glanced at the welt under the young man's eye then asked, "So you give any thought to what we talked about the other day?"

"Me a cop? I don't know."

"Better than having some mook bash your brains in," Officer Reilly replied.

He glanced at the old man standing listlessly next to Brian and regretted his words.

"Sorry, Brian. I just don't want to see you walking on your heels in ten years."

"I know, Paddy, and I appreciate it. I'll think about it." After a moment of silence Brian looked at the snowflakes that had just began settling on the officer's greatcoat.

"Well, I gotta get Da home."

Reilly watched as the two men made their way down Third Avenue; the old man shuffled unsteadily, while the young one padded alongside.

An hour later in the tiny apartment he and his father shared, Brian dozed in front of the television. The eleven o'clock news droned somewhere in his semiconscious. A commentator gave the lead-in to a story about a police officer's funeral. Brian's eyes opened. Video of the event filled the screen. Brian pushed down his recliner's footrest, leaned toward the television and turned up the volume. The camera panned a sea of blue uniforms then held on a flag draped coffin while the whine of bagpipes floated through the gathering. The image of a young woman dressed in black filled the screen then shifted to a wreath of flowers. Draped across the floral ring was a ribbon that read: "Daniel Lugo, EOW November 18, 1973."

VALLEY COP

North Hollywood, California, 1983

A Camel dangling from his lips, Officer Melvin Snyder pulled at the collar of his wool shirt and adjusted his necktie. With his other hand he guided the Plymouth through traffic. Reflections from headlights, streetlights, and storefronts flashed off the black-and-white as it rolled down Ventura Boulevard.

"Last night of probation kid...if you don't screw up, that is."

"I'll try not to," Brian said, looking out of the cruiser's passenger window. His eyes met with those of a tow-headed little boy who was trying to get a look inside the police car, which was alongside his mother's minivan. The young police officer's clean-shaven face broke into a grin. Celtic blood showed in his looks. Brian waved at the child, who beamed and held up a small pink hand. His well-groomed mother looked at her delighted son and smiled apprehensively at the police officer.

Brian turned back to his mentor and announced, "Did I tell you? I got my request. I'm on the transfer to Seventy-seventh Street."

"You requested to work Seventy-seventh Street? For crissake, kid, why? Same paycheck here as there, you know. What's wrong with the San Fernando Valley?" The veteran cop's words mixed with a steady stream of smoke that disappeared out of the police car window. "I thought I taught you better than that."

Brian could feel heat rising up his neck and spreading to his ears. A sheepish expression crept onto his face.

"I dunno, just do, I guess," he mumbled.

Snyder was not surprised. "This kid's gonna be a star," he recalled telling his sergeant. He was more than just a little bit proud of his probationer. "Just gotta be a big city gunfighter, huh?" he said.

Brian smiled inwardly.

Several weeks prior, knowing the time was rapidly approaching when he would be involuntarily transferred or "wheeled" to another

6

division, Brian had requested to be sent to LAPD's Seventy-seventh Street Division. He wasn't sure why. He knew "77th" held a distinctive place among Southern California's cops, due in part to the 1965 Los Angeles riots. There was a common belief among young cops that in order to be a real LA police officer you had to experience the notorious division. Perhaps that was it.

The light turned green and Snyder released the brake pedal as a silver Mercedes-Benz streaked through the intersection, narrowly missing the minivan in the lane next to them. Brian's moment of reflection was over.

"You're mine, asshole!" Snyder said.

He gripped the top of the steering wheel and spun it to the right while gassing the car. A slight squeal could be heard over the engine as the car whipped around the corner and accelerated toward a pair of taillights moving in and out of traffic ahead.

"This guy's flying," Snyder said above the roar of the engine.

He mashed the gas pedal to the floor and quickly closed with the violator's automobile. Brian sat up a little straighter in his seat and concentrated on the silver car, now encumbered by traffic. As soon as he could read them he scribbled the plate numbers onto the small pad of paper affixed to a metal stand between the seats, then he looked up and noted the street numbers. The cruiser's headlights illuminated the interior of the Benz, which was stopped in traffic directly in front of them. Two eyes watched the police car from the Mercedes' rearview mirror. Traffic opened up and the Mercedes slowly pulled ahead.

"Light him up."

Brian flipped the toggle switch on the center of the dash, and immediately red lights reflected off the glossy surface of the car ahead. The driver pulled to the curb without hesitation.

"15A85, show us on a traffic stop on a silver Mercedes, Laurel Canyon and Magnolia."

Brian dropped the microphone on the car seat as he opened the door and stepped to the curb just as the police car stopped. The Radio Transmission Operator or RTO repeated the information as Snyder exited his side of the car. Brian shined his flashlight into the interior of the Mercedes as he worked his way up the passenger side of the car. The driver looked straight ahead, his head slightly bobbing back and forth. Brian glanced at the plate-glass window of the business behind him. He was momentarily startled by his own reflection. He felt a drop of sweat run down the middle of his back under his ballistic vest. It was after 10:00 p.m. and still over ninety degrees in the San Fernando Valley. He flipped another droplet of sweat off his nose with his thumb.

Snyder approached the driver's side and tapped on the tinted window with his flashlight. As the window came down a familiar odor of booze and stale cigarette smoke seeped from the passenger compartment. Watery eyes looked up into Snyder's light.

"Good evening, officer. Was I speeding? I just, I'm going home now, I only live…" The driver's speech was a little thick and had a trace of a slur.

"Sir, may I see your driver's license and registration, please?" Snyder asked.

After some fumbling, the driver held his license out the window. Snyder looked at it, glanced over his shoulder, and checked traffic. Then he stepped back, and spoke the words no one wants to hear.

"Mr. Keen, I need you to step out of the car, please."

"Oh, alright," Mr. Keen said.

Keen squirmed out of the comfort of his tan leather bucket seat and stood. He gently bumped the doorpost, steadied himself with the roof of the car, then shuffled toward the sidewalk on expensive-looking loafers. The short, dumpy, middle-aged man made a haphazard attempt at tucking in his white dress shirt and straightening his necktie.

Snyder led Keen through a field sobriety test. He was unable to walk a straight line, or stand on one foot without losing his balance. After he failed to touch his nose with his eyes closed, Snyder had seen enough and nodded to his probationer. Brian stepped behind the intoxicated man and gently handcuffed him. He glanced at the bald spot on top of his arrestee's head. *Poor guy spray painted his head,* Brian thought as he placed the little man in the backseat of the police car.

"Sir, may I call my wife?" Keen's foul breath mixed with his expensive cologne and burnt tobacco.

It struck Brian as unusual to have an obviously successful businessman twice his age call him "sir." He thought of an admonition he received from his first training officer. *Remember, it's not you that people respect or hate. It's the uniform.*

Brian closed the door, walked around the car and slid onto the backseat opposite their arrestee. His partner dropped the cruiser into drive and headed to North Hollywood station.

By the time their prisoner was booked and the reports were finished it was past midnight and end of watch. Brian completed the evening's log and was walking toward the locker room when he passed Mel in the hall. Already changed into street clothes, Mel was no doubt hurrying to a local watering hole in hopes of beating last call.

"Night, kid, see you in a couple days," Mel said over his shoulder as he exited the station's back door.

"Good night, Mel," Brian said as he pushed open the locker room door. Several minutes later, while sitting in front of his locker polishing his boots, Brian pondered his partner's question. *You requested to work Seventy-seventh Street? For crissake, kid, why?*

Brian wondered. Was he trying to convince himself of his worth—or was he responding to a greater need, someone else's? With the question not yet resolved, Brian O'Callahan placed his boots in his locker and slammed the door shut. Unbeknownst to him, forty miles across town, the muzzle flash from a .357 Magnum pistol had just set a sequence of events into motion that would fall before Brian like a line of blood-splattered dominos.

SCOOBY'S TUNNEL

As Brian prepared for his drive home, twenty miles south of him in 77th Street Division a radio call was broadcast.

Any 77th unit. Shots fired in the area of 67th Street and Kansas Avenue. Any unit respond code-two.

Pistol Pete Rhodes and Speedboat Willie Washington were southbound on Vermont Avenue at Florence Avenue. Feeling his partner's hard blue eyes on him, Speedboat Willie flipped a quick left onto 67th Street.

"12A67, we're at scene, show us code-six in the area of 67 and Kansas," Pistol Pete said into the microphone. He clipped the microphone back onto the dashboard of the cruiser and studied his surroundings. "Slow down Willie, easy. Smell that?"

"Yeah, I do," Willie replied, licking his lips. Gun smoke hung in the air like in a public park on the Fourth of July.

Willie and Pistol Pete rolled down the shadowy residential street lined with circa-1940s bungalows. Most of the small wooden homes exhibited neglect, others abuse. It was common knowledge that the intersection of 67th and Kansas hosted street drug dealers and their customers at all times. Day and night, boys pumped bicycles up and down the streets, keeping an eye out for the police. The youths reported back to young men who stood glaring defiantly at the officers—at least those without reason to fear arrest did. The others moved furtively between the houses, glancing in the direction of the police cars, ready to break into a run at the sound of an opening car door.

Not this night, though. The streets appeared abandoned.

"Fuckin' ghost town, man," Pistol Pete said. "Whoops… Here we go… Stop!" He saw someone sitting on the curb.

Speedboat Willie reacted instantly. His spit-shined boot jammed the brake pedal and the Plymouth jerked to a stop. Pistol Pete braced himself with a hand on the dashboard as a collection of paper coffee cups rolled out from under the seat.

"Damn, Willie, you're a perfect example of why there aren't any black NASCAR drivers."

Willie grinned and said, "Yeah, well, you ain't no Junior Johnson yourself, man!"

With raised eyebrows, Pistol Pete glanced at his partner and best friend. Then he looked out the open window of the cruiser. "Let's see what this guy has to say."

Pistol Pete was looking into the face of a teenaged boy a few feet from the open window. The youngster was seated with his back to a fire hydrant. Sporting expensive basketball shoes, his feet were extended into the street in front of him. He was wearing an oversized white t-shirt and khaki pants. His hands were in his lap and held a clear coin bag containing several off-white objects.

"Hey man, you seen...?" Pete hesitated, then muttered "Shit" as he snatched the microphone and said, "12A67, I need an additional unit, a supervisor, and an ambulance to my location."

Willie leaned against the steering wheel to see the kid, then slipped the car into reverse and backed up about twenty-feet, putting the figure in the car's headlights. He adjusted the car's light switch so only the parking lights were on, then both men slid out of the car. Pete, his hand on his holstered pistol, slowly approached the youth, while Willie peered into the night for any movement. Pete directed the beam of his flashlight on the boy, then at the ground around the figure.

He stooped and took a closer look at the young man's face. Darrel "Scooby" Browne's mouth was slightly agape and his dead eyes stared ahead. Just below the edge of his hairnet and above his right eye was a black hole. The edges of the hole were dark red, and a gray swirl about the size of a quarter surrounded the tunnel into his brain.

"Nice shot," Pistol Pete said, then he keyed LAPD's newest technology advance, a handheld radio referred to as a "Rover."

"12A67, do we have an airship up?"

From Pete's radio came a voice shaking like someone being beaten on the chest. *Air Ten is in route with a one-minute ETA.*

There had been just enough urgency in Pistol Pete's voice to cause officers throughout the division to hesitate and listen to their radios. Those not engaged in capers of their own moved immediately in the direction of 67th and Kansas.

While Willie looked for witnesses, Pistol Pete made a closer examination of Scooby's wound. The bullet's relatively clean point of entry was in contrast to the gory mess where it exited, leaving the back of the boy's head looking like the projectile took a large portion of his skull with it.

"Big fucking gun," Pete mused.

WELCOME TO 77TH

B rian woke with the late morning sun in his eyes. His Murphy bed squeaked as he rose and pulled the yellowed shade down over the offending window. He had recently moved to downtown Los Angeles. He'd kept his move a secret as he figured that most police officers would not understand why a young and single cop would forgo an upscale apartment in the suburbs for a one-room merchant's apartment on Broadway above a line of dilapidated storefronts. But to Brian O'Callahan, the sounds of car horns and buses were the sounds of home.

After a cup of coffee, he telephoned the front desk at Seventy-seventh Street Station. An officer with a slow, casual drawl gave him straightforward directions to the station.

About twenty-five minutes later Brian stepped into the musty stairway and locked the door to his apartment behind him. The wooden risers squeaked and groaned under his weight. At the foot of the stairs Brian glanced at the old barber's pole to his left then let his hand trace along the cool stone façade of the building as he stepped onto the sidewalk.

After a short stroll down Broadway, he entered the lot where he had made parking arrangements and located his VW Bug. Twenty minutes later he bumped up a gateless driveway into Seventy-seventh Street Station's employee parking lot. It was surrounded by a rusty chain-link fence that held windblown trash in various levels of decay plastered along its bottom. The lots fractured asphalt was divided into parking spaces by filthy, chipped paint. He parked next to a decrepit pickup truck with a Marine Corps sticker in the window then dug into his pants pocket and retrieved his "999 key." Turning the item over in his hand he thought it curious that one key should open the back doors of every police station in the city. He pushed the key back into his pocket, clipped his identification card to his shirt, and climbed out of his Beetle. He slammed the door shut with a hollow "whump." Brian noted his oxidized red car fit in line with the rest of the wrecks in that section of the lot.

"Howdy!" a voice called from two parking spaces over.

A tall, athletic man unfolded himself out of a primer-gray El Camino with rusted chrome wheels. A coiled rope hung on the rifle rack in the rear window of his vehicle. The man shot a brown stream of tobacco juice onto the ground and wiped his mouth with the back of his hand then busily began collecting items from the seat, stuffing them into a green canvas bag with "Flying U Rodeo" embossed on the side. He stood up straight and shoved a blue-steel revolver with a huge barrel into the waistband of a well-worn pair of Wrangler jeans. He grabbed the gun's mahogany grips and wiggled it into a comfortable spot. The pistol held tight due to a buck-stitched belt and large ornate western buckle. The man pushed the wad of tobacco to the other side of his mouth, then squinted over the top of the El Camino at Brian. He grabbed his canvas bag with one hand and a pair of glossy black army boots with the other. Then he closed the truck door with a light kick. The cowboy waited at the tailgate of his truck, looking at Brian with a friendly expression on his face. As soon as Brian walked up to him the cowboy turned toward a two-story, red-brick structure that sported a line of small rectangular windows that ran the length of the first floor about seven feet from the ground.

Brian stopped and took in his new home away from home. Built in 1925, the station, like the surrounding community, had seen better days: he would come to learn that its appearance reflected perfectly the men and women who worked there; run down, neglected, and fiercely proud.

The two men walked side by side toward the building.

"Ya jes transfer in?" the cowboy cop asked.

"Uh huh," Brian answered, nodding his head.

They stopped at a scuffed and dented light-blue steel door. The cowboy looked at the door, then at Brian.

"Ah'm Quint King an' this here's the asshole of the beast. It's where all the turds come out." The corners of his drooping red moustache rose slightly.

Brian stepped forward. "I'm Brian. Here, I got it. Your hands are full." He pushed his 999 key into the lock, and after a little jiggling pulled the door open.

"Thanks, pard, that rascal's kinda tricky, ain't it?" Quint said. "Well, see ya around, Bri." He turned sideways to clear the door then turned to his right, took two steps and opened a heavy wooden door with a small wire mesh-window. Above the door was a sign that read: "Detectives." Quint King, cowboy cop, looked back at Brian, grinned, and then stepped through the door.

Brian found himself in the station's north corridor. To his right, the hall ended at the door that led to the detective's tables. To his left, the industrial green hallway ran about seventy-five feet east, terminating at the blue bars of a large jail cell door. Down the left side of the corridor was a long maple-colored wooden bench. Three handcuffed black men sat on the bench facing the wall.

Brian could see several police officers standing in the hall beyond the benches. As he walked toward them, he passed an opening in the interior wall about the size of a small garage door. Sitting at a desk facing the hall was a buxom, dark-skinned woman with brightly painted red lips. She paid the newcomer no mind and clicked away on her keyboard with three-inch red acrylic nails. Brian's eyes met those of an officer walking toward him holding a stack of teletype paper in one hand and a small paper cup of coffee in the other.

"Watch commander?" Brian asked.

Without slowing the cop glanced at Brian's ID card then lifted his chin to his left shoulder.

"Right down there."

"Thanks," Brian said and continued down the hall.

He came upon two holding cells, or tanks. Both had gray steel doors and large windows that allowed officers to see inside. The first was empty, with the door ajar. As he passed the second window, an enormous black woman lifted her shirt and pressed two of the largest breasts Brian had ever encountered against the glass.

"Hi baby, you want some a'this, white boy?" she cooed.

Her blue-black areolas and nipples stuck fast to the filthy window while two gigantic orbs of flesh rotated around them. A pair of officers looked into the cell as they squeezed past Brian.

"Real nice, Mom. I can't take you anywhere," the shorter of the two said.

They both chuckled and continued on their way. One of the men chained to the bench turned toward Brian.

"Yo, say, officer, can you find out when I'm getting booked? I been sittin' here fo' three hours."

The other two nodded in agreement.

"I'll check," Brian answered.

He continued down the corridor until he reached a group of officers standing outside the doorway of the cramped watch commander's office. Brian looked into the small room, took one step through the threshold, and then paused to look around. Across the room was an open door that led to another corridor. The room itself was cluttered with file cabinets and the walls were covered with charts, department publications, and bulletin boards. The sound of ringing telephones seemed constant. On his right, facing the center of the room, Sergeant Leonard Brooks sat at a large metal desk. Brooks held a telephone to his ear with a fist big as a canned ham; with the other he scribbled on a pad of paper. He wore a short-sleeved uniform shirt, and on each sleeve the insignia of a Sergeant II stretched around his arms.

"All right, thanks," Brooks said, then dropped the phone into its cradle.

He regarded the wooden box on the corner of his desk. A stack of papers rose above the confines of the box and spilled like a deck of cards across the plastic mat that covered the top of the scratched battleship gray desk. Across from him at a smaller wooden desk sat Sergeant Montgomery Price.

"Hey man, you wanna gimme a hand with some of these reports?" Brooks asked.

"Yes, sir." The nondescript little man in his mid-thirties jumped to his feet and scooped up the stack of papers from the basket.

"An' you don't hafta call me sir, we're both sergeants, man."

Brian looked at Sergeant Brooks and thought, *He looks like a sir to me.*

Brooks's large round muscles were attached to short arms and wide shoulders. Skin the color of coffee with two creams stretched across his shaved head. A gold-capped incisor shone every time he spoke or smiled. It seemed that Brooks did neither without cause.

Brian didn't know that Brooks was a police legend, a legend created the night he was working off duty at the Olympic

Auditorium downtown and told a ranked heavyweight fighter to "sit his ass down." The fighter took exception to being spoken to in such a manner and sheared off Brooks's front tooth with a punch. It's said that Brooks spat out pieces of his broken tooth then with one punch ended the fighter's promising career. Later that night at a police activity known as choir practice, Brooks and several other off-duty cops stood drinking beer around a fifty-gallon drum filled with burning wood. In a show of admiration and intoxication one of the coppers slung his arm over Brooks' thick neck and exclaimed: "Leonard, he's not a man. He's a fucking lion, King of the Beasts." The handle stuck.

Sergeant Brooks turned his eyes to Brian. "Whatcha got, young man?" he asked. Then he directed his attention back to the crime report on his desk.

Brian took three more steps into the room and stood ramrod straight in front of Brooks's desk.

"Good afternoon, sir. My name's Brian O'Callahan. I'm here to check in."

Brooks looked up. "You the kid from North Hollywood?"

"Yes, sir," Brian replied.

Brooks took a long look at the strapping young man standing in front of him. He eyed the thick, rounded shoulders, the bump on the bridge of Brian's nose, and his large raised knuckles.

"O'Callahan, you a fighter?"

Before he could answer, an authoritative voice growled, "With a name like O'Callahan I hope you're not a drunk."

A trim, gray-haired man with his arms folded across his chest leaned against the doorway opposite the one Brian had entered. He was wearing a suit and a captain's badge was clipped to his belt. Brooks and Price watched and waited for the new guy's response.

Brian's face broke into a wide smile. "No, sir," he answered.

Captain Kevin Sullivan looked Brian over. "We've heard good things about you, O'Callahan. Just don't step on your dick, lad." Captain Sullivan flashed a smile then disappeared into the south corridor.

Brian turned back to Brooks, feeling a little hot in the face.

Brooks said, "Charlie at the front desk is gonna set you up with a locker and stuff. No orientation this month, so just give him your days off request. Lieutenant's got you working a report car. You got any problem working a U boat?"

"Anything you want, sir," Brian said.

Brooks looked up at Brian. Seeing no sarcasm, he stood and held out his mitt of a hand. Brian pushed his forward until their hands met. The shake was firm and neither man went for advantage.

Brooks smiled. "You can call me Leo."

Montgomery Price's head snapped up. It seemed to him improper for a junior officer to address the watch commander in such a familiar manner. Perhaps what really bothered him was that Leonard Brooks had never told him to call him Leo.

From a third doorway located behind Price's desk a middle-aged officer poked his head into the room. Beyond the officer, Brian could see what he assumed to be the station's front desk.

"Watch commander, six-four," the desk officer drawled.

Then he looked at Brian and winked. A raised white scar ran the length of his jaw from his chin to his right ear. Brooks nodded and reached for the phone. With his other hand he pointed at Brian, then at the officer and back at Brian.

"Charlie Bender. Good ta meetcha. C'mon."

Being slightly bowlegged stole an inch or two from Charlie Bender's lean frame. He wore his hair in a style once called a Balboa, straight back with fenders on the sides and a small pompadour in the front. Charlie tossed a cigarette into his mouth, effortlessly caught it between his lips, flipped open a Marine Corps Zippo lighter, snapped it to life in one fluid motion, lit his smoke and then led his new charge down the north hall. One of the men on the bench looked up at Charlie as if to say something, then just hung his head. The woman in the tank rushed to the window, then stopped dead in her tracks.

"Hi, Charlie," she said in the same husky, cooing tone.

"Hello, darling," Charlie said with a smile.

They continued down the corridor and went out the way Brian had come in. They crossed a small area reserved for loading and unloading prisoners, and took a dozen steps to a small building that appeared temporary in nature. They went into a dank room packed with weightlifting equipment that adjoined a larger locker room filled with tall gray lockers lined against lime green, peeling and water-stained walls. Two additional rows of lockers stood back-to-back in the center of the room. Several filthy fluorescent tubes hummed above. On two walls, a row of grime-covered windows near the ceiling allowed only opaque light. It was a perfect accompaniment to the musty odor of damp wool and rodent piss that permeated the air. The concrete floor was the same level as the parking lot. Brian noted the watermarks on the bottom of the lockers.

A group of officers in various stages of dress were standing together in silence, watching Charlie and the new guy approach.

Charlie said, "Hey, fellers."

A chorus of greetings came from the group.

Then Charlie reached into his pocket and pulled out a small gray key. He paused and took a long look at Brian, then inspected the key in his palm. He slipped it into the keyhole of a locker in the middle of the outside row of lockers. He turned it, then lifted the chrome handle that released the door. It squeaked open.

The locker was empty except for a Polaroid taped to the inside of the door. Charlie opened it all the way and stepped back, allowing light to fall on the men depicted in the snapshot. Two smiling faces shined forth, one a thin, Latino man in his late twenties, the other a younger Charlie Bender. Brian was instantly drawn to the dark-eyed police officer standing next to Charlie. He liked the man's pleasant features and wondered if he'd met him somewhere. Then a wave of insecurity came over Brian. He thought, *They look like real cops. What am I doing here?*

"A buddy of mine works at the Academy gave me a call, said he'd been keeping tabs on y'all and that yer good to go. This here's my partner Danny's locker, or was his. Ain't been used fer ten years. Guess it's 'bout time."

Charlie Bender's eyes lingered on the image on the door.

"I'll take this old picture if you don't want it."

Charlie held his hand out. "USMC" was tattooed in fading blue block letters on the inside of his right wrist.

"No, please," Brian said. "I'd like to keep it, if you don't mind."

Charlie drew his hand back and studied the young police officer for several uncomfortable seconds. "Suit yerself. Got some maps and the like for y'all inside." Charlie closed the locker and handed the key to Brian.

Brian noticed the number plate at the top of the locker had been pried off. "Charlie, what's the locker number? There's no number."

Charlie turned and walked away.

"That's locker 32, bud," Pistol Pete Rhodes said.

Brian looked in the direction of the voice and saw several men trying to make sense of what they had just witnessed.

"He's been holding that key ever since his partner, Danny Lugo, was killed. Nobody had the balls to ask for it," Pistol Pete continued.

"Well, I don't know why he wanted me to have it."

"You know Charlie?" Pistol Pete asked.

"No, I just met him."

"That man there is a bona fide hero and a bad mutha fucker," Speedboat Willie chimed in.

Everyone nodded in agreement.

"Dude's got two Medals of Valor. One was for the rescuing a child from a fire, an' the other he won the night Danny got killed," Pistol Pete told him.

"He doesn't talk 'bout that one, though," Speedboat Willie added.

"I understand he was some kind of war hero in Vietnam too. He only says, 'Right place at the right time' if you ask him," a Hispanic officer joined in.

"Got that right, Manny," Speedboat Willie said.

"Some guys say that locker's kinda like, ah, haunted or sumpthin," rumbled a brutal-looking man with a dark six o'clock shadow.

"You're fuckin haunted, Butch," said a tall blond man just as large as the brute but not nearly as scary looking. "Come on, partner, let's get suited up."

"No, really, Lenny, Oco says Danny's spirit is still here. Says he's looking for sumpthin. Oco's a Indian, they know about that kinda shit, too," Butch Caldwell insisted.

"Yeah, it still makes my skin crawl if I'm sitting here alone next to that locker," the Hispanic officer said. "Sometimes I wish I had one of those upstairs lockers by the roll call room."

"Yeah, but you're not a supervisor or old-timer, Magana, so you can forget about one of those lockers, bud," Butch said.

Ignoring his partner's editorial on locker assignments, Lenny

Custer asked, "Brian, O'Callahan, right? Well, O'Callahan, let us know if you see any ghosts, will ya?"

At that the group broke up and went their ways. Brian opened the locker and took one last look at the photograph and at Charlie Bender's flawless jawline. He detected the slight fragrance of men's cologne as he gently closed the door.

On the drive home Brian could not get the photograph off his mind. The face of the officer with Charlie appeared every time he blinked. He wondered why Charlie had given him the locker. Perhaps the hero expected Brian to be an exceptional officer. He hoped not. Ever since he could remember, Brian feared letting down someone who trusted him.

NUTHER DAY IN THE HOOD

In a small white house several blocks southwest of the Seventy-seventh Street police station two brothers stood face to face.

"You ain't my daddy, man," Mo-Mo said.

Maurice Oswald "Mo-Mo" Jefferson stepped over his older brother's outstretched legs and walked toward the front door. Dee watched as Mo-Mo skulked out the door and slammed it behind him. A thin dark woman sat watching from her overstuffed vinyl chair. Her eyes followed Mo-Mo to the door, then met Dee's.

Norma-May Haynes stood, looked around the small room, then drew a deep breath, and exhaled forcefully. Her second son had recently been jumped into the local gang. The night it occurred Mo-Mo had come into the house badly beaten, drunk and defiant. His behavior had grown worse since.

"He's gonna die out there. One day the po-lice gonna knock on the door and I'll know."

Worry and poverty betrayed Norma-May's age. The single mother looked much older than her forty-four years. She shuffled across the room in her blue fluffy slippers, then bent and picked up a pair of white sweat socks from the floor. "Lord," she said under her breath.

Her oldest son, Dimetre Wallace, or Dee, as he had been known since kindergarten, didn't respond. He held a beer bottle to his lips, drained it, got up, took three steps, and was in the bungalow's tiny kitchen. Dee dropped the empty bottle into the trashcan next to a humming refrigerator plastered with aged children's drawings.

On the wall next to the appliance a calendar with a colorful photograph depicting a Halloween scene caught his attention.

Looking at the orange jack-o-lantern and black cat arched behind it he thought, "October already."

His eyes drifted to the fridge and focused on a black-and-white photo affixed to the door with a strip of yellowing tape. In the photo a young boy in boxing trunks beamed while holding his gloved hands above his head. A handsome Latino in his late twenties smiled at the camera, his arm draped over the boy's shoulders. Dee's gaze lingered for a moment longer then he moved to the sink, braced his hands on the white chipped surface, and locked his elbows. He rolled his muscular shoulders and worked his thick neck from side to side. Dee stopped and looked out the window over the sink at the hazy afternoon sky.

"Gonna be another smoggy day," he called out to his mother as he perused the backyard. Several slats were missing from the decrepit wooden fence that enclosed the neglected area. Dee remembered how as a boy he had eluded many a foe by running from his front yard, squirming through that hole, and racing down the alley. It seemed a lifetime ago. A single-car garage sat in the corner of the yard, its large door opening on the alley. Nothing of any value was kept in the structure any more. Dee pushed off from the sink and stood up straight. He made two fists, threw a quick flurry of punches into the air and then slid his hands into the pockets of his sweatpants.

"I'll clean up that backyard tomorrow, Momma," Dee said over his shoulder.

"Thank you, baby." A weak smile crossed the woman's face.

Mo-Mo had since lunged off the home's wooden stoop and hopped over the low chain-link fence that surrounded the front yard. On the short side for his eighteen years, Mo-Mo's squat body was well balanced and agile. He joined his best friend, Trevon "Tre" Williams, on the sidewalk.

Where Mo-Mo was thick and built like a gymnast, Tre was long-limbed and loose-jointed. If Tre ever stood erect he would have been a full head taller than Mo-Mo, but the seventeen-year-old gangster maintained a perpetual slouch, giving the appearance that the two boys were the same height.

"Sup, Mo," Tre said.

"Sup," came Mo-Mo's reply.

"Dee home?" Tre asked. "Saw his car."

"Yeah, nigger thinks he my daddy."

"Man, Dee, O.G., he know wassup, homes," Tre replied.

"Umm huh... but he ain't my mutha fuckin' daddy... always

tryin' to tell me to do this or that."

Both boys abruptly stopped talking and looked up as a black Buick Regal rounded the corner from Hoover Street at a snail's pace. It was a scene all too common in their South Central L.A. neighborhood. The boys' heartbeats quickened and their minds raced as they looked for an avenue of escape. The Buick's chrome wheels glinted as the lowered automobile cruised in their direction. Four heads could be seen through the smoky tint of the car's windows. Tre's right hand went under his baggy T-shirt.

"I think that's Baby-K's ride," Mo-Mo whispered.

As the vehicle rolled toward them, Mo-Mo squared himself to it and held his arms out from his sides. His fingers were contorted into symbols, which to other gang members indicated a specific gang affiliation. The gesture, known as throwing up a sign, was a challenge to an outsider and an acknowledgment to an ally. A teenaged mother raced from her porch to where her toddler sat on a tricycle. The woman grabbed the child by the wrist and dragged her to the relative safety of her house. Others on the street stopped whatever they were doing and watched intently as the scene unfolded in front of them.

Four hard, grim faces peered out of the Regal as it crept past the boys. A blue handkerchief hung from the rearview mirror. The front passenger lowered his window and gave a slight nod. He wore dark wrap-around sunglasses and a scowl on his face. The gangster's kinky black hair was done into rows of braids held together at his neckline with small blue plastic barrettes. Mo-Mo breathed a sigh of relief and Tre's hand emerged empty from under his T-shirt.

"They rollin' deep," Mo-Mo said.

"Yeah Baby-K, he Tootie's boy," Tre answered.

Mo-Mo slowly slid his fingers across Tre's outstretched hand. The car disappeared down the street while the friends in baggy pants slipped between two houses and into an alley.

In a few minutes' walk, the alley opened into a gravel and asphalt parking lot that was about the size of two tennis courts. It was situated between Hoover Street and a long, low, white stucco building. Painted across the face of the structure in blue lettering was "Hoover Street Gym, the Cradle of Champions." From the gym they heard the rhythmic pop of speed bags and the thump of fists against heavy bags. A man with a boxer's head stood beneath an ancient hooded light fixture in the doorway smoking a cigar. He smiled at the boys and waved.

"Hey, Boomer," Mo-Mo said.

Tre waved at the man, then asked Mo-Mo, "Dee train here now?"

Mo-Mo kicked at one of the weeds that pushed up through the cracked pavement and said, "Nah, he mostly down at Main Street Gym. His trainer keep his fighters there."

"He had any fights lately?" Tre asked.

Mo-Mo shrugged his shoulders then broke into an easy jog followed closely by Tre. Soon side-by-side they loped out of the parking lot to the sidewalk and turned south. In a few minutes the boys were outside a small grocery market on Hoover Street.

Kim's Market and Liquor Store was like many other neighborhood establishments that once provided for urban families across the country. Few such emporiums remained in the Los Angeles area except in crime-ridden neighborhoods, where major supermarket chains feared to locate.

The store was housed in a dirty white clapboard structure located on the corner of Hoover and 81st Streets. An old wooden screen door faced Hoover. The rickety door's ancient metal screen was so clogged with rust it barely let in light. Next to the door was the building's only window, a large plate glass affair that was obscured by poster-sized advertisements and iron bars. Beneath the window, a cracked sidewalk, daubed with dried wads of chewing gum, led to a littered gravel parking lot.

The dimly lighted structure was not much larger than a two-car garage. It had the odor of old wood, overripe fruit, and sour milk. Just inside the store a fan hung from the water-stained ceiling, its grimy wooden blades emitting a slight grating sound with each rotation. Directly to the right of the entrance an ancient cash register sat atop a glass display case. Behind the register hung a calendar with the photo of a beautiful Asian woman surrounded by fall foliage. A glass display case ran the length of the store to the back wall. Its dusty shelves were covered with hairnets, blue curlers, blue shoelaces, and blue handkerchiefs. The front of the case was plastered with posters of seductively clad women holding malt liquor bottles. Behind it were the tobacco products and a selection of spirits that ran from cheap rotgut to premium scotch and cognac.

Along the back wall were three refrigerated cooler cases stocked with a diverse assortment of beer, malt liquor, cheap wine and soft drinks. Two shelves were devoted to a limited collection of milk, margarine, cheese products, and lunchmeats.

In the center of the store perpendicular to the display case were two rows of freestanding, wooden shelves which created three aisles. They were stocked with sundry grocery and household items.

Tre pulled the screen door open with a squeak and the boys stepped into the store, allowing its spring to slam the door behind them. Mr. Kim looked up from the register and studied the boys. Next to him an elderly Asian woman was counting out candies laid on the counter by a small girl with mucus-encrusted eyes. The old woman pushed ten pieces of candy toward the little brown fingers waiting at the edge of the counter. The crone picked up the remaining five pieces and put them in her apron pocket. She limped to the register and, crowding the man out of the way, dropped a handful of change into the coin tray then eyed the two boys.

She pointed a wrinkled index finger at Tre. "No, you go! You go, you no pay! You bad boy!" she shouted.

Tre proclaimed his innocence at the top of his lungs while the woman yelled relentlessly at him. Meanwhile Mo-Mo walked to the back of the store, looked up at the convex mirror affixed to the ceiling in the corner of the market, then turned down the cooler aisle. The broad shouldered Korean man glanced at Mo-Mo but was distracted by the fuss being raised between his mother and Tre. The grocer fingered the leather grip of the K-Bar knife tucked into his rear waistband as he monitored the argument. After several minutes of mutual yelling, Tre abruptly shrugged and walked out of the store. Simultaneously Mo-Mo emerged from the cooler aisle and followed Tre out the door. As they crossed Hoover Mo-Mo handed Tre a 40-ounce bottle of malt liquor. While Tre unscrewed the top, Mo-Mo ripped the seal on the corn chip bag he had just retrieved from under his shirt. Mr. Kim pushed open the screen door and watched the boys cross the street. He considered giving chase then shook his round head and looked abruptly toward the sky. A distant buzz became a roar as a blue and white helicopter appeared above. With nose tipped down, the Jet Ranger cut diagonally over the neighborhood. As the roar faded back to a buzz, the sound of racing car engines and sirens grew closer. The grocer wiped his pale, sweaty face with his apron and disappeared into the market.

Tre took a long pull on the bottle as his eyes followed a caravan of black-and- white police cars as they bounced through the intersection at 76th Street and Hoover. Without comment, the pair walked down Hoover Street and passed a lot encircled by a ten-foot-high chain link fence topped by loops of razor wire. Within the compound, automobiles sat in various states of disassembly. Most had no wheels, and rested on the ground or on oil-soaked blocks of timber. A gravel driveway that smelled of petroleum and dirt led to the rear of the lot and a single-bay garage. Piles of used tires leaned against the structure.

In front of the garage a group of men were positioned around a card table. One of the group, an old man wearing a railroad engineer's hat, sat on a milk crate rubbing his gray whiskered chin while two middle-aged men in baseball caps shared a bench seat salvaged from one of the wrecks scattered about. The fourth man was seated in a folding chair, his gleaming shaved head as black as his unlaced work boots and an ample belly filled out his greasy overalls. The group's attention was focused on a line of small black tiles that lay on the table. Within reach of each man was a bottle or can wrapped in a brown paper bag. A gate stood open and was guarded by a 30-foot lumberjack holding a tire high above the street. Parked at the giant's feet was a faded teal blue 1965 Chevrolet tow truck. "Tom's Garage" was painted in red letters on the door.

"There go you boy Tom," said the old timer in the engineer's hat.

The overall clad man looked up and waved at the boys. Mo-Mo lifted his chin an inch in response.

Tom Jefferson watched the boys walk down the street, then stuck the stub of a cigar in the corner of his mouth. His bloodshot eyes studied the tiles in front of him, then he looked back up. All the men watched Tom closely as he sat chewing his cigar in thought. "That boy headin' for trouble," he rumbled.

JUICED

B rian O'Callahan waited patiently for day-watch roll call to begin. He preferred working at night but he had adapted quickly to the 7:00 AM to 3:45 pm shift. It was mid-October and as Brian began his second month at 77th he was beginning to feel comfortable. He didn't even mind that he had been assigned the desk or a report car for the entire first month or that he was working on Sunday.

Patrol roll call was held in a spacious high-ceilinged room directly over the watch commander's office and front lobby. Old-fashioned globe lights cast a yellow hue over the eight rows of wooden tables and benches that faced the front of the chamber.

The floorboards creaked under the weight of heavy boots as the watch wandered in. Seating was determined by seniority. The back row was reserved for the saltiest of dogs and worked forward to the pups. As they waited most sipped from paper cups of brackish coffee from the vending machine downstairs. Several sat with rag and brass polish in hand, rubbing their badges to a rich gloss. Brian settled in the third row and looked out the French doors to his left. His eyes took in a string of palm trees which lined the street below and disappeared into the hazy morning.

A commotion arose in the back of the room as a troop of sergeants entered through the double doors. The acting watch commander, Leo Brooks, led the parade. As assistant watch commander Sergeant Brooks performed the duties of Lieutenant Philo Wiener in his absence. A large wooden table overlooked the room. It stood on a raised platform that allowed the watch commander to look upon the uniformed gathering. Leo walked purposefully to the front of the room and took a seat at the table. His polished scalp reflected the overhead light as he scanned the worksheet in front of him. Without warning the Lion looked up, his amber eyes surveying the scene.

"Roll call!" he growled and silence fell over the room.

Patrol roll was conducted in two stages. Leo first called out a pair of officer's names, then after confirming they were present, he gave them their car assignment.

"Washington, Rhodes," he said.

"Here," came two voices in unison from the back row.

"12A67," Brooks said.

Brooks worked his way down the list of cars and officers without looking up.

Then at last, "Bender, O'Callahan," he said.

Brian felt a jolt of adrenaline. He was going out with Charlie Bender.

"Here, sir," he called.

A smile flashed across Leo's face, a glint of gold between his lips.

Brian's voice had carried across the room louder than intended and several heads turned to look at the new guy. A warm flush came over Brian's face.

He glanced in the direction of Charlie Bender. Charlie, the picture of confidence and cool, had the cuffs of his long-sleeved shirt unbuttoned and flipped back. He took a drag off his cigarette, returned Brian's glance with a wink, and shot a smoke ring across the room.

Brian's enthusiasm about working with Charlie Bender was well founded. Only that morning he heard two probationers saying, *I always wanted to work with him, but they let him pick and choose whoever he wants for a boot. If he doesn't want to work with anyone he just has the watch commander put him on the desk.*

With roll complete Leo opened a blue spiral notebook and read aloud. "Detectives are still looking for the black Buick Regal with tinted windows, used in that drive-by last week on the 'Avenues,' where the little boy got shot off his swing. Suspects are four male black gang member types. Weapon used was a possible Mac-10 or Uzi. Any information to Detective Davy Treats."

"How's the kid, Leo?" called a voice from the back row.

Leo glanced up at Speedboat Willie Washington, who was fluffing up his modest head of hair with an Afro pick.

"Says here he died this morning, Willie. After roll, go back and talk to Dapper Davy, see if you can get any more information on this for us."

Speedboat Willie nodded and pushed the hair pick into his back pocket. Leo flipped the notebook shut.

"Ok, that's it. Let's go relieve morning watch early, so they can get to church."

Chuckles filled the room.

Several rookies in the front row jumped to their feet and raced out of the room and down the stairs and lined up in front of the kit room window in the hall. The rest of the watch followed at a leisurely gait. The kit room was a small space that harbored the daily equipment necessities for the patrol officers. It was off limits to anyone but the officer assigned to it, who doled out radios and shotguns through the rectangular portal. A pasty-faced officer with a receding hairline and Clark Gable moustache pushed the portal shutters open and leaned out of the window. He reminded Brian of the guard at the gates of Oz.

This guard was kit room officer "Radio" Rick Thomas. When Radio Rick wasn't combing his curly, oiled hair back or smoking long brown cigarettes, he was performing all manner of tasks around the station. In truth, 77th would not have functioned without him. Aside from maintaining and issuing equipment, Radio Rick was the court liaison officer. This daunting task required that he ensure 77th officers received the hundreds of court summonses that flowed into the station each week. Most importantly, Radio Rick was a golfing pal of the court liaison officer at the downtown courthouse on Temple Street. That relationship had on many occasions saved the butts of officers who for one reason or another had failed to appear in court as ordered. Rick knew everyone and had the amazing ability to procure anything. He issued two "Rover" radios and a pump 12-gauge shotgun per car, as well as a fingerprint kit if asked for.

So equipped, the officers moved to the parking lot and called out their unit designations to morning watch officers who had worked the car they were now assigned. Coppers from both watches exchanged pertinent information and car keys. O'Callahan located the officers assigned 12A69 and made the transfer. After conducting a safety check on the shotgun, Brian loaded it and slid it into the horizontal rack along the edge of the front seat. He filled in the information boxes of his log and started the car. He checked the unit for damage and confirmed the emergency equipment was in good working order. Short bursts of sirens throughout the lot indicated others were doing the same. Then he leaned against the car and kept a lookout for Charlie Bender.

Brian saw his partner crossing the parking lot, a cigarette dangling from his mouth, a cup of coffee in one hand, and a shotgun over his shoulder.

"I got a shotgun already," Brian said.

"Good. That'n's yours an' this'n's mine," Bender said.

He quickly checked and loaded the shotgun, then affixed a tooled leather pouch to the butt of the gun. After wedging the gun between the door and the driver's seat, Charlie flipped his cigarette onto the ground and settled behind the wheel.

"We ready, partner? Let's get ta goin'."

O'Callahan nodded and said into the mike, "12A69 days is clear."

12A69 days clear, good morning. Hi, Charlie, replied a pleasant female voice.

Charlie grinned at Brian and raised his eyebrows up and down. He downed his coffee, threw the empty cup over his shoulder into the backseat, and slipped the cruiser into drive. 12A69 slowly pulled onto the street.

"We're gonna find this ride. Looks like it was some of our local fellers. Me 'n' you gonna tree 'em if we kin."

Charlie removed a folded piece of paper from his breast pocket and handed it to Brian. On it was a detailed description of the murder vehicle and suspects that Leo had discussed in roll call.

Throughout the watch, when not responding to a long list of radio calls, Bender and O'Callahan prowled the alleys and streets looking for the black Buick Regal.

Any 77th Street unit to handle, a 311, man in traffic, possible narcotics suspect, Manchester Boulevard and Vermont Avenue... code-two.

"Buy that call. A naked drug fiend can only mean one thing round here, Brian...PCP."

Brian reached for the microphone as Charlie flipped his cigarette out the window, gunned the engine, and headed up Vermont toward Manchester.

An authoritative male voice came over the radio. *Units*

responding to Manchester and Vermont, your call is now an assault with a deadly weapon in progress. Any unit to handle code-three.

With the call upgraded to an ADW, Brian's body prepared for conflict. His stomach turned over and he felt an ache in the small of his back. Charlie activated the lights and siren and pushed the car a little harder.

Ahead Brian could see traffic backed up, and pedestrians milling around in the street. The police car made a hard stop. Brian grabbed the mike and reported them at scene, or code-six. He jumped out of the car and jogged to Charlie's side.

An enormous man stood in the center of the street. He was glassy-eyed and bathed in sweat. His dark brown face glistened with beads of oily perspiration; he stared straight ahead, a vacant expression on his face. Such behavior in itself warranted a police response. Several other facts struck Brian as significant; the man was holding a baseball bat over his head in a two-handed grip, half a dozen cars with smashed windshields and windows sat abandoned in the intersection, and the giant was stark naked. A semicircle of officers stood talking quietly to the man.

Donte "T-Bone" Boucher was a graduate of Manual Arts High School, and he had once been a major NFL prospect at the University of Southern California. Unfortunately, he never finished his college career. One evening during his senior year, after smoking a cigarette dipped in phencyclidine, T-Bone disrobed and took a stroll down Fraternity Row. The sight of a naked colossus turning cars on their sides and knocking down "No Parking" signs with forearm rips was great entertainment for many fraternity brothers. But the USC campus police took a dim view of it. T-Bone put two campus cops and three Los Angeles police officers in the hospital before Butch Caldwell rendered him unconscious with a bar-arm chokehold. Things went downhill for T-Bone after that. His days were now spent looking for his next high. The hapless behemoth was a common sight in holding cells and alleys around town.

In slow motion, T-Bone lowered the bat and walked to a late-model white Cadillac parked at the curb. He stood in front of the car, slowly raised the bat above his head, and brought the barrel down on the hood ornament.

The force of the impact sent pieces of metal and plastic flying.

He raised the bat and smashed it down on the hood of the car again and again, increasing the speed of his strokes, chopping away at the car like Paul Bunyan gone berserk. Officers surrounded him but provided a wide berth. Several cops held guns, should T-Bone select a flesh-and-bone target.

Amid the noise of smashing metal, sirens, radios, and the police helicopter hovering overhead, Officer Charlie Bender studied the scene. Brian stood next to Charlie and marveled at the destruction being played out in the middle of the street. T-Bone showed none of the rage one would expect from a person driven to violence but reminded Brian of zombies portrayed in "B" movies. Only T-Bone was real, and something had to be done.

PCP users were often referred to as "Sherm-heads" after the brown Sherman cigarettes they dipped into liquid PCP and smoked. Tales of Sherm-heads "going off" were common fare among police officers. Brian had heard the stories. It seemed everyone had tales of suspects with the superhuman strength and inability to feel pain demonstrated by those who'd ingested the animal tranquilizer. Just the day before, Lenny Custer had entertained Brian and half a dozen others in the locker room with an account of a radio call he and Butch Caldwell had recently responded to. Lenny, a gifted storyteller, stood like a librarian reading to a group of first graders. The cops were mesmerized.

"So we knock on the door and no one answers. We peek into the kitchen window and see this naked guy sitting in a pool of blood on the tile floor. His back was to us so we went in the front door and snuck up on him. There was a butcher knife on the floor next to him, and I cover the guy while Butch kicks the knife away. Then I look at my partner's face. He's as white as an Englishman's ass and standing there with his mouth hanging open."

"Shit, Butch's mouth is always open," Scooter Kellerman chimed in.

Butch shot Scooter a Neanderthal glare. The smirk on the smaller officer's face vanished.

"Fuck you, you little weenie," Butch snarled.

"Hey, you guys! I'm telling a story here…you wanna hear it or not?" Lenny asked.

The group fell silent.

"So Butch looks at me and says, 'This guy's eating his dick!' I step around in front of the guy and his face is all smeared in blood and he's staring straight ahead with that Sherm-head look on his face and he's chewing away on something. I look down and his crotch is just a mass of oozing blood where his Johnson Bar should be. I look closer at his face and here's the guy's helmet is hanging out of his mouth."

"Oh fuck me. What'd you guys do?" moaned Scooter.

Six contorted faces waited for his answer.

"Me 'n' Butch can handle ourselves but we sure as hell weren't gonna try and wrestle some guy that just ate his dick. We called an RA and waited till he bled out and tipped over. Then we cuffed him an' helped load him on the paramedic's gurney. You might say the brother was 'Bad to the Bone!'"

"Oh no, I can't hear this shit," said Speedboat Willie as he stood up.

Often officers try to top war stories with ones of their own. No one tried to top Lenny's. The fun over, everyone went about their business. Brian sat alone in front of his open locker, dumfounded and wondering what he would have done.

Back in the present the question was no longer rhetorical. Brian couldn't imagine how T-Bone could be subdued without injury to all involved.

Speedboat Willie Washington and Pistol Pete had just arrived on scene. After taking in the scene Speedboat walked over to Bender. "What ya think, Charlie, ol' Bone is really juiced?"

The two veterans were formulating a plan when Charlie turned to his youthful partner.

"You play any football?"

"No, I boxed," Brian said, a bit perplexed by the question.

"That'll do. Okay, I'm gonna get this feller's attention. Brian, you get behind him. When I give the sign, you run at Bone as fast as you kin, hit him at the waist, and wrap your arms around him."

"Then what?" Brian asked.

"Hell, then you hold on for dear life, partner!"

Charlie pointed at Brian's gun belt.

"Throw your Sam Browne in the trunk. We got enough guns out here. I don't want this feller getting yours."

Brian ran to the car and removed his pistol and equipment belt and laid it in the trunk of his police car. He returned to find his partner briefing several officers on his plan. Brian took in how calm and assured Charlie was. He was a picture of control and confidence.

Charlie looked at Brian. "Partner, after you get 'im on the ground, roll onto your back if you kin. Don't worry 'bout the bat, it ain't more'n a stub now... let's go."

The group of officers, now formed into an arrest team, fanned out around the maniacal titan. Wood and paint chips stuck to his moist chest and shoulders as he stood holding what was left of his bat. The club had been battered down to little more than a handle about six inches long. T-Bone stood next to the battered car as rivulets of sweat ran down his naked torso. He was panting and making deep guttural noises. Charlie walked directly in front of T-Bone and stood about ten feet away with his wooden straight stick in his hand. In his other hand he held a silver metal whistle. Brian concentrated on the small of T-Bone's back. Brian told himself, *Drive through him, wrap him up.*

"Hey!" Charlie shouted, then gave a long blast on his whistle. Two intense eyes locked with his. Charlie nodded his head. Brian's mind focused on the task. He closed the fifteen feet between himself and his target, accelerating as his left shoulder drove into the small of the man's back. He continued to pump his legs. The impact lifted the suspect from the ground as his head snapped back with an audible crack. Brian reached around T-Bone and pinned his arms to his sides. He kept his feet moving until T-Bone was driven face first onto the pavement. In one fluid movement Brian twisted his torso, flipped himself onto his back, and pulled the crazed behemoth over. The chemical smell of ether, mixed with a musky odor of perspiration, filled Brian's head. He could feel T-Bone trying to move his arms. Brian's grasp was slipping. The crunch of boots on asphalt and the jingling of keys were followed by the breath being crushed out of Brian. As soon as Brian knocked T-Bone to the ground six police officers charged in and jumped on top of the two men. The "dog pile" held the suspect in place while others tied his legs together at the ankles. With two officers on each arm, T-Bone's ridged hands were wrenched behind him and he was cuffed. The sound of the handcuffs ratcheting shut on T-Bone's wrists resulted in immense relief for Brian. Brian gulped a breath of air when Speed Boat Willie and Pistol Pete pulled T-Bone off him. Like a pair of ranch hands securing a calf for branding, they looped a nylon cord around the suspect's ankles and clipped it to the chain of the handcuffs. To an onlooker the whole affair must have seemed like a scene out of *Gulliver's Travels.* With his hands and feet pulled to his wet and gravel-coated buttocks, the prize was hoisted and carried to a nearby police car.

Nervous laughter filled the air as the cops dusted off their uniforms and rearranged their gun belts. Someone broadcast the all clear, known as a code-four, and normalcy was restored. Reports were taken, witnesses and victims interviewed. Brian stood at the open trunk of his police car snapping the straps that held his Sam Browne to his under belt. Several officers smiled at him as they passed.

Speedboat Willie Washington walked by with a big gap-toothed grin. He pointed at Brian. "Alright, man."

Charlie approached Brian, popped a cigarette into his mouth and fired it up with his Zippo. After taking a deep drag he let the smoke trickle out of his mouth as he studied the young officer standing next to him. "Y'all okay?"

"Yeah, I'm good, Charlie.

"Y'all done good kid. Willie and Pete are gonna take this arrest," Charlie said. "Hell, by the time they finish the reports ol' T-Bone will have received a diazepam shot at the hospital and be restin' comfortably, wondering what the heck happened."

"What's diazepam?" Brian asked.

"Medicine they give Sherm-heads. It brings 'em down… you know, back ta normal. Heck, when they come out of it they don't remember anything.

The partners climbed into their car. Charlie drove a few blocks and then parked at the feet of the 30-foot Lumberjack who towered over "Tom's Garage."

"Don't clear us jus' yet, Bri. I'll be right back. I gotta talk to a feller."

Charlie got out of the car and adjusted his Sam Browne as he walked toward a group of men sitting around a card table playing dominos.

"Hey fellers, y'all seen Tom?"

Four sets of eyes studied the officer.

"He yonder up into the garage there," said the toothless old man in the engineer's hat.

"Preciate ya," said Charlie.

He turned toward a gray cinderblock building with two large wooden doors propped open. A Motown tune played from a dusty radio hanging on a nail above an oil-coated desk. A coat hanger was inserted where the antenna once was. Charlie took in the odors of the enclosure, exhaust fumes mixed with the dusty smell of oily rags, and stepped into the shop. Several grimy fluorescent lights hung on chains from the rafters, emitting a low hum. Charlie noticed a pair of large legs protruding from under an old Chevrolet Impala. They were clothed in oily coveralls with patched knees. A worn out pair of unlaced army boots with the sides blown out covered a pair of huge feet.

"Dang, Tom! I do believe that's the same radio y'all had in Vietnam. Matter of fact, them boots look a might familiar, too."

The wheels of his creeper squeaked as Tom Jefferson rolled out from under the car. He wiped a wrench with a filthy rag as he measured the police officer standing over him. Charlie held his hand out. Tom rubbed the palm of his hand on his soiled coveralls, took Charlie's hand, and pulled himself to his feet.

"Well, I'll tell y'all sompin' Mr. Po-lice…a po' man gots po' ways, and dat dere's a fact."

"Poor my granny's night-cap. Y'all got the first dollar y'all ever earned and don't give me that 'please masah don't beat po ol' Tom,' crap either."

"Oh, think so, do ya?" Tom said with an uproar.

"Well, least ways y'all would if ya hadn't run around the neighborhood makin' babies when y'all got back to the world."

"Now thas a damn lie an' you know it, Charlie! I got me a daughter with my wife and then my boy Maurice, that's all."

The two men studied one another for a moment, then embraced.

"How y'all doin, Tom?"

"It's cool, my brother. I got no cause to complain. Wassup with you, man?"

In lieu of answering Charlie smiled, shook out a cigarette, and pulled it from the pack with his teeth. He shook out another and offered it to Tom, who gingerly pulled the offering from the pack with cracked and greasy fingertips.

"I'm looking for a ride…a black Regal."

Tom looked over his shoulder toward the men sitting around the card table and took a step deeper into the garage. He looked inquisitively at Charlie.

"Buncha gangsters did a drive-by up on Second Avenue the other day. Missed their target an' kilt a little chap on a swing. Car was described as a clean black Buick Regal with tinted windows and chrome wheels. I hate to ask, but…"

"Hey, man, I understand," Tom said in his quiet baritone. "Killed a little boy… thass a damn shame. I'll see what I kin find out, man. When you comin' by and play some dominoes so I kin take some of that money yo' pockets is filled with?"

"Man, I know better then to play tiles with a scandalous ol' cheat like y'all."

"You must be thinking o' some other fool, man. I know you ain't talking bout me."

They looked into one another's faces as they held a hand shake. Then Charlie released Tom's grasp and started toward his police car. He then stopped and faced the men sitting around the card table.

"Watch yerself now, fellers. Ol' Tom's as crooked as a dog's hind leg."

"Man, get yo' ass outta here, man. I'm fittin to put the dog on ya!" Tom yelled. His lips stretched and rolled up into a gambler's smile.

WORKIN' KILLINGS

In April, 1973 Detective Davy Treats was assigned to Robbery Homicide Division. Those working RHD handled crimes of significant public interest or consequence and were considered a cut above the average investigator. Among them Dapper Davy was a star, so it came as no surprise when he was assigned the murder of Officer Danny Lugo.

It was believed by most that Danny Lugo had been shot and killed by one of the three assailants who robbed Kim's Liquor Store but Davy wasn't convinced. There was no eyewitness to the actual head shot he took from his own gun, so Detective Davy Treats placed the Lugo investigation between the others he was assigned. For two years he worked tirelessly on the case until there was nothing else to be done. Even still he dug. He re-interviewed witnesses and spent long hours poring over every piece of evidence. On a rainy day in April 1975, his captain called him into his office, reminded him that the Lugo case was considered closed and directed him to focus on other assignments. Davy acknowledged his boss, pulled on his raincoat, popped a piece of chewing gum in his mouth, and walked downstairs. A memorial for LAPD officers killed in the line of duty loomed thirty feet outside the front doors of the Police Administrative Building. Davy exited PAB and walked to the edge of the square reflection pool. Four black stone obelisks rose from the water and affixed to the pool's four walls were slabs of polished black stone that were engraved with the names of every Los Angeles police officer killed in the line of duty. Davy knew many of the names; some had been friends and partners. After several moments Davy looked down at the wet stone and immediately found Danny Lugo's name. Tears and rain mixed as they ran down his face.

Davy didn't know how long it had been before his partner, Mark "Pig Pen" Morris, walked up to him and without a word led Davy out of the downpour and through the double glass doors of the headquarters building. Davy sloshed through the lobby and down the hall to Personnel Division. There Davy Treats stood dripping onto the linoleum floor as he completed a transfer request to 77th Street Homicide. He never provided a reason, but 77th's Captain Sullivan was delighted to have the highly regarded detective on board.

Eight years later, while Brian O'Callahan was wrestling his first Shermhead, Dapper Davy Treats was working on the drive-by shooting in which five-year old Toby Perkins had been shot in his front yard. Killings were on the increase, fueled by the advent of the profitable and addictive "rock "cocaine. In 77th, violent death was approaching epidemic proportions. Despite the gravity of the investigation Davy found it difficult to concentrate on it. Reaching across his desk he picked up a one-page report and two manila coin envelopes and walked to his partner's desk.

"Preach, take a look at this," Dapper Davy said, and dropped the piece of paper onto Leon "Preacher" Pruitt's desk.

Pruitt slid the paper forward so it no longer obscured the image of Jesus pressed under the clear blotter on his desk. He studied the document for a long moment then looked up at his partner. In response, Dapper Davy emptied the envelope's contents onto Preacher Pruitt's desktop. Pruitt pushed the two deformed pieces of lead and copper around on his desk with the tip of his pencil, then looked back at the report, then to the items on his desk. Davy touched one with his fingertip.

"This one came out of Scooby."

"My Lord," Preacher Pruitt said in his rich, soft voice.

"You guys have anything new on the Perkins case?"

Both men's heads snapped up from the desk into the beefy face of Nick Stupin. He stood with his hands on what would have been his hips, if he'd had any.

"Well?" he said.

"What's the matter, Nick, the media beating down your door?" Dapper Davy said, then straightened his black and blue silk tie. He knew darn well that the media had no interest in anything that happened in South Central Los Angeles, including the murder of a five-year-old child.

"Sorry, the old man's after me on this one," Nick said.

Pruitt dropped the items from his desk into their respective envelopes, set them in the top drawer of his desk and closed it. "We went to the autopsy on Friday. Got a couple things we need to follow up on today," he said.

"I'd like to find that car," Davy added. "Got a call from dope; they said the white chunks we recovered in the yard were that high-powered cocaine. Called it Freebase or something like that."

"Same stuff that kid Scooby at 67th and Kansas had, huh?" Nick said.

"Yep, starting to pop up all over," Pruitt said.

Nick started to walk away, then turned. "So what's in the envelopes?"

"Just a thing we're working on. Nothing important, Dick Tracy," Davy said.

Nick pointed a chubby middle finger at Treats and walked away muttering. Dapper Davy shot Preacher Pruitt a triumphant smile.

Pruitt opened the drawer, retrieved the two envelopes, and handed them to his partner.

"We need to find that shooter," Dapper Davy said. "I knew his gun would show up eventually."

Davy unwrapped a stick of gum, folded it and placed it in his mouth. He began chewing vigorously. He did his best thinking in this manner, and Preacher Pruitt left him to his thoughts. Then Davy looked at his watch, picked up the phone and dialed the inside line to the watch commander.

"Leo, this is the dapper one…ha, ha, yes, I am a beautiful man. Hey listen, are the foot beats working today? I need to talk with King. He working? Can you get him in here? Yes, now, this is big city police work, mister. Leo, you kiss your children with that potty mouth? Ha, ha, Okay, thanks pal, bye."

Dapper Davy placed the phone in its cradle. He worked his gum slowly while reflecting on the gloomy accommodations designated for 77th Street's homicide squad. Twelve homicide detectives worked in the cramped corner, which was walled off from the rest of the station. Archaic oak desks shared the workspace with gray metal institutional looking worktables. A similar group of wood and metal bookshelves were arranged along the red brick walls.

An interior wall separated the homicide squad room from the rest of the investigative personnel assigned to 77th Street. Known as the "tables," the cavernous open detective squad room occupied nearly a quarter of the ground floor of the station was generally loud and cluttered. Uniformed officers mingled among the detectives and used desks not being utilized to complete their arrest reports. The chaotic, community atmosphere that prevailed did not exist in the homicide squad room adjacent to it. The mood on the homicide side of the wall was serious. Homicide detectives kept their room neat as a pin and all investigations were locked up in file cabinets at the end of the workday. The office door that led to the rest of the station was kept locked when the homicide bay was not occupied.

"What a dump," Dapper Dan said, picking a piece of lint from his slacks.

Preacher Pruitt looked up, grunted, and then went back to work.

Twenty minutes later a tall officer with a big red moustache sauntered into the homicide squad room. He had a pleasant look on his face and a loose-jointed way of moving.

"Howdy, Davy, what's cookin'?" Quint King asked. "Leo says you needed ta see me."

Quint sat down in the chair in front of Davy's desk, kicked his long legs out, crossed them at the ankles, and laced his fingers behind his head.

"Hi, Quint. Yeah, you know about that shooting a couple months ago at six- seven and Kansas?"

Quint nodded, "Yup. Scooby got it right between the runnin' lights, ah heard."

"You heard anything about it on your beat?" Davy asked.

Quint had worked the foot beat at Vermont and Slauson Avenues for three years and before that worked divisional gangs when they were known as 77th CRASH, an acronym for Community Resources Against Street Hoodlums. Davy knew that Quint King could get the inside line on just about anything on the street. Quint smoothed out his moustache.

"Not much. Heard it was a dope thang. Scooby was a Hoover Crip. Figure he was selling rock cocaine, same stuff that comedian was makin' when he set himself on fire. Jammed a guy last week with a big chunk of it. He threw it down and my partner picked it up and asked what it was. Guy says, 'It's not mine.' Well, we knew sure as shootin' it was sumpthin. Showed it to some dope cops, who said it was rock cocaine. Looked like a chunk of wax to me.

"Yeah, we're seeing it, too. Stuff's supposed to be more addictive than heroin," Davy said. "Listen, Quint, I sure would appreciate it if you could shake the bushes for me and see what you can find out on this."

"You bet, Davy. Got anything ya can share that might hep?" Quint said.

"Not a lot. We're looking for a .38- or .357- mag revolver, might be a Colt Python."

Quint whistled between his teeth and studied Davy's face.

"Nice gat. If ah find it can ah keep it?"

"No, but I'll buy you and your wife dinner at the Room at the Top if you do."

Quint gathered himself and stood. "Nah, ah'll take some beer n' barbeque, though. Hot, spicy, sweet and salty, jus like my ladies. Ah'll get on it, Davy."

Quint King turned and walked toward the door. Davy watched him move away and chuckled.

"That cowboy's even a little bowlegged," he said to Preacher as Quint left the room.

SITTIN' ON A POSSIBLE

The same day Dapper Davy showed the bullets to Preacher Pruitt, Brian sat in a police car with his fingertips pressed against his temples making little circles. It was hot for October and the afternoon sun was shining in his face. He had not been sleeping well, and had a headache. As a boy he had been plagued by bad dreams, and they had recently returned, worse than ever. At least he had been working with Charlie Bender for the past week.

Charlie glanced toward Brian from the telephone booth, then hung up and jogged to the police car and climbed behind the wheel.

"We're in business, partner. Jes talked with an ol' Marine Corps buddy o' mine. Says that black Buick s'poseta be parked in a garage between 81st and 82nd Street jes off Figueroa."

Charlie threw the car into gear and sped off with tires squealing. He braked hard and made a slow turn into an alley. Old tires, couches, trash, and the skeletons of several dried up Christmas trees made navigating the dirt strip a challenge. About a hundred yards in Charlie rolled to a stop. The alley was lined with dilapidated single car garages that sat behind the similarly run down houses that faced the street on either side.

"It's supposed to be on the left hand side, in one of these garages. Put us code-six and grab the tube."

Brian grabbed the mike and said, "A69, show us code-six in the alley south of the eight hundred block of west Eighty-first Street."

The RTO repeated then acknowledged Brian's location as he unlocked the shotgun and slid it from the rack.

The alley was just wide enough to open the car doors and get out. As the two officers worked their way down the overgrown corridor, they peeked between the cracked slats and missing boards of the old wooden garages that lined the way.

"Charlie," Brian whispered.

He pointed to what looked like a pair of barn doors. They were secured with a shank of rusted chain that ran through holes cut in each door and a shining pad lock. In a gap between them, the glint of chrome shone in the sunlight that poured through an opening in the structure's rusted metal roof. Charlie took a quick peek, looked around the alley, and signaled Brian to follow him. They crept around the garage and looked through a broken windowpane. A glossy black Buick Regal was clearly visible inside. The two hustled back to the police car and quietly drove back to Figueroa.

"12A69, can you have two available 77th units meet me at Eighty-first Street and Figueroa?" Charlie broadcast.

Within two minutes Speedboat Willie Washington and Pistol Pete Rhodes were there. Several seconds later, Quint King and his partner, Scooter Kellerman, arrived from the station.

Charlie briefed the group on the situation and laid out his plan. "I figure we can sit on the car and see if anyone shows up. If not, in a couple hours pm watch comes down an' we kin hand it off to them."

He spit on his fingertip and using it as his writing utensil, drew a map of the area on the hood of a dusty police car showing each team of officers where to wait. Brian watched the group studying the map. He was reminded of a bunch of kids back drawing out a football play in the dirt with a stick.

"Think we should call a supervisor, Charlie?" Quint asked.

"Who's workin' today?" asked Charlie.

"Just Price," Quint answered.

"Oh, that guy's a slap dick, man, he'll screw this up for sure," said Scooter Kellerman. To punctuate his assessment, he pushed a long stream of tobacco juice out of his mouth between pursed lips.

"Yeah, okay, tell you what, les jes sit on this ride fer a bit, then we'll get a pm supervisor out here," Charlie said. "Give this guy some room. We'll let you know if there's any movement."

Just then they monitored a broadcast. *Units at Fig and 81st, Air Ten's gonna be overhead. Anything we can help you with, sir?*

Brian looked up and said, "In the Valley you can't find an airship to save your life. But these guys are everywhere out here."

"Yep, the ghetto bird knows where to fish, man," Scooter said.

Charlie spoke into his Rover, "Yes, sir, ya kin, but I need y'all to give us a little space. We got a possible 187 vehicle in a garage 'bout halfway down the alley west of us. It's a black Buick Regal. We're gonna set up on it. You fellers'll sure come in handy if it moves."

Over the radio came a vibrating voice, *Roger that, sir. We're near LAX air space so we'll move off and hang as long as we can.* Immediately Air Ten gained altitude, until it was a speck in the sky.

"Preciate cha let us know if you got any pedestrian movement in the area," Charlie said.

The officers dispersed to their designated positions. Charlie then backed the police car deep into a lot and parked under a pair of pepper trees. He exited the car, opened and closed the trunk then returned in a few moments with binoculars. He tossed the glasses into Brian's lap.

"Okay, partner, you're up."

Charlie wiggled himself into a comfortable position behind the steering wheel and closed his eyes. Brian looked at his partner's profile and examined the jagged line halfway between his chin and ear. It appeared that Charlie Bender's face had exploded and had been patched back together.

"This scar ain't shit. You should see what a little girl named Donna Mae did to my heart," Charlie said in a sleepy voice.

Brian jerked his head around and stared out the windshield of the car.

"Sorry. I was…well, it's just a nasty scar and I was wondering about it," Brian said.

"Got myself shot a number of years ago in a robbery when my partner Danny was killed. Y'all got his locker," Charlie said in the same sleepy voice. "Blowed a purty good hole in my face, what with my teeth and bones an' all flyin' out. Guess I was a dang mess… Actually the doctors did a right nice job o' sewin' me up. Hell, when I was a kid back home in the mountains my Uncle Roy got hisself shot in the face with a shotgun. They's out huntin and… well, he took a full load a number-six shot point blank. Never even took 'im to the doctor. Way my grandpa put it, 'We ain't got no money for stupid doings.' My grandmamma sewed him up best she could an' packed the hole with lint soaked in kerosene. He healed up fine 'cept I always thought his head looked a little like a kidney bean after that. Uncle Roy's an ol' man now an' I heard he's still picking shot outta his face. So I figure I ain't got it so bad."

"Charlie, why did you give me your partner's locker? I mean, after all those years, then you just gave it to me."

Charlie opened his eyes and rolled his head slowly toward Brian. He held his gaze for a few seconds, then looked out the windshield. He removed his pack of cigarettes from the under the sun visor and lit one, snapped his Zippo shut and studied the silver rectangle for a moment.

"Didn't know I was gonna til I did, Bri. I had another locker key in my pocket but when we got in the locker room I got a feeling like Danny tol' me ta give it to y'all. Seemed a good fit to me too, so I jus did."

"Sometimes I feel like I know him. Or like he's watching me," Brian said.

"Yeah, he'd do that. Jus' listen to 'im, Bri. Figure he's been waitin' on ya. We both have."

Brian was stunned. He wanted to ask, *Waiting on me? What the heck for?*

But he didn't. He had a feeling he would find out on his own.

The radio brought them back to the problem at hand.

12A69, this is Air Ten. I got a pedestrian walking up on your vehicle location. He's wearing a white shirt, dark pants, and white shoes. Okay, he's walking into the alley. Guys, he's paying a lot of attention to his waistband. Use caution. All right, got a second suspect exiting the house in front of the garage. Male, black, white shirt, tan shorts, looks like he might be wearing a beanie. He walked into the garage from the south side. I got the guy in the alley. He's wearing shades and looks like his hair is braided. He's opening the doors.

Brian held the binoculars to his eyes and peered forward. Charlie fired up the police car and buckled his seat belt.

Air Ten, both your players are in the garage. Okay, guys, he's pulling out. Looks like he's heading west towards Hoover. I got two occupants in the car.

The black Regal rolled slowly out of the garage, made its way out to Hoover Street, and turned north. From where they waited, one street south, 12FB3 was in the best position to follow the Buick. Quint guided his police car into the alley and pulled in behind the suspect car. Scooter notified communications division as they approached 81st Street.

Back at the station an officer working the front desk heard Scooters broadcast and announced over the divisional public address system, *12FB3 is following a 187 vehicle Eight-one and Hoover. Approach from the east.* Rovers were immediately turned up, and heavy footfalls and jingling keys could be heard throughout the halls. Within seconds, the sounds of screeching tires, racing engines and sirens filled the early evening air.

The Buick weaved through a couple of side streets and turned north on Vermont while slowly picking up speed. Quint and Scooter followed at about three car lengths. Within seconds Speedboat Willie and Pistol Pete filed in behind them. To Brian's frustration, Charlie hung back about fifty yards.

Air Ten, 12FB3 and two units are following a possible 187 vehicle northbound at Vermont from 82nd Street. Vehicle is a black Buick Regal with two black male suspects.

"All right, nigger, chill," Baby-K said to the driver of the Regal. "Jus' be cool, turn here. Muthafuckers, they on us."

"Man, we should jus' stop, they ain't got shit," Tre said.

"Fool, we both strapped, whatchu mean they ain't got shit? An Tootie kill yo ass if the po-lice gets his gun." He looked at the large revolver lying on the seat between them. "So drive over by my momma's house, lotsa homies 'round there."

"I didn't know it was his," Tre pleaded while driving with one eye in his rearview mirror.

With three units, the airship and the world on the way, Speedboat Willie keyed his radio's microphone. "Okay, Charlie, it's your baby. You ready?"

"Roger that, Willie. Let's light 'em up at Florence. Fewer houses to run to," Charlie responded. "You copy that, airship? Vermont and Florence."

Air Ten, copy.

Brian could feel his heart pounding. The junction of Florence and Vermont was a broad commercial intersection, with designated left turn lanes and a concrete island dividing north and southbound traffic. Two corners held fried chicken restaurants; a large grocery chain store was on another. The fourth corner was home to a strip mall with mostly vacant store fronts. Just as the Regal, traveling in the curb lane, entered the intersection, Quint closed with the Buick then activated the overhead red lights. A puff of smoke blew from the black car's exhaust, and it lunged forward. Halfway through the intersection Tre made a hard left turn across traffic and arced back into the southbound lanes. Motorists in both directions, used to such scenes, jammed on their brakes and sat motionless, awaiting the police cars that would follow.

Tires squealing, the Regal accelerated back the way it had come while Scooter and Quint sailed straight through the intersection. Willie and Pete missed the mark too and were forced to continue north until they could turn around. Quint King was not about to drive to the next break in the divider. He bounced his black-and-white over the concrete island, tearing loose the muffler in the process, and headed south on Vermont, dragging his exhaust pipe and leaving a rooster tail of sparks.

Charlie had anticipated some evasive action from the suspects and Brian realized why he'd hung back. Charlie weaved between several stopped vehicles and flipped a U-turn as the Regal gained distance. Bender stomped on the accelerator and the rear wheels of the old Plymouth boiled smoke. He insisted on always driving one of the old ones. Without power steering or fancy light bars, they were built when Detroit was still putting out muscle cars. Each car had a shop number painted on its doors and in large block letters on the roof. This old Plymouth was shop number 81007 and was Charlie's favorite. They quickly gained on the Buick while the officers behind watched the amber flashing "tin cans" on the roof of shop 81007 get smaller and smaller.

In a clear voice the RTO broadcast, *All units on all frequencies stand by. 12A69 is in pursuit of a black Buick Regal. 12A69, what is your location now?*

"All right, man," Baby-K said looking back toward their pursuers. "Take Butt- long."

Budlong Avenue was a less-traveled thoroughfare that traversed 77th Street Division north to south. It ran through residential neighborhoods and was a favorite of bad guys hoping to avoid the "Po-Po."

Air Ten... Okay, guys, the vehicle is now north on Budlong from Manchester and picking up speed. Charlie whipped around the corner, drifting like a dirt track stock car. The sound of the carburetor was amplified by the fact that every day Charlie flipped the cover of the air cleaner over to allow more oxygen to the fuel mixture. Brian could hear the carb sucking in air. The radio frequency was relatively quiet, considering that every unit in the division and some from surrounding divisions were in the vicinity speeding up and down the streets. Every driver was either trying to catch the pursuit or anticipating its course by paralleling it. Only Brian's broadcast and Air Ten's commentary were heard. He held onto the dashboard while the police car bounced along the potholed street. The roar of the engine and whine of the siren drowned out everything else. The Regal made a series of right turns. As the pursuit wound through the neighborhood, balls stopped being bounced, bikes stopped being pedaled, and little girls with two jump ropes for double-Dutch stopped turning. Children stood on the sidewalks and watched the show. Young men picked up their brown paper sacks and stood on porches. Some walked into their houses and made telephone calls. Everyone had seen it before, and everyone enjoyed it immensely.

"Bri, this guy's made three right hand turns," Charlie said. "He's gettin' ready to bail. Get ready. I'll take the driver, y'all bloodhound the passenger."

The Regal made another right turn and disappeared around the corner. The next time they saw it the car was rolling, unoccupied, both doors open.

Okay, units, the suspects are out of the car. Driver wearing a white t-shirt and tan shorts is eastbound in the alley, Air Ten broadcast. *Passenger white shirt, dark pants is northbound through the houses. Use caution, guys, the passenger's got something in his hand.*

Charlie jammed on the brakes and skidded to a stop just inches behind the Regal. Brian grabbed his hand held radio and bailed out of the passenger side of the police car. As he ran past the Buick, Brian looked into the car to make sure no one was inside. Charlie took off down the alley after the driver while Brian stopped on the sidewalk at 67th and Kansas wondering which way to go. A calm came over him. The Rover radio he'd slipped into his back pocket came to life.

Officer at 67 and Kansas, your passenger ran north between the yellow house and white one, large tree in the front yard...chain link fence in front, Air Ten broadcast.

Brian quickly identified the houses, made note of the address, and jumped the fence as Air Ten confirmed his choice. Quint King stopped behind Brian and Charlie's car. He began setting up a perimeter over the radio, placing units at key intersections and mid-block. The observer in the airship assisted Quint by reading off the shop numbers painted on the tops of the police cars and directing them to gaps in the perimeter.

Driven by fear, Tre ran as hard and fast as he could. Soon the lactic acid built up in his legs and his lungs burned. Everywhere he looked police cars cut off his escape. He heard the sounds of racing engines and police radios. A helicopter circled above him. He felt like a rabbit being chased by a pack of wolves, and to run made him vulnerable to the eagle above. He reached into his waistband and pulled the deep blue revolver free. He climbed a fence and dropped into a well cared for backyard. Parked against the fence was an ancient pickup truck on flat tires. He pulled the driver's door open, pushed the gun under the front seat and slammed the door. He ran to the house, stepped onto the back porch and tried the door. It was unlocked. He walked in, pulled his t-shirt over his head and tossed it aside. He went into the living room, where a large woman in a housecoat and slippers sat watching television. Three children were huddled next to her. The woman and two of the children never took their eyes off the TV screen. The third child, a boy about five years old with large expressive eyes, turned his head and looked at the stranger standing next to the couch. The woman reached out and slapped the back of the child's head. He returned his gaze to the television, rubbing his head.

Air Ten to ground units, the driver ran to the rear of a gray stucco house three doors west of Vermont. There is a truck parked in the backyard. We lost him on the orbit but he never popped out onto 67th Street. Looks like he bedded down.

Charlie had learned long ago to keep his suspect in sight during a foot pursuit and to let him burn out. This was now the case, as he had seen the suspect topping the fence. Through a knothole he saw him disappear into the house. Charlie stifled a cough and took a deep breath. He held it for a second, and then slowly let his breath flow out his nose.

With his breathing somewhat under control he pulled his Rover from his back pocket and made a broadcast. "12A69, I got the suspect inside the gray house."

The observer in Air Ten acknowledged Charlie and directed officers to the front of the residence and another team to the rear to meet him. As soon as the other officers were in place, Charlie and the two coppers with him climbed the fence in the corner of the yard as far away from the door as they could. They crept up to the rear door and listened. No sound of commotion, only the sound of a television commercial jingle could be heard. Charlie, pistol in hand, opened the door. He could see the head and shoulders of a woman seated on the couch still watching television.

"Where is he?"

The woman never took her eyes from the soap commercial. "We don't know nothing. Don't want any of all y'alls mess, neither."

Charlie looked at the little boy and winked. The boy returned the wink and looked at a closed door across the room. Charlie caught the attention of the other officers and pointed to the door. He and one of the officers stood on either side of the door while the other covered their backs. Turning the knob, Charlie pushed the door open and looked around the tiny bedroom. About five feet away a heap of blankets heaved up and down on the bed. Holding his pistol to his hip with one hand he jerked the blanket off the bed with the other. Curled in a fetal position, out of breath, and covered in perspiration, lay Trevon Williams. He opened his eyes.

"What?" he asked.

Then Tre saw a flash of light and experienced a feeling he likened to being tossed around in a clothes dryer. He felt pain and the bite of steel on his wrists. Two officers dragged him out the front door of the house.

Charlie said, "Airship, we got one in custody. Do you have a visual on my partner?"

Negative, sir, we lost him on the last orbit between the houses west of Kansas, said the observer.

Quint radioed, "12FB3, ah'm on 67th at Kansas, we are Shop 83712, guide us in."

The observer said, *Roger that, 83712, make a right there....The house with the big tree... You got it.*

Scooter and Quint exited their police car and looked between the houses. They could not see any officers. Then all hell broke loose.

FRONT SIGHT

While Scooter and Quint were searching for Brian, he was creeping between houses with his senses on high alert. He heard a hollow crack then saw a figure climbing a weathered cedar fence between the houses. Perched atop the fence, the man stopped and looked toward Brian. Their eyes met. Then Baby-K swung his leg over and disappeared from Brian's view. For a moment Brian considered waiting for additional officers but felt like he was being pushed from behind and could not stop. Bent at the waist, he made his way to the fence ten feet beyond where Baby-K had scaled it. He peeked between the dog-eared slats and saw no movement, so he clambered over the fence and dropped as lightly as he could onto the other side. His eyes scanned the yard for cover as he drew his stainless steel .38-caliber revolver. Brian held his pistol in a two-hand grasp at a 45-degree angle from his body as he slipped up to the corner of the yellow stucco house. He listened for a moment. Nothing. He stood back from the wall and took small steps to the side, making an arc around the corner of the house.

Around that corner Baby-K hugged the stucco house and faced the direction he had come from. In his hands was a .45 caliber Mac-10 sub-machine gun. He held the rectangular box by its long vertical grip, which doubled as a magazine. With his finger on the trigger and his other hand on top of the gun he waited for Brian. In an attempt to pump up his courage Baby-K whispered to himself, *I'm not going back to the joint, but if I do I'm goin' as a cop killa. Come on muthafucker, Ima smoke yer ass.* Brian rounded the corner and saw the stubby barrel of Baby-K's gun. Without hesitation he brought the front sight of his pistol up to eye level and took a large side step. Baby-K stood ten feet away, pointing the Mac-10 at Brian. The young police officer's eyes focused on the front sight of his revolver, which he placed in the center of the gangster's oversized white t-shirt. The weapon's orange front sight came into view as

Brian's finger found the trigger and began to press; the hammer drew steadily back. Brian's eyes were so fixated on the sight that he could see the small, machined grooves in it and a speck of shoe polish from his holster. Brian's peripheral vision disappeared; all he saw was gun sight and t-shirt, as if he were peering down a tunnel. His world slowed to a crawl. The hammer fell, and his gun fired. Brian didn't hear the shot and didn't feel the gun buck in his hands. He crouched and duck-walked toward the t-shirt, which became larger and larger. He could see flashes coming from the suspect's gun, but heard and felt nothing. He closed and continued to press the trigger. Red dots appeared on the gangster's white shirt. Still Brian closed.

Baby-K had begun shooting as soon as he saw the police officer, long before raising his gun to eye level. As he fired, the machine gun's muzzle rose until rounds were clipping branches from the tree behind Brian. Baby-K felt the first bullet slam into his chest, then the next. Fear and confusion replaced bravado while fire belched out of the hand of the officer. It was like a dream--a bad one. His confidence broken, Baby-K turned and tried to run.

"Oh, no, you don't!" Brian heard himself say.

Brian placed the front sight between the gangster's shoulder blades and raised the rear sight until it was level with the front. His finger found the trigger again and he slowly applied pressure. The muzzle rose and a .38 police special round moving at 900 feet per second slammed into Baby-K's upper back. The projectile splintered a thoracic vertebra, then sent lead, copper, and bone fragments through the killer's heart and lungs. Baby-K felt a bolt of pain and a push forward. He fell face first onto the grass.

The exchange had taken no longer than four seconds. To Brian it seemed timeless. He stepped behind a large tree and reloaded. He snapped the cylinder closed and slowly walked toward the prostrate body. With the muzzle of his revolver trained on the center of the bloody t-shirt, he pushed the machine gun away from Baby-K's twitching hand with the toe of his boot, then holstered, grabbed the gangster's wrists, and handcuffed him. Baby-K tried to stand but his legs would not cooperate. All he could do was raise his head and when he did, he saw a black shiny boot next to his face. A man's face replaced the boot. Baby-K was terrified for in the face he saw the eternity and horror of Hell. He struggled to roll onto his back, to take a breath, but he felt himself sliding toward the inferno. His soul began its imperishable scream. Brian stooped and looked the dying killer in the eyes. He had seen the wave of horror pass over the young man's face. A light rose from within the boy; it filled his eyes and then disappeared. Baby-K's eyes remained open, glazed and lifeless. Brian searched the body for additional weapons and didn't find another; for some reason he was disappointed about that and wondered why.

Brian broadcast in a calm, controlled voice, "12A69, I'm to the rear of 1203 West 67th Street. I need an R.A., a supervisor, and two additional units to my location."

Quint King couldn't believe what he had just seen. He'd watched over the fence and been witness to the entire event. Now he heaved himself over the fence and made his way up to Brian.

"Hot damn, pard... You all right?"

Brian turned deliberately and faced Quint. His face was dark, then changed slowly to light, as if a shadow had passed overhead. His eyes reminded Quint of a wolf snarling over its kill. Quint's words froze in his mouth.

Within minutes the yard was filled with uniforms. Charlie walked through a side gate and stopped. He folded his arms across his chest and took in the scene. Brian was seated on the back steps of the yellow stucco house, expressionless, watching the scramble of activity around him. Yellow crime scene tape was going up. Two officers started an incident log and witnesses were being identified. Ten feet from where Brian sat, a male black in his mid-20s, with braids in his hair, wearing a large white blood-soaked t-shirt, lay motionless on a thick green lawn. His machine pistol lay on the grass about five feet beyond his outstretched hand. The bad guy was on his stomach, chin on the ground, head up. His eyes stared straight ahead but saw nothing. He wore one white basketball shoe; the other lay seven feet beyond him. Charlie stepped under the yellow tape, nodded to the officer keeping the log, and walked up to Quint. He took a close look at his partner's handiwork.

"Looks like a bearskin rug, don't he?" Charlie said. "How's the kid?

"Ah'll tell you what, that feller ain't no kid like ah ever saw," Quint said. "Shoot, he did a dang number on that guy...Ah'm sportin' a woody here, Charlie."

Charlie looked at the smooth-faced twenty-nine year-old police officer sitting on the porch, then glanced skyward. He walked over to Brian.

"You done good, Bri. Don't worry about a thing, I'm gonna stick with y'all. Don't talk to anyone else 'bout this here shooting til Lieutenant Cicotti gets here. Then do what he tells ya. Fess up 'zactly what happened."

Brian looked at Charlie with impassive eyes and grinned. Charlie had not seen that grin for ten years. He put his hand on top of Brian's head.

Two LAFD paramedics pronounced Baby-K dead and were packing up their gear when Sergeant Monty Price arrived from the station. Although he really didn't like being in the field he knew ranking officers or "brass" often respond to officer-involved shootings. He didn't want to miss an opportunity for some face time with the big boys. Price tried to cross into the crime scene but was stopped by an officer with long sideburns.

"Sorry, Sarge, we got the scene locked down, waitin' for Cicotti. Can't let you in. He'd eat me alive. "

Price glared at the copper. "I have to examine the area, officer, now get out of my darn way."

"You go stomping around that crime scene, you're gonna wish you hadn't, sir," the officer said.

Price rolled his eyes then pushed past the officer and walked to where the machine-gun lay on the ground. He picked it up and fiddled with it in an obvious attempt to remove the magazine. He looked at Charlie.

"You know how to unload one of these?"

"What the fuck are you doing? Jesus Christ on a crutch, put that fucking thing down!" said the man in the Brooks Brothers suit. "Why are you in the crime scene?" Dapper Davy Treats walked close enough to Price to smell his minty-fresh breath.

Price looked at Davy's suit. He was not sure who was chewing him out or what his rank was, but he appeared important so Price searched for a better target for his wrath. He gently placed the weapon on the ground and looked at the body on the ground.

"Who shot this man?" he said.

All eyes moved to Brian. Price walked up to the stoop and stuck his face in Brian's.

"You shot this man in the back? Why? Let me have your gun."

"Hey, Sarge, easy now, it's a good shooting, ain't no need to get worked up. Y'all don't need his gun, les just wait on Lieutenant Cicotti," Charlie said. "I'll keep an eye on him."

"You cowboys think you run the show, don't you?" Price said.

Charlie's eyes hardened and he took a step toward the little sergeant and spoke just above a whisper.

"First of all, I ain't no cowboy, Sarge, and second, yer barkin' up the wrong tree. So jes settle down an' everything's gonna work itself out."

Price took several steps back from Charlie. Everyone was watching the exchange between the veteran officer and the sergeant. No one saw the shadow return to Brian O'Callahan's face.

"Hey, you want my gun, come on over here and get it," Brian said. He stood boring holes into Sergeant Price with his eyes.

Monty Price's mouth dropped open. He was looking into the face of the greatest tormenter of his youth. The redheaded villain, Alex Brawn, had played a huge part in making Price's childhood a living hell. His broad, freckled face twisted into a cruel smile. A vision of being held down and having his belly slapped until it burned bright red filled Monty's head. He saw Alex's lips pucker and closed his eyes as a long stream of vile-smelling spittle filled his eye sockets. Monty turned his head and the warm spit ran down his cheek into his ear. With his eyes pressed tightly closed he took a step back and stumbled over the dead gang member behind him. Leo Brooks caught the sergeant by the arm. Price opened his eyes and looked at Leo, then back at his tormenter. Brian's face looked back without expression. Monty Price brought a finger to his cheek and ear. They were dry.

"Charlie, take the kid to the station, put him in the captain's office. Get him a cup and stay with him. You know the drill. Go on, Brian, everything's fine, son," Leo said.

All eyes were on the thin sergeant whose feet felt like they had been cemented to the ground. Montgomery Price was petrified. A thick brown arm draped over his shoulder.

"Monty, Monty, hey, man," Leo said.

Price looked blankly at Leo.

"Come on, let's talk."

Leo led Monty Price away to his car, talking quietly, his arm still hanging over Price's shoulder.

Again the shadow passed from Brian's face. He looked wide-eyed at Charlie.

"Come on, Bri. I'll buy y'all a cup o' joe." Charlie started toward the front of the house. Brian fell in silently behind him.

AMONG LEGENDS

Forty-five minutes after being in a fight for his life, Brian O'Callahan was sitting on a lumpy black vinyl couch in Captain Sullivan's office. He looked at the plaques and awards hanging on the dark paneled walls. No sooner had he read them than he forgot what they said. Despite efforts not to, he was reliving the recent events. He saw the action in single, freeze-frame exposures. A hollow feeling embraced him. He had been drained of all emotion; he thought but did not feel. *I killed a person. Damn. He had a gun. I saw it. But I shot him in the back. He was a fleeing felon. He was a little kid once. He's an asshole. It was like I was a different person. What if they don't believe me? Everyone says it was a good shooting.* The point/counterpoint discussion in his head went on, interrupted only by the occasional face popping into the room, asking if he needed anything. Charlie sat across the room in a chair that matched the couch. He recognized Brian's blank stare and set jaw, and leaned forward with elbows on his knees and hands folded together as if in prayer.

"You know anything 'bout farmin', Bri?"

"Not much. I grew up in the city."

"Yeah? I grew up on a small farm in Virginia, near the Shenandoah Valley on the hip of the Blue Ridge Mountains. Lived up in a little holler in a place called Arnold's Valley. Ever been ta Virginia? My people followed game and Indian trails into that little valley a couple hundert years ago. Hell, I don't expect I left that holler more'n six, seven times my whole life 'til I joined the Marines."

Charlie stopped, fired up a cigarette, took a drag and looked at his lighter as it rolled over his fingers. "Got my first pair of new shoes in boot camp."

O'Callahan looked at the old Zippo and was struck by how large and strong Charlie Bender's hands were. They could have belonged to a man twice his size... or Brian's father. Around his right wrist Bender wore a bracelet of tooled and braided copper. Brian was mesmerized by the workmanship. Charlie saw the bracelet had his partner's attention, and held his wrist out toward Brian.

"Like that, do ya? It's old, was my granddaddy's and his daddy's. Maybe further back thin that. S'poseta have power. Think it does, too. Cherokee charm. Y'all look like an ol' boy I knew back home. He was Cherokee an' Scot- Irish. Lotsa that blood in our mountains. He used to get the same look on his face as you, mostly when he flew with the eagle."

"What?" Brian asked. "Flew with what eagle, Charlie?"

"He was what the Indians called a shaman, or somethin like that. We jes said he was magic. He'd go into trances, mostly up top some cliff or knob. You knew he was up there 'cause ya could see the eagle jes a-floatin around above 'im. Once I got my dad's glass and watched him for 'bout an hour. Jes sittin' there.

Next thing I look up an the dang eagle is sittin' on a rock pile 'bout ten feet from me, jes a-staring sideways at me like they do."

"What did you do?" Brian asked.

"I set that glass down an' put back to my work."

"You believe in stuff like that?"

"I believe there's a passel o' things in this world that we don't know nuthin' 'bout. Jes 'cause we don't, well, that don't mean they ain't real. My granddaddy believed, and he was a sight smarter than anybody else I ever knew."

"You think I had an eagle with me today?"

Charlie took a deep drag from his cigarette and held it, then blew a slow stream of smoke across the office.

"Well, y'all was up agin it today, an' it 'peers to me somethin' or someone was watchin' out fer ya. Maybe it was God, or maybe he sent his angel."

"Or a demon," Brian said.

There were two light knocks on the door. As it opened a very tall man in a wrinkled charcoal colored suit walked in. His thick black hair stood straight up from his scalp in several cowlicks. Brian thought he looked like Abraham Lincoln. The man looked at Charlie, then at Brian.

"You must be Brian O'Callahan, because that old hillbilly jarhead sure isn't." He motioned with his thumb toward Charlie Bender, then crossed the room in one huge step and held out an enormous hand. "I'm Lieutenant Bruno Cicotti. I'm from Robbery/Homicide and I'll be heading this investigation."

Taking his hand, Brian looked into Lieutenant Cicotti's face. Two eyes the color of graphite peered out from under weathered lids. *I'm shaking Lieutenant Cicotti's hand,* Brian thought. Cicotti's reputation preceded him.

In his thirty years with the Department Bruno had spent twenty-three as an investigator, and twenty of those he spent conducting investigations of officer- involved shootings, known as OIS. Over those years he'd honed an expertise rivaled by none. Cicotti was recognized as the last word on OIS investigations from coast to coast. He had the ability to walk onto a shooting scene and within minutes decipher the most convoluted, emotionally charged crime scene imaginable. He saw things clearly when all others were blinded by the moment. His skills made him invaluable to LAPD.

Bruno's greatest asset was his ability to read people. You didn't even try to lie to Bruno Cicotti. If your shooting was solid--within California law and department policy--you had nothing to worry about. If you had committed a crime, no lawyer could save you from him. If you were a political football or your shooting was the result of an error in judgment, Lieutenant Bruno Cicotti was your only hope.

Cicotti set a large leather briefcase on the floor next to the desk. He peeled off his coat and draped it over the back of the chair at the desk. He rolled his right shirtsleeve up to his elbow in precise 2-inch folds while appearing deep in thought. A double shoulder holster rig held Cicotti's signature tools of the trade: twin six-inch, ivory-handled revolvers. The finish of the pistols was a deep satin blue set off by the creamy texture of ivory. On another man they would have appeared cumbersome, gaudy and unwieldy. On Bruno Cicotti they were perfect, and rumor had it they were not just for show.

Cicotti loosened his thin black tie, then meticulously laid out pencils, writing tablets, and a cassette tape recorder on the desk. Head down, he gathered his thoughts. His arms were locked as he leaned on his palms, which he placed at shoulder width on the blotter. He looked up through his heavy brows.

"I need some coffee. How 'bout you, Brian? Charlie, would you grab us a couple cups and on your way out tell Detective Lang we're ready to go in here?"

About two minutes passed, then Cicotti's partner, Detective Robert Lang, entered the office holding two paper cups.

Two hours later, Brian stood and shook the two investigators' hands. He felt like he had just said confession to the pope. As Brian turned the doorknob to exit the room Cicotti called out to him.

"Brian, how long have you worked with Charlie Bender?"

"About a week, sir."

"He ever tell you about his old partner Danny Lugo?"

"Not much, sir. He told me a little bit about the shooting when Officer Lugo was killed."

"Ok, Brian. We'll give you a call in about a week and have you read your statement," Cicotti said. "Close the door as you leave, son. Goodnight."

As the door clicked shut, the two investigators stared at one another, Lang with his arms folded across his chest, Cicotti in his familiar arms-extended-palms- down-on-the-desk position.

"You ever see anything like that before, Robbie?" Not waiting for an answer, Cicotti added, "Up against a machine gun at point blank range, that kid put six rounds in the asshole's ten ring. Kid's got a guardian angel."

Brian sat exhausted in front of his open locker and stared into it. *"Where is that smell coming from?"* he wondered. He had noticed the fragrance of cologne in his locker the day it was assigned to him. It was faint at first, and he assumed it was coming from one of the adjoining lockers. The musky leather scent had become a comfort as it wafted out each time Brian opened his locker. He breathed it in and recalled the soothing feeling of Charlie's hand on his head this evening. Brian dragged himself into the bathroom. His mouth was rank from coffee. He cupped his hands and filled them from the pitted chrome faucet then slurped the water from his hands. He repeated the process, and this time he splashed water on his face. He looked into the cloudy locker room mirror above the sink and examined his bloodshot eyes, then glimpsed someone standing behind him. Brian turned around and saw that he was alone, but the familiar odor of cologne hung heavy in the air. He told himself it was just his imagination. He didn't entirely buy his own explanation.

415 MAN ON A SCOOTER

L A was finally cooling off as Halloween approached. A week had passed since Brian O'Callahan had gunned down the murderer Toby Perkins. Quint King thought of the incident often. He glanced at his watch. "Almost noon," he thought. It occurred to him it would be nice to have a partner like Brian. His current partner made the days drag on. As Quint drove, in the seat next to him Scooter Kellerman was still gloating over the hang time of his last fart. He was driving Quint out of his mind. They had been partners off and on for several years and there was no question about Scooter's capabilities as a police officer. His tactics were solid, but Scooter had issues.

Quint recalled how many times he had been drawn into precarious situations or internal investigations because of Scooter. He thought of the recent investigation he had suffered through, in which Scooter and Quint were accused of accepting gratuities from a business owner on their foot beat. The sergeants conducting the investigation didn't have much to go on, so they were fishing, trying to coerce one officer to provide information harmful to the other, or "roll over," as coppers called it. When the sergeant suggested to Quint that the investigation had uncovered damaging information on him, he hoped to induce Quint to offer an explanation, thereby incriminating himself or his partner. It was a rather common ploy and Quint was not taken in by it. He simply denied any wrongdoing. But when the overweight, middle-aged sergeant wearing a bad suit and scuffed cowboy boots tried the tactic on Scooter, things became heated. Quint recalled Scooter's account of the interview.

"Officer Kellerman, we have proof that you and other 77th Street foot beat officers have taken gratuities during the course of your duties. What's your response to that?"

Scooter let a little tobacco juice dribble into the coffee cup he was holding, and wiped his mouth with the back of his hand. "Well, I tell ya what, Sarge, if you got me then book me. I don't know anything about any gratuities being received. You ever been on my foot beat? What could possibly be out there that I would want? Cheap jewelry, a wig maybe?"

"How 'bout money, officer?" said the other sergeant.

"I make more money than most any one of those poor slobs on my beat. You come in here telling me you got this and you got that. Guess what, that's all you got, because if I was guilty I sure wouldn't roll on myself. An' if you think I'm gonna roll another copper to take the heat off me then you got another think coming'."

Scooter punctuated his diatribe with a squirt of tobacco juice into the coffee cup. The rolls of fat under the sergeant's crimson face shook as the enraged man rose to his feet. He leaned over the desk, his face inches from Scooter's.

"Ok, tough guy..."

The other IA sergeant jumped to his feet and placed a hand on the man's shoulder, as good partners do. He looked at Scooter.

"Officer Kellerman, that's all for now. We'll get back with you if we need anything," the other sergeant said.

The allegations against Scooter and Quint were never proven. Scooter, however, took a two-day suspension for insubordination and felt completely vindicated. Quint did not. He was angry that Scooter had dragged him into the situation in the first place. Scooter could turn anything upside down with a few choice words. Quint learned early in his career that an officer's most valuable and dangerous weapon was his mouth. Like a bullet, once fired, a word couldn't be taken back, and Scooter Kellerman had no trigger control on his tongue. Just the sight of the tall gaunt officer approaching a dispute sent officers already on scene into flight.

Quint recalled a summer evening when several units had responded to a "neighbor dispute." The call's origin was a noise complaint leveled by a woman unhappy with the mariachi music being played at the quinceanera next door. In truth, the root of the problem was a cultural rift. Dispute calls of this nature were common as the tide of Hispanics flowed into LA's lower-income black neighborhoods. When the first police units arrived the lines had been drawn and the potential for a full-blown riot was real. After yelling several derogatory comments at the partygoers and enlisting some help from local neighbors, the person reporting (PR) was working herself into frenzy. Her pent-up fears and prejudices toward her neighbors were now being voiced in the form of racial slurs. Several Latinos from the party took exception and met the challenge with slanders of their own. Tempers were heating up.

Speedboat Willie and Pistol Pete tried to calm the PR. Willie's quiet demeanor and disarming smile soon had the woman laughing and feeding him a plate of fresh peach cobbler. The crowd broke into small groups and headed back to their yards. Only a few young hotheads hovered around, not wanting to miss an opportunity for trouble should it materialize. Manny Magana and his partner Diane Erickson dealt with the partygoers. Manny's incredible good looks and physical size coupled with his mastery of Spanish had both men and women mesmerized. He towered over them and spoke in a firm, gentle, and respectful manner to people who were not accustomed to such treatment. Manny had what is referred to in police vernacular as "command presence."

His partner, Diane, was a blond former All-American track star who also spoke fluent Spanish. She carried herself with confidence, had a quick smile, and knew how to talk with people. Soon the tipsy celebrants were eating out of the officers' hands. A major disturbance had been averted. Then a black-and-white police car skidded to the curb and Scooter jumped out of the driver's side. Several hours earlier Scooter and Quint had handled a similar call at the same location. Scooter pulled on his black leather gloves as he strode towards the party.

What did I tell you people was going to happen if I got called back? Scooter barked.

Two hours and a Help Call later, the situation was finally in hand.

The party was bad but several minutes ago Scooter had crossed the line with Quint. While on a traffic stop, Quint stood guard as Scooter spoke with the driver of a car they'd stopped for a minor traffic infraction. Without warning, Scooter reached into the car, grabbed the motorist by his coat, and with his other hand repeatedly slapped the man across the face. Known as a bitch or gangster slap among police officers, it was reserved for getting the attention of smart-ass gang members.

Needless to say, such a tactic was not common during a traffic warning. After administering the corporal punishment, Scooter turned and walked back to the car. As soon as his partner climbed into the passenger seat Quint put as much distance between himself and the traffic violator as he could.

"What was that all about?"

"Oh I've had problems with that guy before. He needed a little tune-up, that's all." Scooter looked at his wrist and stopped talking. He loved nice trinkets, and used his off-duty job in the downtown jewelry district to procure those goodies. One of these was a Rolex watch.

"Where's my watch? Oh shit, it musta come off when I slapped that guy."

The violator was long gone, and so was Scooter's Rolex. Quint suppressed a smile. *What goes around comes around,* he thought. Quint was brought back to the present when twenty minutes later they were summoned to the station. Ordinarily when officers are abruptly called to the station they conduct a soul search to recall any occurrence during the watch that would warrant a command appearance before the Watch Commander. This time no such search was necessary. Here we go again, thought Quint. He drove in silence. Once there, Scooter walked up to Watch Commander Lieutenant Philo Wiener as nonchalantly as possible.

"What you got, boss?"

Lieutenant Wiener looked at Scooter and pondered the question, as he seemed to do with all questions.

"Not a thing. Check with the desk."

Quint felt a weight lift from his shoulders. He looked toward the front desk. Leaning against the threshold that led to the front desk stood Charlie Bender. His sleeves were rolled up, tie open, a cigarette dangling from the corner of his mouth. Twirling on his right index finger was Scooter's watch. Charlie let out a barely audible whistle. Scooter looked at his watch then back at Lieutenant Wiener, who had taken no notice. Smiling, Scooter walked up to Charlie and reached out for the watch. Charlie dropped it in his own shirt pocket and motioned for Scooter to follow him into the sanctuary of the hallway.

"So this feller comes into the station. He's holdin' a washrag filled with ice to his face. He plops this here watch down on the front desk and says, 'Jus give this watch to Officer Kellerman and tell him to leave me alone.' Guy seemed all right. Joe Lunchbox type. Somebody wore this feller out purty good, too."

Scooter's smile melted like an ice cube in a microwave oven. He looked down at the floor.

"Can I have my watch, Charlie, please?"

Charlie snuffed his cigarette on his boot heel, field-stripped it, then put the butt in his trouser pocket. He pulled the watch out of his pocket and tossed it to Scooter.

"Look at ya, smiling outta the side of yer mouth like a shit-eatin' hound. I ain't gonna cover for y'all again, Scooter, an' thas a fact."

Scooter put the watch in his pocket and mumbled thanks to Charlie then slunk away down the hall.

"Looks like a whipped pup, don't he?" Charlie said to Quint.

"Tell ya what, Charlie, ah'm 'bout shit full of this. Every time ah turn around IA's looking up our ass or he's got some private business to do or something like this happens. Guy's a train wreck looking for a place to happen. Ah love him like a brother but, dang, enough is enough."

"Buy me a cup a mud, cowboy, and I'll tell ya what ta do." Charlie put his hand on Quint's shoulder and guided him to the coffee machine in the hall. Quint placed an 8-ounce Styrofoam cup under the spout of the machine, dropped a dime into the slot and depressed the button until the cup was full of very dark coffee.

"Charlie, this thing's getting purty slow, better get 'er cleaned out," Quint said.

Charlie took the coffee from Quint's hand, glanced at the suspect machine and tossed a fresh smoke between his lips. "I'll talk to Leo, see if I can get y'all hooked up with Brian O'Callahan."

"I thought he was your partner?"

"Nah, I jes work with 'im once in a while. He's assigned to the P2 pool. They ain't gonna give me nuthin' but these fuzz nuts coming outta the academy. That's why I stick around the desk most o' the time. Gettin' too old fer these young 'uns."

"Well, whaddaya think 'bout O'Callahan? He's no more'na colt hisself," Quint said.

"Brian's a good 'un, listens and learns fast. Purty good in a scrap, too."

"No doubt about that. Don't forget ah seen him in action. The night O'Callahan smoked Baby-K he looked like Wyatt Earp out there. Member ah told ya how afterwards he kinda gave me the creeps, 'cause he looked so cold. Didn't seem the way a kid would react, ya know?"

Charlie looked into his coffee. "Yeah, heard he kinda took Lieutenant Cicotti by surprise, too.

"Ah guess that's the way some folks is wired," Quint said. "When ah was a boy my daddy was a Texas Ranger. He and his partners used to talk about the old days and some o' the Rangers that were myths. One of them ol' boys was still alive. Guess he was purt' near eighty. Ah seen 'im at the cattle auction or church social or somethin, an' he jes looked like a nice ol' man. Real quiet feller, too. My daddy said, 'Don't let his way o' goin' fool ya, son. That old man took on cattle thieves, bank robbers, and border bandits all by hisself in a day when you had no backup to speak of. He'd kill a bandit just as soon look at em.' Ah jes couldn't see it."

"One night we was in town, me 'n' my mother. Some yahoos from the oil fields, roughnecks we called 'em, were in the store. They was kinda liquored up an' talkin' loud. My mother was a looker, ah guess, but nobody ever said nuthin' to her on account of Daddy. Plus in those days you didn't talk fresh to ladies anyway. Well, one of 'em, a big buck in his twenties, started in on her, making kissin' sounds and all. Ah was jes a li'l kid, but was fixin' ta give it a try when this here fella lifts the hem of my mother's dress with the toe of his boot. He starts to say something, then whack! Drops on the floor, out cold. That ol' Ranger had seen the commotion and he jes snuck up on that ol' boy and with one punch he pole axed him. The other roughneck pulled a sheath knife outta his boot and started toward that Ranger. Purty as you please that ol' feller cross drew a single-action Colt revolver, swung it up and shot that fella below the right eye in one motion. He holstered his pistol, pulled his hat off, an' took my momma by the arm an' walked her an' me outside to a bench on the porch. He said, 'You jes sit here for a minute, Missy, Ah'll have someone tend to ya straight away.' Then he looked at me with the most kind, sweet old face and said, 'Boy, this here your momma?' Ah managed a nod. 'You take care of her like you been doin, son, Ah'll be right back.' He patted me on the head, put his

Stetson back on, an' walked back into the general store. Turns out the asshole he shot was a parolee outta Huntsville Penitentiary and had a long history of misbehaving. Couple counties away he was suspect in a bar fight where he cut up some cowboy purty good. That ol' man put him outta business with not much more thought than stompin' a bug. Cold as a well digger's ass one minute, then warm as a West Texas wind the next. Man was like two different people. That's what O'Callahan reminded me of that day."

Charlie slapped the counter top of the front desk. "Now that's a tough ol' cob. I ain't sure Brian's up to that jes yet, but he's good ta work with, funny and easy goin'. Seems a good fit for both y'all, Quint. Plus he knows how to treat folks."

"Well, that would be a nice change. Sounds fine. Ah'd appreciate you putting in a word with Leo or the lieutenant," said Quint.

"Thanks for the coffee, cowboy."

Quint looked over his shoulder at Charlie and said, "You bet, pard."

Two weeks later Brian O'Callahan and Quint King partnered up.

THE BEGINNING OF A BEAUTIFUL RELATIONSHIP

After their first mid-day watch roll call as a team Quint thought he would see how his new partner mixed with noncriminal members of the community. He already had a pretty good idea how Brian handled bad guys. They walked out the back door of the police station and headed toward their car. Quint wiped away a piece of grime blown into his eye by the dry Santa Ana winds that were whipping up trash in the parking lot and fires in the mountains surrounding much of Los Angeles. Quint looked into the brown hazy sky then fixed his eyes on Brian.

"Ten am to six forty-five pm, can't beat these hours, eh? Ever work a foot beat, Brian?

Brian inhaled and prepared to answer but without waiting Quint entered into a monologue reserved for new foot beat officers.

"It's a little different from patrol cause most o' the time we're jawbonin' with good folks. Matter of fact most o' the people in 77th Division are good God-fearin' people. That's kinda the trick ta working a foot beat, figuring out who's who an' working with folks. You'd be hard pressed to find anyone in this division that hasn't had someone in their family murdered, an' they need to feel like somebody's here to help. Just racing from call to call like patrol cops don't allow for no bond to be developed between the community an' the police. Ends up kinda makin' us look like an occupation army. Workin' a foot beat, though, we got time to stop an' jes chew the fat with folks and make 'em feel like somebody cares 'bout their lot."

Quint let his words sink in, then added, "We got a boxing gym here in the division, the Hoover Street Gym, and they do a lot of work with local kids. Like ya ta meet the owner. His name's Al Spencer but everyone calls him Boomer. Guess he was a pretty tough guy in his day. Hell, he still is. We're always hearing 'bout Boomer breaking up fights or grabbin' purse snatch suspects. Good man, and he also has an ear fer what's going on in the neighborhood. We're gonna drop in on him right now if yer okay with that."

"Sounds good to me, Quint. I'd like to see the gym."

Dee Wallace was in the gym that morning.

"Dee, y'all need to come on home, man," Boomer told him. "Come work out wif us, man. I'll talk to Joey, he cool."

"Boom, Joey doesn't give a shit where I work out, man. Muthafucker hasn't got me a fight in six months. He's got some good-looking kids in his stable. Guess he figures I'm done, man. I'm not though. I feel strong an' my legs are good. I've never been really knocked out. Shit, man, I'm only twenty-nine. I got some good year's left in me."

"Thas right, man, you still young an' ready. You jes need to train an' get a little confidence back, man. That Perez fight, you gotta get past that, man."

Boomer was right. Eighteen months earlier, an up-and-coming middleweight named Jesus Perez had rocked Dee badly. Perez caught Dee under the heart with a crushing left hook in round six of a fight Dee was losing on points. It stopped him cold in his tracks. Perez followed up with a barrage of punches. Dee stood taking the blows. He couldn't move his arms. He was out on his feet, and in a place he had never been before. He saw the gloves coming and felt their impact in a cloudy kind of way. His mouth was hanging open when a short right hand caught him on the chin. That was the last thing he remembered about the fight. Dee had fallen against the ropes, eyes open and vacant. His knees buckled a couple of times as a half-dozen punches slammed into his head and body. The referee stepped in, determined Dee unable to protect himself, and declared a technical knockout. After two subsequent fights Dee should have won, it was clear to Joey La Barber, Dee's manager, that Dee was done.

Joey had handled Dee since he was eighteen, and liked him. A friend from Joey's East LA neighborhood, a cop named Danny Lugo, had introduced the two of them. At the time, Dee, an undefeated amateur, glowed with potential. Joey liked the kid instantly despite his gang affiliations. Lugo made Joey promise to take care of the kid. Joey insisted the boy train at the Main Street Gym in downtown L.A., in part because it was where Joey trained all his fighters, but also to get him away from his gangster pals. He started the youngster out with caution by booking him fights that were not beyond his skill level. Dee learned quickly. After a year he had won seven fights. He was an up-and-comer.

Then Dee seemed to lose his edge. His downward spiral coincided with the death of his mentor, Danny, but neither Dee nor Joey ever appeared to make the connection. If either man did, he never mentioned it to the other. Dee's training waned and he had fewer and fewer fights. It was getting tough to find him good fights. When the opportunity for Dee to fight Perez arose Joey discouraged him but Dee insisted. Since that disastrous fight, Joey just tried to keep Dee from ending up punch drunk and destitute. Six months ago he quit booking him altogether and Dee didn't seem to care.

The telephone number of the Main Street Gym was scribbled on the wall above the pay telephone behind Boomer. He walked over and dropped a dime into the coin slot.

"I'm fittin to call Joey right now." Boomer held the phone to his ear and put a stubby finger in the other.

"Hey, Joey, this here Boomer down at the Hoover Street. Yeah, man, wuss up yerself. Say, listen, man, I was talking wif Dimetre Walker…yeah… What choo think of him trainin' down here again? No, man, he's gonna come back, man. You watch an' see. Yeah, I'll train him, get him lotsa sparrin' in, too. No, man, he's fine. All right, then, I'll holler at y'all."

Boomer hung the phone on the wall. "All right, my brother. Get some rest an' be here tomorrow morning early. Joey said he would get you a fight when I said y'all was ready."

Boomer's attention was drawn to the door as Quint King and another police officer walked in. The gym became noticeably quieter.

"Boomer, meet my new partner, Brian O'Callahan," said Quint.

All eyes were on Brian. The smells of the gym brought Brian back to a happy time in his life. He breathed in the sour, musty odor of sweat, leather, and cigar smoke hanging in the air. As quickly as it had stopped the staccato notes from speed bags slapping against plywood and the thump of tightly wrapped fists against heavy bags began again. He took in the bustle around the large open room as trainers returned to shouting directions and encouragement to fighters, and the snapping of leather jump ropes on the grimy gym floor echoed throughout the gym. Posters of past fights covered the peeling walls. Brian had grown up in places like the Hoover Street Gym.

"Hey, how ya doing, young man," Boomer said, holding out a club of a hand.

Brian shook Boomer's hand and said, "Al 'Boomer' Spencer. It's an honor to meet you, sir. I saw you KO Jimmy Riley at the Gardens in 1967. What a combo!"

"Now, you too young to remember that fight."

"I was there to see my da fight. You were on the same card," Brian told him.

Boomer studied Brian O'Callahan's face and searched the damaged vaults of his mind.

"You Seamus O'Callahan's boy?"

Brian smiled and nodded. Boomer put his hands on Brian's shoulders and looked him up and down. Quint's jaw had dropped as he witnessed the exchange. His new partner was full of all kinds of surprises.

"Irish Seamus O'Callahan. I'll be damned. Yeah, I see it, too. Mmm-huh, I see it." Boomer looked at Quint and said, "His daddy was the finest light heavyweight I ever saw. Hell, he was one of the best there was." Boomer stopped and reflected. "An' a good man, too. It was a damn shame what happened. Jes wasn't right. I'm sorry."

"Long time ago, sir. My da thought a lot of you, too."

Boomer smiled, showing a gap where the front tooth clipped off by Jimmy Riley had been, and shook his head.

"Mm-mm-mm, I'll be damned. And there ain't no need to be callin me sir. I'm Boomer to y'all."

Dee stood five feet away, listening to the conversation. He wanted to leave but the officers' presence held him there. Everyone in the neighborhood had heard of Officer Brian O'Callahan. He had killed Baby-K. There was even word that a hit was out on him, ordered by some OG shot callers. Dee watched Brian and a feeling of uneasiness grew within him. Not because of the shooting, but because something about the officer reminded him of Danny Lugo, something he couldn't exactly put a finger on.

"Dee, this here is Brian O'Callahan," Boomer said to him. "His daddy and I was friends back inna day."

"I know who he is," Dee grumbled.

"Dee here," Boomer went on, "he fittin' to train wif me for his comeback fight. He gots lots of talent, Brian."

Brian took a step toward Dee and held out his hand. Dee felt every eye in the gym on him. He put his hands in his pants pockets and mumbled, "Hey," then locked eyes with Brian, who continued to smile warmly. In the police officer's smile lurked a ghost from Dee's past. Dee's eyes fell away for a moment. Then he glanced up but couldn't hold his gaze.

Ignoring the slight, Brian simply responded, "Makin' a comeback, huh? Great, Dee! If you need any sparring partners give the station a call. It's been a while since I've been in the ring, but a chance to work out in the cradle of champions would be great," Brian said.

Boomer said, "Oh, man, that would be great, Brian! Dee, hear that? Some fresh meat, man."

"Yeah, well, I think the officer might be in over his head." He turned to Brian. "This isn't the YMCA, turkey," Dee said.

Several voices in the background shouted their approval of the disrespect just shown the police officer.

"What you mean turkey? It's not Thanksgiving for two weeks," O'Callahan replied with a smile.

A couple of hoots came from boxers who were following the exchange from a distance.

Dee rolled his eyes and exhaled an audible burst of air between his lips.

Quint could feel the tension building between the two men. "Well, hey, Boomer, we gotta get on back to work. Brian wanted ta meet you and see the place. Come on, partner," he said.

"All right, then," Boomer said, pumping Brian's hand. "Brian, I'm fittin' to take y'all up on that offer. What time's good?"

"I have roll call at ten o'clock in the morning so six or seven o'clock, Boomer. See ya, Dee."

The two officers walked out the door and into a gust of dry, gritty wind.

"Your dad was a boxer, huh?" Quint said. "Heard you were too?"

"Well, I wanted to be one, that's for sure. My da wouldn't have it, though. He used to say, 'Boxing is what you do when you can't do nuthin' else.'"

"But he taught you to box, didn't he?" Quint asked.

Brian hesitated then gestured across the street toward two women standing face-to-face and yelling at each other on the sidewalk. The smaller of the two appeared to be nine months pregnant. She was skinny as a rail except for her enormous belly and bulbous buttocks. Dressed in a filthy white t-shirt, sky blue spandex shorts, she was hurling insults at her adversary and moving her head in chicken-like gestures that caused her four-inch hoop earrings to swing to and fro. Quint stood at the police car and monitored the exchange. The target of the pregnant woman's ire was a rotund woman who stood menacingly with her hands on her hips, chin extended toward her antagonist, demonstrating a fierce war face. The big woman's listened for a bit then her mouth worked furiously as she spit out a barrage of profanity the likes of which Brian had never heard.

"We better break this up before it gets ugly," Quint said

As the officers approached the two women, Skinny kicked off her fluffy blue slippers and bounced on the balls of her feet. In a seemingly effortless move, she jumped into the air and kicked the much larger woman in the face with both feet, one after the other. She landed butt first on the sidewalk and sprang to her feet, bouncing, her hands up like a prizefighter. Her adversary flew backward and landed on a pair of substantial buttocks. She sat on the ground adjusting her wig and made no move to counterattack; the big lass clearly had had enough.

"Holy shit!" Brian yelled. "Did you see that?"

"Whoa, now, gals, that's enough now," Quint cooed.

He took the gaunt aggressor by the upper arm.

The hapless behemoth no longer looked fierce. She rubbed the blubbery side of her face then rolled to her hands and knees in preparation to stand. Brian took hold of one plump hand and helped her to her feet. She pulled her hand free.

"I'm fine, jes let me loose. You don't need to be grabbin' on me."

She turned and took several steps down the street, then stopped and faced her aggressor.

"Bitch, you baby gonna look like a monkey, jes like you!"

With that she turned and walked briskly down the street. The skinny pregnant woman made a half hearted attempt to pull free.

"Fuck you, bitch! Ima fuck you up next time I see you!"

"Now that's enough, darlin'. What's this all about?" Quint asked, already knowing the answer.

"That bitch wanna talk about how my baby daddy her man an' she don't want me knowin' him an' all. Fuck her, I told her, I don't know that mutha fucker, he jus' my baby daddy."

"All right now, okay, ya want me to call an ambulance or something?" Quint asked.

Her anger having run its course, she looked at Quint, then Brian.

"No, I'm fine now. Can I go?"

"Well, your friend doesn't seem to want to file a report and she didn't look hurt, so yes, you can go," Quint said.

"That bitch ain't my mutha fuckin' friend. She my sister."

The rawboned woman let a glare linger on her face for a moment then waddled away.

Quint put a pinch of dip in his mouth and smiled at his new partner.

"Baby daddy drama. Ah love it. When my wife was fixin' to foal she couldn't get outta a chair but this li'l gal can jump up and do a flying kick like some kung fu master! Well, they say the Santa Ana winds make folks go crazy, so today oughta be interesting."

They both laughed all the way to their foot beat. Most of the day they walked, and Quint introduced Brian to the places and faces he would soon come to know intimately. He met Korean wig merchants, Jewish furniture salesmen, and African-American bankers. As they walked Quint waved to motorists and young men working the drive-up windows at the three fried chicken franchises along Vermont Avenue. Local drunks stood up straight and nodded earnestly as the two officers passed by while a steady stream of children hit them up for goodies. It seemed Quint and Brian could find no limit to the things that just cracked them up. A bond built quickly and within a couple of hours it was evident that they would make a great team. As end of watch approached they walked to their police car feeling like they had known each other for years. The streetlights were on as Quint drove down Vermont Avenue toward the police station, all the while looking down side streets and into passing automobiles.

With a grin, Brian turned to Quint. "Quint, this is between you and me, okay?"

Quint looked straight ahead with both hands on the steering wheel. He prepared to keep a straight face.

"Well, the first day I was in the division, I was working a one-man report car-- you know, a U-boat. I was driving down the street and heard a god-awful scream come from this old building. I slammed on the brakes and ran up the staircase and swung the door open. The room was filled with people sitting on folding chairs watching this girl rolling around on the floor in front of them, screaming. In front of her was a man dressed in black holding his arms out with his eyes closed, shouting toward the ceiling."

Quint smiled. "Man, you didn't."

"Yep. I burst in on a church service, all ready to save this girl from the spirit. Everyone was shouting amen, and hallelujah, waving their arms in the air. Nobody even looked my way. I slipped outta there and never said a word to anyone. I felt like an idiot!"

Quint broke into another laugh, took a deep breath, and looked at Brian. "Man, you are an idiot. Ya gotta stop, partner. Ah'm getting cramps in my face!"

Quint wiped tears from his eyes as he stopped at a red light. To his amazement, a dwarf stepped out of a corner liquor store into the street and crossed in front of the police car. The little man was dead serious as he stopped and faced the police car with his hands held out to his sides. This in itself would have been of interest to most anyone. But today the diminutive SAG member had been working a bit part in a western being filmed in Hollywood. After work, rather than return his costume to wardrobe, he chose to wear it on the bus ride home. So as he faced the police car and gave Quint King and Brian O'Callahan his meanest snaky-eyed look, all from under a ten-gallon hat. He wore a white bandanna and a red silk shirt with mother-of-pearl snaps. To complete the ensemble he sported a pair of tiny woolly chaps and cowboy boots.

Strapped to his hips were two chrome-plated shooting irons with white bone grips.

"Ummm, Quint? Do you see…?" Brian said.

"Don't say another word, man…Only in L.A. could this shit

happen," Quint said.

In a flash the little gunslinger drew both pistols, cocked the hammers back, and pointed them at the police car. Instinctively both officers' hands went to their holstered pistols and flipped open the safety snaps, but neither drew their guns.

"Quint, those are real guns," Brian said.

"Maybe, but this little fucker's gonna have to shoot first, partner, 'cause they ain't no fuckin' way ah'm gonna shoot a black dwarf dressed like Hoss Cartwright."

It was a standoff. The tiny pistolero lowered the hammers of his guns, twirled them several times, and plopped them into the tooled leather holsters. Then he turned and walked toward the far curb, spurs jingling.

The light turned green but Quint sat at the intersection until the motorist behind them beeped her horn. He drove several blocks before either one of them spoke.

"So whaddaya think, partner? He chicken out or just cut us some slack?" Brian said, feigning seriousness.

"Hard to tell. He looked like a purty tough hombre. Ya know, Ah'm glad he wasn't riding a pony, 'cause, well, ah think ah might a just shit my pants. Don't suppose ah could 'a helped myself," Quint said with a grin.

Brian nodded his head and wondered if this was how things always were. The police car bounced into the parking lot at the station and Brian signed them off.

"12FB3, we're end of watch. Good night."

"Well, that was fun. Wanna do it again tomorrow?" Quint said.

"I can't wait to see what's in store," Brian said as he opened the door and began unloading their gear.

LOCKER ROOM TALK

Forty-five minutes later, Quint slammed his locker shut and said to his new partner, "Ya know, at first nobody wanted that locker, then it just never got assigned. Ah heard Charlie wanted it left as some kinda memorial to Danny Lugo. Doesn't it give ya the willies, man?"

Brian finished tying his tennis shoe then looked at the photo on his locker door.

"Not any more. Little bit at first, but no… I guess I'm honored that Charlie wanted me to have it. And it sounds weird, but sometimes I feel like Officer Lugo is watching out for me."

"Yeah, well, it makes my ass slam shut every time ah look at it," Quint said. "Guys said that not long after Lugo was killed they would come into the locker room at night and think they seen Danny sittin' in front of that locker. After he returned to duty Charlie used to sit there and talk to hisself or Danny or somebody fer hours. You ever see anything?"

"Hmm… me? No, I mean, it's just a locker, Quint," Brian said.

Quint knew he was being lied to. "You worked with Charlie a lot when you first got here. Don't s'pose he ever told you bout the night Danny got killed."

"He told me his partner had been killed, and that's all. I have heard bits around the station from cops, but I never heard the whole story," Brian said.

"Yeah, magine not. Charlie don't talk much about it to anybody. He an' Danny were tight. Used to say if one of 'em farted they both felt better."

Quint leaned against the bank of lockers and spit tobacco juice into his grimy coffee cup with his eyes fixed on the photo in Brian's locker. "Ah'll tell the story the way ah heard it. It was 'bout ten years ago. They rolled past Kim's liquor store down on Hoover and 81st. Front door was closed but the lights were on, should have been open.

Jus didn't look right ta Charlie an' Danny, ya know? So they thought they'd take a look. They walked in on a damn robbery in progress. Assholes had the owners down on their hands and knees. They was fixin' to start shootin' 'em when Danny cleared the door." Quint spit into his cup again and sneaked a glimpse at Brian, who was watching him intently. "Bad guy covering the door had a sawed-off shotgun an' fired both barrels. Dropped Danny right inside the door. He tried to get up and another dirt bag walked up to 'im. He's gonna finish Danny off. Has his pistol pointed at Danny's head when Charlie flew in the door. Charlie jumped over Danny and hit the guy pointing his gun at Danny so hard the asshole dropped his gun and flipped over the counter. Then Charlie shot the guy with the shotgun twice in the face. Killed him graveyard dead. A third bad guy, a lay-off man, came into the store and shot Charlie in the back and ass. By then Danny'd crawled into the store and was leaning up against the glass counter with his gun in his lap, trying to lift it up. The asshole Charlie slammed came around the counter and pulled the gun from Danny's hand."

Brian's head was spinning. He looked into his open locker and could see muzzle flashes through a deep haze of gun smoke as Quint spoke. Brian was there. He knew what happened next.

"Detectives figure that's when Danny got shot point blank in the face with his own gun. Strange thing, Charlie didn't recall seeing Danny shot. Who knows? Guess it was kinda like a defense mechanism, him forgetting that. Danny carried a .357 Colt Python. A beautiful gun, an' Danny loved it. Charlie was lyin' on the floor bleedin all over, but he emptied his gun into the asshole holding Danny's gun. Then the lay-off man shot Charlie again while he sat on the floor trying to reload. Hit him in the jaw an' blew his face apart. That's why he's got that nasty scar. Bad guy must have thought Charlie was done, so he started out the door. Hell, anyone but Charlie Bender woulda been done, too. Mr. Kim, the owner of the store, said Charlie got up off the floor and dragged hisself out the door." Quint stopped and reflected, "Funny thing about Mr. Kim, he's a pretty good guy and was some kind of Korean Marine who fought in Viet Nam, but the dicks said he wasn't a very good witness. They felt like he was holding something back." He shrugged and shot a squirt of brown juice into his mug.

"Anyways, Ol' Charlie caught that lay-off man as he was getting into the car around the corner. He jumped on asshole's back, put his two-inch revolver against the guy's head and pulled the trigger five times. By the time he finished there wasn't a whole lotta head left. Somehow Charlie made his way back into the store. When the first back-up unit arrived he had Danny lying across his lap an' was trying to put his partner's head back together. During the whole fracas somebody picked up Danny's gun an' ran off with it. Never recovered that dang thing, neither. It'll pop up; they always do.

An' would you believe it? The department went after Charlie for shooting that asshole five times in the head...un-fuckin' believable! Gave him the Medal of Valor and found his shooting out of policy. An' if that weren't bad enough, Charlie pulled a gun on a hospital security guard who tried to keep the guys from taking him to Danny's funeral. They dinged him for that, too. But Charlie was there."

Quint stared into the muck in his coffee mug then added, "I sure as hell wouldn't wanta be the feller caught with Danny's gun, that's for sure."

Something was missing from Quint's account of the incident. Brian felt his mind being drawn into the darkness of his locker. A grainy image of an officer lying against a display case, gravely wounded but alive, materialized. Brian blinked and looked again; the figure was gone but the smell of cologne hung heavy in the locker. Beads of sweat formed on Brian's forehead and his chest was pounding. He wiped his face with a t-shirt and looked at Quint.

"You smell that?" Brian said.

Quint studied his young partner and sniffed the air.

"Yeah, you mean your cologne? That English Leather stuff? Sure. I thought it was kinda funny, you wearing that brand o' smell good, same stuff Lugo used to wear."

Brian wasn't wearing cologne.

RETRIBUTION

As Quint spoke of Danny Lugo's death, several blocks away Mo-Mo Jefferson strained to see through the rapidly descending mist. Being so close to the ocean it was common for fall's dry air to give way to a damp coastal fog. A halo encircled the streetlight overhead which cast its filtered light onto Mo-Mo and the parking lot. Two veteran gang members, the type often referred to as "Original Gangsters" or "OGs", were loitering in the lot of Kim's Liquor Store drinking from bottles in brown paper sacks. Their eyes were on Mo-Mo as he approached.

"Yo homes, wassup man, you Mo-Mo, ain't you?"

One of the men drew on a cigarette that illuminated his face inside the hood of his coat. Mo-Mo recognized the drawn features of "Wishbone." Mo-Mo and Tre had seen Wishbone riding in the black Buick regal with Baby-K the day the little boy was shot. He walked cautiously up to the pair. Wishbone stood under a peeling billboard, his back to the brick wall, while the other man squatted next to him, alternating pulls on his bottle and a cigarette. Both men were in their late twenties.

"Yeah," Mo-Mo responded.

"Come here, nigger. Iss cool, man. We need to talk wif y'all," Wishbone said.

Mo-Mo stepped closer, his senses heightened; he knew a vague liaison in a secluded parking lot could quickly turn deadly.

"You Crippin, man!" Wishbone said. "What y'all youngsters fittin to do 'bout that mutha fuckin po-lice that killed Baby-K? Y'all mutha fuckers need to get busy wif that, man."

"That was four or five weeks ago man," Mo-Mo said.

He looked into the cold eyes of Wishbone, who forced a cruel, gap-toothed smile. The hooded face of the second man became visible for a moment when he drew hard on his smoke.

Wishbone's face contorted into a vicious mask. "Look here,

muthafucker, I don't give a shit how long ago that shit went down, we fittin to give it up to any nigger that stitch that O'Callahan mutha fucker up… Understan'?"

The best Mo-Mo could muster was a nod. Wishbone turned to this drinking partner and mumbled something Mo-Mo could not understand. The dark figure stood and held a glass pipe out to Mo-Mo. Without hesitation Mo-Mo took the pipe and held it to his lips. He didn't know why he did, but felt it was expected of him and he wanted to make an impression on these two OG shot callers. Wishbone held a flame to the bowl and Mo-Mo drew in the vapors from the pipe. A warm surge filled his lungs, and almost immediately a wave of euphoria enveloped him. Within a minute Mo-Mo felt better than he had ever felt in his life. He saw everything perfectly. He took a second hit from the pipe. Wishbone handed Mo-Mo a piece of rock cocaine the size of his thumb nail and told him to keep the pipe. It never occurred to Mo-Mo that neither of the older men had hit the pipe. He put the still warm glass object in his jacket pocket and the rock in his front pants pocket and peered into the fog. He could feel the thick air flow over him.

"Y'all put it out, man, an we'll take care a you, li'l brother."

Mo-Mo may have smiled; if he did he didn't know it. But what he did know was that someone had finally recognized his worth. He was tired of being Dee's little brother. The way he felt at that moment he could do anything. He might even shoot that cop himself. Mo-Mo floated with the fog down the sidewalk, making plans and paying no notice to the vehicle parked in the far corner of the lot.

After Mo-Mo disappeared into the haze Wishbone sauntered over to the lone car in the lot, a late model Buick 225. At the driver's window he stooped said a few words and then shuffled off.

A few hours later Mo-Mo stood back and admired his creation, *Kill Kallahan.* He'd painted the words on the side of an uninhabited clapboard house. It was one of several cryptic challenges he'd strewn throughout the neighborhood in the dark. The blue spray enamel stood out against the white chipped paint of the house. Mo-Mo's other handiwork was visible on nearby walls, fences, sidewalks, and abandoned cars. His calls for revenge were expressions of hate, including *Fuc 77th, Kill LAPD, Fuck the Police, and LAPD 187.* In the morning everyone would know his gang's cry for retribution. He made it big and painted it where everyone could see that the Hoover Crips were not going to be punked by anyone. Not even the LAPD. He was calling out the cop who had murdered his homie, letting them all know that they were not the only people who could kill. Mo-Mo felt good. Wishbone and the others would be pleased. Mo-Mo thought about the rock in his pocket. He knew demand for the little white rock was growing daily in the hood. Once somebody smoked it, they wanted more, and Mo-Mo now understood why. He'd hit the pipe for the first time tonight and since that moment his mind had not strayed far from it. He put the spray can in his coat pocket and headed toward home. As he walked through the mist he saw a car's brake lights flash in front of an apartment building. A shadowy figure stepped onto the sidewalk, passed under the streetlight, and stopped at the car. After several seconds the car disappeared into the fog and the figure moved back toward an apartment building. *"Cool, Tre out,"* Mo-Mo said to himself as he continued down the sidewalk. Soon Mo-Mo stood in front of an eight-unit apartment building perched above a carport. There was no landscaping on the property other than a couple of scraggly shrubs that stood alone in well-worn patches of dirt. He kicked at the fast food bag at his feet then slipped past the three junkers parked on the driveway and peered into the darkened carport at the top of the drive.

"Wassup, Cuz."

"Sup, homie."

Tre stepped from the shadows. The two friends shook hands in a choreographed manner called a "dap." They had used the intricate series of hand slaps and clasps since they were in elementary school. It was theirs.

"How long you been out, man?" Mo-Mo said.

"Jes got home last night. Had me up in Eastlake," Tre said. "My lawyer and probation officer got the case against me thrown out. Mutha fuckers talkin' 'bout chargin' me wif murder. Man, I dint kill Baby-K, fuckin' po-lice did. Shit, man."

"Yeah, that shit was fucked up, man. I know a dude he fittin to make that shit right."

"Man, somebody trippin'. Gonna kill a police? Nah, man, Baby-K was sprung, man, he been smokin' that rock. Fool pulled his shit on the police and got smoked. I was there, I heard the cops talkin' 'bout it. Mutha fucker that shot him, he even had the po-lice trippin'. Said the mutha fucker be like a for real killer or sump'n."

Mo-Mo's buzz was gone and he was feeling down. Tre's talk didn't help.

"Yo, wanna smoke, man? I got us some base here. Shit's crazy."

"Nah, bro, everybody in Eastlake talkin' 'bout that shit. Say you hit it once and y'all hooked. Say they got girls givin' up trim to get it. Fine bitches, too. Mutha fucker do anything fo' it. Nah, I'm down wif some bud and a 40, bro."

Mo-Mo was feeling agitated and changed the subject. "Nigger, where's the strap? Dee find out I took his gun he gonna sock me up.

"He ain't gonna miss it, man. He leff it up in the attic long time ago, he prob'ly forgot all about it. It's cool. I stashed it over where I got arrested. We can go get it tomorrow or the next. Nobody gonna find it. Besides it ain't Dee's gun it's Tootie's. Baby-K recognized it an tol me."

"Dee had it man an we gotta go get that shit, cuz!"

Mo-Mo's hand went to his coat pocket and felt the smooth shape of the pipe. He retrieved it and moved toward the carport and stopped. He broke off a little chip of the waxy white rock and set it in the bowl of his small glass pipe, then turned his disposable lighter on high, held the flame over the rock and dragged lightly on the pipe. The white chip began to melt then vaporize. The intoxicating gas was drawn to a chamber beneath the bowl. He held a fingertip over a small hole in the stem of the pipe, which restricted the airflow and allowed the cavity to fill with white smoke. Mo-Mo held the flame to the rock until he could no longer stand the heat. Then he took his finger off the small hole and sucked the vaporized cocaine deep into his lungs and held it. A wave of euphoria returned but this time not quite as perfect as the first time. He placed another piece in the pipe, fired up his lighter and went looking for the perfect feeling again. Tre watched his best friend and shook his head.

"You a damn fool, Mo," he said.

Mo-Mo leaned back against the apartment building and tripped.

The next morning the neighborhood was found to be covered with gang graffiti and threats on the life of Officer Brian O'Callahan. This was of great interest to everyone, especially the members of the Los Angeles Police Department, and the officers of 77th Street Station.

By noon Captain Sullivan was spreading a dozen Polaroid photographs across his desk. Jimmy Graham, the CRASH sergeant, Lieutenant Philo Wiener, the on duty watch commander, and Detectives Dapper Davy Treats and Preacher Pruitt sat around the captain's desk. Davy held a note pad on his lap.

"Who took these?" Graham asked.

"Charlie Bender, working A67 this morning," Captain Sullivan said.

"Should have called a CRASH unit," Graham said.

"Why would that be, Jimmy?" Sullivan said. "Your boys been taking classes in photography? I called you in to take a look at these photos and maybe share some information and decide how we're going to be handling this problem."

Graham flushed, while Dapper Davy and Leon Pruitt shared a grin.

"Don't you think this is something Detective Headquarters or Gangs should be handling, Captain?" Lieutenant Wiener asked.

Graham nodded his agreement.

Sullivan said, "Well, the point is, these hooligans have made a threat against one of my officers. I'm more than willing to put together a multi-front response to this threat. But understand this, it's my division and I am sure as hell going to take some action."

"Captain, I'm just saying perhaps we should not go off half-cocked on this, maybe let CRASH gather some intelligence and determine whether or not it is a viable threat at all," Wiener said. "Let things cool down for a while. Maybe transfer the officer out of the division."

Kevin Sullivan was the son of an Irish immigrant and was a second-generation LA copper. His father had been a member of a special detail formed by the chief of police to address gangsters in Los Angeles in the 1930s and 40s. He looked at his watch commander and thought, *This guy and guys like him are going to be the tip of the spear one day. When that time comes it will be a dark day in LA.*

"Philo, it's my guess that when you were in school and a bully pushed you around you ran and hid until you could tell your teacher." He turned to the others. "No, gentlemen, we're not going to be waiting around for one of these thugs to work up the stuff to try it and we are sure as fuck not going to run away from it by transferring the officer. For Christ's sake, what kind of signal does that send to the community, to the gangsters? We're going to find out who made this threat and we are going to deal with him. We are going to make it so hot that somebody is gonna give him up. Nobody threatens to kill a Los Angeles police officer without expecting the wrath of God. I hope I have made myself clear on that point. Graham, Davy, and Preacher nodded. Philo Wiener sat red-faced, his eyes on the photographs on Captain Sullivan's desk. Jimmy, Philo, I appreciate your input. You are excused. Leon, Davy, you two stick around."

Wiener and Graham glanced at the captain then at the two detectives, who avoided eye contact with them. They stood and slinked out of the room. After the door closed Sullivan stared at it for several seconds.

"There's your new LAPD, specialized and spineless. Pick out a sergeant, ten officers, and four detectives. I want tough coppers who know how to write and won't go out of control on me. Have a list of names on my desk today before 1800 hours and those people are to be assembled in my office at 1800 tomorrow. We are going to put some real pressure on these hoods. I want you two to work out a strategy. Do you have any questions?"

"Not a one, skipper," Dapper Davy said, picking up his notes.

"No, sir," Preacher Pruitt added.

While Sullivan was laying out his plan to the two detectives, across the hall in the watch commander's office, Lieutenant Wiener sat at his desk talking on the telephone in a low voice. Sergeant Monty Price was listening on the extension and watching the door. Neither man realized that nothing occurred in that office that Radio Rick didn't pay attention to. Rick sat in the kit room arranging equipment, his door ajar, listening to Wiener whine to Price's uncle, Deputy Chief Gregory Griefwielder. Radio Rick could just about touch the bald spot on the back of Wiener's head. Captain Sullivan got a full report on the call.

That afternoon while the finer points of Captain Sullivan's response to Mo-Mo's graffiti were being worked out, the men and women of 77th Street patrol took matters into their own hands. In a world where violence reigns supreme, a threat against one police officer was perceived as a threat against all officers. Day watch supervisors directed their charges to provide extra patrol in the area identified on the Divisional Reporting District map (RD map) as RD 1267. Twelve indicated the numerical designation of Seventy-seventh Street Division among the eighteen geographic divisions in the city. Sixty-seven was the sector within the division that encompassed the streets where the offending inscriptions had been scrawled. Shortly thereafter, citizens residing in RD 1267 witnessed an invasion of black-and-white police cars. All the free time 77th personnel had was spent in the roughly ten square blocks frequented by the Hoover Crip gang. Any male black between thirteen and twenty-five years of age remotely resembling a gangster could expect to be jacked up. Officers began developing leads obtained from those who owed them a favor. Anyone caught in possession of minor amounts of dope or with an outstanding warrant reluctantly traded clues for freedom. Vice and narcotics cops played *Let's Make a Deal* with their informants. CRASH officers too went to their local sources and developed theories. By nightfall everyone knew the heat was on.

In the meantime Dapper Davy and Preacher Pruitt sat at their desks in homicide and pieced together the task force. Time was short. Sullivan had allowed not much more than 24 hours to put the whole thing together. They needed a leader—someone smart enough to operate within the parameters of law and policy but courageous enough to extend himself into the gray area when need be. They needed a leader that officers would follow, obey, and fear. Most importantly, they needed a man who knew how to get results, and who if he took a hit knew how to stop the bleeding. Detectives Treats and Pruitt looked over the roster of supervisors assigned to 77th.

"How about Abe Palmer?" Pruitt asked.

Davy smiled. Abe Palmer was an icon at 77th Station. His exploits were legendary among street cops and dated back to the

Watts Riots.

"He's got the Special Problems Unit right now. Why don't we just use SPU?" Preacher Pruitt asked.

"We could, I guess. Let's get Abe in here and see what he thinks," Dapper Davy said. "SPU working today?"

A homicide detective sitting nearby overheard the question. "Yeah, I just saw Abe in the hall talking to a couple arrestees."

Preacher turned in his chair and looked out the door to the detectives' tables in the next room.

"Hey, anybody seen Sergeant Palmer? See if you can find him, and ask him to come on down to homicide, will ya?"

"Yes, sir, saw him up by the tanks a couple minutes ago. I'll get him," a youthful voice called back.

Three minutes later a powerful voice filled the room. "Whaddya got for me, Preach?"

Palmer stood in the doorway of the homicide office. One of the department's last Korean War veterans, his steel gray flattop haircut, piercing eyes and thin prominent nose gave the impression of a giant bird of prey. He ambled across the homicide office like John Wayne and stopped at Dapper Davy's desk. He looked at the personnel rosters, RD maps and crime statistic sheets spread across it.

"Looks to me like you boys are up to something," Abe said. His voice sounded like the rumbling of freight cars.

"Working on it, Abe. Sit down," Dapper Davy said.

Palmer grabbed a straight-backed steel chair, spun it around, and straddled it. He rested his square chin on his arms, which he folded across the back of the chair. A toothpick poked from the corner of his mouth. Dapper Davy couldn't believe the man in front of him was old enough to have fought in the Korean War. But Abe Palmer had fought with the 1st Marine Division in 1950 under the legendary Chesty Puller. He had survived the engagement at the Chosin Reservoir, one of the most famous battles in the history of the United States Marine Corps. Like Charlie Bender, Abe was a war hero.

"Ok, shoot," he said.

Dapper Davy laid out the situation as he saw it. "Captain Sullivan wants to put pressure on these gangsters and re-instill some healthy respect for law and order."

Abe nodded and pushed his toothpick to the other side of his mouth. "How you planning on doing that Davy?"

"Sullivan directed us to put together a task force of a sergeant, ten officers and four detectives to basically get these little pricks' minds right. We would like you to head that detail. Detectives will provide the task force officers with crime reports that have good suspect descriptions and occurred in and around reporting district 1267, where the graffiti was painted. Task force personnel will hit the gang hangouts and dope locations in the area where the graffiti was painted and arrest anyone who fits the descriptions on those reports."

Palmer listened intently and said nothing.

"Task force members will bring the suspects in to the station and detectives will interview, photo, fingerprint and book the little thugs."

Abe showed real interest. "Book them for what?"

"Book them for the crime where they match the description," Preacher interjected.

The old warhorse sat up straight. He had a quizzical look on his face. "Are we talking probable cause bookings?"

"Yep, PC bookings exactly," Davy answered with a smile.

"Damn, we haven't done those for years; are they still legal?" Palmer asked.

"Sure. We can hold anyone we determine to be a possible suspect for up to seventy-two hours. During that time we can present the case to the city attorney or district attorney for filing. If we get a reject we've at least got fingerprints and recent photos on every gangster in the area. Plus the dip-sticks spend a couple days in the slam while we get a chance to sweat 'em for information before kicking them loose," Preacher said.

"And some of these descriptions are rather vague," Davy added, "So after shithead is released the next time your guys see him ditty-bopping down the street they can rip him off again for another crime."

Abe Palmer emitted a low growling chuckle. "A life sentence one day at a time, eh?"

"Exactly," answered both detectives simultaneously.

"Couple of months of that should get these little shits minds right about putting a hit on a cop," Abe said.

"And drive down crime in the area at the same time," Preacher reckoned.

"So, Abe, what do ya think?" Dapper Davy asked.

"Fuckin-A, count me in," Abe said with a wicked grin.

"Great," Davy said as he handed Abe and Preacher a roster with the names and serial numbers of every officer in the division. "You can have anyone you want long as you can control 'em."

Abe Palmer's gray eyes hardened. "I don't think that will be a problem, Davy boy.

"No, I don't guess it will be, Abe," Davy said with a wry smile. "Let's get to it then."

Eight officers were quickly settled on. The chosen made an excellent mix of experience, talent, and restraint, so far. The three leaders studied the roster.

"Any ideas, anybody?" Dapper Davy said.

"How 'bout these two?" Abe asked. His pencil tapped on the mid-day watch roster.

"I don't know if that's such a good idea, Abe. I'm all for Quint but his partner is the guy these guys have threatened to kill," Davy said.

"Tell you what, Davy, the kid is solid. Leo said he and Quint are working out to be a dream team--one of the strongest cars we have in the division," Preacher said.

"I been hearing good things about him, too," Davy answered, "but if he gets into another shooting out there lots of people are going to second-guess our picking him."

Palmer worked the toothpick around in his mouth and pondered the conversation. "Well, shit, guys, I don't think I could stand it if some slap dick from the building or the Los Angeles Times thought I had not made the most prudent decision. That just scares the shit outta me." He stood, hitched up his gun belt, looked down at the list on the desk, and put his fingertip on Brian O'Callahan's name. "Let's put him on the list. If the old man doesn't want him, then all right. Otherwise, give the kid a shot, I say. Plus, Charlie Bender likes him and if he's okay with Charlie, he's good with me."

Three days after Mo-Mo painted his threats all over the neighborhood he and Tre watched a black-and-white cruise past the carport. The teens lurked in the shadows, hoping the passenger officer would not light them up with his handheld spotlight. The neighborhood was feeling the pressure in a way that created pride among some and angst among others. The Hoover Crips were drawing heat, and in doing so showed their threat was being taken seriously by the cops, and maybe even scared them a little. It was good for their reputation, and the boys in the hood walked a little taller. The attention brought out the bravado in some and they pushed the officers as far as they dared. Some even threw gang signs at the passing police cars. Others threw rocks and bottles. Young criminals, many already with a killing or two to their names, toyed with the idea of being the one to take out O'Callahan.

Later that evening while waiting in line to buy some fried chicken Tre and Mo-Mo were approached by a buffed-up ex-con. Tre recognized him immediately.

"Yo, little brothers, y'all need to be cool man," he admonished them. Y'all bringing all kinds of heat into the hood. Y'all fitting to do a cop, you don't paint it all over the damn neighborhood--just do it.

Mo-Mo said, "Fuck those muthafuckers. I ain't scared."

"Well, you sure as hell should be, little brother," the man said.

Tre perceived a veiled threat in the man's voice. He took hold of his friend's arm. "Chill, cuz," he whispered.

Mo-Mo glanced at the dangerous looking man and turned towards the restaurant counter.

"We hear you Tootie," Tre said then he moved next to Mo-Mo.

Andre "Tootie" Hicks. He was the source of all the rock cocaine in the neighborhood. More importantly Tootie was a shot caller and responsible for much of the violent death that plagued the hood. What Tre didn't know was that Tootie befriended Baby-K in prison and it had been Tootie who put the hit on the cop in the first place.

TOOTIE

Social changes in the 1980s brought forth opportunity seldom before seen in South Central Los Angeles. Prior to then, LA's African American community had been, with few exceptions, financially and socially restricted to the south and central sections of the city. Recently, busing had been instituted in LA schools. Kids from the ghetto had a whole new world opened up to them. Equal Opportunity laws as well as Affirmative Action programs were becoming widely enforced throughout the city. Parity in the work force was a long way from a reality but things were changing for black Americans in Los Angeles. Many hard working and deserving African Americans were finally getting a chance--perhaps not for themselves but, hopefully, for their children. A few other, less-deserving individuals were seeing the color line erode also. The lucrative cocaine trade crossed color lines, and mid-level cocaine dealers were finding that places like West Los Angeles and Beverly Hills held great potential for profit.

Andre "Tootie" Hicks was just such a person. Prior to being sentenced to prison in 1975, his criminal endeavors and social activities had been pretty much restricted to the neighborhood he grew up in and he would never have considered frequenting an upscale, predominantly white neighborhood.

It was now November 1983, twenty months after his release from prison and Tootie sat watching the wide screen television he had recently purchased. He felt good. Since his parole, his little business venture had grown with surprising speed. Money was coming in steadily--more money than he had ever seen. His street connections could move as much product as he could supply.

He recalled how in 1979, while incarcerated in San Quentin his cellmate, Beppe Fazio, filled Tootie's head with stories of truckloads of cocaine from Colombia headed to California. He had described how everyone in LA used cocaine now. Fazio said even a major television news network had pronounced cocaine safe to use. He told of the nightclubs, luxury cars, jewelry, yachts, mansions, and all-night parties with girls who looked like movie stars that came with the territory. For a twenty-four-year-old gang member who'd spent most of his life in lockup or foster homes, it seemed an impossible dream. Tootie had become Fazio's understudy. He listened carefully to his teachings. In the time they were housed together, Tootie did anything Fazio asked. He also did a big job for an East Coast family and established himself as a reliable and ruthless hit man.

The lecture Beppe had given Tootie not long before the mobster's parole came to mind.

Man, I don't know why you soul brothers insist on shooting the hell out of each other over turf and pocket change, Beppe had admonished his cell mate. *With this new freebase the market is getting even bigger. I'm talking serious money.* At the end of his sermon, Fazio gave Tootie a phone number. *Gimme a call when you get out. I can use a tough nut like you.*

A year later, after nearly six years in the penitentiary, Tootie returned to the hood with that phone number in his pocket. Many of the guys he knew were dead or in prison, the hustles remained the same, and opportunity was zero. He spent much of his time looking for familiar faces while standing in front of Kim's Liquor Store. One May afternoon in 1982 Tootie saw just such a familiar face. He borrowed a little cash from an old homie, drove to his mother's home, and used the phone number Fazio had given him. Within an hour of that call he sat in his bedroom unwrapping a package of white powder. Tootie purchased the items he needed: a few bowls, a scale, baking powder, a butane stove, a pickle jar, a couple wooden spoons, a funnel, and a package of plastic coin bags. There was not much to the process known as "rocking up." The baking powder and water medium removed the impurities in the cocaine when heated together and resulted in a central nervous system stimulant that was nearly pure in quality--and more addictive than anything ever seen before.

Nearly two years had passed since Tootie borrowed that forty dollars. His enterprise had grown to include cooks, deliverymen, and a network of street dealers who worked for him in several South Central neighborhoods. He sold his product throughout the city now, but still ran his operation out of his mama's house near Manchester

Boulevard and Vermont Avenue. Her home was a tidy little bungalow built in the 1930s on a street where all the yards were well kept and palm trees lined the sidewalks. The area's residents were mostly elderly blacks who had moved into the neighborhood after the "white flight" of the 1950s. Many of their children still lived in the homes that were mostly owned free and clear of the banks. Police cars were seldom seen on the quiet little side street west of Vermont Avenue. Tootie no longer lived in his mother's home but in a waterfront apartment in Marina del Rey, about a thirty-minute drive from the hood. He commuted to and from the old neighborhood when necessary in his jet black 1982 BMW 700. When he did, his car was parked securely in the garage behind his mama's house.

Tootie had invested in his old neighborhood, and was rapidly becoming a major employer of its youth. He hired local gang members to patrol the streets, sell product, and keep the money flowing. Kitchens to rock up the cocaine were set up in houses. Local children were given bicycles and "boom box" radios as gifts for letting dealers know when the police were nearby. Dope money was paying the rent. A network of pagers and phone numbers was established. Young men were hanging out around telephone booths at all times of the day and night.

Teens who not long before had sped up and down the streets on stolen bicycles now rolled in customized Cadillacs, BMWs, and Mercedes. Most of the automobiles were in marginal mechanical and legal condition but they all had nice wheels and high-dollar sound systems.

All this success was not without its problems. Rock cocaine generated a lot of money and created a lot of addicts. Greed and need were things Tootie always had to deal with, and deal with them he did. He just did not tolerate problems. A street dealer who shortchanged him might get a warning in the form of a beat down by some local thugs or by Tootie himself. A second offense resulted in the dealer's execution. Tootie almost always performed those killings himself. Having no middleman eradicated any chance of a hired gunman talking to police. Also, providing his own muscle bolstered his reputation and made him more intimidating to his rivals. But most of all, he handled his own problems because he enjoyed it.

Since childhood, Tootie had savored the feeling of dominance he felt when an adversary groveled at his feet. He loved driving his fist into another boy's face. When he'd shot and killed the neighborhood ice-cream man during a robbery, he was thirteen years old. Caught and placed in a juvenile facility, he felt remorse only at being caught, and for some time afterward he lay awake at night visualizing the look on the elderly man's face after he shot him. Most exhilarating were hits he'd made in prison—fast, well-planned, and very personal. He'd held his victims close and stabbed them repeatedly. Killing brought a sense of power and Tootie thrived on it.

When Tootie instructed Wishbone to put the word out on the street that the police officer who had killed one of his few trusted enforcers he had not anticipated Mo-Mo's graffiti. Now Tootie's business was being disrupted. Cars were being stopped and searched, front doors kicked in. Everyone on the street was being squeezed for information. His dope and money were being confiscated and people were going to jail. It was only a matter of time until someone talked, and Tootie feared being used as a "Get out of Jail" card. He had to do something. A week after Tootie ran into Tre and Mo-Mo and warned them to "be cool," he managed to obtain Tre's pager number from one of his contacts.

When Tre's beeper went off he walked to the corner public telephone and called the number.

"Yeah?" said a voice.

"Sup, you page me, man?" said Tre.

"Um-huh. Lookie here, man, I told y'all once to be cool. Y'all need to tell your homies to chill with that kill the police shit, nigger," said the voice. "You hear me?"

Tre was immediately sick to his stomach and his hands began sweating. He recognized Tootie's voice. "I told them--"

"Shut up, fool, an' listen to me. You tight with that Mo-Mo, right? I hear he done all that crazy shit with the paint. You tell him to cross that shit out now, and go to the police an' tell 'em he done that shit 'cause he was trippin' and he was sorry. You tell 'im, man. This here madness gonna stop right now."

The line went dead.

Tootie knew he had made a mistake in ordering a hit in that manner. He would let things settle down then would take care of this

O'Callahan himself.

Tre made a halfhearted attempt at placing the telephone on the hook, but left it hanging by the steel cable as he turned to walk away. He looked behind the store, where two police officers stood in the gravel parking lot talking to a prostitute. A little girl stood nearby. Tre guessed her to be the working girl's child. A second black-and-white rolled down 81st and crossed Hoover. As the car passed Tre he caught a hard look from the passenger. *Time to do a ghost,* Tre thought, knowing that if he stuck around he would soon be kneeling with his hands behind his head and ankles crossed. He traversed Hoover, ducked into the alley, and jogged up to his apartment.

"That was Tre. He's a Hoover. I heard he's slinging outta that yellow apartment building on Eighty-first Street." Pistol Pete turned in his seat in time to see Tre cut into the alley.

Speedboat Willie drove into the parking lot and stopped next to Quint and Brian's police car. He looked in his rearview mirror.

"Yeah, an he ain't hangin round to talk with us, either," Speedboat said. "Let's see what Quint and Brian got, then maybe we can find Tre."

Quint was conducting a sexual assault investigation. The victim, a prostitute named Tasha French, claimed she was forced to perform oral copulation on a motorist she'd flagged down on Figueroa Boulevard. As she related the incident to Quint, Brian's eyes were drawn to the hem of Tasha's black mini-skirt. Her thick black legs met at her knees, and it was difficult to determine where her legs ended and the skirt began.

"Can you tell me what happened?" Quint asked.

"Mutha fucker wanted me to suck his damn stinky dick!" Tasha said.

"Wait, dear, start from the beginning," Quint said.

A little girl with braided hair and a faded pink dress quietly moved closer to the conversation. She stood with one bare foot atop the other.

Tasha's voice rose. "He come drivin' up an open the do' an' I gets in. He gots his thang out an' a knife in his hand. Mutha fucker grab me by the arm an' say, 'Suck my dick, bitch, or I'm gonna cut you throat.'

Alarmed, the little girl said, "Momma, whatchu do?"

The woman spat on the ground, looked down at her copper colored toenails which extended beyond the ends of her sandals and said, "Child, I'm alive, ain't I?"

The child looked at her own dirty toes and nodded. Quint dared not look at his partner for fear of laughing. Brian took the little girl by the hand and led her away from the interview. He stopped and knelt on one knee in front of her.

"What's your name, honey?"

"Kimmy," she said in her tiny voice.

"Partner," he said to Quint, "me and my friend Kimmy here are gonna see what they have to eat in the store."

Pistol Pete and Speedboat Willie were crunching their way through the gravel toward Brian and the little girl.

"Whaddaya got?" Pete asked.

"Business dispute."

Brian stood then looked down at the waif who stared up at him with large, moist eyes. "You hungry, sweetie?" he asked.

She pulled her thumb from her mouth, rubbed the corner of her eye with the heel of her hand and nodded.

"Come on, let them talk to your momma. We'll get something to eat."

Brian led the little girl into the liquor store. Immediately Brian felt a presence. A Korean man with a large head and pasty complexion looked up from the cash register as the pair entered. The man stood erect and held his shoulders back as if preparing for an inspection. His almond-shaped eyes glanced into Brian's then settled on his badge. Brian smiled at the man, then scanned the small store. The child, who lightly held onto his hand reminded him of a small bird.

"You get anything you want and bring it up here," Brian said.

A shy smile appeared on her face. Then she disappeared into the rows of junk food.

"You new one. I Mr. Kim," the Korean man said.

Not knowing whether he had been presented with a question or a statement of fact Brian just nodded.

"You make me think maybe someone else. You no look, but... You make me think him. What kind cigarette you smoke? Here, I give you."

"No, thank you very much, I don't smoke, sir," Brian said.

"You no call me 'sir.' I Mr. Kim."

Kim bowed deeply. Not sure what to do, Brian returned the bow, then held out his hand.

"My name is Officer O'Callahan, but please call me Brian."

Kim shook Brian's hand vigorously. He never took his eyes off Brian's badge. Behind the counter a small boy sat on a wooden crate reading from a textbook. Next to him the elderly woman squatted over a hot plate, stirring a pot of rice.

"That Missy Kim, my mother, and he grandson. Very smart," Kim said.

The old woman looked up, smiled, exposing a mouth of stained brown teeth, and then went back to her cooking. The boy appeared to be around six years old and was missing his front teeth. He smiled but averted his eyes.

"Hey, what happened to your teeth, young man? Don't you brush them?" Brian said.

"No, they fell out," he said.

The child's voice was a gentle whisper that Brian strained to hear. His proud grandfather put his hand on the boy's shoulder and smiled at Brian.

"I know. I was just teasing you," Brian said.

The smile left Kim's face as the little girl in the pink dress came to the front of the store.

"She's with me," Brian said.

"Her mama bad lady, very mean. She make lots of trouble," Kim said.

"Well, perhaps, but not this little thing. She's my new friend."

The little girl kept her attention on the bag of chips and the red soda pop she held in her hands and stood as close to Brian as she could. Kim's face softened.

"Is that all you want, Kimmy?" Brian asked.

A faint smile crept over her face. Brian enjoyed the irony of the girl's name.

"Okay, Kimmy… Mr. Kim, what do I owe you?"

Kim looked at Kimmy and back at Brian.

"You give me fifty cents, please."

"Is that all, Mr. Kim? No, I insist, I'll pay for her."

Kim looked at the little girl and patted her hand.

"No, you name same as me, Kimmy ...You go, eat. No pay, Officer Brian, you no pay Mr. Kim's store."

"You are very kind, Mr. Kim. Thank you."

"You come back, Officer Brian, we talk. I tell you about Korea. About ROK Marine. I once very strong. Brave like you."

The grocer turned and pointed to a photograph hanging on the wall behind the counter. It depicted a fierce young Asian man in a military uniform standing next to an American soldier. As Brian walked back to his partner he considered Mr. Kim's words. *Brave. That remains to be seen,* he thought.

THE GANG TASK FORCE

Ten hand picked officers sat quietly in the back few rows of the roll call room at 77th station. The group, now referred to as the "Gang Task Force," represented Captain Sullivan's response to Mo-Mo's threats. They were attending the regular patrol roll and were slated to work the same hours as pm's, 3 pm to midnight. When roll ended Sergeant Abe Palmer stood.

"My squad, stick around."

Within minutes the task force had compressed to ten officers sitting around their leader. Holding a sheet of paper, he looked over his reading glasses and spoke to the troops.

"Ok, we've been hitting 'em pretty good so far. Dapper Davy said they are even getting some positive identification on suspects you're bringin' in. In the past week the dicks have put together ten felony filings with the arrests you've made. Good job guys. A lot of assholes are going to spend Thanksgiving in jail tomorrow."

Abe looked in Diane Erickson's direction. She smiled, basking in the fact that she was considered one of Abe's "guys."

"Tonight I want to put some pressure on a few dope pads these gangsters are running. Let's start with a swoop on the yellow apartment building between Figueroa and Hoover on Eighty-first Street," Palmer said.

"Oco, you and Spinner set up in the alley with Butch and Lenny," Palmer said.

A murmur of approval rolled through the room. Oconostatota "Oco" Blackstone was a barrel-chested, full-blooded Cherokee Indian. Rumor had it that as a probationer in Hollywood Division back in the early '70s some smart-assed officer had taken to calling him Chief. Oco did not approve of the handle. One night at end of watch, while sipping a beer at a local watering hole, Oco let him know. He held the hapless officer by his ankles and bounced his head off the floor several times, and said, *I'm not a chief. I am a warrior.*

Copy that?

From then on he was referred to as "Oco," which his mother had called him and he approved of. If Oco was the powder, his partner, Ward Spinner was the primer. Everyone who met Ward came away positive that the psychiatric screening procedure utilized by the City of Los Angeles had a hole in it. Ward Spinner was known to friend and foe as "Mental Ward," or just plain "Mental."

The second team assigned to intercept any suspects fleeing in the alley was Butch Caldwell and Lenny Custer. Lenny looked like the boy next door-- if you lived next door to Baron von Frankenstein. Despite his looks, though, Lenny Custer was smart, in an evil scientist sort of way. His partner, Butch Caldwell, was as close to a pit bull as a man could come without requiring rabies shots. It was said that Butch looked like a 1938 Ford Coupe with its doors open. However, such things were never said to Butch. He had teacup ears, a broad flat nose, a perpetual six o'clock shadow and a forehead like a slab of granite. Butch was a sensitive fellow, and took critiques of his appearance to heart. Therefore, if an officer did not want to be choked unconscious by a tree trunk arm he kept his opinions to himself where Butch was concerned.

"I sure as hell wouldn't want to be one of those poor guys that runs into the alley," Pistol Pete Rhodes said.

His partner, Speedboat Willie Washington, shook his head and smiled.

Speedboat Willie was a division favorite. He constantly pushed the department's grooming standards with his large Afro hairstyle but was able to deflect any orders to cut his hair with a broad infectious smile. Willie was an accomplished marine mechanic. He also owned the fastest ski boat any one of them had ever seen. What really endeared Willie to the others was the fact that he didn't ski, and couldn't swim, but loved to drive his boat. His idea of fun was dragging half-drunk cops around any body of water at maximum velocity. He gladly paid for the gas and the beer just for the joy of seeing a fellow copper splatter on the water at fifty miles an hour.

Butch glowered at Pistol Pete and said, "You could pistol whip 'em there, Petey boy."

Willie's partner, Pete had earned his nickname "Pistol Pete" several years earlier, when in the heat of battle he smashed his prized six-inch Colt revolver against a thrashing criminal's head. Unfortunately, the pistol was cocked and his finger was on the trigger. The collision of bone and steel caused him to tighten his grip on the gun. The result was loud. When the smoke settled, the suspect surrendered to the ringing in his ears and the belief that Pete had shot him. Pete fell onto his butt with a three-inch groove in his forehead and a new nickname. It was commonly believed that the department policy of having all revolvers altered so they could not be thumb cocked resulted from Pete's negligent discharge. Among 77th coppers, the order was referred to as the "Pistol Pete Edict." Pistol Pete chose not to take Butch's bait.

Palmer cleared his throat and said, "Pete and Willie you guys pre-deploy east of the location. Quint, you and Brian set up to the west. Manny and Diane will slide by the apartment like they were on regular patrol and see what kind of activity there is. Questions?"

"Boss, that place is mostly Sherm-heads, isn't it?" Manny asked.

"Was, but we've got some rock outta there lately. Dope cops say some Crip named Tre has been slinging outta the carport in the front. He and a guy named Mo-Mo," Palmer said.

"I hear Mo-Mo's just a base head," Lenny said.

"Tre, is that Trevon Williams, Sarge?" Quint said. "He was in the Regal with Baby-K when my partner's shooting went down."

"What the fuck is he doing out?" Butch chimed in.

"They dropped the case," Brian said.

Every eye in the room looked at Brian, who somehow felt responsible for the district attorney's rejection of the case.

"Why?" asked Lenny.

"*Furtherance of Justice* is what the detectives told me," Brian said. "I'm not sure what that means."

"Nobody knows what that means," Lenny said.

"Oh, give me a fuckin break," Butch muttered. "It means the case wasn't a slam-dunk and the D.A. didn't want to work for a conviction."

"Yeah, well, the asshole's lucky he didn't meet my partner that day," Quint said, putting his hand on Brian's shoulder.

"Fear not, boys, what goes around comes around. Mr. Tre, will I'm sure, some day receive his due," Lenny said.

"Lenny's right," Abe Palmer said. "We hook 'em and book 'em

and let the judge cook 'em. Unless, of course, they wanna go the hard way."

"Hey, Sarge, my brother works for the Department of General Services. Why don't we just get a wood chipper and a sewage pumper?" asked Mental Ward.

Everyone waited for it.

"Yeah, we can hook them together and park in the alley. When we catch these gangsters we just throw them in the chipper and they squirt into the sewage truck tank. We can have a fertilizer business, like that fish emulsion those Japanese gardeners in Gardena use. We'll use old forty-ouncers for containers. Very ecological."

Mental Ward smiled proudly. His weak eye wandered around the room.

Sergeant Palmer stared at Ward for a couple of seconds. "Not just yet, Mental, but thanks for playing. Oco, watch that guy."

Oco smiled and patted Mental on the head. "Yes, sir."

Abe Palmer struck a pose, his hawkish eyes engaged each officer in turn, and his voice took on a somber, powerful tone.

"Keep this in mind, people. These gangsters are vicious. That is evident by the number of murders we have each year. The only reason these little thugs are not shooting cops wholesale is because they are afraid. When they go out and start painting 'Kill the Cops' on the walls that means someone is thinking about it. That means the fear is waning. Fear is the world's greatest motivator. Let these gangsters lose their fear and we're gonna be handin' out a shitload of flags. You were picked because you know how to do it right. So go out there and instill some fear."

Coffee was gulped, and specifics were worked out among the teams.

"Brian, I need to see you in the hall for a minute, son," Palmer said. "Oh, by the way, those of you complaining about how slow the coffee machine downstairs is, may have noticed it is working fine now. Radio Rick cleaned it out this morning. It was all clogged up. Apparently it was packed full of cockroaches. But he got most of 'em."

"Didn't taste like cockroaches, just was kinda slow. Glad Rick fixed it," Butch said.

"Wonder if he took any pictures?" Mental said as the detail

headed for the door.

Brian stood at the top of the stairs just outside the roll call room and waited for Sergeant Palmer.

"Hi, Brian. I got this for you." Palmer handed him a folded document. "Your shooting board is scheduled for next week. Did you know that?"

"I didn't know. Seems kinda fast. It's only been a month and a half. Charlie said they sometime take almost a year," Brian said.

"Charlie tell you to go to the board?" Palmer asked.

"Yes, sir, he said it keeps the brass honest. They're not as ready to screw you over if you're sitting there watching them. They know you'll take whatever is said back to the division. Charlie said there are no tapes of the board meeting and some captains will go in there and roll over for the board then say to the officer later, 'I did everything I could for you, son.'"

Palmer studied the young man in front of him. He twitched his toothpick between his teeth.

"Well, sounds like good advice to me, Brian. I don't think you need to worry too much about our captain. Sully and I worked together when he was your age. He's solid as they come," Palmer said. "Go hook up with Quint and grab a bite before it gets dark and you get tied up with arrests."

Brian went out to the parking lot and walked up to the group of officers standing around their police cars.

"How 'bout the Mexican place on Vermont?" Oco was saying.

"Ok, but don't order the shrimp. Couple guys got sick eating *camarones* there last week," Pistol Pete said.

"Isn't there a good Mexican place in Gardena, near Western?" Brian asked.

"Yeah, that's a great place! Sounds good to me. Haven't eaten there in a couple years," said Mental.

"Hope it's not full of fucking motor cops," Butch grumbled.

Quint said, "Well, if it is, we'll just send you and Mental in and you boys can sit down next to them and stare, Butch. That would put anyone off his feed."

Mental smiled, Butch growled, and everyone else agreed that it would. Quint and Brian climbed into their cruiser and pulled away from the group.

"You know how to get there?" Quint asked, looking at his partner curiously.

"Yeah, I think so," O'Callahan said as he turned onto the southbound Harbor Freeway.

Still looking at Brian, Quint asked, "It's kinda outta the way for a new guy, pard. When did you go there?"

"I don't know, but I must have been there some time..."

Quint didn't reply.

A fifteen-minute drive south on the Harbor Freeway delivered the line of police cars to the town of Gardena, and after a short drive from there they arrived at "Mi Abuela's" restaurant. They parked side by side in the back of the lot after ensuring that no other police cars were present. They filed into the restaurant, each making a visual sweep of the clientele. A stout Mexican woman with a gold-studded smile and a faint moustache came from behind the Formica lunch counter. She led the bunch to the back of the restaurant, where they could see the register and the front door, and where no one could walk behind them. She had been feeding *los policia* for many years and knew where to seat them without asking.

As the waitress dropped menus in front of each officer, Brian noticed that despite being thick around the waist the middle-aged woman's dark brown arms were thin and sinewy. While the others scrutinized their options, Brian immediately ordered chili and cheese tamales then engaged the waitress in polite conversation in Spanish. Some minutes later, after scribbling everyone's orders onto a small writing pad, she dropped it into the pocket of her starched white apron and walked from the table, wondering how the white policeman had come to speak Spanish so beautifully.

Diane's partner, Manny, said, "Brian, you must eat here a lot. The cheese and chili tamales aren't even on the menu."

"No, I just like 'em, and I figured they might have them."

"Where did you learn to speak Spanish so well, Brian?" Diane asked.

"I grew up around a lot of fighters who only spoke Spanish and we learned some in the Academy. Plus I have a guy working on my apartment who speaks it." Brian stopped and mulled the subject over in his mind. "But lately it seems I just speak it better. I mean, I open my mouth and it comes out."

"I hear you live downtown. Won't be long you're gonna have a girlfriend who carries the laundry on her head and be eatin' chorizo and eggs for breakfast," Mental said.

"I got your chorizo and eggs hangin'," said Manny.

Mental took a large scoop of salsa with a tortilla chip and moved his eyebrows up and down as he pushed it into his mouth.

"I thought I smelled pork," a heavy-set, bearded man wearing Ray-Ban sunglasses said as he clumped past the officers on his way to the restroom. Vest, jeans and boots, his oily ensemble could be smelled across the room. On his belt hung a ten-inch sheath knife and a chrome dog chain that ran from the belt to the wallet in his back pocket.

"Yeah, and your mama eats bacon, asshole!" Mental said.

The man flipped Mental the bird and continued on his way as the waitress brought a tray of beverages to the table.

"I am sorry. That man, he always says something to the police. He is *muy malo*. Sometimes he comes in with many motorcycle men. They are not nice. Make lots of trouble," the waitress said.

"I gotta piss," said Butch, rising from the table.

Mental looked up at him as he crammed a fistful of tortilla chips into his mouth. Lenny followed his partner.

As the whoosh of the men's room door sounded, all eyes looked in that direction. Lenny stood outside the restroom with his arms folded across his chest. Everyone in the restaurant heard the crash of a metal trash receptacle, some heard the shuffle of heavy feet on a tile floor. The officers heard a toilet flush, and after several minutes some muffled words. The men's room door flew open, propelled by the biker's face. It was covered in red. Blood flowed from his smashed nose, and water streamed down his long hair. Butch had the collar of the man's heavy jean vest in one hand and grasped the chain between the biker's handcuffed hands with the other. A gash on the biker's eyebrow gaped, allowing the lid of that eye to hang over his eyeball. Butch was wearing the man's Ray-Bans and had his knife in his back pocket.

"We can run this mutt over to Gardena Police Station and book his ass after chow. Won't take a minute." Butch said. "Might need to see a doc first."

Butch flexed his arrestee's wrist, which caused him to move

forward on tiptoes. As they exited the restaurant Butch whispered in the man's ear. "Well, it looks like this little piggy is taking you to da market, pal."

"Looks like more than a minute's work to me," said Lenny, shaking his head. "Abe's gonna be pissed."

"Well, the man had lost his fear," Mental said. "Butch helped him find it."

Butch returned as the waitress was carrying a large platter of food to their table.

"I'm sorry, miss, I was going to the bathroom and that man pulled a knife on me. I'll clean up the bathroom if you want."

Putting the steaming plates of food in front of each officer she said, "Si. I told you he was a bad man. I'm glad you are not hurt, *señor*. No, we will clean. It's no problem."

Diane put a small bite of rice into her mouth, chewed carefully and swallowed. She blotted her pink lips with a napkin then directed a question to Butch.

"Where's the brain surgeon?"

"I got him hog-tied in the car, he ain't goin anywhere," Butch answered, looking over his plate. "Man, this looks good!"

By the time they were done eating, the sun had set and the task force stood next to their black-and-whites in what little light filtered out of the restaurant's windows.

"Well, what now?" Pistol Pete asked no one in particular. "Lenny and Butch are gonna be outta pocket for a while. Think we should go ahead with the swoop?"

In the absence of rank, like water, leadership reaches its own level. Quint, the group's natural leader, put the final touches on the night's plan. "Since Lenny and Butch are outta this, Pete an Willie set up in the alley with Oco an Mental. As soon as yer in place let us know. Diane and Manny, when ya hear that the rear of the location is secure drive past the apartment building an do a little reconnaissance. Then set up down the street east of the location. Me an Brian will set up west of the location. When we're all in place ah'll give the 'go-get-em.' Let's broadcast on tac-five so we don't tie up the division base frequency. Ah miss anything?"

Heads shook as an officer from each team turned the knob on his Rover to channel five. Without further comment the officers walked to their respective vehicles. Engines fired up and the five cars bounced out of the parking lot one at a time and headed back to 77th Street division.

Unaware of what would soon befall them, Mo-Mo, Tre, and T-Bone Boucher lounged in the dark cavern beneath the targeted apartment building. Above them, the light fixtures attached to the ceiling were dark. The bulbs had either been broken by vandals or stolen for use in someone's apartment. Whatever the case, it was a regular problem and the building manager had given up on replacing them. Due to the plague of crime in the area the un-securable garage was no longer used to house cars. The oily concrete floor was littered with all kinds of trash and the air reeked of urine and mold. In the farthest corner of the three-sided cave, Mo-Mo and T-Bone sat huddled in the darkness on an old couch. Tre squatted in front of them on a plastic milk crate someone had lifted from Kim's Market. Mo-Mo watched intently as T-Bone drew on the coke pipe. T-Bone liked the feeling he got from rock but loved to mix it with PCP. After drawing on the pipe he handed it back to Mo-Mo and unwrapped a half smoked brown cigarette from a piece of foil. The smell of ether filled Tre's nostrils.

"Oh man, T, you fittin to trip, Bone," Tre said.

T-Bone smiled, showing a mouthful of rotten and broken teeth. He was known as a Sherm-head but loved all kinds of drugs. Earlier in the day, T-Bone had deposited himself on the stoop of a friend's home drinking malt liquor and huffing gasoline fumes from a rag. Now, after smoking the pure cocaine, he felt a growing rush within.

In another world on the same street, two Los Angeles police officers cruised with their headlights off toward the three men. Diane adjusted herself in the seat as the rectangular building came into view. The carport faced the street and above it on either side was a lighted window. Diane envisioned the silhouette of the building to be a head, the windows eyes, and the pitch-dark grotto below was its gaping mouth. She had a feeling of foreboding as she strained to see into the carport. The cars on the driveway obstructed her line of sight so all she saw was a dirty apartment building straddling a dark orifice. Just as she reached for the microphone to advise the others, her eyes caught a light flickering in the depths of the darkness. She made out at least two figures.

T-Bone took two long hits on the phencyclidine-dipped cigarette and in seconds was completely at the mercy of his environment. His enormous body trembled but stayed otherwise motionless. Awake but conscious of only basic stimuli, his mind became primal, deleting all cognitive thought.

Tre stood with the intention of putting distance between himself and the smoldering volcano just as Diane Erickson radioed that she saw forms in the carport. Manny flipped a U-turn at the intersection and waited for Quint's signal.

Quint keyed his mike. "We good ta go?"

Each team indicated that they were.

"Let's get em!" Quint called.

Two engines roared then tires squealed as the police cars converged on the unsuspecting trio.

Tre stood just inside of the carport and dipped a cigarette into a jelly jar filled with amber liquid. Mo-Mo drew on his pipe and T-bone sat staring into space. Two children were playing on the sidewalk with a flat basketball when the headlights shone into their eyes. Manny and Diane's cruiser jerked to a stop behind the Cadillac in the driveway. They kicked the doors open and ran toward the carport.

Lights flashed, doors slammed, and heavy footfalls sounded on the driveway. "Police! Freeze, everyone! Get your hands in the air!" a woman's voice yelled. The only ones who froze and put their hands in the air were the six-year-old boy and his five-year-old sister.

"Go on, kids, go home right now!" Manny said.

He passed the children and headed toward a teenage boy holding a jar. Tre looked wide-eyed at the officer moving toward him, then threw the contents of the jar at him. PCP drenched Manny's face and burned his eyes. From the smell, Manny knew he was in trouble. He didn't even realize he had slipped and fallen. Tre dropped the jar, leaped over the officer, and took off toward the rear of the building. Seconds later Brian and Quint stopped behind Manny and Diane's abandoned cruiser. They jumped from their car and sprinted to the figure on the ground. Brian stepped around Manny and in a few strides was on Tre's heels. Quint stopped next to where Manny now sat and radioed the officers in the alley.

"We got one headed your way, on the west side of the building."

Mo-Mo stood up and in the darkness and confusion he slipped out of the carport and around the east corner of the building. He headed for the alley forcing himself to walk. Pistol Pete and Speedboat Willie saw a silhouette and ran toward it. Mo-Mo saw them too. He pushed down on the rusted chain link fence that separated the apartment building from a vacant lot and jumped over it, then kept walking.

Speedboat Willie yelled, "Hey, man, come here!"

A bolt of adrenalin shot through Mo-Mo. He broke into a run, crashing through the weeds. He didn't know the house that had once stood in that lot had a basement. The hole was covered with debris from the recent demolition of the house, and Mo-Mo crashed through it like an animal falling into a pit trap.

"Where the fuck did he go?" Pistol Pete shined his flashlight at the spot he had last seen the suspect.

Speedboat Willie joined in and scanned the lot with his flashlight, then trained it on a pile of debris. "Check that big pile of junk over there, Pete."

The two officers jogged over to what was left of the home. They stood five feet from where Mo-Mo lay at the bottom of his concrete sanctuary. He listened to the officers talking above him.

"I didn't know they tore down this house," said Willie.

"Me neither. It was here yesterday. Guess the owner decided to just go ahead and tear it down after those assholes painted graffiti all over it. Tore it down before someone burned it down. Place was a shambles anyway," Pistol Pete said.

As the drama unfolded out front, Brian was closing on Tre behind the apartments. Just before he reached the alley, Brian kicked Tre's heel and caused the teen's legs to become entangled. He lost his balance and fell face first on the oily, compacted dirt surface of the alley. After tripping him, Brian over ran Tre, rebounded off a decrepit garage door, and turned, searching for the suspect. He caught sight of Tre pushing himself up off the ground and Mental's boot connecting with the side of the gangster's face. It was a kick any NFL place kicker would have been proud of. A thud combined with the clack of Tre's teeth slamming together. Mental backed up and was lining up for another shot when Brian grabbed him by the arm.

"That's enough! He's probably already dead, Mental!"

Mental Ward bent over, lifted the unconscious gangster's hand, and dropped it to the ground. He looked at Brian and smiled. His weak eye wandered down the alley.

Out front, Diane Erickson was trying to help her partner to his feet. If the officers had never swooped in, shined lights in his eyes, and yelled in loud voices, T-Bone may have spent the evening semi-comatose on the smelly couch in the carport. But they did, and that changed everything. Diane never saw the monster emerge from the cave behind her. Quint heard Diane cry out and turned in time to see T-Bone lift her over his head then throw her head first through the windshield of the old Coupe Deville that rested on blocks in the driveway. Diane lay motionless, legs on the hood, half in and half out of the car. Her torso was slumped over the steering wheel, and her head rested on the torn and stained front seat.

Quint yelled at the top of his lungs, "Officer down! Get up here fast!"

Quint leaned into the smashed windshield and shined his flashlight on Diane. T-Bone lurched between them and throttled Quint with both hands. Kicking his feet and trying to gain purchase on the ground, his right hand went instinctively to his pistol, the other hand tried to pry the huge fingers from his throat. Pressure began building in his head; he could not breathe and had the sensation of floating. For a moment Quint thought, *So this is how it feels to be guest of honor at a necktie party.* A crack sounded in his neck. Quint focused on his right hand, which was still squeezing the wooden grips of his pistol. He pulled the gun from its holster, pushed the muzzle into his hangman's rib cage and jerked the trigger. Then it was darkness.

Diane Erickson stirred, then climbed through the shattered windshield and dove onto T-Bone's back. Her right arm around his enormous neck, she tried to set her hold by grabbing her right wrist with her left hand. T-Bone felt nothing that could be called pain. He only responded to sensations. He sensed Diane's weight on his back, released Quint who slumped to the ground, and grabbed the object of irritation and threw it away from him. Officer Diane Erickson hit the support post in the carport so hard the building shuddered. She spun around the pole and her head went through the stucco wall of the carport. She lay still. On the ground and nearly blinded by the chemicals in his eyes, Manny felt for and grabbed T-Bone's tree trunk of a leg. Deep in his poisoned brain T-Bone felt the impulse to flee. He walked unsteadily, dragging Manny, who clung to his leg like a child riding his father's foot.

Quint's gunshot had echoed down the side of the building into the alley. Brian told Mental to stay with their arrestee and then sprinted toward the street. Oco drew his pistol and ran down the opposite side of the building. As he ran, Oco stumbled over an abandoned shopping cart, lost his balance, and dropped his pistol. He broke his fall by grabbing a metal pipe that had served as a fence post for the rusted chain link fence that ran the length of the building. The pipe moved in Oco's hands. He pulled it free from the ground and felt the heft of the concrete clod at its base. At that moment Oco saw a huge figure lumbering along the building toward him. Oco had no time to find his gun, so he lifted the pipe and held it on his shoulder like a baseball bat. He stepped into the shadow of the building and saw the figure picking up speed. When T-Bone was about ten feet away, Oco lifted his lead leg and brought the pipe around his body in an arc performing a perfect home run swing. Just then, Manny lost his grip on T-Bone's leg and slid to a stop on the filthy sidewalk. Before he passed out, Manny remembered hearing a crunch. When fifteen pounds of concrete slammed into his chest, T-Bone's feet continued toward the alley but his torso came to an abrupt halt. His smashed sternum was driven inward until his heart pressed against his spine. His right lung was collapsed by the time his skull fractured upon impact with the cement sidewalk. A surgeon said later, "Either the gunshot or blunt force trauma should have killed him, but in his condition Mr. Boucher did not go into shock."

CLEANING UP THE CLUSTER

Tre was dragged to a waiting police cruiser and stuffed inside; his swollen face intermittently bathed in the reds and yellows of the rotating lights of emergency vehicles. Through a pain induced haze he heard the back door of the police car open and felt someone slide onto the bench seat next to him. Tre had sight in one eye, and cocked his head to see who had joined him, half expecting to see Mo-Mo. But he looked and pulled away frantically, trying to put distance between himself and the creature next to him. The huge brown and black pit bull terrier filled the backseat with his mass and emitted a low growl. The dog's eyes reminded Tre of a shark he'd seen on television peering out of the water as he rose to eat a chunk of meat the filmmakers used as bait. The dog's eyes, like the shark's, seemed sightless, merely tunnels into a savage brain.

In his horror, Tre's mind clicked back to when he was five years old. *He had been playing in the alley with Mo-Mo when they saw a huge brindle pit bull dog running toward them. Tre ran, pumping his legs as fast as he could. He recalled the sharp agony as teeth clamped onto the back of his leg. In an instant he was on his face, being dragged down the alley. For a moment he beast's teeth released him, then they took a better purchase on his buttocks. Bolts of pain shot through Tre's body as the dog shook him like a rag doll. The only reason he was not mauled to death was that Dee had arrived and crushed the dog's broad, thick skull with a baseball bat. For years Tre woke screaming from dreams of the dog eating him as he lay helpless, pulling at the beast's cropped ears.*

Throughout his childhood Tre harbored the belief that one day the pit bull would find him again; now he had. The dog was back to finish the job. But how could that be? It was dead and lived only in his mind. His hands cuffed behind him there was no escape. Tre raised his feet and pressed his back to the door. The cur opened his broad jaws and a flash of white teeth tore into Tre's abdomen. Before

116

he felt anything he heard the ripping and popping of his intestines. The smell of fecal matter filled the car as the brutish head pulled great mouthfuls of bloody entrails from Tre's midsection. Steam rose from Tre's ruined body and clouded the windows. Blood dripped from the creature's muzzle when he stopped to view his victim's agony. It shook its gore-covered head and lunged forward, burrowing deep into Tre's mutilated torso. Tre's pain was only matched by his horror. He closed his eyes and endured the pain. Then a car door slammed shut. Tre opened his eyes. Oco was at the steering wheel and Mental Ward was sitting next to him. Tre looked into his lap, expecting to see a grisly mess of tissue. He saw his pants and a seat belt.

"Man, this guy doesn't look too good, Oco," Mental said. "Maybe we should get another ambulance for him. I think he might croak on us... I don't need that, man. Call an RA."

Tre exhaled. The officers couldn't imagine how good he felt.

Several feet away Brian walked from the police car to the gurney Quint was strapped to. He slid Quint's Sam Browne from under him and put it, along with his partner's service weapon, in the trunk of their police car, then hurried back to the gurney as Quint was lifted into the RA.

Sergeant Palmer had arrived on scene within minutes after the melee and was trying to sort things out. He stood next to the RA giving directions to a pair of officers when Brian climbed into the ambulance.

Abe cut his orders short and called to Brian, "O'Callahan are you hurt?"

"I'm riding with him," Brian said.

"No, Brian, you need to stay here," Abe Palmer said. "The dicks are going to need to talk to you. I'll get someone to go with him."

Brian seated himself next to his partner then regarded Abe. Someone closed the doors of the ambulance and it pulled away.

Abe watched the vans tail lights fade down the street then got about his business. He had three injured officers, two suspects en route to the hospital, a huge crime scene, and an OIS to supervise. It was going to be a long night.

"What a cluster fuck," Abe said under his breath.

Butch and Lenny had been driving north on the Harbor Freeway when they'd heard the help call. In their effort to get to the scene they broke just about every rule of the road, and screeched to a halt at the yellow crime scene tape as the RAs bearing T-Bone pulled away from the curb.

"Where the hell were you two?" Sergeant Palmer asked.

Lenny provided an abridged answer while Butch stood looking hangdog.

Palmer endured the explanation then said, "I'm on my way to the hospital. You guys make yourselves useful here. We'll discuss this later."

At the hospital, a trauma team worked feverishly over Diane Erickson. She had suffered broken bones throughout her body. They immobilized her spine and then focused on her fractured skull. Her traumatized brain was swelling and the medical staff raced to prep her for surgery.

Captain Sullivan hurried through the Emergency Room and approached a group of officers. Their attention was concentrated down the long hall, where several people in green scrubs were pushing Diane Erickson on a hospital gurney through a double door at the end of the hall. As the doors swung closed behind them Sullivan read the placard on the doors: "SURGERY."

At the other end of the hall, Quint King sat up in his bed. He wore a neck brace but felt pretty good. Brian sat quietly next to the bed. A thick-wristed middle-aged nurse wearing a "La Raza" t-shirt and flowered scrub bottoms adjusted Quint's bed.

"That should make you more comfortable, officer. Doctor says you suffered soft tissue damage to your neck. But you should feel better in a week or so."

"Hell, ah've had broncs snap my neck harder than that," he drawled.

"I don't think you will be doing any of that for a while, buckaroo," she said, unimpressed.

The nurse tucked the sheets under Quint's mattress, then headed toward the figure in the bed next to Quint. She jerked the curtain that slid on an overhead track between the beds thereby separating the two patients.

"Hello, *mijo.* You feeling better?" the nurse asked.

Manny's eyes tracked the nurse. A half hour ago when she'd

administered him a diazepam shot, Manny had called her "Mommy." Now he lay strapped to the bed with leather restraints and with a starched white sheet pulled to his waist. His uniform was in a blue plastic trash bag at the foot of his bed.

"I gave you a shot. You should be back to normal soon," the nurse told him. She tousled Manny's dark, wavy hair, then smoothed it.

Next to Manny sat Scooter Kellerman, happily reading the girlie magazine he kept in his duty bag for just such occasions. He looked up at the large Latina nurse.

"He's feeling much better. All he could do at first was grunt like a piggy. A few minutes after you gave him the shot he started to come around."

"Hmm. You're a lot of help, Scooter," she said.

She plucked the magazine out of his hands and as she walked from the room said, "You can pick your smut up at the nurses' station when you leave."

"No problemo, Iris, you can have it. I got more," Scooter called.

Quint and Brian heard the exchange between Scooter and the nurse and shared a grin. Neither of them heard Abe Palmer and Bruno Cicotti come into the room.

"How you feeling, Quint?" Cicotti said, "Up to a little conversation?"

"Yes, sir, lieutenant." Quint came to attention in a seated position.

"Relax, Quint. Just want to talk a little and see what you remember. Sounds like it was a mad minute to be sure," Lieutenant Cicotti said as he settled into the chair Brian had vacated as soon as the two supervisors walked in.

Quint eased just a bit. "You bet, Sir. It got kinda western, that's for sure."

Cicotti turned to Brian. "Hi, Brian. I need to talk with Quint. Would you go with Abe? Later you can tell me what you saw, son."

"Yes, sir." Brian slipped between the curtains into the hall, followed by Abe Palmer.

"How's he doing, Brian?"

"Better, sir. They think he's going to be fine. Sergeant, I'm sorry about leaving the scene, but I didn't know how bad Quint was and..."

The veteran sergeant clamped Brian's shoulder.

"Not to worry it's common for an officer to refuse to leave his partner's side. Hell, I remember the Lugo-Bender shooting. Charlie Bender had three bullets in him and was nearly bled out. It took four people to pry him away from Danny."

Abe hesitated, his features softened as he looked at the wide-eyed young man standing next to him. "Sometimes you kind of remind me of Danny. He was a good kid. Sad thing, Danny's death; Charlie's never completely recovered from it. I think the fact that Danny's revolver is still out there being carried around by some puke grates on Charlie."

"His wife gave him that gun when he graduated from the Academy," Brian said.

Abe shot Brian a quizzical look then said, "Sure would like to see it recovered." He hitched up his gun belt. "Sorry, I don't know how I got to talking about that."

Brian was glad the old sergeant had.

Cicotti pushed his head between the drapes and said, "Brian, there's a little office the nurses let me use. Let's see if it's free."

Brian followed the tall man in the wrinkled suit into a small, windowless room. It seemed even smaller when Cicotti closed the door. Cicotti conducted a short interview, and was soon satisfied that he had gleaned any pertinent information that Brian possessed. But something else weighed on his mind. Cicotti knew a campaign against the officer's shooting of Baby-K was being organized downtown, sparked by a phone call from Lieutenant Wiener to Deputy Chief Griefwielder, who would be the head of Brian's shooting review board.

"So, Brian, are you nervous about your board?" Cicotti said.

"Well, a little, sir. But Charlie explained how it works."

"Uh huh. Do you know what the board looks at?" Cicotti asked.

"Yes, sir. They review the drawing of my weapon, my tactics leading up to and during the shooting, then each shot I fired is looked at individually."

Cicotti was impressed with the textbook answer Brian provided, and was glad to hear that Charlie Bender was watching out for the youngster.

"That's right, Brian. The board makes a recommendation to the chief of police, who then makes his determination, and sends it to the Police Commission for their final approval. Generally, the commission agrees with the opinion of the Chief. So don't panic if the board is a little tough on you. It still has to get past the Chief. Did Charlie tell you anything else?"

"Yes, sir. He said to watch my temper and my ass around Sergeant Price and Lieutenant Wiener."

"That sounds like some very good advice, son."

CONDUCTING BUSINESS

On the day after Thanksgiving, Westwood Village was already taking on a Christmas look. Business owners were busily hanging lights and festive decorations. "The Village" was an upscale collection of restaurants, shops, and theatres conveniently adjacent to the UCLA campus. Wedged between the San Diego Freeway, Sunset Boulevard and the University, the Village was a favorite meeting place for students and affluent Angelenos from nearby West Los Angeles, Brentwood, Bel Air, and the independent city of Beverly Hills. It was not unusual to see a recording artist or movie star in one of several bistros in the Village enjoying the trendy fare, leisurely atmosphere and cool ocean breezes. Recently, another group of citizens had found the quaint setting to their liking. On weekends it became common to see gang members loitering on the sidewalks and cruising the streets of Westwood. The age of innocence was running out in upscale Los Angeles.

Tootie Hicks and Beppe Fazio sat at a sidewalk café in the center of the Village sipping coffee and discussing business. Since his parole, Beppe had been living in an apartment near the UCLA campus. He liked LA, and business was good. Colombian cocaine was moving into California in record quantities, and much of it went to the beautiful people of Los Angeles. Hollywood personalities, musicians, business people, professional athletes, lawyers, and even politicians were snorting "snow" until their noses bled. Now the drug was making its presence known in the poor neighborhoods of town, too, in the form of freebase or rock cocaine. The addictive capacity of rock was creating a dealer's market like never before. Historically, strong intoxicants like heroin, high proof distillates, and malt liquors have had a significant customer base in poor urban neighborhoods. The powerful seductive high of freebase certainly met that bill and a disproportionate number of African-Americans were now becoming addicted. Some believed it to be a sinister plot to keep the black man down, while others simply saw it as a way to riches.

"I got some business to attend to in the hood tonight, man," Tootie said. "Some fool is messin' with my business an' I'm fittin to school his ass."

"Tootie, why are you still doing your own muscle? I know you're bringing in all kinds of dough. Let some homeboy make a couple bucks and risk his ass."

Tootie shrugged his shoulders and thought of the little fool who had caused such a mess in the hood.

Despite Beppe's misgivings, the man across the table impressed him. He had always been moved by violence and nerve. Growing up in a tenement on the lower east side of Manhattan in the 30s and 40s, Beppe had lived in the midst of bloodshed his whole life. As a boy he loved to listen to stories of New Yorks mobsters. Men like Lucky Luciano and Don Vito Genovese were his childhood heroes. While most young boys his age wished they were riding the range with Roy Rogers, Beppe longed to wield the power of Chicago's Al Capone.

Tootie eyed the young coed waiting on his table.

"Excuse me, pretty miss. Check, please."

The waitress flipped back her blond hair and gave Tootie the smile she saved for special customers. She let her fingers trail along his neck as she walked away.

She was back quickly with his bill, complete with a personalized smiling flower over the "i" in Cindi. Next to that was her phone number. He left his usual tip, a twenty wrapped around a vial of white powder. Tootie slipped the receipt into his pocket and focused on the problem at hand.

With a shipment due in a few days, he was intent on putting an end to the police problem in the hood. He was losing dope, losing dealers and, most importantly, he was losing money.

"It's no big thing man. The po-lice been hittin the hood hard cause some silly ass niggers been actin the fool. I jes gotta get some shit straight, thas all," Tootie said.

"So pay da cops to look the other way. Look at it as taxes or the cost of doin' business."

"I ain't givin those mutha fuckers shit, man," Tootie said.

"Fine, kid. Just watch you don't draw too much heat running

around shooting da place up. That's not good business."

Unbeknownst to Beppe the man across the table's hate of the police and need for revenge over rode his business sense. He was going to deal with the cop O'Callahan who had killed his protégé and was making such an impression in the hood.

Tootie, in his navy Adidas sweat suit, and Beppe, his maroon silk shirt unbuttoned to the middle of his hairy chest, were gangsters from different times and places, but alike in their ruthlessness. Both wore heavy gold chains around their necks. Tootie's was thick-linked and had a gold medallion with a diamond encrusted dollar sign embossed on it. Beppe's was a braided rope with a gold malocchio charm dangling from it. Beppe stood and picked up the canvas gym bag Tootie had put on the ground when he sat down. It felt right. He would make certain when he got back to his apartment.

"Ok, kid, see ya in da funny papers." Beppe slung the bag's strap over his shoulder and walked away.

An hour later Tootie pushed the automatic garage door opener and parked his BMW in his mother's garage. He'd paid for his mom and a friend to take a Las Vegas trip so the house was his own. The neat little cottage was decorated with French provincial furniture and photographs of her two sons. Tootie's older brother, Gabriel, had been shot and killed by a rival gang member as he walked from his girlfriend's home one summer evening. As Tootie rummaged through the sideboard drawer looking for a phone number, he came across a photo of two boys. The grade-school brothers had their arms over each other's shoulders and beamed as they stood together, with the Pacific Ocean as a backdrop. Fourteen years after Gabriel's murder Tootie was still tortured by this photo. He fingered the silver bracelet around his right wrist. It had been his brother's, and was Tootie's most prized possession. Finding what he was looking for, he unfolded a piece of paper as he pushed the drawer closed with his knee. He then dialed the number scribbled on the paper.

"Yo, wassup? Look here, man, I'm fittin to drop by your crib an' pick up my shit. All right, then, 'bout fifteen minutes." Tootie hung up without saying goodbye.

He walked into his old room and took a set of car keys from a box on the dresser, put the keys in his pocket, walked out the front door, then made sure it and the steel mesh security door were both locked. He walked a block and slipped the key from his pocket into the door of a late-model Buick 225, commonly referred to in South Central as a "deuce-and–a-quarter." Tootie kept the car parked near his mother's home to use when he was in the neighborhood. Although car theft and burglary from motor vehicles were rampant in the area, Tootie's green Buick was never touched. Most drug dealers insisted on cruising the streets in high-priced customized cars--styling for the ladies. There were no girls in the hood Tootie was interested in, and he'd learned early that such a car in this neighborhood was to the police what a red cape is to a bull.

After his abrupt telephone conversation, Dee walked into the small hallway in his mother's home and pulled down the attic ladder. He looked up into the attic and thought back to the day in 1982.

Dee! Hey, man, wassup!" Tootie said.

Dee stopped. His heart jumped to his throat at the sight of the light complexioned, muscular ex-con in front of him.

"*Tootie? Hey, cuz, you're home now, huh?"* Dee asked.

"*Yeah, man, jus got out.*

Say, man, I don't s'pose you can front me some bank until I get my thing together?" Tootie asked.

"*Sure, man, I got a little bit, I can help a brother,* Dee said.

He pulled a roll of bills from his pocket peeled off a couple and gave them to Tootie, who pocketed the money and started toward a dented old Chevy Impala parked at the curb. He pushed the key into the trunk lock and the lid popped open with a hollow sound. He lifted the spare tire and reached under an oily mat. Tootie looked around the immediate area, then when he assured himself that no one was looking, handed Dee a large shoebox.

"*Hang on to this for me, man, I'll come get it later."*

"*Hey, look, Tootie, I don't mess around any more'."*

"*Chill, nigger, jes put it away. I can't have it at my crib right now, man an you know you the only one I can trust to keep it."*

Dee's stomach tightened. He tucked the box under his arm, and headed home. Once home he'd taken a kitchen knife and cut the tape on one side of the box. He looked into the box and was not at all surprised to see the gun. It was still beautiful and frightening. Dee re-taped the box, climbed the ladder to the attic, and pushed it into the far corner with a broomstick.

He didn't like Tootie then, and now almost two years later, he still didn't like him. Dee rued the day he had loaned Tootie forty bucks and first took custody of the shoebox.

On occasion Tootie had come by and picked up the box then returned it a day or two later. Happy to be rid of the gun and hopefully for good, Dee climbed into the darkness and aimed his flashlight into the farthest corner of the small attic. Seeing what he needed, he crawled to a cardboard box filled with magazines. He lifted out the magazines and shined the light into the box. His stomach rolled over and knotted. *Where is it?* he thought. Dee's mind raced first to Tootie, then to his little brother. Dee was on the bottom rung of the ladder when he saw Mo-Mo limping for the front door. He had injured his ankle as a result of his fall into the basement and it was painfully swollen.

"Mo, where you think you're going?" he said.

Mo screwed his face up and said, "What?"

"You know what. Where's the strap? Man, that gun's Tootie's, and he's comin' to get it right now," Dee said.

"I gotta go, man. Tootie mad at me fo' some reason. Tre told me."

"Where is it, Mo?" Dee said, walking closer.

Mo-Mo's head was spinning, and his heart was racing. He put his hands up, thinking Dee was going to punch him. "I let Tre use it. He had it when he an' Baby-K got jacked. He hid it over near where he got arrested."

"That was over a month ago, man. Why the fuck didn't you go get it?" Dee yelled.

"I didn't know it belonged to Tootie an Tre keeps gettin busted," Mo-Mo whined.

"This nigger doesn't play, man. He's gonna want his shit," Dee said.

The brothers stopped talking when they heard the deuce and a quarter's heavy door slam. Mo-Mo's face faded two shades. He limped to a couch by the window and sat down.

"All right, man, you be cool. I'll talk to Tootie," Dee told him.

Dee walked out the front door and met Tootie at the fence. Mo-Mo watched through the window. The two men exchanged words, and then Tootie looked toward the house. He spun on his heels, walked to the trunk of his car, and opened it. He put something from the trunk into his waistband then smoothed his oversized black silk shirt over it. Mo-Mo considered running out the back door, but he wouldn't get far with his injured ankle. The ex-con headed toward the house with a grim look on his face. Dee walked backwards in front of Tootie, trying to calm him. Mo-Mo was near panic when his momma walked into the room from the kitchen.

"What's troubling you, child?" she said, putting a hand on his forehead.

"Nuthin', Momma, jus go in your room, please," Mo-Mo said.

Dee backed through the front door followed by Tootie. Norma May Haynes screamed when Tootie pulled the 9 mm pistol from his waistband and chambered a round. Mo-Mo curled into a ball on the couch and held his hands over his head. Dee tried to think.

"Nigger, you Mo-Mo?"

Tootie held the barrel of the pistol an inch from Mo-Mo's head. His mother lunged at Tootie but was intercepted by Dee. She wiggled and twisted. Dee was just too strong. She dropped to the floor, sobbing.

"Momma, wait, he's not gonna shoot Mo, are ya, Toot?" Without waiting for an answer he hurried on. "Toot, look here, brother. I'll make it right, man. Don't kill him, man, please! My momma's here, homes."

Tootie took a look at the wailing woman on the floor then at the professional boxer three feet from him. His mind moved back from the edge of murder. He turned back to Mo-Mo.

"Nigger, you was told to paint that silly ass shit off the wall an you didn't. Now I hear you stole my property? You're a real mutha fuckin bother."

"Toot, he didn't know it was yours, man. I'll get it back," Dee said.

Tootie glared down at Mo-Mo. "No, this mutha fucker's gonna get it. And he gonna go down an' tell the po- lice that he painted that shit on the wall, an' he sorry, an' he ain't gonna kill nobody."

Mo-Mo lowered his hands and nodded his head. Tootie brought the pistol down against the side of Mo-Mo's temple and eyebrow; blood flowed instantly.

"Cause if you don't, Ima come back here an' kill yo' punk ass.

127

An' I don't care if you sittin' in yo' momma's lap. You hear me, muthafucker?" Tootie said.

He brought the gun down across the top of Mo-Mo's head again and took a step away from the couch. Mo rolled onto the floor, exposing his midsection. Tootie couldn't resist one more lick. He kicked Mo in the stomach, then left him bleeding and retching, but alive.

Twenty-five minutes later Tootie was driving along the Pacific Ocean. The beach always made him relax. He recalled the day he and his brother had spent at the beach. Two busloads of inner-city children had been treated to the outing courtesy of Los Angeles Parks and Recreation. Despite living only a few miles away from the ocean, for many of the children this was the first, and for some, the last time they would ever see it. The day was spent running through the surf in cutoff jeans, digging holes in the sand, and eating gritty peanut butter and jelly sandwiches. Tootie had loved it. He thought about the waitress's phone number in his pocket and smiled. *Life's a whole lot better with money,* he thought. He pulled into the gated drive of a luxury waterfront apartment complex and pushed several numbers on a pad next to the security gate. It opened, and Tootie parked in his assigned spot. As he stepped from his car he heard a deep voice behind him. He spun around, and his hand instinctively slipped under his shirt.

"Easy, brother, I was just saying I like your ride, man," said the very tall African American man.

Tootie relaxed and said, "Thanks, man."

Tootie had seen the man around the complex and recognized him immediately. There were several professional athletes living in the apartment building. This one played basketball at the Forum in Inglewood.

"Elvis Tubbs. Nice to meet you," the man said, holding his hand out.

The two men performed the three-part handshake popular with blacks across the country, then made small talk as they walked toward their respective apartments.

"It's nice to see a brother doing well," Tubbs said. "I'm in 1123. Stop by any time, man."

"All right then," Tootie said, pointing a finger at Tubbs as he walked away.

Each man felt he had just made a good contact.

In his apartment, Tootie poured himself two fingers of cognac and fired up a joint. He pulled back the full-length curtains, opened the sliding glass door to the small patio, stepped outside and gazed at the boats bobbing in their slips below him. He hit the joint hard, drew the smoke deep into his lungs, and held it as long as he could, then lowered himself into a wicker chair and exhaled. The pungent smoke mixed with the cool, damp salt air. After half an hour, Tootie felt refreshed. He went back to the living room and settled onto his plush black leather recliner and took out the receipt from lunch and dialed the phone. A young female voice said, *Hello?*

In his best Barry White voice Tootie said, "Hello, you fine thing."

THE BOARD

Shooting Review Boards were held in downtown Los Angeles on the top floor of the Police Administration Building. The six-story structure was commonly referred to as Parker Center in honor of former chief of police William Parker who led the department from 1950 to 1966 and was credited with the LAPD's rise to fame in the late 50s and early 60s. PAB was where the Department's elite and powerful prowled the halls. It was looked upon with awe and considered a mystery to most rank-and-file police officers. To Charlie Bender, PAB was where those who didn't have the stuff to be street cops hid and rode on the coattails of officers who did. The building was encased in reflective windows, and therefore known to residents of South Central as the "Glass House." Many a pilgrimage from South Central to the Glass House was made, as PAB also housed Men's Central Jail.

Charlie and Brian stepped into the elevator then turned and faced the doors, which closed six inches from Charlie's nose. There was a casual conversation going on among the four people behind him. Charlie glanced to his right and Brian looked back at his mentor.

"Charlie, do you think--"

Charlie shot him a stern look and gave his head a minute shake. From that point there was silence in the elevator all the way to the sixth floor. Both men could feel eyes on their backs. The doors opened, and Charlie stepped from the elevator, then turned and faced the remaining occupants.

"He's just a kid, fellers. He doesn't know that you don't talk shop in the Glass House elevator."

There were strained chuckles among the uniformed men as they exited the elevator behind Charlie and Brian. The first three all had silver stars on their collars, which meant they were command staff officers. Each glanced at Charlie and tried to read his highly polished nametag as they passed. The fourth wore two silver bars on each collar. He was a captain. Charlie and Brian had seen him when they entered the elevator and they had acknowledged one another with quick smiles.

"Hi, skipper," Charlie said.

Captain Sullivan put a hand on Brian's shoulder and said, "I see ya brought moral support, or is that immoral support?"

Brian wasn't sure how to answer so he remained quiet.

Sullivan turned to Charlie. "Just can't miss an opportunity to thumb your nose at authority, eh, Charlie?"

"The department shrink said I needed a hobby, boss."

"I see," Sullivan said.

Charlie held his hand out. Sullivan took it and shook it earnestly, all the while he kept his hand on Brian's shoulder.

As the three men walked down the hall toward the boardroom, Charlie and Captain Sullivan talked of the good old days. Brian watched the scar below Charlie's jaw stretch as he spoke. The sight of it made Brian sad, and fueled a profound affection for the man, though he didn't understand why. They stopped outside the boardroom. Men in suits, others in uniform, milled around the hall outside. A uniformed sergeant appeared from inside the boardroom. He propped the door open, nodded to the group, and people began filing in.

Sullivan looked at his watch. "Won't be long now, lad. It's nearly time."

Charlie put an arm around Brian's shoulder and whispered in his ear. "I wish I could go in with ya, but asides the shooter, only board members, RHD investigators, and use of force experts are allowed in. Remember what I told ya, Bri. Don't say a word unless somebody asks y'all a question. Then answer only that question—short and sweet. Y'all are just here to witness the review of yer shooting. Look 'em in the eye but don't stare 'em down. Smile if something is funny and everyone is laughing, but otherwise keep yer poker face."

Captain Sullivan cleared his throat. "Charlie, don't be such a mother hen. I'll watch out for him. You just wait out here and behave yourself."

Brian smiled a smile Charlie had not seen in ten years and said, *Este nada, mi hermano.*

The young police officer then followed his captain into the

chamber.

Charlie watched the door close behind the two men. *That's right, Danny. Y'all look out for that boy in there*, he thought.

"The kid inside?" Lieutenant Cicotti asked.

Charlie's head snapped around to see the familiar face.

"Not like you to let someone sneak up on you, Charlie. Must have been deep in thought," Cicotti said.

Charlie ignored the good natured ribbing. "How's this thing looking?"

"Shooting is solid and in the long run it won't be a problem. That prick Griefwielder will stir the pot. Fortunately he doesn't know much about tactics or understand shooting policy. Mika Slate from the Tactics Unit is on the board, and the big boss thinks Slate hung the moon. They might go after Brian's tactics some, but they always do. Got to hand it to that kid; he had some balls going after a suspect armed with a Mac-10. His guardian angel must have been with him that night."

"Somethin' like that, Bruno," Charlie said.

Cicotti's partner, Robbie Lang, shuffled his feet and looked toward the room.

"Well, better get in there," Cicotti said.

"See y'all guys."

Thirty-five minutes later the doors opened and the occupants filed out, talking among themselves. Among the group was a paunchy man in his late fifties. His thinning hair was coiled on top of his head like a cinnamon roll. The ginger tint of his comb-over was in sharp contrast to the man's pallid complexion and gray eyebrows. Deputy Chief Gregory Griefwielder peered over his shoulder back into the room. He did not seem pleased. Close behind were Brian, Cicotti, and Slate, who did. Griefwielder glanced over his Benjamin Franklin bifocals at Charlie then waddled down the hall toward his office.

Brian walked up to Charlie, fighting a smirk.

"How'd it go, Bri?" Charlie asked.

"Good," he answered.

Sergeant Mika Slate, a square-jawed former Marine, approached, took Charlie by the hand, and then pulled him into a bear hug.

Slate released his. "I'll tell you how it went Charlie, Captain

Sullivan did the shooting overview and made his recommendations to the board. Without even addressing the captain's presentation or recommendations, Griefwielder went after O'Callahan. He says,'*Officer, I have scrutinized your actions quite closely and am aghast. What do you have to say for yourself?* Everyone in the room was shifting around in their seats, shuffling papers and trying to think of something to say."

Cicotti took up the tale. "Brian stood up and walked to the board table. Sure he's going to go off on the Deputy Chief, I'm thinking, oh shit, here we go. In a low, calm voice Brian gave a textbook rational for his shooting. It was as if he were reading my mind."

"Griefwielder just sat there mumbling with those liver lips of his," Slate added.

They all laughed at Slate's description.

Embarrassed by the conversation, Brian used the pause in conversation to ask, "Where's the restroom?"

"Down by the elevator," Cicotti said.

The three men watched Brian walk down the hall for a moment then resumed the recap of the hearing.

"Did the board buy it?" Charlie asked

"Fuckin-A, they did," Slate said. "When he finished you coulda heard a rat piss on cotton. Then one of the board members says, 'Well, I don't have any questions. Does anyone else?' Griefwielder just sat there looking like his puppy got hit by a car. Never said another word. It was a thing of beauty."

Cicotti said, "Kid threw a damn shutout; Drawing and Exhibiting: in policy, no action. Tactics: no action. All shots: in policy, no action."

Down the hall Brian approached Sergeant Price and Lieutenant Wiener, who were standing in the hall outside Griefwielder's office. Brian stopped inches from Price and addressed him.

"Sergeant, I was out of line the day of my shooting when you asked why I shot Baby-K in the back. I would like to offer my apology."

Monty Price's face was as pale as his uncle's had been when he exited the shooting review. Try as he might, Price could not look the young cop in the eye.

All he could muster was, "Fine," which he directed to the floor.

Captain Sullivan approached, with Bender, Slate, Cicotti and Lang.

"Lieutenant Wiener, I would like a word with you, if you please," Sullivan said.

The two men stepped from the group and rounded the corner. Sullivan's voice could be clearly heard.

"Pogue lieutenants are a dime a dozen, but hard working police officers are not. It is hard enough to get fine young men like O'Callahan down here without you trying to run them off. In the future, should you have a problem, kindly follow the chain of command and bring it to my attention. And while we're on the topic, if you don't like any of my decisions, march into my office and let me know about it rather than whining behind my back to the Deputy Chief."

All eyes were on the pair as they returned, except Brian, who glared at Price. Wiener walked directly into Griefwielder's office. Sullivan, Lang, Cicotti and Slate said their good byes and walked off toward the Chief's office as the elevator bell rang. The doors opened and Price scuttled in. Just as the doors were closing Price saw a hand grab the black plastic bumper. Charlie Bender and Brian O'Callahan stepped into the stainless steel cube.

Brian stood next to Price. Staring at him but speaking to Charlie he said, "Partner, you never told me Danny Lugo was a Physical Training instructor at the Academy." Brian cocked his head so he could look in the sergeant's eyes. "Matter of a fact, he was your P.T. instructor, wasn't he, Sergeant Price?"

Monty Price stared straight ahead. Charlie watched the terrified sergeant, then directed his attention to Brian, whose features had become dark and cruel.

Brian continued, his voice taking on a sarcastic edge. "Recruit Price had a little accident during combat wrestling when he was in the Academy." Brian watched impassively as more color drained from Price's face.

"A classmate got Monty here in a bar arm and choked him out, caused him to, oh... how would you say it? Let loose, I guess. Another classmate started calling him 'Poopy Pants.' Danny stepped in and put an end to the name-calling. That wasn't enough for recruit Price."

Monty Price moved so close to the elevator doors that moisture from his breath collected on the stainless steel.

Brian continued, "His uncle was the captain at Internal Affairs back then, got that classmate and the kid that choked him terminated and had Officer Lugo transferred to 77th Street. Right, Sarge?"

Price was having difficulty breathing and loosened the collar of his shirt. He gasped as the elevator bell sounded and when the doors opened, he bolted into the lobby and ran to the men's room.

Charlie turned to Brian. "Looks like ol' Poopy Pants had ta go purty bad. How'd y'all dig that stuff up on 'im?"

"A little birdie told me in a dream, *jefe,*" Brian said softly.

Thirty feet away Monty Price sat against the tiled wal panting in the men's room. He could hear his Self Defense Instructor, Officer Lugo, yelling, *Fight,*

Price! Don't give up! You gotta fight!

MY BABY AIN'T SEEN NOTHING

The day after Tootie's visit to his home, Mo-Mo walked into 77th Station and confessed. He spent much of that day and the next painting over his handiwork under the watchful eyes of Butch and Lenny, who found great joy in pointing out any inscriptions that needed additional attention.

A week later, Tre was released from the hospital. Mo-Mo was waiting in front of his apartment when Tre returned home. Despite Tre's injuries Mo-Mo convinced him of the urgency of the situation, as the alternative to not finding and returning Tootie's gun was both their deaths. That evening, the two friends slipped down the alley where Tre had run trying to avoid arrest. They stopped at the fence he had scaled a month and a half ago. With a leap and heave, Mo-Mo flung himself over the fence in one fluid motion. Since his injury, Tre was experiencing severe headaches and dizziness. Tre adjusted the black patch that covered his empty eye socket and took hold of the dog-eared slats at the top on the wooden fence. He managed to get one foot on top of the fence then wavered. Mo-Mo grabbed Tre's shirt and pulled him down into the yard. Once safely in the yard Tre pointed to a 1958 Chevrolet pickup sitting on concrete blocks.

"Over there in the truck, under the front seat."

Mo-Mo worked the handle and pulled the door open. The hinges moaned with resentment at being disturbed.

"Shhh, man, someone call the po-lice! Jes be quiet, Mo!"

Mo-Mo fumbled around under the seat until his fingers felt the cold touch of the steel. He pulled the revolver out of hiding and examined it under the moonlight. "Got it."

He slid the barrel into his waistband as he and Tre walked past the gray house, down the driveway and onto 67th Street. They turned down the dark sidewalk, passing the home they had been behind. Dee was waiting for them in his car down the street and saw the two boys heading his way. He also saw a car slow and pull alongside them, its headlights off.

"Where you from?" a voice called from the darkened vehicle.

Anyone who lived in the hood knew those words to be a precursor to gunfire. Tre stopped and let the car keep moving while Mo-Mo stepped slowly backwards, adding a couple more feet between himself and the old Chevrolet Impala.

"We ain't from nowhere, man, jes visiting my auntie," Mo-Mo said. "We fittin to--"

Mo-Mo stopped talking when he saw the shotgun barrel pointed out of the backseat window. That was just as it spewed a foot of flame. He pulled the revolver from his pants and pointed it at the car. The gun seemed to shoot itself, as the hammer continued to fall even after all six rounds were discharged into the car. The Impala lurched forward then slowed as the left front tire squealed against the curb. The car came to rest several yards in front of Dee who threw his car into gear, and stepped on the gas pedal. Mo-Mo still had the pistol pointed at the car down the street when Dee pulled over and pushed open the passenger door.

"Hey, man, get in the car! Come on, Mo!"

Mo-Mo threw the pistol into the car and turned to Tre, who was staggering toward the car bent over at the waist with both hands to his abdomen. Mo- Mo helped him into the backseat, leaped into the car and they sped off. As he drove, Dee thought of the scene he had just witnessed. He imagined all the commotion that was now going on and the questions that were being asked. He wondered what had been seen and what would be told. His mind was racing. He drove up the long ramp that led to the emergency room at the USC Medical Center. As he reached the turnaround he stopped abruptly. Mo-Mo opened the car door, pulled the front seat forward, reached under Tre's arms, dragged him onto the sidewalk and laid him down. Two paramedics were wheeling a patient from their rescue ambulance and stopped to watch.

Mo-Mo looked at them. "We gonna park the car, man! Go get a doctor! We be right back!"

He jumped into the car and Dee slowly drove off. The brothers stayed east of Main Street on surface streets and headed toward home. As they rode, Dee told Mo-Mo what to tell the police if they were stopped.

"Just say Tre got shot on Hoover and we drove him to the hospital, that's all, man. You don't know anything about how it happened."

The best Mo-Mo could muster was a grunt; too many thoughts were vying for his attention. Despite the violence of everyday life in South Central, Mo-Mo was frightened. Tre had been his friend as far back as he could recall. After several minutes of silence, he asked, "You think he's gonna live?"

"Doctors are pretty good at USC. They say so many gangsters get brought in with bullets in them the Army sends doctors there to learn because the hood's like a battlefield."

Back on 67th Street, Dapper Davy and Preacher looked into the Impala. It appeared each occupant had been hit at least twice. Judging by the wounds and damage to the car, Davy figured the shooter had used a damn big gun, too. Then something occurred to the veteran homicide detective.

He looked thoughtful, then directed his attention to the job at hand.

"We got any wits?"

"Not a whole lot yet. We have some little kid who said he saw two guys in his yard. He's with Quint and O'Callahan," said Preacher.

"Hmm, could be something," said Davy as he walked to the other side of the car.

Lieutenant Wiener approached the detectives with Sergeant Price in tow. "Do we need all these officers here? We are dropping calls and have cars from three divisions handling calls in 77th Street."

Dapper Davy looked at the wide-hipped, narrow-shouldered lieutenant for a long moment and measured his response. "Talk to Detective Stupin, lieutenant. We have no control over it".

Wiener walked briskly off, asking officers their assignments as he passed them.

"What a prick!" Dapper Davy mumbled. "Guy's a fuckin bean counter, only concerned with the numbers."

"He won't be around long. Neither will his little pal, Sergeant Price," said Preacher.

"I heard he had a nervous breakdown or something," said Dapper

Davy.

"Yeah, he was leaving the Glass House after O'Callahan's shooting board yesterday and collapsed in the men's room," Preacher said. "They found him semi-conscious, lying in front of a urinal. He's back to work today but I hear he's going on loan to Internal Affairs."

"Sounds like a vice caper to me. They do a rape kit on him?" Dapper Davy asked with a chuckle.

"A little compassion for your fellow man, partner," Preacher said.

Several houses down the street from the Impala, Quint and Brian stood talking with a little boy who appeared to be about six years old. He said his name was Anthony and that he had seen "everything."

"I heard a noise in my yard and looked out the window. Those boys had a gun, they found it in my grandpa's truck, I seen em," Anthony said.

Brian squatted down next to the little boy. "Do you know whose gun it was?"

"Mm-huh. Yes, it was that boy the po-lice chased in our house only now he's got a pirate patch on his eye. He's the same boy got shot." Anthony said.

"Same boy that got shot tonight? You mean in the car down the street?" Brian asked.

"No, the boy that got shot by them in the car," Anthony said.

"Anthony wiped his runny nose by pulling his forearm across his face and recounted the sequence of events. What most interested Brian was the child's description of the pistol. Somehow he knew it was Danny Lugo's Colt.

Brian reached into his pocket, retrieved a piece of hard candy, and handed it to the little boy. He had developed the habit of keeping a bag of candy in his duty bag after seeing a juvenile detective pull some candy from her handbag while talking with a little girl who'd just witnessed her father's suicide. She told Brian sometimes it was like putting a Band-Aid on an axe wound, but as least it was something when you felt helpless. Anthony ripped the paper off the root beer barrel and without hesitation popped it into his mouth.

The boy's mother came out of the house in a rage. "Child, you get yo butt in the house now! I'm fittin to snatch you bald-headed, boy! Now get!"

Anthony crouched as he scrambled past his mother, hoping to avoid any low- flying slaps.

"Hello, ma'am, my name is Officer O'Callahan and this is my partner, Officer King. We need to talk to Anthony. He witnessed a murder and can help us find the man who did it."

"Mmm-huh, my baby ain't seen nothing. So y'all might jes as well go on, 'cause he ain't talking to y'all no mo'."

"How 'bout this, we leave and come back later through the backyard so no one sees us? We only need a few minutes."

"Officer, don't you understand? My baby talk to you and those boys they gonna come back here and shoot up my house and kill my family and where y'all gonna be when that happens? They ain't nobody can stop 'em."

Quint and Brian had no answer to her exclamations, because she was right. Witnesses were often killed in South Central Los Angeles, and their names just became new numbers on a long list of victims. The detectives tried to offer protection, but gang members responded in a ruthless manner and had little fear of the penal system.

"Ma'am, how 'bout if Anthony tells my partner and me what happened? We won't tell anyone who told us, not even the homicide detectives. You will never need to go to court, and none of your names will be on reports. That way we will at least have some information to go on. Can we do that, you think?" Brian looked into the woman's frightened, distrusting eyes. The corners of his mouth softened and his eyes lost their authoritative edge. "Please."

She relented before she knew she had. Her eyes went soft and her shoulders dropped.

"Y'all come 'round back in a hour," she said then went to her house.

"Hot damn, yer good, partner! Too bad yer such a choirboy, 'cause with that tongue you could throw yer rope 'round a whole passel o' pussy."

Brian just started toward the street thinking about the gun.

Quint caught up and pondered the situation as they walked. "What the hell is the matter with this country? How could we let these little thugs run roughshod over the whole system?" he said.

"I guess they think they can rehabilitate them," Brian answered.

"Rehabilitate? How in the hell do you rehabilitate some little psychopath that blows a little kid off his tricycle and has absolutely no remorse? These killers are like mad dogs and you know what you do with a mad dog: take 'em out back a' the barn and put one in his head. And you don't do it as punishment, you do it so the dang thing don't maul anyone else."

A black look came over Brian O'Callahan. He stopped and faced his partner. "The biggest motivator for man is fear. If there is no fear of retribution then what's to stop people from responding to their most primitive impulses?"

"That's right, Brian," said Lenny Custer.

Brian and Quint turned and directed their attention to the two big cops standing on the sidewalk a few feet away. Lenny and Butch Caldwell were maintaining the east perimeter of the crime scene and had overheard Brian and Quint's conversation.

"Yeah, Lenny's got a theory," said Butch. "It's called--um, what's it called, Lenny?"

"The Theory of Immediate Gratification," said Lenny.

Quint and Brian were intrigued, as were Dapper Davy and Preacher, who had joined the group.

"Pray tell, master," said Preacher.

Delighted to have an audience, Lenny cleared his throat. "My theory can only flourish in a moral or ethical void--an environment with no positive role models, no repercussions, and no hope. A person responds only to stimulus. See car, want car, take car. It's that easy. See pussy, want pussy, take pussy. It is the motivation of unbridled greed and lust."

"And our country is becoming a spiritual desert," said Preacher.

"God's the biggest fear factor there is," said Lenny. "No fear of God, no fear of hell, why not pop a cap in some kid's head for looking cross-eyed at you? Life comes to mean nothing."

"This is all quite intriguing," said Monty Price, who had been eavesdropping. "But the lieutenant wants everyone not critical to this investigation to get back into the field and clear.

Dapper Davy said, "Well, looks like this meeting of the 77th Street Brain Trust is now adjourned."

Everyone went about his business without responding to

Sergeant Price. He stood alone on the sidewalk, looking at Brian O'Callahan's back.

But Brian stopped abruptly and turned toward Price. "Feeling better, Sarge?"

Sergeant Price averted his eyes and walked away on wobbly knees.

Brian trotted to catch up with Quint, who was standing next to Davy and Preacher's unmarked Plymouth. He was filling the homicide detectives in on the witness, Anthony. "So we'll give y'all whatever he gives us, but we can't give the kid up as a wit."

"I don't know if Nick Stupin is gonna go for that. We'll do our best to protect his ID. But if this goes to trial and the court orders us to reveal our source then we don't have any choice," said Dapper Davy. He brushed his wool slacks off with the horsehair whiskbroom he kept in his police car.

"That's not good enough, Davy," said Brian.

Davy's head snapped up and his eyes flashed. "Oh, really? Well, it's just gonna have to do, young officer, as it's my case and I call the fuckin' shots."

There was silence, and Davy immediately regretted his response, but he was not accustomed to being called to task by police officers with less time on the job than his socks. A faint smile bent Brian's lips but never reached his eyes.

"Yes, sir, sorry. Guess I got carried away." Brian started toward the cruiser then turned. "Oh and I think your killers weapon was a Colt Python.

Dapper Davy and Preacher snapped to attention.

What...why do you say that?" Davy asked

"Just a hunch sir." Brian said. Then he walked away.

A few minutes later Quint climbed into the car next his partner. "You know, Davy didn't mean nuthin.' He jes gets a little high-spirited."

"Quint, what Davy says or means really isn't my concern. Point is partner, we can't give him that kid's information, period. Even if he says he'll protect that kid his word has qualifiers. What I heard from him was, he would protect Anthony as long as it didn't make any hardship for him. Christ, this is someone's life we are talking about. These assholes will kill this kid and you know it. I'm not gonna have that on my head just to solve some homicide where one piece of shit smoked another piece of shit."

"Partner, I think you were a social worker in another life."

"I'm not sure what I was in another life, but in this one I sure feel pulled in different directions."

"Why you say that?" Quint asked.

"I don't know. Sometimes I do things or say things and it feels like someone else is doing it. Like I'm on a rail and my actions are already determined.

"Like thinking the murder weapon on this caper is a Python?"

"Sometimes I know things, Quint. It's like I've already been there before. Weird, huh?"

Quint drove for a bit, shot a stream of tobacco juice out of the window, then turned to his partner. "Yup, but you sure as shootin got Dapper Davy's attention."

Quint and Brian ate dinner, then drove to the alley behind Anthony's home. They parked several houses away and found a likely spot to scale the fence.

Both cursed the size of their recent meal as they struggled over the fence and dropped unceremoniously to the ground.

"You handle this, partner. The li'l feller likes you, and Momma does, too." Quint said

An hour later Brian had the entire sequence of events, complete with suspect and vehicle descriptions, on micro cassette tape. Quint looked at the rickety wooden fence with apprehension, and said, "Let's walk 'round front and have the technician from latent prints dust that old pickup. He ought to be here by now."

"Yeah, and we can play the tape for Preacher and Davy."

"Sure you want to do that?" Quint said.

"Yeah, why not? There is no personal information on the tape and it can't be used as evidence because I won't testify to its authenticity or tell whose voice is on it. And I told Anthony not to talk to anyone but you or me."

"Davy's gonna be hot," said Quint.

Fifteen blocks away, sitting alone in his car, Dee turned the pistol over in his hands. He was accustomed to inexpensive and mistreated firearms that, when the trigger was pressed, responded with rough, grating metal-on-metal movements. Not so with the piece of art he held now. Its finish so deep it gave the appearance of being wet. He stared at the gun for a long while then wrapped it in an old t-shirt and carried it into the house. Two days later Tootie came by and picked it up. Dee hoped he'd seen the last of the gun and Tootie too.

A FULL DAY

With his Use-of-Force board behind him, Brian felt comfortable enough to accept the invitation from Dee's trainer Boomer Spencer to spar. Seconds after walking into the Hoover Street gym Brian felt he had found an asylum. He'd maintained a steady regimen of running and calisthenics since graduating from the Academy and worked the heavy bag in the Academy gym regularly. He was excited, as he had not worked out in a boxing gym for years. The sights and smells brought back memories of his childhood, when he had followed his father from gym to gym and city to city. The rapping of the speed bag and grunt of fighters as they bullied the heavy bag, and the sound of shuffling feet as they moved on rosined canvas-covered plywood rings filled his ears. Boxing had always been a part of Brian's world, and he felt returning to it might bring some balance to his life. The rounds bell rang and brought him back to the moment.

Brian asked directions to the locker room from a group of men standing next to the ring. A short Hispanic fighter pointed to a door, which led Brian to a small gamy smelling dressing room. Brian pulled his two-inch revolver from his waistband, dropped it into his bag, and slid the bag into an empty locker. After changing into his workout gear Brian closed the locker, placed a heavy padlock through the handle, and affixed the key to the laces of his well-worn boxing shoe. Brian walked into the gym, stopped, and took measure of the people around him.

"Hey, Brian, good to see you!" Boomer said, feinting a left hook to Brian's mid- section.

"Morning, Boomer, fantastic to be here, sir. I already feel at home."

Boomer's smashed face bore the scars of a thousand battles, but his eyes remained bright.

"You are home, my brother," he said. "Say, man, I know it's been awhile, but Dee needs to put in some light rounds. You feel like mixing it up?"

Brian spotted Dee warming up on the heavy bag. "Sure, sounds great. Let me get my hands wrapped and get warmed up."

"Sho'nuff, man, give a holler when you ready."

Boomer walked across the gym to Dee. "Get geared up. You gonna go a couple with Brian over here. Nice 'n' easy, work your combinations, body, head, body, head. Take it easy on him. I don't know what he got, man."

"Hell, he hasn't got shit, that's what the white boy's got." Then he yelled, "Hey officer, it's been a while since you were here. Thought you got smart and changed your mind."

Brian continued to wrap his hand and didn't acknowledge Dee's wisecrack.

"Easy man, the boy comes from a fightin' family. He might just surprise yo' ass," Boomer told Dee. "An watch his left, he wears his gun on that side so he's a southpaw."

Dee scoffed as he pulled a heavy padded groin protector to his waist.

Several minutes later Brian stepped between the ropes. He was wearing a gray sweat suit with "O'Callahan" stenciled on the front and back, and wore his father's head protection, which was an old-fashioned open- faced affair. Dee sported the latest in boxing head protection, the red leather helmet made famous by Muhammad Ali, with pads that came down from the temple area and protected Dee's cheekbones. Both men wore gloves, twice the weight and padding of those used on fight night.

"All right, y'all, nice an' easy for a couple rounds. Brian, Dee's gonna work some combos, but keep him honest, now. He gets lazy, sting 'im," Boomer said.

Brian bounced on his toes and threw light punches at the air. Dee looked like bull preparing to charge. The bell rang and both men met in the center of the ring. Dee threw a couple of jabs in Brian's direction, both deflected by Brian's right glove. Dee bent to the left and threw a hook at Brian's ribs. Brian blocked that with his elbow and slid away as Dee let loose with a straight right hand intended for Brian's head. The punch missed its mark, and Brian responded with a sharp jolt to Dee's body. Dee waded in, throwing a barrage of punches at his opponent's body and head. Brian let Dee's first punch slip over his shoulder, he rolled under another, and slapped the third punch away. He covered up and let Dee's body shots bounce harmlessly off his arms. All the while Dee and Brian circled, advanced, and withdrew like fencers. Dee sent a right hand at Brian's chin, but the punch grazed harmlessly off his shoulder. The gym was coming alive with voices as fighters, trainers, and onlookers moved toward the ring for a better view of the show. Boomer stood in the corner shouting directions to Dee. When the bell rang, he stepped between the ropes and made some adjustments to Dee's tactics while he washed his mouth out and caught his breath. Brian put his hands on the top rope, leaned over and pushed his mouthpiece forward with his tongue to allow more air to pass into his lungs. He felt better than he had in months. Boomer moved next to Brian and whispered in his ear while massaging his shoulder muscles.

"That's great, man, jes what he needs. Keep it up. Throw some counterpunches, man, make him work for it."

Brian banged his gloves together, and moved toward Dee as the bell rang again. Dee opened up on Brian with several combinations. Most punches Brian dodged, ducked, or minimized. Every time Dee slowed, Brian tagged him with a well-placed counterpunch, always pressing him. Dee had expected to humiliate the policeman; instead Brian seemed to be hitting him at will. The two men clinched and Dee pressed his sweaty face against Brian's.

"Okay, pig, you wanna play?"

Dee pushed Brian away and shot a hook to his opponent's jaw. He followed it up with two left hooks to the body. Brian reeled and crouched against the ropes. As Dee raced in to administer more punishment Brian catapulted off the ropes and threw a short uppercut, powered by his legs as he rose. The punch caught Dee squarely on the chin. Had Brian not been wearing sparring gloves the blow would likely have knocked Dee down, if not out. As it was, the punch sent Dee staggering back. Brian did not pursue his advantage. Instead, he held up his glove, and spit his mouthpiece into his other.

"I need a breather. This guy's killing me, Boomer," Brian said.

"Yeah, take a break."

Boomer put his hand on Dee's shoulder. "Did you see what happened there, Dee? It's not just about punching, man, you gotta be smart. Can't jus come rushin' in like that. How ya feel?"

"I'm good."

Dee looked over his shoulder at Brian, who was stepping out of the ring. Several people acknowledged the display of skill and sportsmanship they had just witnessed.

An hour later, after finishing his workout, as Brian sat on a bench removing the wraps from his hands Dee approached.

"Hey, thanks. You gave me a good look today, something I been needing. You coming back?"

Brian had a welt under his right eye and a glove burn on his chin. "Dee, I'm here for ya, bud. I'll see you tomorrow. But I'm gonna need to train more, 'cause I was really blowing snot bubbles out there today."

Dee looked at the man sitting in front of him. The feeling of familiarity he had the first time they met returned but he still couldn't place it. "Alright, cool, man. Thanks."

Brian walked to the dressing room, changed and was heading toward the front door As he passed through the gym, several heads nodded and a couple of hands waved. Brian sensed his father walking next to him and someone else too.

By 10:00 am Brian was suited up for midday's roll call. He plopped down next to Quint just as Sergeant Palmer began roll.

"King, O'Callahan, after roll go on down to homicide and meet with Dapper Davy and the Preacher."

"Sarge, hope it isn't another dang task force. Last time ah just about got my head pulled off," Quint said.

"Yeah, well, at least it was over fast for you. I'm still writing reports on that cluster. And you guys were supposed to be a handpicked team. Good thing that little base head came into the station and did a *mea culpa*. If the task force had gone much longer I'm not sure I would have had any coppers left."

"Sarge, Dapper Davy said we cleared a shitload of crimes and drove the crime stats into the cellar," Speedboat Willie said.

"I heard that's why the captain kept us all together on middays," Lenny added.

Abe flipped the toothpick end over end in his mouth, then

clamped it between his incisors and spoke through clenched teeth.

"Even a blind squirrel finds a nut once in a while, Willie. The captain kept you knuckleheads together so we can keep track of your crazy asses. Hell, he pulled me off SPU until further notice, just to ride herd on you guys."

"I think you just love us, Abe."

"Like a dose of clap, Mental," Abe replied.

Abe Palmer did a double take on Brian's face. "What the hell happened to you, O'Callahan? Momma catch you poking' fun at some honey?"

"No, Sarge, I don't have a girlfriend."

"Well then?" Palmer said.

"Just doing a little training over at Hoover Street Gym, sir," Brian said.

"Christ, son, I don't know whether to tell you to be careful or call Boomer and tell him to be. Watch yourself over there."

Mental launched a crumpled piece of paper across the room. It bounced off Brian's head. He ignored it, and Scooter's cat calls.

"I will, sir."

"How can this guy be such an altar boy one minute and so ruthless the next?" Pistol Pete whispered.

"I don't know, but I'm staying on his good side, brother," said Willie.

Oco overheard the conversation. He had a theory but learned years ago to avoid such topics with pragmatic people such as police officers.

"All right, let's focus on the Aves today. The Daily Occurrence Sheet has some information on a crew ripping off Mazda RX-7s on the west side of the division."

"Probably some Rollin' 60s gangsters," said Butch Caldwell.

"Or da Rasta men off West Boulevard and 69th Street," said Mental Ward.

"Nah, those guys just sell ganja and run scams," said Manny.

"Well, I'm glad you guys got it all figured out, so it shouldn't be a problem to go rip off a couple rollers. Butch, Lenny, try to keep your hunting party here on the reservation if you don't mind. Oh, one more thing, guys. Dapper Davy said anyone who wants to buy a Reporting District for the homicide lottery better get down to his office. Says he's got a couple good RDs left."

"They're all good in 77th, Abe," Quint said.

There was agreement among all on that point.

After roll Quint and Brian headed toward the Homicide office.

"What's the homicide lottery?" Brian asked.

Quint picked a piece of tobacco off his tongue and flicked it away.

"Ya know how the division is divided up on a grid map and each square is called a reporting district and each one has a number? Every year Dapper Davy raffles off RDs at five bucks a pop. Whoever has money on the RD where the last homicide of the year occurs is the winner. He also has a contest for the number a homicides on the books in 77th. At 00:01 January first the copper who bought the RD where the last homicide occurred and the copper who picked the final number of homicide victims for the year each take a third of the pot. The remaining third goes to the station fund."

"Does an OIS count?" Brian asked.

"Yeah, ah guess so. A police shooting where the guys dies is still a homicide. Last New Year's Eve two pm watch guys nearly went to knuckle junction 'cause this little pooh-butt gangster took one in the ten ring, staggered across Crenshaw, and died on the other side of the street. Problem was he was shot in one RD and died in another. Fellas are a bunch of ghouls."

Quint and Brian walked into the homicide squad room to find a line of officers standing in front of Dapper Davy's desk. Preacher and Davy were hustling numbers like a couple of Wall Street stockbrokers.

"Davy, we ain't waitin' in line to see you. Purty as you are, we kin wait!" Quint said.

Detective Dapper Davy Treats looked up, handed the lottery operation over to Preacher Pruitt.

"Quint I'd like to speak with your partner...alone."

"You bet Davy. I'll just hang around and help Preach scalp these tickets."

Quint joined Preacher Pruitt and Dapper Davy led Brian to an empty interview room. Once inside Davy closed the door and seated himself at a small wooden table across from Brian. He dropped a manila envelope onto the table, unwrapped a stick of gum, folded it and popped it into his mouth. He chewed for an uncomfortable minute without speaking.

Davy learned long ago to trust his intuition. He seldom disregarded a gut feeling and he had one about this young police officer across the table from him. He poured the contents of the bag onto the table and slid them toward Brian.

"So tell me about your Python hypothesis."

Brian counted eight clear plastic coin envelopes. Each contained a bullet that was deformed to some degree. Davy watched Brian's eyes moved from each piece of lead and copper to the next until they froze on one. Brian picked that envelope up by the corner and examined its contents. Brian felt like he had been hit by a lightning bolt. His hand trembled and the bag slipped from his fingers.

Pointing to the remaining projectiles with a pencil Davy said, "This one was dug out of a dope dealer just before you transferred in here. The rest came from the guys in that Impala the other day here." Davy picked up the bag that had drawn Brian's attention. This other one here was removed from a victim ten years ago. Ballistics indicate they were all fired by the same pistol.

"A .357 Colt Python," Brian said.

Mind telling me how you knew that?

"I'm not sure how. I just do," Brian said. He felt nauseous and had an excruciating head ache.

"Brian I think you know a lot more than your telling me; why?"

"Cause you'd think I was a nut if I told you."

"Try me son"

Brian burst like a melon dropped from a roof. "Ever since being issued his locker I have had premonitions and dreams about Officer Lugo, his murder and his Colt Python."

Davy was silent. He knew there was more and waited for it.

"In the back of my mind every time I conduct a search Lugo's gun is what I'm looking for."

Brian felt like a drunk who had just thrown up; relieved but dizzy and weak. "I see his face in my dreams, I see his wife and son. I feel and know things there is no rational explanation for. Call me crazy but I know this is the bullet that killed Danny Lugo."

"Brian if there is one thing I've learned it's that's there is a shit load of stuff out there I don't understand and no one can explain. I have used clairvoyants to find bodies, had witnesses hypnotized to find clues even had a gypsy woman read my victims cards. So don't expect me to sell wolf tickets for what you just said. I don't give a damn if you get you information from a magic lamp, if you have any more premonitions I want to hear them.

Dapper Davy hesitated the asked, "I don't suppose you dreamed who has Lugo's gun have you?

"No but if I see him I'll know him."

"Fair enough. Now let's get your partner in here and talk about something else."

Davy stood and opened the door and waved Quint over.

Quint shuffled in and sat next to his partner.

"Guys, after Brian's shooting a number of lips around the hood have loosened. We even have a line on the third suspect in the drive by where the little boy was killed. I need you guys to give me a hand locating this other player. His name's Ray-Ray. Ever heard of him?"

Quint sat with his legs crossed at the ankle, his hands behind his head. He searched the perforated tiles of the ceiling for an answer. "Hmmm... Might maybe know the name, little turd that lived over on 80th went by that handle. Haven't seen him in a while, he caught a juvenile case a couple years ago but he's out now. There's other Ray-Rays but he's the only Hoover I can think of by that name."

Davy started chewing faster. "Remember what he went for?"

"Some kind of gun charge, I think. Yep, he shot another kid outside school for disrespecting him or somethin' like that. Went down at the bus stop in front of John Muir Junior High," Quint said.

"Sure, I remember that one," Davy said. "He hosed down an RTD bus full of people to get this kid that beat him in a fistfight a couple days before." An incredulous look came over his face. "He's out?"

"Yep, ah was talking to a couple CRASH cops at court the other day and they were tellin me about him gettin out. Said the evil little prick was already gettin into shit."

"How do they release someone who shoots up a bus?" Brian asked.

Quint slowly shook his head. "Some bleedin heart liberal social worker must have figured a couple years in Eastlake Juvenile lock-up cured em of killin' people. Couple of coppers called all the local newspapers and television stations the day that shootin went down. Heck, in the real world some gangster sprayin down a bus full of kids is news. Not around here. Not one outfit said a dang thing. Now he's out and about."

Dapper Davy scribbled some notes and looked at Quint, who was sitting straight up, drumming his fingers on the tabletop in thought.

"As I recall Ray-Ray used to run with that kid Tre who tossed PCP in Manny's face. Mental punted his sorry butt across the alley. Did you get a load of that guy's eyeball, smashed flat and hangin' outta his head? The guys brought the photos into the hospital to cheer me up. Dang, that was a full helping of ugly! Little fucker tried to tell the detectives the devil did it. Purty close--it was Mental Ward," Quint reminisced.

Davy cracked his gum. "Yeah, I remember, he was the same kid that was in the black Regal Brian and Charlie chased. Too bad you didn't smoke him, too, Brian."

Davy smiled. Brian did not.

"That's about all ah remember on Ray-Ray, pard," Quint said.

"Great. I talked with Abe and he said you guys can do some legwork for me if you have time. I didn't bother asking Wiener after the ass-chewin' he got the other day at the building."

"You heard about that?" Brian asked.

"My boy, the only creature that's a bigger gossip than an old woman is a cop," Davy said.

Dapper Davy got up, opened the door of the little room, spit his depleted gum into the waste basket outside the door, and then walked to his desk. He sat down and began writing on a yellow tablet.

Quint and Brian assumed the meeting had ended so they exited the interview room and headed for the office door.

Without looking up Davy addressed Quint. "Any luck on that .357 we talked about?"

Quint stopped at the doorway. "Nuthin' yet, but ah got my nose to the ground," he said.

Brian's face felt like it was wrapped in a hot towel. He kept walking.

Meanwhile the rest of the midday watch crew were scouring the western portion of 77th Street Division for stolen automobiles. Oco and Mental cruised down Third Avenue and passed a silver Mazda RX-7 parked at the curb. To the average person the car would have attracted little attention, but to a sharp street cop it screamed "stolen car," or as the coppers called them, "G-Rides." Mental was driving as Oco rubbernecked the car and grabbed the license plate number as they passed.

"You see that ride, man? No front license plate, factory wheels and tires have been replaced with junkyard rubber--plus that li'l baby needs a bath. We got one, I'll bet code seven on it," Oco said.

Mental drove to the next street and made a right turn while Oco ran the license plate. He pulled to the curb close enough to Third Avenue that they could keep an eye on the Mazda. The license plate on the Mazda came back registered to a 1976 Honda.

"Yessss!" said Oco. "I knew it! Let's call the guys in and set up on this bad boy."

Several minutes later Butch and Lenny were positioned one street south and east of the Mazda while Willie and Pete set up south and west of the car. Oco talked with the other units on a tactical or restricted frequency set aside by Communications Division for such circumstances. He made sure all routes of escape were covered. The weather was warm for a December afternoon, even for Los Angeles. Oco wiggled himself into the seat and slid his handcuff cases to either hip, allowing the small of his back to rest against the seat. He gazed at the robin's egg sky while Mental held a pair of binoculars on the Mazda.

After sitting quietly for an hour, Mental looked over at his partner. "Hey, Oco, whaddaya think of O'Callahan?"

"I don't know. He's a good cop, especially for the amount of time he has on the job. Quint and Charlie like him and he sure as hell can hold up his end of the deal in a fight, guns or fists. Guy's a warrior, that's for sure."

"That's what I mean--how's he know all that shit? Don't you think he's kinda spooky the way he acts sometimes? I see him just staring into his locker like Charlie used to do. I always thought that fuckin' locker was haunted. And those eyes of his when he gets pissed? Holy shit."

Oco studied his partner for several seconds. "Do you really want to know what I think? I'll tell you, but if I get any of your wisecracks I'm gonna pull this knife in my boot and turn you into a gelding."

Mental lowered his binoculars.

Oco went on. "I have long had a feeling about that locker, and I get a strong sense of spirit when O'Callahan is around. Back home I had an uncle who was a shaman--that's like a priest--and he spoke of a people who lived in hidden places in the mountains called the *Nunnehi.* The Nunnehi were gifted with knowledge, but were often confused and susceptible to spirits who entered them and made the Nunnehi do their bidding. Perhaps O'Callahan is like a Nunnehi."

"Like possessed, you mean? You believe in that stuff?"

"Sure, and so do you. Otherwise you wouldn't have asked."

Mental tossed Oco's words around in his head and pulled an enormous bag of sunflower seeds from a paper sack he brought with him. He was still pondering the idea a couple of hours later when Butch's voice came over the radio.

"Oco, I think we must have got burned. It's almost 1500. Wanna call it?"

Oco looked at his watch, then at Mental, who was sitting contently amongst the scores of sunflower shells that littered his lap, the car seat, and the floor of the cruiser.

"Let's give it a few more minutes, you guys, okay?" Oco said.

"We're good," Pistol Pete chimed in. "But my partner has to go potty patrol pretty quick."

"Fuckin' amateur," Mental said as he reached into the backseat. He held up a Gatorade bottle half full of yellow liquid. "Hasn't Willie ever been on a stakeout, for Christ's sake?"

"Maybe he's afraid he'd get stuck in the bottle opening," Oco said. "You ever seen the Johnson bar on that brother? Looks like a radiator hose."

"No, I have not, partner, and I'm a little worried that you have." He spit a mouthful of seeds between his legs onto the car floor. "I gotta stop with the seeds, my tongue feels like a pickle." Mental brought the binoculars up to his eyes again and then sat up straight. "Oh shit, we got a player getting in the ride. He's black, light complexion, wearing what looks like an army jacket. Looks young. It's eighty fucking degrees out. Why do these guys always wear those big-ass jackets?"

"Trade secret," Oco said.

Oco put out the information to the other cars. Then advised Communications on base frequency of their situation and requested an airship. The Mazda pulled away from the curb, then made a U-turn midblock, and headed south.

"Comin' atcha, guys," Oco said into the microphone.

Mental floored the police car and sped south on Third Avenue. He and Oco saw two police cars blast through the intersection and whip in behind the Mazda. Mental closed the distance between the two black-and-whites.

"Let's hold off lighting 'em up until the airship shows," Oco broadcast to the lead car, driven by Lenny Custer.

"Roger that," Butch returned. He reached across Lenny, took hold of the seatbelt and buckled his partner in.

Lenny looked down and said, "You got some hairy ass arms partner."

Butch buckled his own seat belt and grumbled, "Blow me."

The Mazda's driver looked into the rearview mirror and the car picked up speed.

Butch was breathing a little faster and felt his pulse quicken. He keyed the mike. "Here we go, this guy's gettin' ready to rabbit. What's the ETA on the airship?"

The RTO came back. "Air Ten is over a shooting in Newton. No other airships available."

After a short pause she came back with, "12X43 and units following the possible code-37, air support is launching an airship with a ten-minute ETA."

The Mazda made a couple of quick turns. When the car blasted through a stop sign, Lenny flipped the toggle switch that activated the light bar. He left the siren on manual, which allowed him to control it by pressing the car horn. As they neared Florence, the Mazda slowed and made a left turn, narrowly avoiding a white US Mail Jeep. As they turned onto Florence, Butch and Lenny could see and smell smoke rising from the Jeep's wheel wells. It sat motionless, a wide-eyed mailman at the wheel. Six car lengths ahead the Mazda weaved in and out of traffic gaining speed, then abruptly drove into the curb lane at about 70 miles an hour. At Western Avenue, the driver, two seconds late on a red light, made a picture-perfect drifting right hand turn, taking up all southbound lanes. Lenny braked at the turn, but the much heavier police car plowed its front wheels and skidded into northbound lanes.

"Shit!" Lenny said.

Butch put one hand on the dash and the other on the doorpost.

The driver of a white Ford Econoline van saw the police car skidding towards him. He had just enough time to grab his steering wheel and take a deep breath before the police car smashed into the side of his van, causing it to spin and roll onto its side. The police car spun 180 degrees and came to rest in the northbound lanes, with light bar flashing, one back wheel on the curb.

"Oco, stay with him! We'll check on X43," Willie broadcast.

Mental made the turn and saw a line of stopped traffic ahead. He could make out a silver vehicle about a quarter mile ahead. He steered the police car to the curb lane. Then using a gas station driveway, he put his two passenger-side tires on the curb and smashed the gas pedal.

"Owwwwwwahhhhh!" he screamed at the top of his lungs. "Here we come, mother fucker!"

Both officers' ticket books, which had been wedged between the windshield and dashboard, broke free and cascaded toward Mental. Keeping one hand on the wheel, Mental grabbed the wayward books and threw them over his shoulder into the backseat. He saw a hole in the traffic and jerked the steering wheel to the left. As they came off the curb the cruiser's front bumper bounced off the roadway. The police car, with lights flashing and siren screaming, whipped into the middle of the street, its tires straddling the double yellow line. Ahead, the Mazda caught a new green at Manchester, cut into oncoming lanes, passed two cars waiting to turn left and negotiated a precise high-speed left turn without ever touching the brakes.

"Damn, this guy's good! I'ma get me one a' those RX7s," Mental said as he pushed the police car through the same left hand turn just in time to see the silver car disappear into traffic.

Brian O'Callahan's voice came over the radio. "12FB3, we are Code-100 on Manchester at Hoover."

"What's code-100?" Mental asked.

"That means he's up ahead waiting, you fuckin' blockhead!" Oco yelled.

"See what I mean? How the hell does O'Callahan know this shit?"

"Oh, I don't think its magic, partner. Perhaps he studied the manual. Would you pay a little more attention to your driving, please, Mental?"

"Oh, yeah, studying--I've heard of guys doing that."

Up ahead 12FB3 was waiting.

"This guy's heading for the freeway," Quint said.

They sat in a parking lot, straining their eyes to the west, trying to pick out the Mazda through the late afternoon traffic.

"Here he comes!" said Quint. "Oh, shit!"

The Mazda was a blur as it blew through a mid-phase red light. It narrowly missed several north—and southbound cars but never slowed. The vehicle flashed past Quint and Brian so fast they could not even make out the features of the driver. The car sped up the on-ramp of the southbound Harbor Freeway.

"Units eastbound at Hoover, you have heavy cross traffic. Use caution. Suspect vehicle is southbound Harbor freeway from Manchester," Brian broadcast as Quint slid their cruiser out of the parking lot onto the roadway and followed the Mazda onto the freeway.

"12FB3, we are now primary unit southbound Harbor from Manchester," Brian broadcast.

Air Twelve's observer came on the air, "12FB3, this is Air Twelve, we're about a minute out. What's your location now?" His voice had a distinctive tremor in it caused by the beating of the helicopter's blades.

"Still south on the one-ten approaching Century Boulevard," Brian advised.

Mental was not about to relinquish lead position in the pursuit without a fight. He raced onto the freeway and hugged the right shoulder and blew past Brian and Quint, who were bogged down in traffic in the number-one lane. As he passed them, Mental turned his head toward Quint and Brian and inserted a middle finger up his nose. Ahead the Mazda was about half a football field from the Century Boulevard exit when the Mazda driver set a course across four lanes of traffic toward the off-ramp. Mental saw his opportunity to close with the Mazda and floored the Plymouth, kicking up gravel and debris from the freeway shoulder. The passenger-side tires of the police car tracked in the concrete water gutter on the right shoulder, guiding it like a child's slot car. Quint, meanwhile, knew he could not make the same lane change as the Mazda without endangering himself, his partner, and a score of motorists. He was already preparing a contingency plan when he saw Mental's car roar within 15 feet of the Mazda's rear. The moment the Mazda entered the freeway exit the suspect driver threw the silver sports car to the left and narrowly missed two large yellow canisters filled with sand. The tubs, installed by Cal Trans, were meant to absorb the impact of a vehicle should one collide with it. The little silver car climbed a brushy berm between the traffic lanes and the off-ramp. The berm acted as a ramp and the car was carried several feet into the air, tearing through the shrubs like a rocket, then it slammed back onto the right lane of the freeway in a spray of metal and asphalt. Under the force of so much kinetic energy the car's suspension compressed to capacity, then drove the vehicle upward. The Mazda was catapulted onto its passenger side wheels. To the amazement of motorists, the sports car proceeded down the freeway on two wheels for about fifty feet. Once the car righted and was on all four tires, the driver sped off undaunted.

Mental was right behind the Mazda and tried to follow. Since his tires were tracking the rain gutter, getting the police car back onto the road necessitated a more forceful pull of the steering wheel; Mental over corrected, and the police car lost traction. A patch of loose gravel on the shoulder exacerbated the problem and the police car went into a spin. The car swapped ends several times; Oco was reminded of riding in Disneyland's Teacups with his daughter. The yellow Cal Trans canisters that the Mazda had narrowly avoided, the spinning police car did not. The car careened into them on Oco's side, causing sand to spray into the air. Mental and Oco came to rest with the rear of the police car sitting in traffic. Despite his efforts to stop, the driver of a large van loaded with fresh baked goods plowed into the police car and spun it off the embankment. The impact caused the rear door of the van to open, and as it fishtailed down the roadway much of its contents flew out the back. Oco and Mental rolled down to the embankment amid a shower of cinnamon rolls and cupcakes.

Ahead the Mazda had cut across the lanes of traffic, and Quint and Brian found themselves directly behind it once again. Red taillights flashed in all four lanes. Just prior to striking a stopped vehicle, the Mazda swerved to the left, out of traffic lanes, then onto the middle divider and sped on. Quint followed. The median between north and southbound traffic was a minefield of roadside garbage and Brian could hear debris bouncing against the bottom of their car.

"Quint, we're gonna get a flat tire for sure driving in this crap."

The police radio was alive with requests for fire department personnel and additional unit responses. Brian joined the group. "Air Twelve, we got our hands full down here. Will you take over pursuit broadcast?"

"Roger, sir, will do," was the response.

Quint had closed the gap between the two cars when the Mazda was kicked up a piece of wreckage. Brian's eyes locked onto the object that seemed suspended in the air.

Brian thought, *That looks like a piece of tail pipe,* just as the windshield in front of him imploded, and peppered his face with glass. The piece of metal did not come through the windshield, but had bounced up and shattered the light bar on the roof. Quint took several quick looks in his partner's direction.

"Ya all right? Wanna pull over?" he shouted.

Brian picked a sliver of glass out of the corner of his eye and flicked it away. He could feel the air funneling through the hole in front of him.

"I'm good, man! Catch this asshole!"

Quint pressed on the accelerator. The Mazda slowed, then angled across the freeway toward the Imperial Boulevard off-ramp. Quint braked hard and looked over his shoulder. Several motorists had stopped or slowed to allow the police car to change lanes.

Brian looked out the passenger-side window. "Clear right!"

Brian waved thanks to several commuters who had just acquired a pretty good story for their next family get-together. Quint stopped at the bottom of the off ramp. The Mazda was nowhere to be seen. On a hunch Quint made two quick turns and found the Mazda sitting unattended in front of a small, pink stucco cottage. Parked directly behind the Mazda was a police car with "cans," as the old timers call them, on the roof. Smoke was coming from under the Plymouth's hood and boiling out of the front wheel wells. Charlie Bender had beaten everyone.

Quint and Brian bailed out of their police car and ran to the front door.

Air Twelve advised, "Use caution, officers entering the pink residence. One officer pursued the suspect inside. No one has exited the residence."

Brian called, "Charlie!"

"Back here, y'all!" came a familiar voice. "House ain't cleared yet, fellers, I'm in the first bedroom on yer left. Got a code-four in here, suspect in custody."

"Standby, Charlie, we're gonna clear the rest of the house," Quint said.

After he and Quint ensured there were no other occupants in the house Brian opened the bedroom door, expecting the usual carnage that occurs at the end of a pursuit. Instead, Charlie Bender was leaning against the wall smoking a cigarette and filling out a field identification card. A young woman wearing a green military jacket was sitting on the bed in handcuffs.

"What's yer name, darlin?" Charlie asked.

The girl wiped a dangling teardrop from her chin onto her shoulder. "Demi Sanders," she sniffed.

Elsewhere in the house excited voices, heavy footfalls, and police radios could be heard. Quint walked into the small front room, and found it crowded with officers. He worked his way to the front door and saw Speedboat Willie and Pistol Pete coming across the lawn.

"How are Butch and Lenny?" Quint asked.

Willie said, "They're a little banged up, but okay. They weren't even transported by the FD. Sure as hell gonna be sore tomorrow, I'll tell ya that."

"Hear anything on Mental and Oco?" Quint asked.

"Nuthin, we drove past 'em. There were all kinds of units with 'em so we headed on out here," Willie said.

"Where's the suspect?" Pete asked.

"She's inside with my partner and Charlie. Fuckin' guy paralleled the entire pursuit on surface streets and beat everyone to the jackpot. How does a fella raised on a farm working mules learn to drive a car like that?"

"Heck, Charlie's a mountain boy. I heard he used to help his father run moonshine back home in Virginia. I think he even drove some dirt track stuff before he joined the Corps," Speedboat Willie said. "I'd like to try that."

"You better stick with boats, cause you can't drive for shit," Pistol Pete said.

"Haulin' moonshine… Dang, that ol' boy never ceases to amaze me," said Quint. "You guys mind takin' care of the Mazda? Me an' Brian will book the driver."

"Did you say the driver was a she?" Willie said.

"Yup, no bigger'n a popcorn fart, either," Charlie Bender said as he stepped through the doorway leading a petite woman by the arm who looked to be in her early twenties.

"Holy cow! I never saw a chick that could drive like that," Pete said.

The girl raised her head and looked at Pete, then cast her eyes back toward the ground.

"Don't be so glum, sister, it ain't no thing," Willie said.

"He gonna kill me," she said.

"Who's gonna kill you, sis'?" Quint asked.

"You'll see," she said.

Brian led her out of the house and helped her into the backseat of the police car. "He gonna kill me," Demi Sanders repeated.

"Who?" Brian asked gently as he pulled the seatbelt across the woman and buckled her in.

Her face only inches from his, she looked directly into Brian's soft green eyes and held his gaze for several seconds. She didn't know why, but she felt a glint of hope.

"If I tell you, you gonna keep him from killing me?" Demi asked.

Twenty minutes later, Brian stood next to the Mazda, taking notes for his arrest report while Willie completed the vehicle impound report. Pete called out impound inventory information to Willie, who had just popped the trunk open.

"Lord Jesus!" Willie said. "Will you look at that?"

The trunk was filled with rectangular bundles wrapped in olive-colored shipping tape. Brian walked closer and stared.

"My guess is each of those bundles weighs one kilogram," Willie said. "I worked dope for five years and if that is what I think it is, I never seen so much coke in my life."

Within seconds several police officers stood shoulder to shoulder around the trunk of the car, gawking. They reminded Brian of pirates admiring a treasure chest.

"The sister's right. Whoever owns this is gonna be pissed," said Speedboat Willie.

LIFE AT THE MARINA

Elvis Tubbs spent over ten thousand dollars on the sound system in his apartment. The music that flowed from it was flawless. Hand- rubbed cabinets complemented the African mahogany furnishings that filled his living room. Tootie Hicks enjoyed the room and Elvis Tubbs's company. It had been about two weeks since Tootie met Tubbs and already he had been introduced to several big sports figures and a score of Hollywood celebrities. He had been to their hangouts, parties, and homes. With the commodities he dealt in, Tootie was a welcome guest and was looking forward to a flight to San Francisco on a private jet to see a basketball game. He nodded at his new friend, who sat across the room with an arm around a Whitney Houston look-alike. Tubbs had met the girl at the Playboy Mansion a few months earlier. He referred to her as "one of my regular freaks." They lounged on an overstuffed couch that ran the full length of the room. Tubbs claimed it to be the only couch he could stretch out on without his feet or head extending beyond an armrest.

"Baby, fetch me a blunt off that table," Tubbs said.

As she leaned forward his hand slid from her waist to her hip. He reached out and cupped a mocha-colored buttock with his other hand. The light from the gas fireplace would have hidden any imperfections in her naked body if she'd had any, which she did not. With her knees on the couch and both hands on the coffee table she looked over her shoulder at Tubbs with a smoky come-on. She lowered her torso to the table and pushed her hips into the air then slightly opened her legs.

"Damn, girl!"

Tubbs opened his silk robe and placed both hands around her waist as he knelt behind her.

The girl placed her face near the glass tabletop and with each push from behind she snorted one of the many lines of cocaine laid out

164

on the tabletop. Tootie was mesmerized by the scene, feeling more excited by the moment. Lying on a leopard-skin rug, he partially sat up, resting on his elbows. He directed his attention to the blond head moving up and down in his lap. He grasped a handful of the silky ponytail, pulled her head to the side, and watched. On a wave of cocaine, marijuana, and cognac, Tootie closed his eyes and floated away to the music of Stevie Wonder.

Pounding on the front door destroyed the moment. Tubbs wondered who it was and Tootie wondered where he'd put his pistol. Tubbs closed his robe and walked to the door.

Tootie pushed Cindi toward the coffee table. "Bitch, clean that shit up."

Tootie found his 9mm pistol under the coffee table, and checked to ensure a round was in the firing chamber while both women cleaned up. What coke remained on the table was swept into a crystal bowl half full of white powder. Cindi grabbed two marijuana cigarettes, a cloudy glass tube, and a chunk of rock cocaine the size of an ice cube. Clutching the items, both naked women scrambled to the master bedroom and locked the door.

"Who's that?" Tubbs said in his most authoritative voice.

"Elvis, is Tootie there? It's Ray-Ray."

Tootie pushed past Tubbs, unlocked the door and jerked it open.

"What chu doin here muthafucker? This better be good, nigger," Tootie said.

The small, thin black man with a heavy braided-gold necklace stood speechless at the sight of Tootie, buck naked, pointing a gun at him.

"Well, wassup, man, talk!" Tootie said, using the pistol for punctuation.

Ray-Ray looked up and down the hall then he stepped into the room carrying a brown paper sack. Tubbs closed the door behind him.

"I was jes droppin off some bank, man, but the po-lice, they outside," Ray-Ray said, looking at the pistol pointed at his chest.

Tootie walked to the window and pulled the curtain back. "Where?"

"They down by yo' car, man. I saw 'em looking inside it wif flashlights an' they writin' things down," Ray-Ray said.

"How they dressed, what are they wearin'?" Tootie asked.

Ray-Ray appeared confused. "They dressed like the po-lice."

"They wearing uniforms, man?" Tootie said.

"Yeah, uniforms," Ray-Ray answered.

Tootie craned his neck to see into the parking lot. "What the fuck do they want?" He pulled on his pants, slipped on his house shoes, and was buttoning his multicolored silk shirt as he walked up to Ray-Ray. "Gimmie the money and hold this."

Ray-Ray handed the bag to Tootie and took the pistol with his other hand.

Tootie glanced inside then threw the sack onto the couch. "I'll be right back."

He opened the apartment door and started down the hall. Elvis Tubbs closed and locked the door behind the gangster.

One of the most difficult things for Sergeant Abe Palmer to learn was the department's policy on supervisors not participating in arrests or related activities. More than once he had been reminded that his job was to supervise police work, not do it. Abe was one of those who never entirely got being a cop out of his system. Today Abe was going to fudge on that rule. He commandeered Manny Magana to do some follow-up stemming from the pursuit and arrest of Demi Sanders the day before and after roll they headed west on the Santa Monica Freeway, toward an address in Marina del Rey.

"I don't know if it's a good location or not, but this chick says the dope belonged to a guy named Tootie," Abe said. "Quint and O'Callahan did a workup on that moniker and came up with some parolee that used to live over on 83rd Street near Vermont. Guy's got a twenty page rap sheet."

"Damn!" said Manny. "They're a good team. Quint says sometimes he feels like he's working with a guy who already put in twenty years on the job in another life."

"Yeah even Dapper Davy has become a fan of that kid."

After a thirty minute drive Abe pulled to a stop. The cruiser's headlights illuminated the front of the large waterfront apartment complex. Abe breathed in the moist sea air as two scantily clad blondes jogged past the car, smiling as they bounced by. Both men watched the girls round the corner and disappear.

As they walked toward the gate Abe said, "We are definitely

working the wrong division, my brother."

"Roger that, Boss. How long you think those two would last jogging at night down Hoover?" Manny asked.

"Not long bud. Let's see. This is the place here."

Abe pushed the intercom button marked "Manager."

A mild male voice answered.

"Yes, may I help you?"

"Good evening, sir. I'm Sergeant Palmer from the Los Angeles Police Department. I'm conducting a follow-up on an incident that occurred in the city. I wonder if you could spare a moment to talk with me."

"Uh, sure. I'll buzz you in. My apartment's the first on the left."

A buzzer sounded and Manny pushed the security gate open. They walked into a breezeway decorated with dark wood-plank siding and fishing nets. Standing next to an aqua landscaping light was a diminutive man in his thirties. He fussed with his well-trimmed moustache and meticulously combed hair as they approached.

"Hello, gentlemen. I'm James Trask, the manager here. I hope I needn't be alarmed. We are so seldom visited by the boys in blue. How can I be of service?"

This guy looks like a Vegas lounge singer, Abe mused.

Abe held out his hand. Trask lightly gripped Abe's fingertips and held them for a second without movement. His eyes were on Manny. Unconsciously, Abe wiped his hand on his trouser leg.

"I'm Sergeant Palmer, Mr. Trask. Thanks for speaking with us."

"Certainly," said Trask, never taking his eyes off Manny. "And who is this?"

"I'm Officer Magana."

Manny hoped Trask would forgo the handshake. No such luck. Trask took Manny's hand in both of his and insisted the lawmen come into his apartment to talk. They did.

James Trask's apartment was beautifully furnished in an ultra-modern motif of black, white, and chrome. They sat in the living room, which had as a centerpiece an enormous saltwater aquarium. Abe made himself comfortable in a black leather chair with chrome armrests.

Trask joined Manny on a couch of similar color and style. "So how can I be of service?"

"We are trying to locate the owner of a car. It's a black BMW 700 series," Palmer said.

"Well, a man with a car like that lives here. What has he done? I mean, I'm not really supposed to give out personal information on our tenants, but if it's serious."

Trask looked at Manny. Manny caught a look from his sergeant and took over the questioning.

"Well, James. I'm sorry, do you mind if I call you James?"

"Oh, no, please do," Trask said. He lightly touched the cuff of Manny's shirt.

"James, we certainly understand your position and would not want you to get into any trouble. Right now we just would like to identify the man. He most likely has done nothing and is not even the person we are looking for," Manny said.

"Oh, so you are looking for leads, huh?"

"Exactly. You are familiar with police procedure, I see."

Trask beamed. "Well, I read a lot, and I just love those old detective stories, you know?"

Manny looked deep into Trask's eyes and said, "Yes, I do, too."

"Well, I can tell you this: I don't know what he's done, but Mr. Hicks frightens me," Trask said.

Manny leaned closer to the delighted little man. "Oh?"

Abe removed his notebook from his pocket and began writing. It turned out James Trask was a very observant person. Soon, the officers had a complete list: Tootie's physical description, daily schedule, visitors, habits, vehicles, a copy of his rental agreement, and a map of the complex. Trask also provided his own hypothesis of Hicks's profession.

"I think he's a drug dealer. He never goes to work and obviously has lots of money. I mean his clothing, it's...well, not my style, but designer clothing just the same. Some men that come to his door look like mafia men, you know, wise guys, I think they call them. And he has offered drugs to several of the ladies who reside here. I do not appreciate that. I mean, sure, it's the eighties and what's a little coke going to hurt? But he's creepy."

Manny gave Trask his business card as he showed them to the door. "If you see anything unusual, or something you think we should know, give me a call."

"Mr. Trask, we would appreciate it if you said nothing about this to anyone," Abe said.

"Oh, no. I wouldn't dream of it."

"Thanks for your cooperation, sir. You say the BMW is parked in space 244 on the north side of the building, right?" Abe said.

"Yes, sergeant."

Trask turned to Manny and took the officer's hands in his. "Officer Magana, it was such a pleasure to make your acquaintance, and I'll call if I see or hear anything."

"Thank you, James. You have been a great help."

With little difficulty Abe and Manny located a gleaming black BMW 700.

Abe looked through the tinted windows at the tan leather upholstery and whistled lightly. He removed an Instamatic camera from his front pocket and took a photo of each side of the car.

"Nice ride."

"Wanna door-knock the apartment?" Manny asked.

"Nah, we don't have anything solid yet. We'll get his parole agent and do a parole search or something after we do a little follow-up on ol' Andre here."

Abe looked up from the car and saw a man walking rapidly toward them. His partially buttoned shirt billowed open, exposing a heavily muscled chest and a row of well-defined abdominal muscles.

"Is there a problem here, officer?" Tootie said.

"No problem. Just looking at the car," Manny said. "Is it yours?"

Abe stepped into the shadows, watching the man's hands, and kept his head on a swivel for additional suspects.

"So what if it is, man? Can't a black man have a nice car? I don't see you fuckin' with nobody else."

Tootie clinched his fists and took a step toward the police officer. It may have been the drugs or a convict's bluff, but it was enough. Sergeant Abe Palmer stepped behind him and drove the side of his boot into the back of his knee, causing it to buckle. As Tootie dropped to his knee, Abe slipped his arm around the man's neck, grasped his own wrist with his other hand, and pulled his arm tightly beneath Tootie's chin. Then Abe leaned back and pulled him off balance. He flexed the muscles in his arms and cut off the blood flow through Tootie's carotid arteries. By the time he could respond, Tootie felt his eyes starting to bulge. He grabbed the arm that was choking him, then tried to lean forward or turn, but each movement seemed to cause the officer's arm to press deeper under his chin. His forehead felt like a taut balloon. His head began to spin. Just as he was losing consciousness, the pressure lessened.

"Now, Mr. Parolee, is this how it's gonna be?" Abe said. "'Cause in a second you're gonna be doing the chicken with a load of shit in your pants unless you chill. I don't know who you are or what your trip is, but I sure as hell will violate your ass and put you back in the gray stone hotel. Now, you let that angry black man shit go, and we will have a civilized talk here. You got that, pal?"

Tootie held gingerly onto the dark blue sleeve around his neck and managed a nod. When released, he dropped onto his rear, gasping for breath. His throat felt like he had swallowed a hard-boiled egg and it had stuck halfway down.

"Stand up, put your hands on your head, and spread your legs," Manny said.

Tootie did as he was told.

"Now," said Manny after conducting a cursory search for weapons. "Is this your car?"

"Yeah, man," said Tootie, rubbing his neck.

"We had a 700 like this taken over in West L.A. in a robbery a couple days ago," said Manny. "The owner lives around here and called the station, said he saw his car pull into this apartment complex. Before you came storming' up here we were getting ready to run the VIN. If the identification number comes back to you we will be on our way. If not, well then, you will be taking a ride with us."

"It's my car, man. I don't know nuthin' 'bout no robbery. If I stole it you think I'd come up to the po-lice and all?" Tootie said.

"You would be amazed at the stupid things people do. Now, what is your name?"

Manny removed a pad of white cards from his shirt pocket and completed his field interview. He ran the BMW's VIN and ran Tootie for warrants. Both were clean.

"Andre, I know you been around and that you're draggin' a tail. So why would you come out here and get in my partner's face like you did? A call to your parole officer would bring you nuthin' but grief. Looks like you got a good job and things are going good for you. Why fuck that up, man?" Abe asked.

Tootie hung his head, feigning remorse.

"You right, sir, I jus been drinkin' a little an' got mad. Can I go now?"

"Yeah. You got any questions?" Abe said.

"No, man. I know what time it is, sarge. You ain't got to explain."

Tootie turned and slinked away tenderly rubbing his throat. Manny and Abe watched him walk from the parking area and disappear into the apartment building. They walked out of the front gate to their cruiser and said nothing until Abe was eastbound on the Santa Monica Freeway.

Manny was pleased with the yarn he had spun with Tootie and was looking for a little praise. "So, whaddaya think, sarge?"

"Well, first of all," Abe stopped talking to pack his lip with Copenhagen chewing tobacco, "I think Mr. Trask wants to have your baby."

"Real nice. I treat a fellow human being with a little courtesy and compassion and this is my thanks."

He wondered what his sergeant would say if he knew Manny had put his home number on the back of the business card he'd handed James Trask.

MERRY CHRISTMAS

Brian and Quint temporarily returned to their midday foot beat just in time for the Christmas rush of shoplifters arrested by security guards employed by stores in the division. The pair spent much of their time booking the petty thieves, thereby freeing up patrol units to handle emergency calls. During the holiday season even warring armies often agreed upon a truce; not so in South Central where the weather remained the same and so did the crime. This is not to suggest that the holidays were not celebrated. At Christmas time, children waited for Santa and on New Year's people rang in the New Year. It's just that in South Central sometimes Santa didn't show and the ringing you heard on New Years were bullets landing on the hood of your car. Two days before Christmas, Quint and Brian were in the holiday spirit as they walked the beat.

"Where in the heck do you buy a black Christmas tree?" Brian asked.

Quint watched a white a car drive down Vermont with a black Douglas fir tied to the roof.

"Over near Crenshaw and Vernon, I think. That's where the 'Afrika with a K' folks hang out. Ya know, those people who walk around dressed in robes and sandals lookin' like they just got off the boat from Uganda or somethin'. Whatever blows yer skirt up, ah guess."

"Well, it's nice to be back on the beat again, dealing with some good guys for a change," Brian said.

"Yeah, well, if ah were a bettin' man ah'd say that ninety percent of the folks in this division were good as gold. Matter o' fact there's probably more church goin folks in 77th than any other division in the city."

Their attention was drawn to a poster featuring a busty Mrs. Santa in fur-trimmed hot pants being placed in the window of Tony's Liquor Store. The model sat seductively straddling a reindeer, ogling a fifth of cognac. Brian and Quint stopped to give Tony, who was hanging the poster, a thumbs up. Just as they were discussing whether to stop for a soda the report of two gunshots ripped the air.

"Shoot, that was close!" Quint said.

The officers looked in the direction of the shots. Quint drew his pistol and peered down the street while Brian broadcast "Shots fired" and their location. They jogged down Vermont while keeping a close watch on traffic for anyone fleeing the scene. As they neared 54th Street, several people standing on the corner pointed east. From the intersection they observed a slight person dressed in a blue sweatshirt, blue work pants, and blue corduroy slippers staggering down the sidewalk. The boy walked a few feet before he tottered and fell onto the walkway of a disheveled Craftsman-style home. The officers cautiously approached the yard where the youth lay panting like a gut shot deer.

A middle-aged woman was parked in her car at the curb. She called out to Quint. "I saw it, Lord God, I saw it, two boys in a white car. They just shot that child down. Lord have mercy!"

She provided Quint with a description of: the circumstances of the shooting, the suspect vehicle, and its occupants. Quint furiously jotted down the information. Brian hurried toward the boy who was lying on his side, mouth agape. His eyes met Brian's.

"O'Callahan. Help," he gasped.

The victim was a local kid Brian had met soon after being assigned to 77th Street. His name was Robert, but was known as "Bee Boo." The personable youngster did odd jobs at Tony's Liquor Store, and Brian liked him. On several occasions he'd spoken with the boy about his future. Brian admired how Bee Boo would forgo money in exchange for food, which he brought home to his two younger sisters. Though often not much more than day-old bread and pastries, Bee Boo was glad to have it. Quint had told Brian that when Bee Boo was a little boy he and Scooter occasionally found him wandering the streets late at night and brought him home. It was common for the boy's mother to disappear for days at a time, leaving the children in the care of whomever she could coerce into it.

Brian and Quint both harped on Bee Boo about his growing involvement in gangs. Several days ago, he had announced to Brian that he was going to jump out of his gang and join the Army. This he would do after graduating from high school in the coming spring. Now, at seventeen years of age, Bee Boo lay in a widening puddle of crimson that oozed off the edge of the walkway onto the lawn. Lost in the moment, Brian watched the blood turn bright red as it absorbed oxygen from the grass. He knelt down as Bee Boo drew a breath, shuddered, and stopped his labored breathing, eyes still locked on Brian's. Something akin to panic rose in Brian's chest. He rolled the limp teen onto his back. After determining that Bee Boo had no pulse, Brian laced his fingers together, placed his hands on the boy's chest, locked his elbows, and applied pressure straight down. Deep red blood flowed between Brian's fingers and pinkish foam frothed from the youth's mouth.

He continued, and with each compression the flow of blood between Brian's fingers lessened.

Quint got what information he needed from the witness and left her in the care of a police officer who had just arrived at the scene. He walked up and looked over Brian's shoulder. "Shit," he whispered. Quint considered telling his partner that the boy was obviously dead, but felt that Brian needed to try.

When the R.A. arrived, a young black paramedic approached and put his hand on Brian's shoulder. "We got it, officer."

Swathed in blood, Brian stood but kept his eyes on the motionless, gore- covered boy. He flicked a drop of sweat from the tip of his nose, replacing it with a bloody smudge. Quint watched his partner and for a moment and saw him as a broken-hearted child. A grizzled fireman with an enormous moustache, wearing a yellow helmet, white t-shirt, and heavy turnout pants, clomped up to them. He slipped his thumbs under his thick suspenders and looked at the blood-soaked police officer. He took in the sizable pool of blood that had begun to coagulate like burgundy gelatin on the walkway.

"Good job, bud," he said to Brian, then added, "looks like you pumped him dry."

Mental, who had just arrived with Oco, slapped his partner on the back and laughed at the firemen's gallows humor. No one else found it humorous.

The black paramedic shook out a white sheet, floated it down over the dead boy. Seeing this, an obese woman struggled down from the front porch where she'd been watching the show. She stepped off the bottom riser and scowled at Brian.

"If y'all ain't taking him to the hospital can't you move that motherfucker next door? I know how you po-lice's is. Y'all gonna put that yellow tape everywhere and ain't nobody gonna be able to come up to my house fo' hours. It don't make a damn bit a' difference if he fell out here or over there. " She pointed a plump, acrylic-adorned finger at the house next door.

People within earshot reacted differently. Some smiled, others shook their heads in amazement. Quint told her to go back into her house. She waddled back to the front porch mumbling under her breath.

The grizzled fireman walked toward his engine chuckling. He said over his shoulder, "Charming. You boys give us a call if you want a wash-down. I know how you motherfuckers is."

"We might just let the dogs clean the blood up. It's full of nutrition, you know, and ghetto elk love it," Mental called out.

The old leather-lunger waved without turning around.

"It's Christmas time, Mental. Where's your compassion for your fellow man?" Oco said.

The young paramedic turned to Quint.

"Ghetto elk?"

"Yeah, ya know, the dogs that roam the streets o' Tombstone at night? Those're ghetto elk," Quint said.

The paramedic glared at Quint for a long minute then walked away. Brian still hovered over Bee Boo's shrouded body. Oco took a pouch of chewing tobacco from his pocket and stuffed a gob into the side of his mouth, then held the bag out to Quint, who did the same.

"You guys know 'im?" Oco asked.

Quint nodded.

As he looked down at the dead boy Mental reached into his shirt pocket and removed a small candy cane.

"I got a candy cane. Should I give him a candy cane?"

"I wanna be there at the Pearly Gates when you try to get in, Mental. Saint Peter will probably have a wanted poster of you," Oco said.

"Just another dead gangster, partner... No humans involved." Mental ripped the paper from his candy cane then popped it into his mouth.

A fireman brought Brian some moist paper towels. "Come on over to the engine, man, let's get you cleaned up," he said in a low voice.

Brian followed him silently.

Later, Manny Magana, who was working with Scooter Kellerman, was preparing to leave the scene and saw an opportunity to entertain some civilized company. He offered to give the two foot beat officers a ride to their car. Brian's shirt was stiff with dried blood and he still had an unsettled feeling in his stomach, but outwardly he appeared to have regained his composure. This was to his credit, because for the past two hours firemen, detectives, officers, and supervisors had made sport of his lifesaving attempt. As Brian bent to get into the backseat of Manny and Scooter's black-and-white, Mental couldn't resist one last barb.

"Well, it wasn't a kill, kid, but you get an assist."

Before getting into the car Quint whispered something in Mental's ear and the grin fell off his face. He walked away and Quint got in next to his partner. Scooter, in the front passenger seat, turned to look at the two cops in the back.

"Well, Manny, looks like we got two bleeding hearts working the foot beat now. Brian, did you know your partner's a social worker at heart? He ever tell you about his great fire rescue?"

Brian looked at Quint, who was not smiling.

"Couple of years ago me 'n' Quint come up on this house that's on fire over on Sixty-ninth Street. Fire department wasn't on scene yet. Seemed everyone was out of the house, but the flames had ignited the house next door. Quint and I run up and bang on the door. A woman and three little kids run out. Well, one of the kids gets about halfway to the sidewalk, yells *'My doll!'* turns around and runs back into the house and slams the door behind her. The house is burning pretty good by now, so Quint runs up to the house, tries the door and it's locked, so he kicks it open, crawls on his hands and knees until he finds the kid in her bedroom. He drags her through the smoke-filled house, scoops her up and runs out the front door. Just as he steps off the front stoop, the water heater or something explodes. It blows the front of that house to pieces. Knocks Quint down, but he gets up, still holding the kid, smoke comin' off him, with his back looking like a porcupine from all the wood that blew outta the house."

Scooter stopped, spit a stream of tobacco juice out his window, and continued. "Quint's staggering towards the curb thinking he just won a medal. Kid's mother comes up to him, jerks the girl outta his arms, and says, *"Gimme my baby, you white devil!"*" Scooter broke into a laugh that sounded like a donkey's bray.

Quint shrugged. "Guess she wasn't much of a police fan."

The car filled with laughter.

"Oh, shit, that ain't nothing," Scooter said, trying to top his own story. "Listen to this one. A couple years ago Quint and me get a 'suicide just occurred' call on Crenshaw. We roll up and the FD is already there. Paramedics tell us the guy's in the bedroom so we head that way. On the way into the room we see a .32 auto and a suicide note sitting on this little table. I stop and read it. The guy that capped himself was all bummed out 'cause he's a fag and nobody loves him and he's a big disappointment to his whole family, that kind of shit, ya know?"

A murmur of understanding encouraged Scooter to continue.

"Me and Quint figured the fuckin' paramedics moved the gun and note. They do that kind of shit, right? We walk into the bedroom and there's the dead guy face up in bed with the covers neatly pulled to his waist. He's got a small hole in the side of his head, no exit wound. So we're all standing around the bed looking at this guy and all of a sudden his eyes pop open. Then he sits up! Holy shit! We all jumped back, one of the paramedics fell over a foot-stool. Scared the shit outta me too--well almost, cause I did squeeze off a little fart in all the excitement."

There was another round of laughter and a hee haw from Scooter.

"Anyway, I ask this guy what happened and what it felt like to shoot yourself in the head. He says *Officer, it's like having a rocket ship fly right through your head. After I shot myself I just laid there for a while, then I got thirsty so I got up and went into the kitchen. In the hallway I realized I still had the gun in my hand so I put it on the table in the hall. I got a drink and got back in bed and waited to die.* I look over at Quint and he's nodding and looking at this guy like he's Florence fucking Nightingale."

"When we get the guy to the hospital we gotta wait for the people from Mental Evaluation to take him off our hands. So Quint here spends the whole time sitting with the guy offering encouragement and reasons for him to embrace life. In the meantime I'm over with the nurses, doctors, and paramedics laughing our asses off while we look at the X-ray. Fuckin little .32-cal bullet hit the side of this guy's noggin and splattered like an egg. Never even penetrated his skull. He shot himself in the head and the extent of his medical treatment is two Ibuprofen and a Band-Aid. After an hour or so, the Mental Eval team shows up and we're getting ready to leave. Quint walks up to this turd burglar and says, 'I have to be going now. Just remember, God is giving you a second chance. Life is worth living.' The guy ponders Quint's warm and fuzzy words, then says, *You know, Officer King, I need a bigger gun."*

Brian chuckled, Quint smiled sheepishly, and Manny stared straight out the windshield.

The police car came to a stop next to Brian and Quint's car, which was parked next to the Zody's Department store on their beat. Manny slipped the Plymouth into park and said to Scooter, "You and Mental are a couple of real humanitarians, Scooter. You guys missed your calling. You should have been doormen at one of Hitler's concentration camps."

Quint and Brian laughed at that one and so did Scooter.

Back in their car Quint and Brian drove straight to the station with little talk. As they unloaded their gear, Marty La Floy, the community relations sergeant, approached.

"Hi, guys," Marty said.

It was ironic that he worked public relations, because to the untrained eye it would appear that Marty La Floy didn't like anyone.

Whenever Marty made any effort to be friendly it was an overture for a solicitation.

"'Lo, Marty," Quint said with his head still in the trunk of the car.

Brian smiled and said, "Hi, Sarge."

Marty hiked his pants up to the bottom of an impressive beer belly.

"Well, it's that time again, Quint. Can I count on you and your partner tomorrow?"

"You bet, Marty, but please tell me you have enough turkeys to go around this year," Quint said. "An' maybe make sure we're gonna be givin' shit to folks that need it."

"Oh, yeah, Quint, we have plenty of everything this year so I don't expect any problems," Marty said. "I told all the clergy members to provide only names and addresses of people who are really poor."

Quint opened the trunk of the police car, grabbed the small toolbox he carried with him, and then turned to Brian.

"Last year Community Relations ran outta turkeys for their Christmas boxes. So a few needy families received two large roastin' chickens instead. Well, ah carried a box loaded with food and gifts up to this home with a brand-new Cadillac sittin' in the driveway. A woman answered the door. As ah'm handin her the box ah can see she's watching soap operas on one of those big-screen TVs. Hell, ain't none a' my business. But as ah'm walking to my car this gal yells, 'A yard bird? Where's my mutha fuckin turkey?' She picks one of those roasters up and launches it at me. Ah moved, but it put a dent in the door of my car. Dang near ruined my Christmas spirit."

Marty La Floy hiked his pants up and grumbled, "Very funny. See you tomorrow about noon," and waddled away.

"Hey, Marty, weren't funny at all, an' you wouldn't need ta be hitchin' up yer britches if you wore suspenders. Get some nice black 'uns ta go with yer uniform."

Sergeant La Floy opened the station door with one hand and flipped Quint the bird with the other.

"Think he smiled," Quint said.

"Man, Quint, you talk to a sergeant like that?"

Quint kicked the car door shut and walked toward the station with his hands full of gear.

"Partner, 'round this outfit, rank gets ya more money. Y'all gotta earn respect. That tub-a-guts been sittin' on the fence handin' out advice since ah been here. Never does a lick a' work himself, neither."

The next day was Christmas Eve, and after roll Quint and Brian loaded boxes full of groceries and presents for the needy into their car. They had spent most of the watch delivering boxes, returning to the station for more and then heading out again. It was getting dark when they stopped in front of a home on San Pedro Street. Quint examined the delivery list La Floy had provided them.

"Says it's a guesthouse in the back," said Quint.

Police officers know they can never be sure what an unexpected knock on a door will result in, so Quint kept his hands free while Brian followed close behind carrying a large cardboard box overflowing with goodies. Quint walked onto the porch of a decrepit shack and knocked on the door. A small face appeared in the window next to the door.

"Mama, it's the po-lice," a little girl's voice said.

Within seconds the window was full of small faces. A woman in her mid- twenties came to the door and stood with it partially open. She peered between the door and jamb.

"Yes, sir?"

"Howdy, are you Mandy Green? We're here to bring ya some grub and gifts for Christmas, if ya want it," Quint said.

Several little hands tore the door open and the threshold filled with children sized from the woman's hip to her knee. Mandy Green straightened the scarf on her head and looked over her shoulder into her home.

"Um, yes, please, thank you, come in," she said.

She rested her hands on the heads of two children, one a boy and the other a girl. They stood wide-eyed on either side of Miss Green, each with an arm wrapped around one of her shapely legs. Brian guessed the two to be about four years of age.

The room was clean but cluttered with secondhand furniture, blankets, and clothing. Still fussing with her scarf she followed the two officers and the horde into a small living room.

"I'm sorry it's a mess... I didn't know... Um, we're kind of crowded..."

"We shouldn't have surprised you like this, miss," Brian said. "Where would you like the box?"

"No please, it's fine, sir. Over there is good, thank you," she said pointing at the kitchen table.

A little boy missing his front teeth stood in his t-shirt and underwear smiling at Brian.

"Wass in that box?" he asked.

"Well, food for Christmas dinner, and Santa gave us some stuff to drop by 'cause he's going to be real busy tonight, you know. So we're helping him."

Brian set the box down on a wobbly wooden table with six mismatched chairs around it.

"How many little 'ins do you have, Miss Green?" Quint asked.

"Well, I have three, and the twins here, they're my sister's, she died, an' I just... Well, they're mine now," she said, nodding toward the boy and girl on her legs.

Two girls of about six and seven stood against the wall holding hands. The older held a Barbie doll that was missing an arm and all its clothes; the other had three of her fingers in her mouth.

The boy with missing teeth pulled on Brian's trouser leg. "I'm Donavan," he announced.

Brian stooped and shook the little boy's hand and said, "Nice to meet you, I'm Officer Brian and this guy with the big moustache is Officer Quint."

Quint smiled and said, "Howdy partner," in his best Texas drawl then he waved to the other kids in the room.

"Children, pick up all your beds and move them out the way-- now," Miss Green said, clapping her hands.

Her eyes met Brian's and she looked down at her stocking feet. She would have been pretty if she were not so worn and weary. With her head still down, she lifted her eyes under long brown lashes and allowed herself a smile.

The girl with the doll stepped from the wall with her smaller sister in tow. She slipped up next to her mother. "Momma, look at his eyes. They so pretty. They green."

"Yes, child, now go pick up your bed," her mother said.

She picked up one of the twins and rested him on her hip. Quint looked around and realized what he had first thought to be random piles of blankets were actually pallets for sleeping. The children hurried about the room and carried, or in some cases dragged, their beds through a door that led to a small bedroom. Brian began to unload the box while Donavan stood on a chair next to him trying to look inside it. As he worked, Brian could feel four other sets of little eyes on him.

"Donavan, now you get on down and don't bother the officer," Miss Green said.

"He's no bother, Miss Green. He's gonna be my helper," Brian said.

The little boy smiled and said, "Uh huh, jes like Santa's helpers."

Brian looked around the room and could see no tree. He handed Donavan a wrapped package.

"Donavan, put this over by where the Christmas tree will go."

Donavan and several others chimed in, "We ain't got no Christmas tree."

"We 'haven't,' not ain't,'" Miss Green said mildly, watching Brian.

"I know. Santa told us to get you one. As soon as we're done delivering our packages Officer Quint and I are going to go pick it up and bring it here."

The oldest girl took her mother's hand said, "Mama, Santa getting us a tree, too!"

Seeing the joy in her daughter's face, Mandy's heart swelled. She bent and hugged the little girl. "Yes, sugar, he is," she answered.

Quint looked into the box. Then he and Brian exchanged looks and, like all good partners, knew what the other was thinking.

"Miss Green, would you please take care of this?" Quint said. "We have to go get the other ones. We'll be right back."

The two Santas in blue walked from the house toward the police car making their plan.

"The gifts are marked age and sex. Let's jes raid a couple boxes here," Quint said.

When Quint and Brian walked back to the shack, their arms were loaded with gaily-wrapped gifts. Donavan who was waiting on the porch, stood at attention, saluting the officers, with his belly button poking from under his tee shirt. Setting their loads on the dirt yard they returned the salute, then retrieved the holiday booty from the ground and delivered it to the kitchen table.

After bidding the family goodbye, Brian and Quint spent the rest of the watch doing Santa's bidding. When they came to a home that clearly was in no need they kept driving and set the box aside for a family that was. Just before end of watch, with a Christmas tree they'd bought hanging out of the trunk of the police car, Quint and Brian returned to the guesthouse on San Pedro Street. They could smell the roast chicken before knocking on the door. A troop of young faces stood, scrubbed clean and gleaming, when the door opened.

"Hi, Quint, hi, Brian," said Donavan. "Momma said we can have the tree by the window."

Little hands reached out to touch the tree as Brian carried it into the room, with Donavan walking behind holding the tip of the tree. Quint carried an assortment of lights and ornaments they had picked up at the Zody's department store on their foot beat. The manager of the store, after hearing why his foot beat officers were Christmas shopping in uniform, had donated the decorations.

"Now, everyone sit. Come eat and we'll decorate the tree after dinner," Mandy Green said. "Will you join us? Now that I have some food to cook, I'm a good cook." A chorus of voices offered encouragement.

Before Brian could respond Quint said, "Sure smells like great home cookin'. We'd be tickled to join ya."

In their absence, she'd taken successful measures to improve her appearance, which wasn't lost on either of the officers.

Quint whispered to Brian, "That little gal cleans up purty good, wouldn't ya say, pard?"

Brian agreed.

Donavan grabbed Brian's hand and led him to a folding chair. "You can sit in my chair."

As soon as Brian sat the little boy climbed into his lap and looked up with a big gap-toothed smile.

"We got a turkey, too, but that's fo' tomorrow, on Christmas," Donavan said.

The dinner was delicious and Brian couldn't remember enjoying a meal more. While Brian and Miss Green talked, Quint kept the children entertained with stories of the Wild West. Brian learned that Mandy was a nursing student currently completing her internship at a local hospital. After dinner Quint and Brian set up the tree then excused themselves and walked to the door with five giggling children underfoot. Brian shook Mandy Green's hand and thanked her for the wonderful dinner. The handshake lingered and neither was in a hurry to release the other. In fact, she leaned toward Brian, then put her lips to his cheek and gave him a light kiss and whispered in his ear, "Thank you, and Merry Christmas, Officer O'Callahan."

The chemistry was not lost on Quint or the children.

"Momma, you kissed a po-lice!" a little girl giggled while

hugging her sister.

The two men stood on the front porch and called, "Merry Christmas!"

Five excited little voices echoed their holiday wish.

Donavan raced out the door and took Brian's hand in both of his. His eyes sparkled the way only a child's on Christmas Eve could. "I wish you were my daddy."

Brian stooped and hugged the little boy. He hoped no one saw his eyes well up.

HAPPY NEW YEAR

Captain Sullivan directed Abe Palmer's crew to work mid-pm watch for one night, New Year's Eve. They were to work the hours leading up to and immediately following the first day of the new year, which were legend in South Central. From sundown to sunup the rules went out the door. Several minutes before and after midnight even the LAPD acknowledged the fact they had no control. Abe walked into the roll call room and slammed a coffee can down on the table.

"I want everyone to see this before you go out on the street tonight. What you will find in this can are bullets, a variety of calibers ranging from .22 to 30.06. Anybody know where these came from?"

The assembly sat quietly, knowing not to interrupt Abe Palmer when he was making a point.

"I picked these up from the roof of the station on January first a year ago. If you have worked here on New Year's Eve before you know what kind of mad minute we have at the stroke of midnight. In war there is an acceptable mortality rate; on this police department there is not. I don't want to see any of you hurt or killed because the citizens of this division think it's alright to open up with whatever piece of hardware they have stashed under the bed. At 2345 hours-- that's quarter to midnight--I want everyone either in the station or under a freeway overpass. There is just too much heavy artillery out there tonight. An 'officer needs help' call is the only reason you could possibly have for not taking cover at midnight."

Palmer picked up the coffee can and slowly poured the contents onto the tabletop. It took a while, and by the time the last projectile bounced onto the table the murmur of voices filled the room.

"Are there any questions?" the room fell silent; even Mental kept his mouth shut.

Leo the Lion sat at the table behind Sergeant Palmer, obviously in agreement with him. Generally the watch commander did not attend mid-watch roll calls, but tonight was New Year's Eve, and Operations South Bureau was at maximum deployment. Lieutenant Wiener was in attendance as well. He stood and faced the watch.

"That doesn't mean you spend an hour sitting around the station, either," Wiener added. "As soon as the celebratory gunfire subsides I want everyone out there again, picking up calls. That includes Abe's personnel. You will be activated to handle radio calls tonight. Questions?"

His eyes scanned the room for dissenters. "No questions. Good, then let's get out there and buy some calls so pm's can have dinner."

"Pm's never have code-seven, lieutenant," Mental said. "Too damn busy."

"Well, I'm sure they find ways to eat and make it up somehow," Sergeant Price chimed in.

There was general discontent in the room. All ghetto cops knew that missing dinner during pm watch was part of the job. This was despite the fact that forty- five minutes was added to the eight-hour workday for every officer to take a break and eat. That Wiener refused to acknowledge the fact didn't make him popular. To make matters worse, it was an unspoken rule that if you missed code-seven you did not put in for compensation. Any officer who did ran the risk of an ass-chewing by the likes of Wiener.

While mid-watch grumbled, on the east side of the division Officers Sonya Sontag and her diminutive male partner, Oliver Ewing, known throughout the division as Littleman, rolled up on two women standing in the middle of main Street punching it out.

"Shit, the Buffalo Gals," said Sontag.

She pulled the cruiser to the curb, then reached for the microphone. Littleman hopped out of the cruiser. "We got this," he said.

Acutely aware of his stature and forever concerned that someone might think less of him, it was common for Littleman to bite off more than he could chew. Sonya Sontag, on the other hand, could do many things most police officers could not. She'd graduated from the Police Academy in the top ten of her class at a time when women recruits were shown no quarter, and she had asked for none. Like any solid police officer she knew her limitations, and the Buffalo

Gals reached far beyond her comfort zone. She requested another unit to meet them at 83rd Street and Main.

The Gals, born Lea and Bea Davidson, had earned their nicknames several years before, the night they'd lowered their enormous shaggy heads and rushed Scooter Kellerman. With over 600 combined pounds of flesh and bone between them, the Gals drove Scooter over a bed, through an interior wall, and into the bathtub of their apartment. Scooter swore afterward that the identical twins had let out guttural grunts and snorts that reminded him of two charging buffalo. Apart from their size and unkempt manes, each of the Gals had been born with kyphosis, a curvature of the thoracic spine. Kyphosis is often insensitively referred to as hunchback. Over the years, the bulges between their shoulder blades became well marbled with thick fat and muscle. The humps were fearsome and pronounced by the time the Gals stampeded poor Scooter.

Lea and Bea worked the docks at the harbor. They were accepted into the Longshoremen's Union fifteen years ago by walking into the "Poop Deck" bar in San Pedro and challenging any man in the bar to fight. After significant damage to the bar--and several longshoremen--they'd made their point. Ever since, they had been loading and unloading freight at the busy Port of Los Angeles. They drank vodka, and when they did they liked to laugh, screw, and fight. It was said among some of the toughest men alive that when the Buffalo Gals laughed they were hilarious; when they screwed it was frightening; and when they fought it became a problem. Just such a problem was unfolding in front of Sonya.

"Freeze! Freeze!" Littleman shouted.

The behemoths were ringing in the New Year with a couple of bottles of vodka and a fistfight. Since they had no common foe yet they punched, kicked, and wrestled one another. Lea had Bea by a tuft of thick wool on each side of her head and was kicking her in the face when Littleman grabbed Lea's arm. He was shocked at the size and tone of her arm. Lea unhanded her sister and turned on the blue flea that was annoying her. She took Littleman by the neck with one hand and the Sam Browne with the other, and pressed him over her head in one effortless motion. Littleman beat her massive arms with tiny fists and kicked his miniature police boots in vain. Bea roared with laughter, then set her gaze on Sonya. Sonya radioed for assistance and drew her side-handle baton.

"Come on, Bea, let's not do this, okay, honey?" Sonya said. "Lea, put him down, please."

Sonya drew her baton back in preparation for a power stroke. Still laughing, Bea lowered her head and charged. Like a matador, Sonya sidestepped the charging Buffalo Gal and delivered a crashing blow to her hump as she passed.

"Ole!" cheered Lea, pumping Littleman up and down.

Bea turned and blinked two bloodshot eyes before charging again. Sonya had positioned herself next to the police car and when she stepped aside this time Bea crashed headfirst into the LA City emblem affixed to the door of the police car. She dropped to one knee, panting.

Ole! Lea yelled again.

Her cheer was made with a little less enthusiasm this time though. She had her eye on the two police officers stepping out of their vehicle. One of those officers was Butch Caldwell. Lea still bore the scars of her last run-in with Butch.

"Lea, knock that shit off and put him down, now!" he told her.

As Butch pulled on his deerskin gloves Lea, with the look of a child having her favorite toy taken away, gently set Littleman on the sidewalk. She rocked back and forth, head down and arms hanging at her side. Littleman recovered some composure and drew a set of handcuffs.

"Turn around and put your hands behind your back!" he shouted.

Lea looked up from under her protruding brows at Butch. He nodded and she complied. Lenny walked calmly behind Bea, who was now rising from her hands and knees and preparing for another charge. Lenny delivered a bone-crunching strike to Bea's right elbow with his wooden straight stick.

"Oww! Shit, mutha fucka that got my funny bone!" Bea bellowed.

She sat up on her haunches and rubbed her burning arm. Lenny slipped his baton under her chin lengthwise and held it against her throat, one knee on the back of her head and a hand on each end of the piece of hickory.

"You gonna play nice, sis, or am I gonna choke the shit outta you tonight?" Lenny said in an even tone.

Bea's bovine lips broke into a wide smile. "Ha, ha, we was jus waitin' on the real po-lice to show up anyway, Officer Custer."

Several minutes later, with both Buffalo Gals corralled and placed in separate cars, a quick sidewalk debrief took place. A caper of such notoriety called for a period of unwinding and fellowship. The officers enjoyed the moment and agreed this incident had been high comedy, and was a good start for New Year's Eve. From that day on Sonya Sontag was known as *La Matador.*

The rest of the night did not disappoint. There was plenty of action to go around. By 2100 hours the police radio was spitting out calls rapid-fire. Every unit in the division was racing around, investigating crimes, completing reports, and making arrests. While in the station, the cops listened to their radios to ensure no outside unit was assigned a call within 77th Street's boundaries. It was a matter of pride. Rather than "drop" a call to an outside division 77th Street officers delivered arrestees to the station, then returned to the field to handle urgent calls. They would complete their reports after the night settled down.

As with the Buffalo Gals alcohol proved a key factor in many of the night's activities. While responding to a "Shots fired" complaint, Quint and Brian came upon a green Chevy Nova being driven at a snail's pace down Florence Avenue. The car drifted from lane to lane, narrowly missing a parked car. Brian activated the red lights and followed the car for several blocks, but it drove on. He gave the driver a couple of shots with the siren. Still the driver paid no heed. Quint had enough.

"Pull up next to this yahoo an' let me get a look at him. Be careful, don't let 'im bang into us."

Brian accelerated until the passenger door of the police car was aligned with the Nova. The driver was a man in his forties wearing a worn Los Angeles Dodgers baseball cap. He stared blankly straight ahead and took no notice of the police officers in the next lane.

"Hit the siren again," Quint said.

Brian gave a blast on the siren while Quint lit up the interior of the Nova with a spotlight. The man sleepily looked to his left then his eyes opened wide.

Quint pointed toward the curb and yelled at the man. "Pull over!"

The driver immediately directed his car to the curb and stopped.

Seconds later, Quint stood on the sidewalk in front of the police car talking with a stocky man in a flannel shirt, and work boots. The intoxicated man leaning against his beat-up Chevy Nova was what cops referred to as a "Joe Lunchbox" type. While he attempted to remove his license from his wallet, he dropped a photo of himself, three children, and a pretty woman on the ground. Quint picked it up as the police radio broadcasted a string of high-priority radio calls.

"That your family, sir?" Quint asked.

"Yes, sir, it is," he said.

"How far away do ya live?" Quint said.

"Um, 'bout two, three blocks, sir," the man said, pointing up the street.

"Gimme yer keys," Quint said.

Watery-eyed and swaying, the fellow handed over a ring of keys. Quint shone his flashlight on them, then tried a couple in the trunk lock of the Nova until the trunk popped open.

"You got another set of car keys at home?" Quint asked.

"Yes, officer."

Quint tossed the keys into the trunk and slammed the lid.

"Walk home and come get the car in the morning when you're sober."

Quint handed the astonished man his driver's license, registration, and the photograph.

"Put these in yer pocket an' don't lose em."

"I can go?"

"Yep, partner, ah ain't putting a workin' man in jail tonight if it can be helped. Now, you get on down the road to yer family," Quint said.

The man took half a dozen steps and turned toward Quint.

"Happy New Year, officer."

"Guy's probably heading to the next bar and has an extra key hid in the wheel well," Brian said.

Quint punched Brian on the shoulder.

"Oh ye of so little faith, that's why we never seen that guy and never recorded nothin' about this stop, pard. 'Cause no good turn goes unpunished. Now let's you an me go handle some of these dang calls. Folks're goin' crazy ta'nite."

For several hours Quint, Brian, and every other copper working that night chased the radio. Quint looked at his watch.

"Well, you best pull into that gas station. It's jes 'bout midnight. We can park under the cover."

The gas station was closed and Brian parked the police cruiser under the covered area. He backed the car into the "L" where the garage and office came together at a right angle. They were protected from gunfire on two sides and from above.

Brian O'Callahan had heard celebratory gunfire at midnight before. But nothing he had ever seen or heard prepared him for the display of firepower that ripped through the night at the stroke of twelve. Weapons of all calibers discharged simultaneously. Orange and yellow muzzle flashes lit the night around them. Across the street a shadowy figure stood on a second floor balcony, pointed a rifle at the sky, and tore into the night with a burst of automatic gunfire. Brian tried to determine what kinds of guns were being fired by their reports. He heard volleys of .22-caliber rounds met with a string of shotgun blasts. Then a fully automatic AK47 ripped into the sky. A semi-automatic pistol fired 16 rounds in concert with a large-caliber revolver that fired six. Twice something went off that sounded more like an explosion than gunfire.

Brian turned to Quint, "Holy shit! Listen to that, will you?"

"Sounds like a cattle-town whorehouse on Saturday night," Quint said. "Think ol' Abe made a good call on this one. Nobody oughta be drivin' 'round in this."

As if on cue, pings on the metal roof of the gas station began. Projectiles that had gone up were coming down.

Brian's eyes searched the night. "I guess what that Japanese guy said during World War II about there being a gun behind every door in America was true," he opined.

The gunfire went on for several minutes then began to taper off and after fifteen minutes it subsided. Only a few die-hard shooters could still be heard. The radio operator continued broadcasting "Shots fired" calls throughout the division. They normally would have sent police cars racing, but now they merely served to entertain the officers, who were monitoring their radios from positions of relative safety.

At 12:35, Brian and Quint figured the coast was clear so they slipped from their fort and headed north on Vermont toward their beat. A call advising of a shooting that had just occurred in the 1100 block of West 54th Street was broadcast. Brian shot Quint an inquisitive look.

"Sure, go ahead on, buy that. We're right there," he said.

Quint broadcast, "12X42, we're Code-six on the eleven hundred block of West Fifty-fourth Street. Have you got any suspect description?"

Brian wheeled a left turn onto 54th Street. As they drove past the clapboard bungalows in the neighborhood they saw a single form standing in the middle of the street about 100 yards from the intersection. The police car approached the figure slowly and stopped about 25 yards away from the form, now recognizable as a black male in his late teens or early twenties.

The radio operator came on the air, "12X42, no further on your call. PR called from a phone booth."

"Somethin's not right here," Quint said as he illuminated the man in the street with the car's handheld spotlight.

Immediately the man raised his right hand and a glint of light shone off the large, dark, revolver being pointed in their direction.

"Shit, get us outta here Bri."

In preparation for backing away, Brian glanced in the rearview mirror. Directly behind them stood another man dressed in black wearing a hooded sweatshirt. He was holding an Uzi machine gun.

"Ambush!" Brian threw the car into reverse and backed directly at the figure behind them. In the same moment, the rear window of the police car exploded. A bullet hole appeared in the front windshield just above Brian's head. The hooded assailant stood his ground, firing until the police car was within several yards. Then he leapt to the side and sprayed the black-and-white as it roared past him. Gunshots sounded like they were coming from all directions as chaos reigned inside the car. Quint felt something strike the car by his feet at the same time four bullets tore through the rear door on the passenger side. The windows shattered as tufts of upholstery, pieces of glass, and shards of metal filled the interior of the car. Brian kept one eye on the front windshield and the other in the rearview mirror. He heard a pop and the mirror disappeared. He continued driving backward at full throttle until he felt they were clear of the ambush. Brian tried a stunt Charlie had taught him. He let up on the gas, stomped on the parking brake, and spun the steering wheel. The police car did a half-pirouette in the center of the street. He threw the car into drive as he released the brake and stood on the gas pedal. Before the last piece of glass had fallen out of the shattered windows, the two officers were back on Vermont. Brian rolled out of the car with his Rover in one hand and his pistol in the other.

"12X42, officers need help! Shots fired at our location 54th and Vermont!"

Quint pulled the shotgun out of the rack and ran in a crouched position to a BBQ stand across the street. He took cover behind a low brick wall, and searched the street where they had just been attacked. No one was in sight.

After firing one shot from the .357 Magnum, Ray-Ray quickly got out of the street. Before he stepped to the curb he fired five more shots into the police car. He looked down the street and saw Q-Tip's muzzle flashes lighting up the night.

"Happy New Year, muthafuckers!" he yelled. Then he took off running.

One street north a silhouette sat waiting in a green Buick with the engine running. As he ran toward the car Ray-Ray pulled the pistol from his waistband, jerked the passenger door open, and slid it under the front seat. He climbed onto the front passenger seat as the driver slipped the car into drive and slipped away.

Duwayne "Q-Tip" Jackson was only 18 years old, but already had a reputation among his homies for being a "hardass nigger." Before his eighteenth birthday he had murdered rival gang members and committed scores of armed robberies. But his most noteworthy deed occurred when he was still in school, when he slashed the face of a girl in class who had "dissed" him. Q-Tip was sadistic and fearless. After emptying the magazine of the Uzi into the police car, he sprinted southbound between the houses, climbing fences and waking dogs. On 56th Street, he tossed the gun onto the roof of a friend's home then continued running between the houses until he emerged onto 57th Street. He saw a police car heading down the street toward him. He crouched and ran back to a crawl space under the house he'd just passed and wiggled into the opening. He lay under the house, breathing in air laden with the scent of decaying wood and wet earth.

The morning of the first day of 1984 filled with sirens. Officers arrived en masse from all over South and Central Bureaus. Quint set up a large perimeter. Sergeant Palmer established a command post on Vermont, and within half an hour three K-9 officers and their dogs began a search for the shooters. Sergeant Leo Brooks arrived with Lieutenant Wiener in tow about forty-five minutes after the incident had occurred. As they walked past the bullet-riddled police car Leo sucked his teeth and rubbed his head.

"Damn miracle those men weren't killed," he said.

Abe Palmer began his situation report to Leo and the lieutenant as soon as they walked up.

"Everyone is okay. Quint set up a good perimeter and we closed this thing up pretty quick. Metro is gonna send another dog to help in the search. I think we've got a good chance of catching these guys."

Before Palmer finished, Lieutenant Wiener broke in, "Do we need all these officers here?"

"Ah, sir, this is an attempted murder of a police officer investigation," Palmer said. "I think we should keep this perimeter tight at least until Major Crimes shows up."

Brushing off Palmer's advice, Wiener turned to Sergeant Price, who had just arrived on scene. "Drive around this perimeter. Any non-essential personnel I want sent back to patrol. All outside units I want released back to their divisions."

Wiener turned back to Palmer. "How do you know this is an attempted murder on a police officer? Maybe they misidentified the car and thought they were shooting up some rival gang member's car."

Leo and Abe Palmer exchanged looks.

"Now wait a minute, sir," Leo said.

"Did our officers return fire?" asked Wiener.

"No, sir," Palmer said.

"Were any officers hurt?" Wiener asked.

Leo said, "Lieutenant, those are determinations we can let Majors make, or at least Detective Stupin. I don't think it is our place to--"

Wiener cut him off.

"This is a no harm/no foul situation as far as I'm concerned. We are dropping radio calls to divisions outside of South Bureau. That's not going to occur on my watch. Let's scratch out a crime report, give K-9 fifteen minutes. If they have not located a suspect by then close this scene down and get these officers back to work."

"Lieutenant, this is wrong!" Abe Palmer roared.

He took a step toward Wiener, who took a step back. Leo grabbed Abe by the crook of his arm and pulled him several feet away.

"Easy Abe, be cool, man," Leo said. "Let me handle this."

"Fuckin handle it then," Palmer snarled, shooting arrows with his eyes.

Quint and Brian were leaning against a police car near the command post when Willie and Pistol Pete approached.

"You guys hear? Fuckin LT's breaking down the CP," Pete said.

"Naw that cain't be right," Quint said rising off the fender of the black-and-white.

"We were there when he told Leo to release the guys from other divisions." Willie said.

Quint muttered something then stepped off with Brian at his heels.

As he neared Leo who was, positioned between Abe and Wiener, Quint said, "Hey, Leo, what's this bullshit about shrinking the perimeter and turnin' all outside units loose?"

"Hold on a second, Quint, I got my hands full right now"

Wiener took the offensive, "You heard what I said. I want this shut down in fifteen minutes, Sergeant Palmer, and I don't want to hear any argument!"

Before Abe could mutter a sound in response Wiener was confronted by a face inches from his own. The young man standing in front of him looked familiar but he couldn't recall where he had seen him.

He heard the young man say, "Remember me, Mr. Wiener? You coached our baseball team? You used to give me rides home, too. Remember? I'm older now but I remember you. I will always remember you."

The memory came to Wiener like a punch in the stomach. He felt himself retch. The boy pulled open the collar of his button- up shirt and exposed a black-blue bruise that ran around his neck. The discoloration starkly contrasted the milk-white complexion of the sandy-haired youth. Wiener tried to speak but his tongue felt as if it had been pickled--thick, briny and sour. Slowly the boy's lips turned the color of a plum. His adolescent face took on the color of boiled meat, and his head abruptly twisted then hung to the side. The blood vessels in the boy's eyes ruptured, as his eyes widened then pushed from their sockets, red and bulging. Wiener gasped and looked to his left then his right. All eyes were on him. He opened his mouth but could only manage a croak. His knees buckled and he dropped in a heap onto the pavement. Wiener forced himself to look up at the boy. Brian O'Callahan stood in his place.

"I know," Brian whispered.

Quint put a hand on his partner's shoulder. "Brian, come on, let it be, pard. Let's don't do this."

Leo and Price moved quickly to Wiener and helped him to his feet. Brian felt like a guest within his own body. Why was everyone looking at him? Suddenly he was exhausted.

"Quint, meet me at the sergeant's car," Brian said. He headed toward Abe's car feeling like he'd missed something important.

Wiener watched him go, then turned to Leo. "Let's go," he said quietly and walked away.

But Leo and Abe looked at Quint for some kind of explanation for what they had just witnessed.

"What the hell was that?" Abe asked. "Brian just walked up and looked at Wiener and the LT came apart."

Quint drew a can of snuff from his back pocket and snapped it open. He took a pinch of the fragrant ground plant and packed it into his lower lip. He rubbed his fingers together, ridding them of tobacco crumbs, and slid his tin back into his pocket. He drew a long deep breath as he cast a look at Brian sitting alone behind the wheel of the police car.

"Well, boys, Brian told em he knew sumpthin, ah'm not sure what that is, but a'm sure as shootin gonna try an' find out, 'cause ah wanna know, too."

Leo followed Wiener to his car. As Wiener slid into the passenger seat, he noticed the dampness of his lap. He folded his hands over his soaked crotch and gave thanks for his dark wool trousers. Leo got into the driver's seat and looked at him, preparing to present an argument in private, but Wiener turned in his seat, away from Leo.

"I don't want to hear a word, Leonard, just get me to the station and don't stop for anything. Just drive," Wiener said.

"Sarge, if you have Charlie work on the crime report at the station, me an Bri will stick around and collect evidence then hook up with Charlie later an help him complete the reports. I wanna make sure we get a good investigation in case somebody decides shootin at the cops is a big thing. If y'all leave us a car since ours is in sorry shape."

"You sure your partner is up to it, Quint? He seemed pretty worked up," Abe said.

"Hell yeah, he's gonna be finer then frog hair in a minute, Sarge. No problem."

"It's gonna piss off the dicks but fuck em. Here take my car, I'll catch a ride with Pete and Willie." Abe tossed a set of shop keys to Quint.

Q-Tip, was unaware that Wiener's order to break down the perimeter was being circulated among the police officers searching for him. His heart was still pounding but his breathing had slowed as he listened to the car engines, police radios, and voices. A flashlight momemtarily shone through the crawl hole of the house he was hiding under. He held his breath but only a cursory visual search was made, then the searcher moved on. He heard men's voices and a dog barking.

"What? No fucking way. Are you shitting me?" someone yelled.

Some muffled talking and the slamming of car doors followed the outburst. After that it was quiet. Even the helicopter was gone. Q-Tip couldn't believe the police had given up so easily. Neither could anyone else. The young killer stayed hidden long after he heard the last police officer then crawled out from under the house. He adjusted the small pistol in his front pants pocket, dusted himself off, and made his way out to the street. He walked west on 57th to Budlong then turned south. Q-Tip strolled along and tried to appear nonchalant.

Back at the station Lieutenant Wiener stood in front of his locker in the upstairs dressing room, slipped out of his wet underwear and dropped them. They made a *"plop"* when they hit the floor. His trousers were damp also. He placed them gingerly on a hanger and hung them in his locker, then picked his shorts up with a pencil and walked bare-assed across the locker room to the trashcan. He tossed the soggy skivvies and the pencil into the trash and returned to his locker. He did not see Mental, who, with the help of his handy-dandy pocket mirror, had monitored the entire sequence of events from behind the bank of lockers. Wiener reached into his open locker, removed another pair of trousers, and pulled them on without underwear. He sat down heavily on the bench and stared into his locker.

Mental knew his little mirror would come in handy, but this was too much to ask for. He slammed his locker shut and emerged around the row of lockers.

"Hey, lieutenant, Happy New Year!" Mental said in his most cheerful voice. He walked into the adjoining bathroom, washed his hands, and tossed a paper towel into the trashcan. He stopped and studied the contents of the can, then reached in and retrieved the soiled skivvies by the waistband. "Whoa! Looks like somebody had an accident. Poor little tyke."

He held the shorts up for the lieutenant to see, then dropped them back into the can. Wiener looked like he was going to vomit. Mental smiled, pushed the locker room door open with his boot and descended the stairs at a jaunty clip. "Looks like my work here is done," he said aloud to no one in particular.

Before heading to his car and his partner, Quint saw that a tow truck driver had their car on the hoist. The truck driver asked Quint where to take the car.

"Ah already got pictures of it so jes haul er off to the station. Wrap it up with yellow crime scene tape if ya would."

Quint climbed behind the steering wheel of Sergeant Palmer's shop next to his partner. "Bri, ya okay?"

"Yeah, I just got kinda dizzy, that's all," Brian answered.

"We're gonna be doing the investigation on this here shindig. You up to it?"

"Yeah, sure, let's do it," Brian said.

Alright, after all the excitement and fancy driving you been doing tonight ah'll drive for a bit. Quint drove down 54th Street to the scene of the ambush.

The partners scoured the scene for witnesses and evidence. They found lots of 9mm cases from the Uzi but none from the pistol.

"Stands ta reason, Bri. The guy had a big revolver and they don't eject casings. After lookin at a couple of the holes in the door of our car, my bet it was a Magnum of some sort. Maybe that .357 Dapper Davy's been lookin' for," Quint deduced.

After completing their investigation, Quint said, "Betcha the shooters went to ground with all the police in the area. My bet's they're waitin for us to clear outta here and then plan on jes strollin on home. Let's set up down the street and wait an see."

They parked with their lights out in an east west alley that intersected with Budlong Avenue several blocks away from the crime scene. Brian got out of the car and secreted himself behind a row of trashcans just south of the alley. From that vantage point he could see any activity on Budlong for a quarter mile north or south. Quint stayed with the car in the alley east of the street facing west. They had created an ambush of their own. All they had to do was wait. No more than twenty minutes later Brian saw Q-Tip walking down Budlong two blocks north of his position. The would-be assassin was moving straight into the trap.

Brian keyed his radio and whispered, "He's coming."

The car was pulled far enough into the dark alley that it could not be readily seen from the street. Quint waited behind the open driver door of the police car with his fingers on the headlight switch and the engine running. He was happy with their deployment. Several minutes passed before Q-Tip stepped into the mouth of the alley. Quint waited until the suspect was directly in front of him then turned on the headlights.

"Freeze! Police! Get yer fuckin' hands up!" Quint yelled.

Q-Tip was bathed in light. He looked into the lights, then over his shoulder as he slowly raised his hands.

"Don't even breathe, asshole!" Quint warned.

Q-Tip thought about the revolver in his pocket. He thought all the cops had left the area. He was too startled to put together a plan, and judging by the tone of the officer behind the lights he was not going to get much of a chance before being shot.

"Eyes straight ahead!" said the voice behind the lights.

Q-Tip's heart was racing. The lights were a little far away. He had always been able to out run the police. If he was going to, it had to be now. He broke into a sprint heading south on the sidewalk and out of the lights. He took half a dozen strides, looked back toward the alley, and never knew what hit him. Brian rose from behind the trashcans and stepped onto the sidewalk directly in front of Q-Tip. When he looked ahead again, Brian had already let loose a sizzling punch that detonated against the side of the gangster's face. Brian heard a muted crunch and felt Q-Tip's nose and cheek collapse beneath the blow. The young man dropped face down on the sidewalk and lay motionless. Brian immediately handcuffed his prey then rolled the unconscious gangster over and searched him.

When he'd seen the attempted murder suspect bolt, Quint broadcast their location and situation, then ran from the alley just as Brian stood and held up the .22-caliber pistol he'd removed from Q-Tip's pants pocket. Quint moved to where Q-Tip lay. He was not prepared for what he saw. Prior to joining the police department Quint King had been a professional rodeo cowboy and was no stranger to blunt-force trauma. As he looked down at the distorted face of the suspect, his mind flashed back to a cowboy whose face had been crushed when a bull stomped his head into the arena dirt.

Quint returned to the moment and noted blood bubbling from their prisoner's mouth and nostrils. "Roll him on his side, Brian, or he's a-gonna drown in his own blood."

Brian pushed the suspect onto his side and Quint took a gray jail blanket from the trunk of the car and propped him up with it.

They could hear sirens heading their way. Quint keyed his Rover. "12X42, Code-four, suspect is in custody, but we're gonna need an RA here, ma'am."

The operator came back, "12X42, what have you got?"

"Ma'am, we got a male, 'bout twenty years old, unconscious with head trauma," Quint said.

She enquired further. "Is your victim breathing?"

Quint looked down on the gurgling attempted-murder suspect. "Well, ma'am, he's tryin'."

Down the street in the shadow of a fruitless mulberry Tootie watched the whole thing go down.

"Damn did you see that cop sock up Q?" Ray-Ray asked. "Must be that fuckin O'Callahan."

Without comment Tootie studied the scene through his windshield. A police car flashed past them headed for Brian and

Quint's location.

"Guess you didn't get O'Callahan," Tootie said.

He guided the Buick to Vermont, flipped on his headlights, and headed toward home.

Twenty minutes later Brian watched as they loaded Q-Tip into the RA. He was frightened. He'd reacted instinctively when the suspect tried to flee. He figured the man had just opened up on a police car with a machine gun, but he was so young. There was good cause to believe he was armed and he'd been warned. But he was just a kid. The voice from deep within him said, *Kids like this kill people every day. He tried to kill you tonight. Fuck him.* Grudgingly, Brian agreed with the voice.

A paramedic stood at the back of the ambulance writing on a clipboard.

"You think he's gonna live?" Brian asked.

The man looked at the form lying on the gurney, then smiled at the young officer. "Yeah, he'll live, but he sure ain't gonna win any beauty contests. What the hell you hit him with?"

Brian held up his clenched left hand.

"You did that with your fist? He glanced into the RA, and then looked warily at the cop in front of him. "You can roll on my calls anytime, man."

The paramedic walked to his partner, said a couple of words, and both men looked back at O'Callahan and smiled. Just before the RA's rear door was closed, Quint put his hand on the door, leaned into the vehicle, and looked into Q-Tip's swollen eyes.

"Happy New Year, asshole."

STRAWBERRY AND THE MULE

Tootie picked up the pager and read the number. It was one of his distributors. He called immediately.

"Wassup?" he grumbled into the telephone. "What? When? An you're jes telling me now? Where is that bitch?"

Tootie began pacing. Holding the phone to his ear, he yelled at Cindi, "Turn that music down!" then turned his attention back to his phone conversation. "Where are you? Meet me at that chicken place on Sepulveda. Yeah, Dinah's. Man, I don't give a muthafuckin' shit what you got to do. It's almost eleven. Be there by noon, fool."

Something was wrong, and Cindi was frightened. In the time she had known Tootie, his temper was something she had learned to fear. When angered he took it out on whoever was nearest to him. She'd been the closest a few times and paid the price.

She turned down the stereo and thought, *I need a hit.* She always needed a hit. It wasn't like when she'd smoked marijuana or snorted cocaine. Then she just wanted more. It was fun and made her feel good. But after she first smoked rock cocaine, she craved it. Now she needed it badly. Her life rotated around her next hit. She had not been to class at UCLA for a month and had been fired from her waitress job about the same time. All that Cindi once loved about life paled in comparison to the pipe. Nothing else could provide the endorphins her system was now accustomed to. The taste of lobster dipped in butter, or of rich chocolate truffles, used to flood her with a feeling of satisfaction and contentment. Now food held no joy. It could not compete. Even sex had little appeal to her. It only served as a means to keep Tootie happy, and provide her with the object of her greatest desire and need.

Tootie slammed the phone down onto the cradle; 1984 was starting out poorly. A vicious look contorted his face. His eyes scanned the room and fell upon the girl, frozen beside the stereo. She was not as pretty as when Tootie had first started patronizing the upscale café where she worked. Now her skin was blemished, and her hair reminded him of the dried grass he'd seen along the runway at LAX. Cindi looked like she had lost about twenty pounds, and her clothes hung on her. He stepped toward her.

"What the fuck you looking at, bitch?"

Like a deer in the headlights, Cindi could not move. She drew her arms across her chest, hunched her shoulders and cowered. Just before closing her eyes she saw his large gold ring. She held her hands up, but Tootie's fist crushed them against her head. His second punch smashed into her mouth. The thick ring he wore split Cindi's lip and caused her to fall forward. She struck her forehead on the corner of the stereo cabinet. In an instant a stream of crimson ran down her cheek and dripped from her chin. Tootie saw her blood on the carpet and kicked her several times, then grabbed her by the hair and dragged her into the kitchen.

"When you done crying and carrying on, clean up this mess," Tootie said. "Shit better be straight when I get back."

He walked into the bedroom and seconds later came out wearing a sweatshirt and pushing the Colt into his waistband. He eyed the girl sobbing on the floor and considered giving her another kick, but he was in a hurry.

Vernell "V-Roc" White was in no hurry to get to Culver City and meet his source. He'd put off telling Tootie about his girlfriend's arrest a few days after Thanksgiving and here it was January. He was frightened because not only was Demi Sanders arrested with 50 kilos of Tootie Hicks's cocaine, but, to make matters worse, she'd driven directly to one of Tootie's safe houses in Compton. Andre Tootie Hicks was a stone-cold killer, and "V" knew it. If he'd known Demi had identified Tootie as the owner of the coke, V-Roc would have left town.

V-Roc had visited Demi at the woman's facility of the Los Angeles County Jail, Sybil Brand Institute, where she was being held pending trial. He'd told her, *I should have known better than to let your country ass make a delivery. Jes be cool and keep your mouth shut, understand?* Demi had only sniffed and wiped a tear from her cheek.

V-Roc hoped he could talk Tootie down. After all, such things were to be expected and the money flow to Tootie hadn't waned. V-

Roc would accept all financial losses and find another house to operate out of in Compton.

A few minutes before he was to meet with V-Rock Tootie stood in the phone booth waiting for the callback. He'd learned in the joint that information was as important as muscle and took pains to develop his own sources of information once he got out of prison. His cousin Shawndra was just such a source, and he didn't mind throwing a little cash in her direction. She had three children but no man, and making ends meet on a clerk typist's salary was near impossible. Tootie picked the phone up on the first ring and grunted into the mouthpiece. For several minutes he listened. He could feel rage welling up from deep within. He hung up the phone and walked to his car in a trance, his mind racing, searching for options. Finally he knew there was only one.

V-Roc sat in his car outside of Dinah's Chicken, pleased with the way his meeting had gone. Tootie had listened quietly while he promised him that he would absorb all the costs, pay Demi's bail, and personally drive her home to the little shack in Georgia where her momma lived. He made clear that the house had no telephone and was in the middle of nowhere, surrounded by peanuts and red clay. To show his earnest, before leaving the restaurant V-Roc pushed a Nike gear bag across the table to Tootie. It contained twenty thousand dollars. "That wasn't so bad," he said out loud. He adjusted the rearview mirror of his Mustang to admire himself and smiled, then shook out his jheri-curled hair, spattering the Mustang's windows with the oily treatment he used to relax his tightly-curled hair. He heard a tap on the driver-side window and looked up into an enormous black hole. In a flash, the car's windows were also spattered, with Vernell "V-Roc" White's brains.

Cindi talked into the bloody mouthpiece. She closed and rubbed her good eye; the other looked like a plum.

"Daddy, can you pick me up? Please, Daddy, I'm sorry, I just want to come home. I don't know where my car is. I loaned it to a friend and he never returned it. I know, Daddy. I think I have to go to the hospital. Yes, I'll meet you in front of the apartments. Thank you, Daddy."

She hung up the phone, picked up a cigarette lighter and the glass pipe. She gingerly held the pipe to her lips. *Just one more time,* she told herself.

James Trask watched the blonde get into a white Mercedes. He jotted down the license number and walked back to his apartment, looking at the drops of blood that led down the flagstone walkway and out to the street, where the girl had stood pacing for thirty minutes. He had not verified it, but he knew the trail of blood would lead back to Andre Hicks's apartment. He'd offered to drive her to the hospital, but she'd refused and said her father was going to pick her up. Trask was no medical expert, but he knew from the look of her that she needed a doctor. Back in his apartment, he pulled Officer Manny Magana's business card from his wallet and dialed the number.

Manny walked into the watch commander's office where Abe Palmer was seated at the small wooden desk. "Sarge, I just got a call from James Trask, the manager at the apartment complex in Marina del Rey. He says he just saw Tootie Hicks's girlfriend leave, and she was beat to shit. He said some middle-aged white guy in a Mercedes picked her up. He got the license plate number. It comes back to a doctor's office in Beverly Hills."

Sergeant Palmer looked up from a pile of paperwork. "So? Narcotics division is handling that case now, and Leo said if we left the division again he was gonna have my ass. And you know what, Manny? I don't want Leo to have my ass. So forget it."

"Might not be a bad time to talk to her, while she's still pissed off," said Manny.

"Well, give them a call over at narco and pass on the information," Abe said.

"Those guys aren't gonna do shit, boss. They'll say, 'Okay, thanks,' and that clue will go in the circular file."

Manny held up a wastebasket and threw in a wad of paper for effect. Abe loved street cops, especially the ones who liked to dig.

"All right. Lieutenant Wiener took a string of days off, and Leo's the watch commander. Let me talk to him," Abe said, rising from his chair.

Leo Brooks rubbed his hairless scalp and looked at the blotter on his desk while Abe Palmer made his pitch.

"So I was thinking we could send King and O'Callahan over there and see if they can get a statement from her. You know nobody digs like Quint, and Brian could get Charlie Manson to roll on himself. I never saw a guy that could talk to people like he does."

"Yeah, and if they don't cooperate he'll punch their headlamps out, shoot 'em, or make 'em piss their pants," Leo said.

Abe looked somber. "You make that sound like it's a bad thing, Leo."

Leo shook his head. "Tell your boys to be cool. With all the shit your team has stirred up lately I can't believe Captain Sullivan or Bureau hasn't shut you down yet. The fucking lieutenant is watching you guys like a hawk, too."

"Hey, did the lieutenant really piss his pants the other night?"

"That's what a little birdie told me. Keep it under your hat 'cause the LT is seriously shaken up.".

"Fuckin' beautiful," Abe said. "That O'Callahan is really growing on me."

As Palmer walked into the hall Leo shouted after him, "Abe, I ain't bullshitting! Tell King and O'Callahan to get a statement and get back."

Leo looked back at his blotter and rubbed his head.

Twenty minutes later Quint was bringing his partner up to speed.

"Beverly Hills?" said Brian. "Why?"

"Some gal that lives with this guy Tootie Hicks got tromped by him, and Abe thinks we might be able to get'er to roll the guy," said Quint.

"Isn't he the Crip that girl in the Mazda gave up?"

"You bet, partner, and we're gonna use that magic tongue of yours to get more dirt on 'im," said Quint. "Ah called the doctor's office where this li'l gal's daddy works. Receptionist said he wasn't in, so ah explained what kinda guy was snorting the doctor's daughter's flank. The doc called back in a couple minutes and said he'd meet us at Cedars Sinai Hospital about 1800 hours."

"Where's Cedars?" asked Brian.

"Bout fifteen miles from here, near West Los Angeles, Brentwood, Beverly Hills, you know, the high-rent district," said Quint. "The hospital of the stars. We got jest enough time to make it."

Doctor Stanley Sykovski stood up when the officers walked into the hospital lobby. He looked like a coal miner in a designer suit.

"She's on the third floor," Dr. Sykovski said.

He led the officers to the elevator.

"Cindi's always been a handful, but in the past few months she has changed. I feel like I don't even know her. Our home is turned upside down, and her mother is a wreck. Quite frankly I hesitated to even come pick her up today at this man's apartment. She's been living with him about a month now. We bought her a Porsche for her birthday and don't even know where the car is now."

He looked around the lobby and said in a low voice, "It's not because he's black, you know, it's because he's..."

"An asshole?" Brian said.

Sykovski pondered Brian's words for a moment then said, "The world is full of assholes officer, wait until you see what he did to my little girl. He's a damn animal! I have a mind to..." he caught himself, and showed them a photo he'd brought from his office. "This was taken during Cindi's sophomore year at UCLA."

Bright-eyed and tanned, the girl in the photo could have been model for a suntan lotion company. The trio stepped from the elevator and walked briskly past the nurse's station. A middle-aged nurse of Philippine descent looked up from her paperwork and watched Sykovski. The perplexed look on her face softened to a noncommittal smile for the two officers trailing behind him.

They entered a room with drawn blinds and dim lighting. There was a single bed, upon which lay a creature who looked nothing like the girl in the photo. Her forehead was bandaged; one eye was swollen shut. Her lip was sutured up to her nose, and one cheek was twice the size of the other. Her right hand had been broken when she protected her face and was in a cast. Brian had seen people who'd gone through the windshields of cars in better condition. Injuries aside, this girl did not look healthy. Brian thought she looked as if life had been drained from her. It was if a vampire had been sucking her blood. He pulled a chair up next to the girl's bed.

"Hi, Cindi. I'm Officer O'Callahan."

Her eye widened and she shook her head.

"Cindi," her father interjected. "These men are here to help make sure this Andre is dealt with. I want you to tell them what happened."

Quint stepped next to Sykovski.

"Sir, maybe she'd feel a little more at ease talking if you stepped out of the room."

Sykovski shot Quint a stern look and walked out of the room.

Brian scooted his chair a little closer to Cindi's bed. "Hon, we are not here for any other reason than to hear what you want to tell us. We are not interested in what you have done, because nothing you did made you deserve this. After we talk, if there is anything we can do to help you, I promise we will try."

Then Brian smiled his soft, genuine smile and put his hand on the girl's forearm just below her IV tube. "Deal?"

For the first time in a long while, Cindi felt safe. The officer's smile warmed her heart. His soothing voice and handsome features calmed her. But his eyes! They reminded Cindi of a kaleidoscope her daddy had given her when she was a small girl. She nodded.

Quint turned on his micro-tape recorder and laid it on the pillow next to the girl's head.

Across town in East Los Angeles, another young girl feared Tootie Hicks.

"Demi Sanders, you made bail," said the LA County Sheriff's Deputy. "Let me see your armband."

Demi pushed her arm through the rectangular opening in the cell. The tough- looking female deputy checked Demi's name and booking number on the wristband. Six hours later, Demi stepped through the doorway into a parking lot. A skinny young black man wearing several large gold chains around his neck swaggered over to her. She immediately did not like him and felt her stomach tighten.

"You Demi? V-Roc sent me to pick you up. He say y'all fittin to get outta town fo' awhile."

His pointed goatee made him look like the devil.

"Who are you? Where's Vernell?" she asked.

"I'm Ray-Ray," he said. "Come on, we gotta hurry. Ima take ya to V-Roc."

He led her to a green Buick parked at the edge of the lot. Demi climbed into the front seat but stayed near the door with her hand on the handle. She never knew anyone was behind her until she felt the barrel of a gun against the back of her head.

OUT TO THE STATION

Tom Jefferson leaned against the wall. He was mesmerized by the battle being waged ten feet away. He had not seen Dee look so sharp since he was a boy. Although Mo-Mo was Tom's natural son, he'd always felt closer to Dee, whose father no one knew.

"That boy sure look good, Boomer," Jefferson said in a rich, slow baritone. "You done put some life back into him."

He took a long sip from the Styrofoam coffee cup he held in his thick hand, and slapped Boomer's hand with the other.

"He jus needed to get his confidence back, man. I always knew Dee had it in him. He jus needed to come on home."

Boomer watched the two men dressed in gray sweats up in the ring. Dee circled, jabbed, rolled, and counterpunched. He was fluid, and his punches were crisp and popped when they struck Brian O'Callahan. The young police officer pressed Dee and kept him honest. Dark rings of sweat spread across their chests and backs.

"O'Callahan, he been great fo Dee. He come in every morning and spar with Dee. He jus like his daddy. Tough as a five-year-old rooster, but he never crow."

"You knew his dad?" said Jefferson.

"Sho did, Irish Seamus O'Callahan. That man would give you the shirt off his back an' he could punch hard enough to shell a coconut. He was a real fine man."

The round bell rang and Boomer looked up into the ring. He threw Brian a towel.

"Y'all had enough, Irish?" said Boomer.

Brian spit his mouthpiece into a gloved hand.

"Yeah, Boom, let Slugger here beat somebody else up for a while. I have to get to work."

Brian walked to Dee, draped an arm around his neck and feinted a punch to his midsection. Dee spit his mouthpiece into the bucket in the corner of the ring and twisted out of Brian's playful hold.

"Boomer, I think you've got the wrong guy fighting next week," said Dee. "Brian ever decides he doesn't wanna be a cop he could be winnin' big purses in six months."

"Yeah, brothers would be lining up to kick my white ass."

Dee laughed. "Yeah, an'those niggers would be gettin' a surprise, too."

"Yea, you both ready fo' a shot at da champ." Boomer said. "Whatchew think, Tom?"

"Boom, I think in y'alls day you woulda knocked 'em both out...bip bap!" He threw two heavy punches for emphasis. "All right then y'all. I gotta go back to work." Tom waved and lumbered to the front door.

"Brian, see you tomorrow 'bout 6:30 then," said Boomer. "Dee, take a fifteen-minute break, then we gonna work on that lef' hook, man. You gonna put Gonzales to sleep wif that, man."

"Dee, where you want to eat tonight, man?" Brian said as he pulled off his gloves.

"I don't know, what do ya feel like?" said Dee.

"Tell you what, why don't you come by my place and I'll make us some big salads, say 'bout eight o'clock. You still got the key?"

Dee nodded and wiped his face with a towel. "All right, cool. Just call the crib if your gonna be late, man, cause last time I waited two hours for you're thin ass."

"Yeah, and you ate everything in the fridge, too."

"Aww man, you didn't have shit to eat in that fridge. I had to walk down to Mickey D's and get a burger," Dee said.

"You're in training. You shouldn't eat that crap," said Brian over his shoulder as he walked toward the door.

Dee watched Brian go, then took a long drink of water from a pop bottle wrapped in white athletic tape. He wondered about O'Callahan. He had never met anyone like him. He was a cop, but didn't act like one. O'Callahan never talked about police work but at the same time, there was no doubt that Brian was a cop. That was sure. Since transferring to 77th Street Division he'd made a name for himself in the neighborhood. Even gangsters commented on how fairly they were treated by "Officer O'Callahan". A few days after New Year's Eve Dee had heard a fighter talking about him in the locker room. *Yeah man, O'Callahan damn near killed that young killer Q-Tip wif one punch, man," said the fighter. "That boy Q-Tip, he ain't no punk, either. He a big strong youngster. I hear that shit and the next day I see O'Callahan over on Fifty-fourth Street walkin' wif Officer King. Wass he doing? O'Callahan be handing out candy to the kids. Man, thas what a po-lice suppose to be like.*

Aside from everything else, Brian reminded Dee of Danny Lugo; and not just because they wore the same aftershave lotion. Dee decided to tell Brian about Danny Lugo and a murderer named Tootie.

Brian pushed open the screen door and stepped into the sunshine.

"Excuse me, Officer O'Callahan," a deep male voice called out.

Brian looked in the direction of the voice and reached into his duty bag simultaneously.

Tom Jefferson said, "I don't mean you no harm. Just wonderin' if you got a minute to talk."

"Sure, Mr. Jefferson. Sorry," said Brian. He set his bag at his feet and turned to the hulking figure.

"How can I help you, sir?"

"You been real good to Dee, seems you and him are friends an' all. Well, I'm his stepdaddy and I been watchin out for him best I can since he was a small boy. An' I been raised in this neighborhood. Only time I wasn't here was when I was in the Marines. Then I was gone over to Vietnam and when I got home seemed there was so much madness in our community. So much changed."

Tom was lost in his thoughts for a moment.

"I'm just saying I care 'bout my neighborhood and my boys. Dee ain't my real son but sometime he seems more like my boy than his brother, who is my child. His name is Mo-Mo. His real name is Maurice, been Mo-Mo for a long time. That boy, he's been messin' 'round with that rock cocaine, an he always on the street. Hangin' out with all those li'l hoodlums, you know. I try to talk to him but he don't want to hear."

Brian nodded his head without a word. He knew Mo-Mo, and had spoken with him on several occasions.

"Seems you really care about folks round here an' I want to help you. Lots of people talk to me and I sees lots going on over at my shop."

Tom pointed toward his garage, with the looming statue in front.

"What happened on New Year's over on Fifty-fourth Street was wrong, and that's the type of thing that makes the police treat people mean, and folks gets mad and then we got us a riot. I don't want no more of that. You caught Q-Tip that night but the other boy he got away. I don't expect Q-Tip tol' you much about that other boy."

"No, sir, he didn't," said Brian.

"Well, the boy you're looking for, his name is Ray-Ray. He used to stay over somewhere on the seventies but now I don't know. Little skinny rat-face boy, he always wears lots of gold chains. He must be about twenty-three or so now. Word is he's done lots of shootin', and not just gang stuff. He works for someone but I don't know who that is."

Brian was shocked and not sure how to respond, so he remained silent. Tom's words were so intimate and powerful. He wished Charlie or Quint were there. They would know what to say and what to do with the information. Tom judged Brian's silence for skepticism.

"If you don't believe me ask Officer Bender, we friends. I'm no snitch. I don't want nuthin' except to get these little hoodlums off the street."

It dawned on Brian that Charlie Bender had visited Tom's garage just prior to locating Baby-K's black Regal.

"No, no, Mr. Jefferson, I believe you, it's just such important information. I can't believe you told me," Brian said.

Tom studied the young officer for a moment.

"Officer, I seen many men die an I seen men lie when the truth would save their lives. I know who to trust, learned by doing business an' fighting in war. Most of all just livin', man. You straight up, officer, and that's plain as my nose. I might maybe ask one thing. You ever get a chance, talk to Mo-Mo. I'd sure appreciate it. I got to get going now." Tom took Brian's hand in his grimy paw and gave it a squeeze, then clomped off in his half-laced combat boots.

Quint King was nearly in uniform when Brian walked from the shower into the locker room and began dressing.

"Hey, Brian, hurry up and get suited up. Captain wants to see us in his office right away."

Brian searched Quint's face for some sign of angst. As usual there was none. Quint was one of the few people Brian knew who almost never became rattled.

"What's up?" asked Brian.

Quint looked into the small mirror hanging in his locker and combed his moustache. "Don't know."

Brian smiled and shook his head.

"What?" Quint asked.

"Man, doesn't anything worry you?"

"Worry don't fill the pail, pard. Jes walk on down to the well and fill it. No water in the well looks like yer walking to the creek."

Quint shot a stream of tobacco juice into the "Arbuckle" coffee cup he kept in his locker for such purposes.

"My partner, the cowboy philosopher," said Brian.

Quint shot a second stream into his cup. "Yup," he said then wiped his moustache with the back of his hand.

Brian grabbed the four pieces of leather that snapped together to affix his gun belt to his under-belt and walked toward the door. He turned and looked at Quint, who was still admiring himself in his mirror.

"You're beautiful, Tex," Brian said. "Now let's go see if there's any water in the well. If there is, I just hope it isn't hot water."

Quint slammed his locker shut. "Hey, ah'm the ol' hand 'round here. Don't go getting sassy."

They stepped into the watch commander's office. Lieutenant Wiener was working his first shift since New Year's Eve a week ago. He looked up from his paperwork and watched the two cross the room but made no comment.

"Skipper wants to see us, lieutenant, might be late for roll call," said Quint.

Wiener nodded with no change of expression or reply. Still, he watched them.

Charlie was leaning against the doorjamb that separated the front desk area and the watch commander's office. "Well, you done it now, boys. Y'all get yerselves up to the principal's office, an' we don't wanna hear no squealing when he paddles y'all's fannies," he said. He took a sip from his Marine Corps mug and gave Brian a tap on the seat of his pants with the toe of his boot as he walked through the doorway. "Go on, scat, young 'un!" Charlie said.

A coughing jag interrupted his laugh. Charlie turned and spit a gob of phlegm into the wastebasket.

Wiener winced and looked away.

"Charlie, I wish you wouldn't do that."

"Can't swaller those big 'uns, LT, I'd choke."

Brian looked over his shoulder at Charlie, who winked at him as he fired up a cigarette.

Charlie always seemed to be able to put Brian at ease. A kick in the pants and a wink from him did more for Brian than any pep talk.

The door to Captain Sullivan's outer office was open. A thin, pretty woman sat at a desk in the middle of the room. Rita Jones looked up from a pile of paper on her desk and motioned them closer.

"You two, the captain's got Lieutenant Cicotti and Detective Lang in there. He was not happy when he told me to get you in here," Rita said.

Batting her lashes at two of her favorite police officers, she lowered her voice and leaned forward.

"Something about the New Year's Eve when you got your car shot up. Guys from Robbery Homicide think you should have called them."

Rita pulled a pencil from her modest Afro and placed the eraser between her lips, while she adjusted the silk multicolored scarf she wore around her head. Then she took the pencil from her mouth and pointed it at the closed door of the captain's office.

"Well, don't just stand there gawking at me," Rita smiled, exposing a row of brilliant white teeth.

Brian knocked on the door then said to Quint, "I have something to tell you about this shooting after we're done here."

The door opened. Brian peeked into the room. Dapper Davy was seated next to the door and Preacher, Nick Stupin, and Robbie Lang formed a semi-circle around Captain Sullivan's heavy oak desk. Seated at the desk was the captain, and towering behind him, with his arms folded across his chest, was Bruno Cicotti.

"Come in, lads," said Sullivan.

He motioned to the pair of straight-backed chairs arranged at the far end of the desk. Now Quint was nervous. Every face in the room was grim. He felt like he had a wad of cotton in his mouth that hung up when he tried to swallow. The small room was crowded, and legs had to be moved in order for Quint and Brian to make their way to the chairs. On the desk in front of the captain was the "Preliminary Investigation Report" Charlie had completed pursuant to the ambush. Next to it was an evidence report and manila evidence envelope that contained the spent bullet casings Brian and Quint recovered that night.

"Did you men complete these reports?" Captain Sullivan asked.

"I did, sir," said Brian.

"I understand you dictated the crime report to Officer Bender and completed the property on your own. What were you thinking?" Nick Stupin blurted. "Why wasn't I advised about this? Do you think you can just roll up and complete an attempted murder on a police officer without making any notifications?" Stupin's beefy face was crimson.

Brian said, "No, sir, I don't, and if you read the box for notifications you will see that I did notify RHD. "

Stupin's voice rose as he said, "Don't tell me to read the report, smart ass!"

"Hold on, Nick, let him explain," Sullivan said.

"I want to know what makes a two-year fuzz nut PII think he can just…"

A calm had come over Brian. He looked around the room and saw mostly downcast eyes. Brian closed his eyes and saw his father straddling a kitchen chair, wearing his sleeveless undershirt and dungarees. From deep within he heard his father's words. *This guy's a bully, only thing to do with a bully is hit him as hard as you are able and keep on hitting him, son.*

In a low voice Brian said, "Detective Stupin, there is no need to yell. I will be glad to …"

Stupin pushed himself up from his chair and pointed his finger in Brian's face.

"Don't tell me what to do, mister! Do you realize what you have done?"

Stupin grabbed Brian's report from the captain's desk. Before anyone could move he threw it in Brian's face. In an instant, Brian was on his feet and grabbed the fat man by his tie and collar. He twisted the bunched material under Stupin's double chin and drove him back into his chair. The chair rocked back on two legs momentarily and groaned under Stupin's weight. Brian released his hold and sat back down. His eyes smoldered.

"Now, Detective Stupin, if you will listen, I will explain," Brian said in a calm, even tone.

Brian had moved so fast, and with such force, that Bruno Cicotti wasn't sure what he had seen.

Captain Sullivan said in a voice that betrayed his true feelings, "Officer O'Callahan, you're outta line!"

"Sir, I'm sorry," Brian said, "but Detective Stupin--or anyone else for that matter won't assault me. As far as I am concerned he crossed the line. I'll take my punishment, but I won't be bullied."

Brian's voice was soft and calm. All the while he never took his eyes off Stupin, who sat motionless, in his chair, just as Brian had delivered him. So intense and seething was Brian's expression that both Preacher and Detective Long found themselves leaning away from the object of his wrath.

"Okay, let's everyone take a deep breath here and we'll start over," said Sullivan.

Brian broke his glare, retrieved his investigation from the floor, and laid the report in front of Sullivan. He glanced up at Cicotti, who had not moved or said a word since Brian and Quint entered the room, and was amazed to see a faint smile pass over the police legend's face.

"Brian, let's hear what happened," said Captain Sullivan. "And it had better be good."

Brian gave a complete account of the incident. After he finished, Sullivan and Stupin exchanged looks. They turned to Cicotti and Long. Not a word was uttered.

Finally Sullivan asked, "Quint, is that how it went down?"

"Captain, that's exactly how it went down. Leo and Abe were there. They'll tell the same story. Wiener told them there wasn't no need to bother RHD with a call."

"Well, that's not how Lieutenant Wiener explained it," Nick Stupin said in a subdued voice.

Detective Lang stirred. "Guys, the captain and Detective Stupin have taken considerable heat from RHD, South Bureau and the Chief's office over this. That's why we're here and why everyone is a little at odds. Shooting at a police officer, from ambush no less, is considered a major crime and RHD would have sent a team out to investigate it."

"That's how we felt too, Robbie," said Quint. "But since the scene was being shut down we did the best we could."

"You did a damn good job of it too, Quint," Cicotti added. "Collected and handled the evidence properly, took photos, hell, you even made an arrest. I don't think anyone here thinks you men didn't give it your best shot."

He looked at Stupin. "Right, Nick?"

Detective Stupin looked at the floor and gave a slight nod.

"King, Callahan, that's all I need," Sullivan said. "Does anyone have anything to say before these two go back to work?"

There was a general shuffling of feet and clearing of throats.

"Then everything's settled?" Captain Sullivan said. "Cause if it is not I'll hear about it right now, and nothing of it later."

After an uncomfortable silence Captain Sullivan said, "Officers, you are excused. Thank you, and would you mind telling the good lieutenant I'd like to have a word with him?"

Quint and Brian hurried out of the Captain's office. Quint gave Rita the thumbs up and they crossed the hall into the watch commander's office.

As they walked through the office Quint saw a gaggle of coppers loitering around the front desk. Lenny Custer, Butch Caldwell, Scooter Kellerman, and Willie Washington were whispering like kids on Christmas morning. They all were profoundly pleased about something.

"You guys seen the Wiener?" Quint said.

"Yeah, he's in the crapper," said Charlie from the front desk.

"Oh, Quint, Brian, come here, you gotta hear this," said Scooter, who then gave Butch a nod of encouragement?

"I don't know who did it, but Dapper Davy's gonna shit when he sees it," said Butch. "You guys know how much Davy loves his truck, don'tcha, and what a tight ass gung-ho Marine pretty boy he is?"

Quint and Brian nodded. Butch displayed a mouthful of hippo teeth.

"Go check out his rear license plate holder if ya want a good laugh."

"Well, let's get a look at this. You comin', Charlie?" Quint asked.

"I seen it a couple days ago but didn't want to spill the beans. I gotta stay at the front desk."

Brian looked at Charlie, who gave him a wink.

Charlie picked up the ringing telephone and answered with his usual greeting, "77th Po-lice."

Wiener had just settled into his desk as the line of officers passed him. Brian stopped in front of him. "Oh, Lieutenant, the captain wants to see you, sir."

Wiener failed to respond. Brian walked from the office. As he exited the station he spotted the coppers standing around the rear of a black Silverado pickup. The immaculately cared for truck had a USMC globe and anchor sticker in each corner of the tinted rear window. The item of such great interest and entertainment was the rear license plate frame. It too had a globe and anchor embossed on it, but also in bold crimson and gold letters were the words "Dapper Davy Proud Gay Marine."

"How long you think he's been driving around like this?" said Scooter.

"I don't know, but don't tell 'im...this is fuckin' classic," said Butch.

Lenny said, "Dan drives right through Hollywood on the way home. He probably wonders why folks are suddenly so friendly!"

"Tell ya what, boys, the Dapper One is gonna have a calf when he sees this," said Quint.

Brian looked around the parking lot and noticed Charlie Bender leaning against the station wall next to the back door. His sleeves were neatly folded, his coffee cup in hand, and a cigarette dangled from his lips. He appeared to be deep in thought and had a pleasant expression on his face. Brian turned back to the group and noticed Manny Magana standing with the men. Manny looked at the plate and had a forced smile on his face as his eyes met Brian's.

Hola pues, Manny," said Brian.

Hola, mi campanero, Manny said under his breath as he passed.

"How's Diane?"

Manny's expression relaxed. "Much better, man, you should stop in and see her. I know she would really appreciate it."

"I will, Manny... Tomorrow, if I don't get any overtime."

"Great, catch you later, man."

The tall, swarthy officer walked to the back door and pushed his key into the lock. Brian watched him until he disappeared into the station. He wondered. The rest of the guys were still standing around Dapper Davy's truck, but somehow Manny's face had taken much of the humor out of the prank for Brian. He collected his gear and walked to the police car that would be his office for the next eight hours or so. Quint ambled up while Brian was performing a safety check on his shotgun. He opened the driver side door, leaned into the car and slid the shotgun into its rack, then stood back up.

"So whatcha got, partner?" Quint said as he loaded his gear into the car.

"I got a name on the other shooter from New Year's Eve," said Brian.

Quint was reaching into the passenger side of the car. Immediately all sounds of activity inside the car stopped. Quint's head popped up above the roof of the black-and-white. Brian had his arms crossed on the roof. His chin rested on a muscular forearm, his eyes on Quint.

"Hell, look at that shit-eatin' grin." Quint said. "Ya look like a pup hound who just treed his first coon. Well, let's have it, pard."

"I think you know him. A guy named Ray-Ray."

"Ray–Ray the Hoover Crip? Where'd ya hear that?" Quint said, while he tried to picture Ray-Ray's face.

"At the gym," said Brian.

"Think it's good info?"

Brian nodded.

"Well, dang, man, let's go do a workup on ol' Ray-Ray an' see if we cain't throw a loop round his young ass." He slammed the car door and headed toward the station.

Brian grabbed the microphone from the clip on the dash.

"12FB3, show us out at the station on a follow-up until further."

He slammed his door and jogged up to his partner. Brian could see Quint was already lost in thought. He was wracking his brain for all the information he could recall on a gangster named Ray-Ray.

SLOW DEATH IN A DINGY ROOM

The smoggy sky glowed orange as the setting sun hung red above the city's skyline. Many of the cars on South Main Street had their headlights on already and were heading home for the weekend. Oco and Mental were discussing where to eat when they heard their call sign over the police radio.

"12A69, unknown trouble… the Topper Motel, 8003 South Main Street. See the motel manager, Code Two."

Oco Blackstone keyed the mike. "12A69, roger." As he returned the mike to its clip on the dashboard, he said, "You know it's gonna be a landlord tenant thing. I hate them, and I hate that fleabag hotel. Ahhh, it's so good to be back in patrol, man."

"Sarcasm does not befit a man of your stature, Oco," said Mental. "Hell, you know we are the backbone of the department. Don't be dissuaded because they treat us like we're the armpit."

"Speaking of armpits, the Topper is a fuckin' armpit," grumbled Oco.

The Topper Motel was indeed in a class of its own. Built in the 1940s, the dilapidated row of rooms was surrounded by a 10-foot chain link fence and razor wire. In the corner of the parking lot in front of the manager's office was a small swimming pool that had been filled with dirt. The inn's clientele was generally restricted to addicts, prostitutes, and drug dealers. At the entrance, a top hat and cane adorned a blue neon sign that buzzed above the trash-strewn parking lot.

Mental flipped an imaginary fare meter on the dashboard. "Here we are, sir. The Ritz."

He slid the cruiser to the curb one address north of the motel and stopped. They stepped from the car and made a quick visual scan of their surroundings. Along the sidewalk, halfway up the chain link fence in front of the Topper, grew a line of greasy-looking shrubs that provided privacy to the parking lot and acted as a net, capturing any trash that blew into it. Oco glanced at the headline of a yellowing piece of newsprint suspended at eye level in the hedge.

Unaware of the two police officers in front of the grimy row of rooms, Tootie was peering out of the window of his. Two men were loitering outside his door chatting. He pulled the drape closed and paced the room, waiting for an opportunity to load the grisly package into his car and get the hell out of there. He pulled back the drape and peeked again then walked to the foot of the sagging, queen-sized bed. For a moment he studied the bundle lying next to the bed.

As Oco and Mental neared the entrance to the parking lot, a transvestite wobbled past them on four-inch red stiletto heels sporting a huge afro-wig and filthy pink V-neck t-shirt tied in a knot just below his ribcage. A long string of plastic pearls hung around his neck and rested against two rows of oiled abdominal muscles. The tightest pair of denim hot pants Mental had ever seen set off the ensemble.

"Good evening, officers," the drag queen said in a husky, honey-coated voice.

"What's going on, Licorice?" Mental asked.

The drag stopped, his eyes darted towards the motel.

"Room 114, baby... two gangsters checked in a few days ago. A couple of animals, that's all I got to say."

"Stick around. Might need to ask you a couple questions," Mental said.

"Oh, baby, you can find me," he cooed. "But that's all the Licorice you get for free."

He adjusted his enormous wig and clicked his way down the sidewalk. Mental and Oco stepped into the parking lot. Oco accidentally knocked over a bottle that had been abandoned under the flickering blue light of the motel sign. An amber liquid foamed out of the bottle, which was wrapped in a brown paper sack. They scanned the parking lot taking in the pair of men talking under an exposed light bulb between the line of lodgings and several parked cars. One, a black man in his sixties, looked in the direction of the two police officers, then scuffled into the room next to 114.

The second, a tall, thin, tawny man, wearing a white turban called out "I called you, sirs."

The two officers separated. Oco engaged the man as Mental stepped into a shadow next to an old Buick. From that vantage point he kept watch on the courtyard and the row of motel windows.

Oco said, "How can we help, mister...?"

"Singh, sir, I am the manager," the man said.

"How can we help you, Mister Singh?"

He pointed a bony finger at the chipped red door of room 114 behind him. "I want no trouble, sir. These men are most frightening. They must go. I want no trouble."

"What did they do?" asked Oco. He kept an eye on the door and adjacent window.

"They took the room for one day, and now they will not leave. The little one says if I call the police he will come back and kill me," Singh said as he tucked a lose strand of his long, gray-flecked beard into his headwear.

"You sure they're in there?" asked Oco. "Looks pretty quiet."

Singh shrugged his shoulders. "I am not sure, sir. If you will please check I would be most grateful."

"Okay, hang on. You have the keys?" asked Oco.

"Yes, sir, here you are." Singh handed the officer a ring with two keys and a blue plastic fob. The fob had a white top hat and cane embossed on it.

Oco walked to where Mental kept watch.

"Manager says a couple thugs checked in and won't leave. Said they would kill this guy if he called the cops."

Mental glanced at Singh, then at the door.

"You got the keys?"

Oco held them up and the officers walked toward the room. Singh followed closely behind. They deployed on the room, Oco at the door, while Mental stood several feet back, watching the window. Oco looked over his shoulder at Singh.

"Mr. Singh, please go to your office. We will come and get you if we need you."

Singh nodded, took half a dozen steps back from the door, and then stood watching intently.

Oco rapped on the door with his flashlight.

"Police! We need to talk to you."

Tootie heard the deep authoritative voice rumble outside his door.

He moved across the room and put his ear to the door. He could make out the unmistakable chatter of a police radio. Near panic, he scanned the room. He grabbed the revolver from the bed and pushed it into his waistband as he hustled to the bathroom. Above the dirty sink a small window was plugged with a piece of painted plywood. Tootie climbed onto the sink. Holding onto the corroded showerhead he kicked the plywood out of the window and into the alley behind the motel. He put his head through the window space, then worked an arm and shoulder through the hole. Tootie heard a loud rap on his door just as he wiggled free from the bathroom window and landed headfirst in a patch of dried weeds. He jumped to his feet, pulled off his silk shirt, wrapped it around the pistol and disappeared down the shadowy alley.

Oco stepped to the side and listened. After a few minutes and no apparent activity from inside the room, he slipped the key into the dented, scratched doorknob and turned it. The lock popped and the knob turned freely. With the door ajar, Oco lit the room with his flashlight. Once he determined it was clear he pushed the door the rest of the way open. The smell of perspiration, curl activator, dirty feet, beer, and cigarettes greeted him. The odor was complimented by a general mustiness and a slightly sweet smell Oco could not readily identify. Mental stepped to the other side of the door and pointed his flashlight into the room.

"Hello, police! Anybody home?" Mental called.

Oco eased into the room, gun in hand, braced against the back of his flashlight hand. As soon as Oco cleared the doorway Mental crossed from the other direction, behind him, utilizing the same technique. Mental walked around the bed and saw a pile of blankets on the floor. He toed it with his boot and found there was a mass under the pile. He held his pistol on the blankets while Oco cleared the rest of the room. Once done, Oco stepped next to the pile of blankets and jerked them away, exposing two large plastic trash bags, taped together end to end and wrapped with duct tape. The black bags conformed to the shape within, which appeared to be that of a small human being, on its side in a fetal position. Mental put his hand on the black plastic mummy and confirmed the contents.

Oco produced a folding knife and made an incision in the area most likely to contain the figure's head, while Mental kept his light on the cut. Oco gingerly opened a small hole in the trash bag. The cut exposed a heavy-gauge opaque plastic sheet. Oco punctured that sheet and pulled it apart. A cloudy eye peered through the slit, its pupil so dilated the brown iris was barely discernable. A rush of air flowed from the hole and carried a thick, nauseating odor to Oco's nostrils. The smell was not yet that of rot but death. It brought back a childhood image of staring into the dead eyes of a freshly killed deer hanging in his father's tobacco barn. The same smell hung in the hotel room as in the barn. Oco blinked, stood up, and staggered backward. "Turn on a light," he said.

Mental pulled a pencil from his shirt pocket and went and flipped the switch next to the door. A shadowy light bathed the room. The glass globe covering the single overhead bulb was obscured by years' worth of dust; and hundreds of tiny winged corpses that had settled in at the bottom of the fixture. A cigarette smoldered in an ashtray, and half a bottle of beer sat on a water-stained nightstand. Oco looked back into the bathroom.

"Bathroom window's open. They might have climbed out the window."

Three blocks away Ray-Ray walked, head down, along Main Street. He stopped and took a long pull on the bottle of cognac he held wrapped in a brown paper bag. As the bottle left his lips with a pop, he glanced up and saw the black-and-white parked in front of the Topper Motel. His intoxicated brain tried to throw off the haze as he stood swaying on the sidewalk. Licorice Jones was across the street from the motel and watched the mean little man. The drag queen meandered across Main, angling toward the entrance to the motel, waving at honking cars, twirling his string of pearls with his other hand. As soon as Licorice reached the seclusion of the parking lot he kicked off his high heels and sprinted toward the open door of room 114.

"Oh, my God! They killed her!" a throaty feminine voice said.

Mental spun around and saw the transvestite looking over Oco's shoulder at the plastic package on the floor.

"Hey! Come on, get outta here! Someone will talk to you in a minute," Mental said.

He placed both hands on the drag's shoulders. "Come on... Out!" He pushed lightly and Licorice gave way.

At the doorway, Licorice stopped, looked over his shoulder, licked his large red lips and said, "Officer, one of those men is outside right now."

"Where? What's he look like?" said Mental. He pushed past Licorice and looked into the lot.

"He's just up the street, near the liquor store. He's got on a white tank top and baggy jeans. He has chin whiskers and lots of gold on. I think he's drunk, but be careful, 'cause he's a mean little bastard."

Mental grabbed his Rover from his gun belt. He had already made a crime broadcast and knew units were in route to his location.

"12A69 to any unit in the vicinity of 83rd and Main Street, a possible 187 suspect was last seen..."

Not far away, Brian turned up the police radio. "...walking south on Main from Manchester. He is a male, black, 5-6 to 5-8, slight build, in his twenties, wearing a white tank top and jeans. Suspect has a beard and is said to be wearing several gold chains around his neck." Brian turned onto Main Street from Manchester.

"Got em! On the sidewalk, about eleven o'clock," Quint said. He keyed the mike and said, "12FB3, we're code-six, Main and Eighty-third Street with the homicide suspect."

Ray-Ray decided he would just slip away, down Manchester to Tootie's cool house about a mile away. He turned just as Brian pulled onto the sidewalk behind him. Instantly, Ray-Ray dropped his bottle and bolted across the street. Quint was out of the car, pistol in hand, and close behind him.

Brian broadcast, "Suspect running east on Eighty-third street."

Then he bailed out of the car and fell in behind Quint. As he ran, Ray-Ray stepped out of his black corduroy bedroom slippers and ran in his stocking feet. He held his sagging pants up with one hand and looked over his shoulder at the two officers pursuing him. Ray-Ray never saw the black-and-white police car in front of him. Cruising with their lights off toward Main Street, Butch Caldwell and Lenny Custer watched the figure running toward them. His white wife-beater undershirt reflected the ambient light.

Lenny looked at his partner.

"Front door takedown?" he asked.

"You got it," said Butch.

Lenny accelerated toward Ray-Ray, who was still more

concerned with what was behind him than what was in front. Ten feet before he reached him, Lenny swerved left and floored the car. Butch kicked the passenger door open and braced it with his size 14-EEE jump boot. Ray-Ray heard an engine and looked east just as the westbound door of the police car flew open in front of him. The window frame caught him across the forehead, and the body of the door slammed into his torso. The impact launched the gangster backwards like a bowling pin. Lenny jammed on the brakes and both officers bounded from the car but there was no hurry. Brian and Quint ran up just as Lenny and Butch got to the prostrate killer.

"Damn, partner, I didn't even see that guy until the last minute! Good thing I swerved," said Lenny with mock seriousness.

Butch lit up the semiconscious face that was staring at the moon overhead. He smiled, "You, my man, are under arrest." He rolled his prisoner onto his belly and handcuffed him.

"That's Ray-Ray," Quint said.

"Who's he?" asked Butch.

"We think he's the second shooter on the ambush the other night," Quint said, looking up at Brian, who was staring intently into Ray-Ray's face.

"Fuckin-A, daddy!" Butch yelled. Then he gave Lenny a high five.

If Ray-Ray had been sober, his collision with the door might have killed him. But aside from bumps on the forehead and the back of the head, he had no other apparent injuries. After being checked by paramedics, he was placed in the back of Butch and Lenny's car. Brian volunteered to keep an eye on him while the investigation continued. By this time police cars from both 77th Street and neighboring Southeast Division were everywhere, looking for the outstanding suspect. An airship hovered overhead, bathing the arrest scene in night sun. Brian watched a sergeant approach. The dark circles around his eyes and widow's peak hairline reminded Brian of an owl. Quint recognized him.

"Sergeant Jim Graham, how's the CRASH business, sir?"

"Hi, Quint. You guys need any help?" Graham asked. "This one looks like a gangster."

"Used to be a Hoover, but I don't know now. They call him Ray-Ray. Ever heard of him?"

226

"Nope, but if you say so. We lost the best gang intelligence officer we ever had when you went back to patrol," said Graham.

"Appreciate that," said Quint, tipping an imaginary cowboy hat.

"If he's a gangster we'll take him off your hands," said Graham. "I'll call a car over right now."

"Nu-uh, boss, this guy's good for a bunch a' stuff round here. We better hang onto him till the dicks get here, at least," said Quint.

Graham looked from Quint to Butch. Butch's primitive glare unnerved the sergeant who excused himself in short order.

"Fuckin CRASH trying to steal our arrestee. Never see those guys when we need a gang investigation," grumbled Lenny.

"Yeah, well, folks say the same 'bout us," said Quint. "Dern cops, never around when ya need 'em."

Brian closed the front door of the police car and looked into the backseat at Ray-Ray. The gangster's drunken and recently battered brain produced a vacant stare. Ray-Ray heard the officer say something, then felt a bolt of excruciating pain shoot through his head. His teeth clamped and ground together, with his tongue trapped between them. Ray-Ray pushed away from the officer with his feet and jerked his head side to side. He felt like a plastic bag had been slipped over his head; he struggled to inhale but could draw no air. Blood filled Ray-Ray's mouth and he gagged and tried to spit. His jaw and throat were seized; he couldn't open his mouth. He was suffocating in his own blood. After minutes that felt like hours, Ray-Ray's pain ebbed. His jaw relaxed, and blood ran out of his mouth and down his white t-shirt.

Brian felt a familiar detachment, a place between consciousness and sleep. He heard himself speak but knew nothing of his words. "You like to shoot at the police, asshole? There's a whole lot more pain where that came from, *puto!* You got an eternity of it coming, *verdad?* Where's my gun, you little fuck?"

Several moments later Brian opened the door of the police car. Oxygen rushed into the car and filled Ray-Ray's lungs. Brian was dizzy. He remembered feeling this way as a child, after spinning himself in circles until he fell to the ground. *Lying down and watching the moon spin overhead would be nice*, he thought.

Quint saw Brian take a couple of unsteady steps and place his hand on the hood of the police car. "Brian, ya okay?"

"Yeah just got a little dizzy. I'm okay now."

Brian cast his eyes on Ray-Ray, who was peering through the rear window at him. *"Tootie huh?"* he thought."

Quint walked over and looked into the car. Ray-Ray looked at Quint and pushed his back against the far door. He looked as if he had seen a ghost. Quint opened the back door and leaned into the car.

"How ya doin?"

The car was filled with the smell of booze, blood, and fear. Ray-Ray opened his mouth to speak, his lips popped from the coagulating blood.

"My head hurts, man! I need a doctor," Ray moaned. "That Mexican police officer was talking to me and my head just started hurting bad, man. I bit my tongue."

"Mexican officer? Where?"

"Mutherfucker was just here talking crazy shit."

Quint stood and walked over to Brian.

"He thought you were Mexican. Ah wonder if he has a fractured skull or somethin'. I seen guys bang their heads purty good at rodeos and walk away fine, then go to bed that night an jes die."

Brian shrugged.

West of the scene, Tootie loped down the alley. He was in his element. How many times had he eluded the law and other dangers via South LA's system of long abandoned, neglected alleyways? To say hundreds of times would not be an overstatement. As a youngster, it seemed he had outrun a police officer, rival gangster, even a homie or business owner at least once a day. At the least sign of danger he would scale one of the dilapidated wooden fences that lined the alleys and fade away between the houses. Ramshackle garages had satisfied his need for hideouts. One garage in particular came to mind. It had served as safe haven many times. Tootie recalled the dusty, sour smell of old wood and rotting eucalyptus leaves in the one-car structure. He remembered the line of glass automotive oil bottles on a shelf shrouded in spider webs. He had a stash of girly magazines hidden in that garage. Many a summer afternoon he'd spent ogling young women by the hazy light that filtered through a filthy window. Tootie turned the pages, a hand in his pants, almost daily until the magazines mildewed and fell apart.

Tootie's thoughts were interrupted by the thwapping cut of helicopter blades. It was fully dark now and the ghetto bird lit up the neighborhood. The aircraft held a tight orbit over the Topper Motel. There was a moon, so Tootie kept to the deep shadows at the edge of the alley. Several times he stopped to allow police cars to race past the end of the alley before he emerged to cross the street. It was not the cops in speeding cars that alarmed him. It was the smart cops who hid in the shadows and waited. Those cops didn't give chase like hounds. They tracked you and lay in wait, like panthers.

O'Callahan was just such a cop. Tootie had scoffed at stories about him but now, in the dark of this dirt and gravel lane, he looked for O'Callahan to strike from a dark place.

HILLBILLY ASSHOLE

Standing in the hallway of 77th Station, Brian O'Callahan slammed the holding cell door and completed the prisoner log. On the other side of the Plexiglas window Ray-Ray, sat on a bench staring straight ahead. His tongue was no longer bleeding, so they decided he could wait for medical treatment.

An hour later Quint was walking down the north hall when Scooter and Manny entered the station with an intoxicated woman in tow. She appeared to weigh more than both officers combined, and her sole piece of clothing was a white t- shirt that stopped at her belly button. As they led her down the hall she sang a Motown medley at the top of her lungs.

As Scooter passed Quint he said, "She's pretty good. I gotta get her to Wardrobe."

Such a procession deserved a second look, so Quint turned to watch the trio proceed down the hall. Manny unlocked the holding cell, pushed the door open, and beheld a hole big enough for a man to crawl through in the ceiling.

"Hey Quint did you have a body in here?" Manny asked.

"Yeah why?"

Scooter stuck his head into the tank, regarded the breach and said, "Not anymore you don't."

Elsewhere in the station Nick Stupin had just heard of Ray-Ray's possible involvement in the New Year's ambush and was having difficulty containing his excitement. He hurried into his office--sat behind his desk and called Captain Sullivan's home. As the phone rang, Detective Stupin heard a noise above him.

Ray-Ray was not sure where he was headed, but he was crawling as fast as he could when he felt the surface beneath him give way. He burst through the ceiling and landed flat on his back on Detective Stupin's desk amid a shower of ceiling tiles and insulation. Nick Stupin let the phone slip through his fingers just as Captain Sullivan answered the phone.

"What the hell!" Stupin said.

Ray-Ray blinked twice and rolled off the desk, dragging most of the clutter with him. Stupin's chair tipped over, momentarily trapping him against a file cabinet.

Ray-Ray was on his feet and halfway across the office before Stupin was able to decipher and react to what he had just witnessed. He kicked his legs and waved his arms like an overturned turtle.

Finally Stupin managed to spit out, "Hey! Stop!"

The telephone receiver lay on the floor next to Stupin's face. Nick heard his captain yelling. Ray-Ray ran toward the doorway that led to the station's south hallway. The corridor passed the Captain's office and connected with the front lobby, and then freedom. Fortunately, the station's custodian, Mr. Toby, had the habit of abandoning his large house cleaning cart wherever it was at quitting time. On this particular day he'd left it just outside the homicide office. As Ray-Ray blasted through the doorway, his stocking feet lost purchase on the tile floor and he piled into Mr. Toby's cart, knocking it over with a significant racket. Ray-Ray lay momentarily confused among dustpans, brooms, buckets, trashcans, and an assortment of spray cans and bottles.

An elderly man in a tweed hat was standing at the front desk reporting a crime. He looked down the hall and whispered, "Oh, Lord!"

Charlie Bender, who was taking the man's statement, leaned over the desk and saw Ray-Ray rolling on the floor with Mr. Toby's tools of the trade. By the time Ray-Ray slipped his cuffs in front of him and was running toward the lobby, Charlie had retrieved his hickory baton and was positioned in the doorway to the south hall. As Ray-Ray ran past the doorway, Charlie took a step into the hall and stuck a foot out. Ray-Ray's legs tangled in Charlie's outstretched leg and foot. He slid on his stomach into the lobby and scrambled to his hands and knees. At a hurried walk, Charlie approached, nightstick in hand. He delivered a blow to Ray-Ray's right elbow, which caved in with a sickening crack. Howling, Ray-Ray rolled onto his back, his feet in the air. Charlie took a step to the side and delivered a second strike that landed across Ray-Ray's left shin. It was later said that the sound Ray-Ray emitted after the second blow put dogs to howling throughout the neighborhood. Leo heard the impact from the watch commander's office. He swore it reminded him of the sound he'd heard the night Big Frank Howard bounced a homer off the Union '76 Ball at Dodger Stadium. Ray-Ray was done running from the police for the day.

The elderly citizen removed his ancient hat and said to Ray-Ray, "You a damn fool, boy, to try that mess in the middle of a po-lice station! You lucky y'all didn't get yo' ass shot."

If Ray-Ray heard him, he never acknowledged it. His screaming continued as he was being loaded into the RA. A group of smiling officers stood on the sidewalk. They all agreed it must have really hurt. The coppers filed back into the station chatting like fans leaving a ball game. Charlie Bender was seated back behind the desk, working on the old gentleman's crime report and talking to a citizen on the telephone. Next to Charlie sat Brian O'Callahan, pencil in hand, diligently at work on another crime report. No sooner had Charlie put the telephone in its cradle than it rang again. Charlie snatched the phone, held it to his ear.

"77th Po-lice," he drawled.

A voice on the other end of the line said, "This is Deputy Chief Griefwielder. Who is this?"

"You don't know? Good!" Charlie dropped the phone back into the cradle, stood up and stretched like an old dog. Then he flipped a cigarette into his mouth, and wandered into the watch commander's office.

Leo the Lion looked up from his paperwork. "What now?"

"I gotta go to privy. Brian's gonna spell me."

Leo directed his attention back to the endless busywork before him.

"Fine."

All watch commanders had a non-public-access telephone line that afforded them the ability to make and receive emergency calls. 77th Street's inside line rang just as Charlie rounded the corner. Leo picked up the phone and, in accordance with inside-line procedure, said the last four numbers of the phone number. No sooner had the words left his mouth than an angry voice filled Leo's ear.

"This is Deputy Chief Griefwielder! Who just answered the phone at the desk?"

Leo looked up at the front desk and saw several officers loitering around, still kibitzing about Charlie Bender's home run.

"Hey, which one of you guys just answered the telephone?" Leo yelled.

His question was met with five angelic looks of innocence.

"Couldn't say, sir. We just had a use of force in the lobby and just about the whole watch had access to the desk phone," Leo said into the telephone.

"Who is this?" Griefwielder demanded.

"Sergeant Leonard Brooks, sir, I'm the watch commander tonight."

"I called a moment ago and was greeted in a most inappropriate manner. When I inquired as to whom I was speaking, the officer hung up. I want you to conduct an investigation and find out who answered the phone, and I want that officer's name on my desk tomorrow. Am I understood, Sergeant Brooks?"

"I'll do my best, sir."

"You do that, sergeant. Now, is Lieutenant Wiener or Sergeant Price working today?"

"No, sir, the lieutenant is off sick and Sergeant Price is on loan to Internal Affairs. Would you like to leave the lieutenant a message?"

"You just find me that officer, sergeant."

The line went dead. Leo closed his eyes, rubbed his head with both hands, and then worked his hands down to his face. He took a deep breath and released it in the form of a long sigh. As Leo sat at his desk, face in his hands, he heard a metallic click and looked up into Charlie Bender's smiling face. Charlie flicked his Zippo and lit a cigarette.

"Hey, Leo, any calls for me?"

"Damn it, Charlie! You gotta fuck with the chiefs, too?"

"Well, Leo, ya know, I'm an equal opportunity pain in the ass. Want me ta call him and cop out? Heck, Greg Griefwielder was one of my boots, jes not one I'm proud of, bless his heart. I kin take the pain."

"No, I got it, you hillbilly asshole," Leo said.

Charlie started toward the front desk, cleared his throat, and faced Leo the Lion.

"I don't care what all the other fellers say 'bout y'all, Leo... Yer okay in my book."

Leo shook his head and went back to his busy work.

Charlie climbed onto his favorite stool. "Thanks fer coverin' fer me, Bri. I 'preciate cha, son."

"You're welcome. Hey, Charlie, you want to come with Quint and me on Saturday night? Dee, the guy I've been training with, has a fight at the Olympic."

"Tom's stepson is gonna fight tomorrow night? I figured he done had enough fighting."

"No, he's really looking good and he's fighting a solid middleweight named Rudy Gonzales. Should be a good fight. I'm going to be in Dee's corner, so you and Quint can sit together. Dee's fighting right before the main event. His manager got him a good spot on the card. I'm sure Tom Jefferson will be there, too."

Charlie took a sip from his coffee mug. "I'll try to get a T/O. Squeeze one outta Leo later. He's a little hot right now."

"Great! I better find Quint and help with these reports." Brian hopped off the stool and took out toward the detective squad room looking for his partner.

He spotted Quint talking with Preacher in the hall. "Hey, Quint, did you see what just happened?"

Quint turned and looked at Brian. His face was grim. Something gripped Brian's stomach. He felt lightheaded. He looked at Preacher, who avoided eye contact with the young police officer.

"What's wrong, Quint? What's wrong?"

The last time Brian had been greeted with such a look it was on the face of a New York police officer. The vision filled his head as he searched Quint's face. He could hear his words. *You Brian O'Callahan? Is Seamus O'Callahan your father? We need you to come with us.* Twenty minutes later Brian was staring down at an ashen face beneath a sheet raised above a cold, rigid form on a gurney. Dried spittle ran from the corner of the corpse's scarred lips into a deformed ear. The battered head was a remnant of the man that Brian worshipped and adored. "Oh, Da," he heard himself whisper.

"Brian," Quint said softly.

Brian snapped back to the present.

"What is it, Quint?" he asked, terrified to hear the answer.

"The body at the Topper was Demi Sanders. Looks like they raped and tortured her before she was suffocated with a plastic bag," Preacher said.

"She was all covered with cigarette burns and bites," Quint said.

"That's not possible. She's still in jail," Brian asserted.

"Someone bailed her out yesterday," Preacher said.

Demi Sanders's face materialized before Brian's eyes. He heard her voice as if she were standing next to him. *If I tell you, you gonna keep him from killing me?*

"I said I would protect her if she talked," Brian said aloud to himself. "He killed her. I promised her..."

Brian blinked hard. His eyelids pressed the tears from his eyes, causing two large drops to slide down his cheeks. The vision was gone. Brian's green eyes glistened with tears, but a light burned behind them. Quint and Preacher were mesmerized.

"Come on, pard, I'll buy ya an Arbuckle," Quint said.

He took Brian by the arm and turned him toward the door. Brian moved like a sleepwalker. A black rage began to well up inside him. He could feel a pulse in his temples. Despite the storm within him, Brian was outwardly calm. His mind was far beyond a normal state. It whirled with thoughts and images, but remained focused. "Where did they take Ray-Ray?" Brian asked.

"Not sure, pard. Maybe California Hospital for MT. Why?" asked Quint.

"Huh? Oh, nothing, just wondering," Brian said. "Let's just finish our reports and go home. All of a sudden I'm real tired."

"All we gotta do is gin up a couple statements for the dicks. They're fixin' to do all the reports," Quint said.

"Good."

Quint decided he had better keep a close watch on his partner for a bit. Brian was quieter than usual as he completed his statement and sipped the coffee Quint had bought. When he was done, Brian dropped the document on the tabletop in front of his partner.

"I'll see you at the Olympic Auditorium tomorrow. Say about 1600 hours."

"Whoa, hold on, pard. Ah'll go with ya," Quint said.

"No, I have to meet someone," Brian said.

Quint hurried to finish and dropped six pages of the neatly hand-printed account of his and Brian's observations on the blotter in front of Davy and turned to go. But Dapper Davy wanted to proof read the statements, so Quint settled into a chair across from the homicide detective's desk, slid his hips forward, pulled a gray metal wastebasket next to the chair, and let out a sigh. Dapper Davy chewed his gum with enthusiasm as he read the statements.

"Where's your partner?" he asked, as he pored over the documents.

"He already left. He got all choked up when he found out who your victim was. But ah checked his statement. He writes great reports, helluva lot better'n mine."

"Yeah, well, he gets upset a lot, I'd say," Dapper Davy said. "Matter a fact, that kid's a hothead."

Preacher turned from an open file cabinet.

"Yes, he's no monk like you, Davy."

Dapper Davy ignored his partner's observation.

"Do you know who put that license plate frame on my truck, Quint?"

"Sure don't, Dapper, but even if ah did don't s'pose ah'd say."

"I'm thinking it was O'Callahan. I know he's pissed off over our argument the other day."

Quint drew out his snuff can and packed his lower lip with fresh dip. He kicked out his long legs and laced his fingers behind his head.

"Ya do, huh? An' why's that, Davy?" Quint said.

"Because I've seen what he does when he gets mad. I know the reputation he's got on the street. He was pissed off and thought he'd exact a little revenge on me," said Dapper Davy.

Quint leaned forward and shot a line of tobacco juice into the trash basket. "Come on, Davy, yer smarter'n that. That ain't Brian's style."

"I think it is. He's got everyone buffaloed. Not me. And I'll tell you: what goes around comes around."

Quint stood up. "Davy, if you need any changes done to our statements I'll do 'em later. I'm all played out."

He took two long strides toward the door and stopped next to a wastebasket. He shot another stream of brown juice into the basket and turned around. Several homicide detectives looked up for

Quint's parting comment.

"Oh, and jus 'cause that prank wasn't Brian's style don't mean he won't stomp a mud hole in the middle of you and that fancy suit a' yers if you take to jerkin' his tail. Let it be, Dapper Davy. Someone was jes funnin' ya and it coulda been anyone. Ah'm warnin' ya, don't pull the cork outta this jug. You'll never get 'er back in."

Outwardly Dapper Davy scoffed. Within, he took note. He'd seen Q-Tip's booking photo and knew what one punch from Brian Callahan could result in.

Quint hurried to the locker room. Brian's locker was ajar. Quint opened it fully and saw Brian's duty gear had been stowed and his personal gear was gone. *Musta left in such a hurry he left his locker open,* Quint thought. Before shutting the locker Quint took a close look at the photos taped to the inside of locker 32's door. He had seen the one of Charlie Bender and Danny Lugo, but was a bit surprised that Brian still had it in his locker. Taped above that was a photo of a young, smiling Brian O'Callahan in green boxing trunks and wearing red boxing gloves. His eyes were swollen, and several red patches shone on his face. In the background was a boxing ring and beyond that a large crowd of people. Brian had an arm around a man who looked to be in his forties. Only his profile was evident, as he was kissing Brian on the cheek and had his arms around the fighter's waist. The man wore a blue wool snap-brim cap, a blue windbreaker, and baggy khaki pants. Scar tissue above the man's left eye caused the lid to droop, his nose was flat and the tip of it was the only portion that rose with any significance from his face. Quint studied the photo. The older man was undoubtedly Brian's father. Taped above that photo was a card. Quint pulled it off the door and examined it. It was a Catholic holy card. As with all such cards a religious scene was depicted on one side. On this card was a painting of a winged angel. The angel was dressed like a warrior of old and held in his right hand a saber, in the other hand a chain. The chain was attached to a prostrate black-winged demon. The demon's head was pinned to the ground by the angel's sandaled foot. Quint looked down the aisle to where several other coppers were changing clothes.

"Hey, any y'all Catholic? " Quint asked.

Manny looked up from polishing his boots.

"I am."

Gregory L. Baltad

Quint handed him the card. "Who's this feller?"

Manny studied the two figures. "That's the Archangel Michael. The other guy's Satan or a demon or something. Michael led God's army against Satan and the forces of evil." He handed the card back to Quint,

Quint took the card and taped it back on the locker door.

"Hmm. Whaddaya know 'bout that."

Standing in front of the locker, Quint had an uneasy feeling. He looked at Manny, who was staring intently at the locker.

Quint said, "I get a weird feelin' every time I walk past this locker."

"Yeah, they say the dead can leave an imprint on things that were important to them." Manny broke his stare and looked at Quint. "Least that's what mi abuela used to say. All I know is that locker gives me the creeps. Has ever since I got to 77th."

Quint's felt the hair rise on his arms. He closed the locker and made sure it was locked.

HOSPITAL

Brian turned the screwdriver and the little red car's engine sputtered to a stop. His car had been stolen several weeks earlier, and he had not replaced the ignition since its recovery. He was reduced to using a screwdriver to turn his car on and off. He looked through the bug-splattered windshield at the neon sign with the red letters that spelled "Emergency." It was five miles from the police station to the hospital and Brian didn't remember the drive at all. A police car was parked next to the emergency entrance but no officers were in sight. He slid lower into his seat and watched the automatic glass doors. After several minutes he opened the VW's door and stepped into the parking lot. He flipped the door shut and slipped the screwdriver into his back pocket. After glancing in all directions, Brian started toward the double doors. He looked through the glass, saw a familiar face, and waved.

Ray-Ray was on pain medication and resting as comfortably as a man with a dislocated elbow and fractured tibia could. Even the weight of the sheet on his shin hurt. He gingerly kicked it off his injured leg and looked down at a lump the size of a baseball between his knee and ankle. Ray-Ray tried to move into a more comfortable position but his movements were restricted as a result of his being handcuffed to the metal rail of the hospital bed. He tried to rest, but when he closed his eyes he saw the Mexican officer's face. Somehow the officer had controlled the pain that shot through his head, and how could he have known about Tootie's gun? The officer's prophecy of more pain played prominently in his thoughts.

"Hey, Miss, when we going to County?" Ray-Ray asked. "They ain't gonna take me to the Glass House all fucked up like this."

Sonya "La Matador" Sontag was stationed next to Ray-Ray's bed slouched on a gray metal chair with green vinyl pads. She held a half-full foam cup of tepid black coffee, and a *Cosmopolitain* magazine lay open in her lap.

239

"The doctors have to examine your X-rays, and they will decide where you will be booked," she said, sitting up in the chair.

"Well, when's that gonna be?" Ray-Ray said.

Sonya peered through the opening in the drapes that encircled the examination area and bed that Ray-Ray was chained to, then turned and shot her prisoner an irritated look.

"Do I look like the doctor? You got a hot date or something? From now on you've got nothing but time pal."

Sonya poked her head out from between the drapes again. A well-built orderly dressed in scrubs was outside the drapes, mopping the floor.

"Have you seen my partner?" she asked.

"Yeah the little dude's over at the nurses' station, tryin' to work it." With a lecherous grin he went back to mopping.

"I need to use the restroom, would you please go get him? I called him on the radio but he must have it turned off or down, she said."

"Bathroom's jes right there," the orderly said, nodding toward the ladies room across from the examination room. "Go on. Hell, that brother ain't goin' nowhere chained to the bed, with a busted leg an' all." The orderly chuckled to himself and pushed the mop down the hall.

Officer Sontag's bladder felt like it was going to burst and the pressure of her gun belt didn't help. She he glanced at the form lying on the bed. Ray-Ray had his eyes shut but a pained look remained on his face. Sonya knew she was on the verge of an accident. She let out a deep sigh and, against her better judgment, set the coffee cup and magazine on the floor and slipped between the curtains. As she walked across the hall, she noticed Brian O'Callahan just outside the emergency room doors.

Seconds later Ray-Ray heard the drapery rings slide on the chrome rail above his head and opened his eyes. They widened, as a rubber-gloved hand covered his mouth and pressed his head into the pillow. With his injured arm, Ray-Ray grabbed the assailant's wrist but a bolt of lightning shot up his arm. He felt something in his ear then he heard a crunch and suffered white-hot pain. The pain manifested as flashes of light and indescribable agony. His body went rigid, then limp. Raymond "Ray-Ray" Dubois never felt anything in this world again. After twisting and turning it, the rubber-gloved hand drew the bloody screwdriver from Ray-Ray's brain and laid it on the bed next to his oozing ear. The rings chimed on the railing again, and then silence.

ALL KINDS OF FIGHTERS

Rudy *El Monstro* Gonzales shadowboxed in the corner of the small dressing room with the low ceiling. He could hear the crowd in the old downtown auditorium upstairs. Built in 1925 and selected as the boxing, wrestling and weightlifting venue for the 1932 Los Angeles Olympic Games, the "Grand Olympic" had seen better days. Designed to house 10,400 patrons, it had a huge ground floor with a boxing ring in the middle and a balcony that extended around the whole structure. The Olympic was an old-school boxing arena with lots of fight game history and Gonzales loved fighting there. He was looking beyond this fight, for after this win he expected to fight Jesus Perez, the top contender for the middleweight crown. As a matter of fact he had expected to fight Perez when he was signed to fight the man he was facing tonight. His manager explained that although his opponent was washed up and no threat, he still offered an opportunity to meet a journeyman fighter; his rival was sure to show him some tricks of the trade while not being too dangerous. He was a good stepping-stone; also he was from Los Angeles, which would increase the gate. Gonzales was not concerned with *el Negro's* fans. He knew that Los Angeles had a rapidly growing Hispanic population and he was sure to have overwhelming support from his own countrymen.

"Este es tiempo, venga Mijo," Gonzales's father (and manager) said as he came through the door.

One of his corner men who had been standing nearby flipped the red silk hood of Gonzales's robe over his shaved head. Gonzales bounced on his toes, rolled his shoulders, and stepped into the tunnel leading up to the ring.

In an equally dingy room two doors down, Brian rubbed Dee's shoulders and arms as he sat on the old padded wooden table; a table where boxers had been rubbed down and stitched up hundreds of times before him. Dee stared straight ahead, occasionally rolling his head one way, then another. His taped hands rested between his thighs. As Brian massaged Dee he bent forward and whispered into the fighter's ear. Brian's words were compressing him, storing energy to be released through Dee's fists. Dee had just finished warming up and was covered in perspiration. He was fit as he had ever been and felt ready, body and mind. Like a racehorse at the starting gate, he waited, his muscles coiled, ready to explode. Boomer leaned against the wall with his arms folded across his chest and a smoldering cigar clamped between his teeth.

Finally, Dee's manager, Joey La Barbara, opened the door, and looked into the room. He caught Boomer's eye, and nodded his head.

"Okay, Dee, let's go to work," Boomer said.

Brian pulled the hood of Dee's robe gently over his head. The black shroud threw a shadow across Dee's face and gave him an ominous look. He hopped off the table and strode to the door, nearly running over La Barbara. Boomer followed him out. He winked at Joey as the entourage passed. Joey fell in behind them. He was not looking forward to this fight. Gonzales's nickname of *El Monstro* was well earned, and he was on his way up. Joey had wanted to feed Dee a couple of stiffs and bring him back slowly, but Boomer insisted they book a fight with Gonzales. Boomer had seen Gonzales fight on several occasions and felt his crouching, hard-pressing attack was a good match for Dee's lateral counter-punching style. A win over Gonzales would be the kind of comeback Dee needed to build his confidence and ensure him some good purses in the future. Against his own judgment, Joey arranged the fight. Now he was hoping he had done the right thing.

Dee walked into the arena. The steamy indoor stadium vibrated with excitement and blood lust. Through a blue haze of tobacco smoke, he strode past the seventeen rows of yelling fight fanatics on the ground floor. Empty paper cups flung from the balcony bounced off the fans below. He made his way to the roped in platform where he intended to surprise Gonzales and all his screaming supporters. Dee stepped through the ropes amid jeers, and cheers. Once in the ring, he no longer heard the voices. Dee's mind was closed to anything that did not directly involve the man standing across the ring from him. Brian poured words into Dee's ear, words that were like coal, and Brian's breathe like a bellows, stoking an already raging furnace. Dee could barely contain himself. When Boomer slid the black robe off Dee's glistening shoulders the audience fell silent. He looked like he had been chiseled out of black marble.

Seated in the eighth row, Quint pushed his cowboy hat back on his head and whistled through his teeth. "Dang, that boy's in shape!"

Charlie Bender, who sat between Quint and Tom Jefferson, nodded in agreement. He punched Tom on his shoulder. "Tom, that young feller looks like he could go bear huntin' with a switch."

An enormous smile spread across Tom's broad face. His hands wrung the program he held like a wet rag. "Yep, an Officer O'Callahan sho got us some fine seats."

The referee, a bantamweight with a crushed nose and a bow tie, called the two fighters to the middle of the ring for last-minute instructions. After a moment the two warriors tapped gloves and returned to their corners. Each stood glaring at the other, awaiting the signal for battle to begin.

At the bell, Gonzales charged across the ring. His blocky form crouched forward with his chin tucked behind a well-developed shoulder. Dee took two steps from his corner and stopped. Gonzales threw a flurry of punches. Dee stuck a jab in Gonzales's face, slipped to the right and threw a straight right fist that crashed into the side of his opponent's head. He followed it up with a hook that caught Gonzales below the heart. Dee felt his foe shudder. Immediately Dee opened up with a barrage of punches, most of which landed within Gonzalez's defenses. Gonzalez continued to press, throwing powerful inside punches that for the most part Dee eluded or blocked with his arms. The round went on in that fashion, and at the bell the crowd was on its feet. Dee returned to his corner and sat on the stool Boomer had placed there.

"You own this guy, man! You can hit him anytime you want. Work him man, all over. Keep him off balance. Don't let him plant his feet and punch."

"Go out there and hit that guy as hard as you can, right on the coconut, Dee," Brian whispered into Dee's ear.

Dee nodded. Brian pulled himself up and stood. He dabbed at Dee's Vaseline- coated ears and face. At the bell, Dee moved toward Gonzalez, who was showing more caution than he had in the first round. Gonzalez jabbed and threw a wide right at Dee's head. Dee bent over, and the punch sailed harmlessly over his head. In a rolling motion Dee came up, driving his body forward with his legs. As they extended, he twisted his torso and let loose a right hand that struck Gonzales's face like a hammer blow. Dee followed up with an unnecessary left that glanced off his opponent's chin as he fell backward onto the seat of his trunks. Gonzales sat stunned, then tipped over onto his side, his glazed eyes wide open. Dee stood over his fallen foe until he felt the referee pushing him toward the opposite corner of the ring. He stood like a junkyard dog on a chain waiting for his foe to get up, but Gonzales never did. Dee Walker had definitely shown him some tricks of the trade.

The announcer called into a microphone, "Winner in the second round by knockout, Dimetre 'Dee' Walker!"

The referee held Dee's gloved hand in the air. Tom, Quint, and Charlie were on their feet, hollering and slapping each other on the back. The crowd screamed at the slaughter while reporters scribbled.

Seated in the front row, Beppe Fazio was impressed and told the man next to him so. Andre Tootie Hicks' was distracted, his attention was focused on a man in Dee's corner.

After the appropriate celebration, handshaking, and hugging, Brian led the group back to the locker room. He opened the door for Dee and his corner crew to pass. As he moved to follow them into the room he felt a hand on his shoulder. His head snapped around, followed immediately by the rest of his body. His clenched fist relaxed when he recognized Captain Kevin Sullivan. In the dark hall next to Sullivan stood Sergeant Price and three men Brian did not recognize. At a distance, two of those men, both uniformed officers, stood eyeing Brian. The third wore the uniform of an LAPD captain.

"Hi, captain. What's up?" Brian asked.

"Brian, this is Captain Sherman from Internal Affairs, and you know Sergeant Price," Sullivan said.

Louis Sherman, a stout, sharp-eyed man with a blond flattop smiled, but Price looked at his feet. Sullivan did not introduce the two burly cops who kept their distance.

"You need to come with us, son. We can't speak here," Sullivan said.

"What kinda lynchin' we got goin on here, fellers?" the unmistakable voice of Charlie Bender called out to the group.

The two uniformed officers stiffened.

Sullivan said, "Charlie, I'm glad you're here. Would you mind sticking with Brian until someone from the Police Union gets here?"

"That won't be necessary, captain," said Sherman.

"Like hell it won't," Charlie said. "Is this an Internal Affairs investigation and are y'all gonna ask questions? 'Cause if it is and ya are, Brian here is entitled to representation.

As he stood in the dimly lit hall, Charlie Bender's scarred face looked like bad news for anyone crossing him.

"That's fine. Let's go," said Sherman. "Officer O'Callahan, are you armed?"

"Hold on now," Charlie said.

"This is an investigation that may lead to serious criminal charges. It would be in the best interests of all that Officer O'Callahan be unarmed during this process. Now let's get on with it," said Sherman.

"Here, I got my two-inch, that's all. Take it." Brian lifted his pants leg, showing a five-shot revolver in an ankle holster.

Sherman looked at the two uniformed officers. On cue they stepped forward while Sergeant Price stepped several paces back from the group. One of the officers stooped down and removed the revolver from its holster while Brian stood with his hands at his side. The other officer directed Brian to put his hands on top of his head. Brian complied and that officer grabbed Brian's fingers, and squeezed them until his knuckles popped. He instructed Brian to spread his legs, and then bent him backwards while he performed a cursory search for more weapons. Charlie saw Brian's eyes narrow and knew what was coming.

"Boss, this is gonna get ugly. Kin I search him?" Charlie asked.

Sullivan nodded, and in an instant Charlie had stepped between Brian and the searching officer.

"I got it, asshole," Charlie muttered to the officer.

To Brian he said, "Okay, Bri, relax, ol' buddy. I got your back. Stay frosty now. Jess stand up and keep yer arms by your side, buddy."

Quint and Tom had just arrived from the auditorium and stood wondering what was going on.

Charlie looked over his shoulder at his friends and said,

"Everything's fine fellers, we jes gotta dance for these gents from IA for a bit. Go on home. I'll give y'all a call later."

He performed a thorough search of O'Callahan's person, then gave the group of cops before him a black look. Boomer and Joey La Barbara stepped into the hall to look for Brian just as he was walking away with Charlie and the grim-faced police officers.

"Brian, where you goin', man? Dee's askin fo ya," Boomer yelled.

As he was being walked away Brian said, "I got to go with these guys. Tell Dee I'll give him a call as soon as I can."

Boomer looked at Quint and Tom inquisitively. Quint held his palms up and shrugged. Tom stood like a statue.

They walked out a back door and stopped at a black-and-white, which was parked next to the captain's tan Plymouth and another unmarked police car.

The uniformed officers got in the black-and-white and started the engine.

"Brian, you ride with me. Charlie, you ride with Captain Sherman and Sergeant Price," Sullivan said indicating the other plain car.

"Naw, I'll drive my car, skipper. Where we going? The Glass House?"

"Yeah, the fifth floor," said Sullivan.

Before going to his car, Charlie took Brian by the arm. "I'll meet ya at the building. Don't say a word to nobody, no matter who they are or what they tell you, until you talk to a lawyer."

Charlie said it loud enough for everyone to hear him.

"We will call a Police Protective League representative when we get to the office," said Sherman.

"Fuck a bunch of union reps. He don't need a policeman. He needs a lawyer," Charlie retorted. He turned to Brian. "Don't let these guys steamroll you. Don't say..." Charlie stopped in mid-sentence.

Danny Lugo had replaced Brian and was seated in the captain's tan Plymouth staring in his direction. Unbeknownst to Charlie his ex-partner's attention was focused on a figure beyond him. In the shadow of the brick auditorium, Tootie returned Danny's scrutiny.

Charlie wondered about the wisdom of giving Brian Danny's locker. After watching Danny and Sullivan's car disappear into downtown traffic, Charlie walked to a nearby phone booth. Standing in the booths dim light he opened his wallet, and removed a dog-eared business card. He looked around, laid the card and a pocketful of change on the small shelf under the pay phone, then punched the number on the card and waited. On the second ring, a mellow tenor voice answered, "Hello?"

"Andy, this is Charlie Bender."

"Charlie, how are you my friend? I haven't heard from you in years. What's going on, bro? I'm guessing this is not a social call."

Charlie related what he knew about Brian's situation. "Looked like a damn lynch mob, Andy. Can you help him?" Charlie asked.

"Driving time from Sherman Oaks, Charlie. I'll meet you at PAB. Find the officer and stick with him until I get there," the voice said.

Andy Tomlinson hung up the telephone. Andy had turned in early and had just dozed off when the phone rang. He kicked off the covers and slid out of bed. Then he glanced at the place where his wife would have been lying, had she not tired of these nighttime calls. A year ago she'd taken off, with his Porsche, most of the furniture, their cabin on Lake Tahoe, and an obscene chunk of Andy's nest egg. She wanted the house too, but he'd owned it before their marriage. Not even in California could she get around that. The settlement did leave him the dog, a surfboard, and his 1967 Chevy Camaro, for which he was eternally grateful, and he'd considered the agreement fair. He shuffled into the bathroom, looked in the mirror, and wondered if he should shave. Deciding against it, he splashed water on his thin, tanned face. At forty-two he still bore a strong resemblance to the blond beach bum of his youth.

Twenty-nine minutes later Andy walked out of his ranch-style home buttoning his Hawaiian shirt. The crisp night air kept him awake until he got a cup of hot coffee at his favorite doughnut shop on Ventura Boulevard. He sat in the Camaro sipping it for a few minutes. The smell and taste of strong coffee from a foam cup in a darkened car took Andy back to his past life on the streets of Los Angeles. He allowed himself a few nostalgic thoughts, then fired up the burnt-orange muscle car. Andy had worked as a Los Angeles policeman for ten years before he passed the California Bar Examination. Not long thereafter he'd joined a law firm that specialized in defending police officers in criminal matters.

Charlie Bender had been the first client of his legal career. Andy retained a vivid memory of the entire episode. A friend at the Protective League had called and explained that a 77th Street policeman had been involved in a shooting, his partner had been killed, and he had killed three suspects. This officer had sustained multiple gunshot wounds and was in the hospital. The friend said the captain at Internal Affairs, a man named Griefwielder, was pushing to have the shooting reviewed by the district attorney and to have the officer arrested. A strong bond developed between Andy and Charlie during the ensuing ordeal.

Tomlinson had never before or since met a man of character and courage like Charlie Bender.

Since then Andy had represented an array of men and women from law enforcement. Some were criminals who needed to be convicted. In those rare cases he did his job and wrestled with the ethical side of doing so. Many of his clients were coppers who had been accused by spouses of wrong doing in the course of divorce proceedings. In these matters he worked with the respective commanding officers and courts to ensure his clients could stay gainfully employed so everyone involved got paid and they could get on with life. Many of his cases involved drug or alcohol abuse; in those Andy did everything he could to diminish the effects of the double jeopardy police officers were subject to. But only "thrown to the wolves" capers would get Andy out of bed and into the night. Those cases occurred when, during the course of his duties, an officer became involved in a situation that arbitrarily exposed him to unreasonable public criticism and a rush to judgment. The causes of such cases were varied. Racial implications, media interest, political posturing, and departmental malfeasance were all factors that could have an effect in these miscarriages of justice. Such public drubbings were the reason Andy had become a lawyer. Now, as head of his own successful firm, he would even take a "thrown to the wolves" case free of charge, or *pro bono,* if it met his criteria.

Moving fast, Andy drove south on the Hollywood Freeway. He left the San Fernando Valley and rumbled through Cahuenga Pass and the Hollywood area. Soon he was looking at the glittering nighttime skyline of downtown LA. He drove through the famous interchange where the Pasadena, Hollywood, and Harbor Freeways met and formed an enormous asphalt-covered cloverleaf and exited at Los Angeles Street. While he sat at a light, a filthy, bloated, shining red face appeared at his window. Andy rolled down his window and emptied an ashtray full of coins into the homeless man's hands. The man's face broke into a toothless smile as he muttered some unintelligible response that Andy took for thanks. The wretched soul dropped the change into a ragged coat pocket and turned toward the motorist stopped behind the Camaro. Andy whipped a right turn, squealing his tires, and parked across the street from PAB in the exposed- girder parking structure known as the "Tinker-Toy building." He waved to the officer sitting in the guard shack, hooked up with a couple of officers walking in the back door of the PAB, and effectively avoided having to check in at the front desk. Andy had developed this technique of entering the building several years earlier, when representing an officer in a high-profile case. Slipping in the back door had allowed him to enter without having to walk the gauntlet of reporters lurking near the main entrance of the Glass House.

Brian and Charlie were seated on a wooden bench in the hallway outside the office of the Commanding Officer, Internal Affairs Division. Many believed the pew's purpose was to allow officers involved in investigations to sit and worry.

Coppers considered it a form of public humiliation, as most people seated there were shunned by passersby and scowled at by IA personnel. Officers waiting to be interviewed were often left sitting for extended periods of time. Andy remembered he'd once commented unfavorably to Griefwielder on the practice of "sweating" officers on the bench.

Griefwielder had scoffed and said, "If it were up to me they would be in stocks out front of Parker Center. Maybe that would loosen their damn tongues."

Charlie Bender jumped to his feet when he saw Andy. He took two steps and shook the lawyer's hand in earnest.

"Thanks, Andy, I 'preciate ya coming," Charlie said. "We're not sure what's going on, but I called you as soon as I smelled somethin' rotten."

"Good to see you, Charlie. Is this Brian?"

"Brian, this here's Andy Tomlinson," Charlie said.

Brian stood slowly and held out his right hand. "Hello, sir," he said.

"Hi, Brian." Andy reached out and shook Brian's hand. In doing so he looked the young man over. He was a big believer in first impressions. His knew his first contact with a client was the last time he would look at him with completely objective eyes. He always made a mental note the first time he met a client, as he felt that he was looking at him in the same manner a jury might. He allowed the handclasp to linger as he looked directly into the officer's green eyes. Brian's grip remained strong. He did not avert his eyes or even blink.

"I see they still have the bleacher of shame. Try not to let the waiting get to you. Brian, have you any idea what this might be about?"

"No, sir," he said.

The attorney was impressed. This young man exuded integrity and honesty. Most remarkable were his eyes. They were those of a much older person, and Andy perceived a wisdom he seldom found in anyone, let alone a young police officer.

"Then the first thing is to find out what they think you did. I'll be right back."

Andy walked into the lobby of Captain Sherman's office. There was a door to the right, which was wide open and led to a nicely appointed office. To his left was another door. It was ajar and he could hear a conversation being held in low tones in the room behind it. He eased through the doorway into what appeared to be a meeting room, and stood at the end of the primary furnishing in the room, a sturdy Mission style conference table. Its glossy rectangular top was finished in a deep walnut color. Facing him, at the far end of the table, sat Sherman.

Captain Sullivan was seated to his right and Sergeant Price loomed directly behind Sherman, peeking over his new boss's shoulder. All three men were intent on the reports spread out before them. Andy looked around the chamber's windowless walls, which were covered in dark wood paneling.

He slipped his hands into the pockets of his baggy khaki slacks and said, "Good evening, gentlemen. My name is Andy Tomlinson. I am Officer O'Callahan's legal representation."

All three men's heads rose abruptly.

Sherman was annoyed at being caught off guard. "It's customary to knock Counselor."

Tomlinson ignored Sherman's jab and continued. "I realize at this point you can only share limited information with me regarding this situation. Perhaps you might tell me what it is you think my client has done."

In the hall, Charlie sat next to Brian and stared straight ahead. The image Charlie had seen when Brian was seated in the police car still loomed vividly in his mind and made his stomach churn.

"Pretty good fight tonight," Charlie said. "I remember Dee when he first started out. Danny thought that kid was gonna go all the way."

Charlie watched Brian for a reaction to his reference to Danny Lugo. He saw none.

"He still could," Brian said. "He's got what it takes, and winning tonight like he did is going to do a lot for his confidence. Confidence plays a big part in boxing-- that and willpower. You have to will yourself to take more pain than the other guy can."

Brian spoke in a monotone, his gaze on the polished linoleum floor. He rubbed the palms of his hands together as he talked, like a child molding a ball of clay.

"Y'all were a big part of his comeback. Matter of fact, the way I hear it from Tom, if this here thing tonight goes to shit y'all could make it as a professional fighter." Charlie chuckled to show he was kidding, mostly.

"My Da said, 'Boxing is what you do when you can't do nothing else.' I guess if I lost my job I could do it again. Heck, I really enjoyed being in Dee's corner."

"I knew your dad was a fighter, and y'all were pretty good but I didn't figure that good."

Still staring down Brian said, "Yeah, I did some fighting when my Da got sick. We didn't have anything and he needed to get his medications. So like he said, it was what I did when I couldn't do anything else."

"How long did you fight?" Charlie asked.

"Couple years. Quit when my Da died."

"So how'd ya do?"

"I won."

"How many?"

"All of 'em. Charlie, am I allowed to get a drink of water?"

"Sure, kid, y'all not under arrest. They just want to make you feel like you are."

Andy walked into the hall as Brian returned from the drinking fountain. He watched Brian wipe a drip of water off his chin with the back of his hand. The attorney took notice of the young officer's hand. He took in his thick fingers, fat calloused knuckles, and meaty palms. Powerful hand, he thought. Andy's lips were pressed together and his brow furrowed. The casual, confident smile was gone. Charlie stood next to Brian as they waited for Andy to speak.

"You know someone named Raymond Dubois?" Andy asked.

"No," said Brian.

"They called him Ray-Ray."

Brian's face turned to steel. "Yeah, I know him. He ambushed me and Quint on New Year's and tortured and murdered a young girl. Quint says he's probably good for a lot more, too. We arrested him last night."

Brian's voice seethed with anger and his eyes blazed as he talked.

"From your face and tone I take it you don't like Mr. Dubois," Andy said.

"No, I don't!"

"Well, then, it's your lucky day, 'cause he's dead." Andy made a head gesture toward the office he had just left. "And they think you killed him."

Charlie and Andy both studied Brian O'Callahan's face and body language for several seconds without saying a word.

Brian looked at them with no expression then a grim smile crept onto his face. "Someone killed Ray-Ray?" he said. "Good. That means I won't have to."

Andy thought he felt the temperature in the hall drop ten degrees. He was suddenly chilled to the bone.

Charlie was mesmerized by Brian's words and face. He had not seen such raw conviction and distilled hate since returning from Vietnam. *A feller gets a look like that when voices of the dead speak through 'im,* Charlie thought.

Andy began again, in an even, controlled voice. "They brought in some big guns to prove you already did. Even got Bruno Cicotti loaned to the case. He's heading the criminal investigation and some little pantywaist named Price is going to assist with the personnel investigation. I'm sure he'll have lots of help, though. He looks like a cherry. The department is going to order you to give an administrative statement. If you refuse they will threaten to fire you for insubordination. Right now you have bigger worries than losing your job. I advise you to say nothing and we will just cross that bridge when we come to it."

Brian hadn't moved but his face remained hard as he stared off into space.

"Brian, were you at the hospital Friday night?"

Brian returned from his trance then said, "Yeah, but--"

Andy held up a hand. "Don't say anything more tonight. We'll get started on this tomorrow."

"I gotta work tomorrow," Brian said.

"No, this is how it's going to go down. Captain Sherman is going to come out in a moment and order you to give a statement, which you are not going to do. As a result he will relieve you from duty, without pay, until further notice."

The young officer turned to his mentor. The hard look on his face was gone.

"Charlie, I didn't kill Ray-Ray. I swear."

Charlie's threw his arm over Brian's shoulder, pulled him close, then he whispered into his ear. "I don't give a shit if ya did, Bri. That asshole needed dying. Remember, being innocent don't mean a fucking thing to these IA guys. If they want y'all's ass they're gonna do everythin' in their power to prove ya did."

He glanced at the only attorney in the world he trusted, let his arm slide off Brian's shoulder, stood straight and squared himself to his protégé.

"Listen to me. You gotta stay tough on this pard. Do everythin' Andy tells y'all to do. Hear me?"

Brian looked at Andy, who had sat on the bench and was writing on a yellow legal tablet, then back at Charlie. "Yes."

A door opened and several men walked into the hall. Among them was his captain, Sullivan, the Internal Affairs Captain, Sherman, and lurking at the back of the pack, the familiar face of Monty Price.

Brian detected the hint of a smirk on Price's pasty face.

LIFE GOES ON

It was a warm day for February. Tre sat on the old couch, watching traffic pass. He'd had a couple of neighborhood kids drag it closer to the entry of the carport to enjoy the sun. He tipped a bottle to his lips and let the malt liquor trickle into his mouth. He held it for a moment, and then swallowed. Since being shot by the rival gangsters and gutted like a fish by doctors, Tre was being careful about what he ate and drank. But the medication worked best when he chased it with a forty-ouncer. The combination of opiate and alcohol didn't stop the pain of being shot. It just deadened his senses enough to live with it.

"Hey man, wassup?" a familiar voice said.

Tre cocked his head to the side to see who was speaking to him.

"Sup, Mo," Tre mumbled.

Mo-Mo looked like he'd lost more weight, and appeared ten years older than he was. His blue jeans had an oily texture and had not been washed for weeks. His basketball shoes were run over on the sides and scuffed. Mo-Mo wore them without socks, and the odor of his feet hung in the air around him. He reached into his pocket and pulled out a handful of razor blade cartridges, still in their packaging.

"You need any blades, man? I'm fittin' to see if Mr. Kim wants to buy some."

Aside from stealing anything of value he could from his mother, Mo-Mo was supporting his rock cocaine habit by shoplifting high-value items like razor blades, cigarettes, meat, and liquor. There was always a market for those things, and he could quickly turn them into cash.

Tre glanced at the cartridges and shook his head. "No, I'm cool."

Mo-Mo sat on the couch and put the brown paper sack he was carrying between his feet. Tre took another swig of malt liquor and handed the bottle to Mo-Mo without looking at him. Mo-Mo took a long pull, then set the bottle on the ground between them. A car drove up, slowed then stopped in front of the apartment house where the two boys sat. The occupants, a man and woman, looked in their direction. Tre struggled to his feet from the sagging couch.

"Want me to --?" Mo began.

Tre cut him off. "No, man, I got it." Mo-Mo was his best friend, but Tre knew better than to let a base head do his bidding. He made sure Mo-Mo was not watching him and reached between the cushions of the couch and retrieved a small zip top coin bag. He picked several small white pieces of cocaine out of the bag and popped them into his mouth. He quickly pushed the bag back into its hiding place, stood, and shuffled down the drive to the car window.

Tre looked up and down the street then asked, "Whatchu need, man?"

The driver held his hand out of the window, a twenty-dollar bill between his fingers. Tre took the cash with one hand and spit a rock the size of a pea into his other. He held it in front of the man.

"Come on, man, that's no twenty," the driver said.

Tre held his hand to his mouth again and spit another, similarly sized chunk onto his palm. The driver picked both pieces from Tre's outstretched hand and drove off without a word.

Mo-Mo took a deep drag of the menthol cigarette he had just lit. He felt agitated and restless. He took another and drag and a long drink from Tre's bottle. Tre returned to the carport and took the bottle from Mo-Mo's hand.

"Easy, cuz. Get your own if y'all gonna be like that. Gimme a cigarette."

Tre sat down and Mo-Mo passed him an unopened package of cigarettes. Tre looked at the cigarette package. "You got any mo?"

Mo-Mo nodded and rummaged in the torn grocery bag at his feet. He pulled out a carton of cigarettes and held it out to Tre. Tre took the box and laid it next to him on the couch. He could feel Mo-Mo's eyes on him.

"Man, that's for all the shit I been givin you, Mo. I can't jess turn you on fo' nuthin. It ain't mine, man."

Mo didn't reply. He just stared at his friend like a dog watching its master eat a hamburger.

"Shit, man." Tre reached into his secondary stash place, under his colostomy bag, and retrieved a small coin bag. Mo-Mo made a face.

"Hey, the po-lice done jacked me three times, an never searched under this funky ass bag." Tre removed a small piece of rock and handed it to his friend. "Here, fool, you want it or not?" Tre asked.

Mo-Mo snatched the rock from Tre's hand and reached into his pants pocket. He had lost his fancy store bought pipe and now used a glass tube two-and-a- half inches long. It had a milky coating on the inside and a brown scorch mark on one end. Stuffed into that end was a small wad of copper scouring pad.

"Hey, man, don't smoke that shit here. Go back there!" Tre said, indicating the carport behind them.

Mo-Mo got up and scurried into the trash-strewn alcove. He put the rock in the scorched tip of the pipe and held the other end to his lips as he put a flame to it. Mo-Mo drew slowly on the tube as the vaporized cocaine flowed into his lungs. The chemicals filled his bloodstream and brought the feeling he craved to his brain. For a few minutes Mo-Mo felt better.

Tre looked down the street and watched a teenaged girl approach. She was pretty and had a look on her face that said she knew it. She rolled a baby stroller in front of her. A chubby brown face peered out from a pile of blankets within the buggy. Tre tried to be nonchalant as he walked to the wrecked Cadillac sitting in the driveway. He opened the door, reached under the front seat, and retrieved a brown paper bundle the size of a large paperback book. The package was wrapped with rubber bands. Tre slammed the heavy door shut and heard the tinkle of glass as a few pieces fell from the car's shattered windshield. He meandered to the sidewalk and waited. As the girl pushed her stroller past him he dropped the bundle into it. The girl walked a few yards and stopped, as if to check on her baby. She tucked the package under a periwinkle blanket, then reached into the toddler's diaper and removed a plastic sandwich bag. She dropped the bag on the sidewalk, straightened the child's blanket, and continued down the street. Tre looked up and down the street before he retrieved the plastic bag. He looked at it and held it to his nose.

"Muthafucker smell like baby shit," Tre said under his breath.

He reached into the bag and removed a fist-sized chunk of rock cocaine wrapped in clear plastic. He pushed it into his pants pocket, wadded up the sandwich bag, and dropped it on the ground. Without acknowledging Mo-Mo he started up the stairs toward his apartment.

With each step, he leaned on the steel rail that protruded from the dirty stucco wall. Tre rested on the landing for a few seconds, then panting and sweating, made his way into his apartment. His mother glanced up from the game show she was watching, then shoveled another spoonful of breakfast cereal into her mouth.

"Tre, we need more milk an' bread. You got some money?"

Tre laid a crumpled twenty-dollar bill on the arm of her recliner. On top of the bill he put a pack of cigarettes.

"Here, momma," Tre said.

She looked up. "Thank you, baby."

He opened the door to the apartment's only bedroom and lay down on the queen-sized box spring and mattress on the floor. He closed his one eye and felt the room spinning. He grabbed a prescription bottle from the floor next to his mattress, dumped two painkillers into his hand, and swallowed them without water. He lay looking at the ceiling, listening to his mother's game show until he dozed off.

Mo-Mo watched Tre struggle up the stairs and gave some thought to following him in hopes of scoring another rock. He stood then decided against it and walked through the alley then wandered down 80th Street toward home. Mo-Mo had not been home for several weeks, not since Dee slapped him around. Dee had accused Mo-Mo of stealing his mother's jewelry and hocking it for cocaine. Mo-Mo did steal some rings and gold from his mother's drawer, but he didn't like being accused of it. When he'd emphasized his denial with a barrage of profanity, Dee slapped his face. Mo-Mo raised his fists in defense and Dee cuffed him again, this time on the side of the head, so hard it nearly knocked him unconscious. His ear rang for hours and was swollen for a week. As he'd skulked out of the front door that day, Mo-Mo told his brother he would be back soon with a gun. Tom Jefferson had allowed his son to sleep in a small trailer behind his garage since then.

As he neared the house Mo-Mo hoped the unpleasantness was forgotten. He was surprised to see a yellow rental truck parked in front and the chain-link gate propped open with a brick. Dee and a white guy were carrying his mother's couch down the walkway toward the truck. As Mo-Mo got closer he looked into the enclosed cargo box of the truck, and saw it was filled with furniture from the house. Dee passed Mo-Mo with his end of the couch and followed the white guy up the truck's ramp.

"Whatchu doing, man?" Mo-Mo asked.

"We're moving," said Dee.

Mo-Mo looked at Dee then at the open front door of the house he grew up in.

"Movin' where?"

"Away. There's your stuff," Dee said.

He pointed to a large trash bag on the porch, and then walked into the house followed by the other man. Mo-Mo started up the stairs behind the white man.

The man turned around. "I'm sorry, but your mama doesn't want you in the house, Mo-Mo."

Mo-Mo squinted his eyes, puffed out his chest, and in his most threatening gangster voice said, "Who the fuck are you? I'll put a cap in yo white ass. Get outta my mutha fuckin way, bitch."

Mo-Mo believed he had filled the stranger with fear. He stepped further onto the porch and tried to bull his way through the door. The stranger grabbed the front of Mo-Mo's shirt with one hand, then placed his foot behind one of Mo-Mo's heels and pushed. With his foot blocked, Mo-Mo couldn't maintain his balance and fell backwards off the porch knocking the wind out of him. The man jumped from the porch and grabbed Mo-Mo by the throat and held him on the ground. Mo-Mo lay gasping for breath and looking up into the most menacing eyes he had ever seen. He knew those eyes, O'Callahan.

"Mo, you just don't learn, do you?" Dee said over Brian's shoulder. "Talkin about getting a gun and scatterin' someone's shit? Your nuthing but a scandalous base head who steals from his own momma. Get your punk ass outta here before you get hurt, boy!"

Brian did a quick search of Mo-Mo's person. Finding only his coke pipe, a handful of plastic cigarette lighters, and several packages of razor blades, he released him. Mo-Mo stood up, rubbing his throat.

"Where am I s'pose to go?"

Dee looked at his brother and sighed. "I don't know, man. You're eighteen now. You've been staying with your dad. Go there."

"He tol me to get out. Said I stole his tools."

"Man, everyone has tried to help you, but you just keep bringing madness into everyone's life. You need to quit sucking on that glass dick."

Mo-Mo looked at his brother, then at Brian. He took a step down the walk then looked around in a daze.

"Where's Momma? Momma! Momma!" he yelled at the open front door.

"Momma's not here, Mo. Now get your shit and go."

Mo-Mo avoided Dee's gaze, while he retrieved everything he owned in the world, and dragged his feet down the walk and into the street. He didn't know what to do or where to go. He sniffed and tasted his tears as they rolled down his oily face. Then something occurred to him. He checked his pants pocket to see if he still had his coke pipe. Assured he did, Mo- Mo trudged down the street wondering if there was anything in the bag Tre might want to trade for.

MONEY MAKER

The toy poodle with champagne-colored toenails lifted his leg and shot a stream onto the wrought-iron fence. Tootie sat on the patio inside the fence sipping a two-dollar cup of coffee. He watched the dog for a moment. "Now why would anyone want a fucked-up little dog like that?"

The woman in the skintight stonewashed jeans shot Tootie a look, then flipped her feathered hair out of her face. She tugged on the rhinestone-encrusted collar. The little dog fell in next to her and they sashayed down Westwood Boulevard. Beppe Fazio stuffed the rest of his bagel into his mouth then turned toward the street, chewing and swallowing simultaneously. He licked the butter from his stubby fingers.

"Don't ask me. Broads like em, I guess," Beppe said. "Hey, what happened to that broad you was bangin'? She works here, don't she?" Beppe looked around the eatery.

"I had to cut that little strawberry loose, man. She trickin' out on Sunset Boulevard or somethin'," Tootie said. "Bitch started trippin' on me."

A cruel smile formed within Tootie. Cindi had run off after he'd had to slap her around. A couple weeks later she showed up at his door begging for him to take her back. He didn't have anything going that night and she looked better than she had for a while, so he let her in. She was still all about the pipe, and Tootie soon lost interest in her. A couple weeks ago at a nightclub in Hollywood he hooked her up with a brother from the neighborhood; when he'd seen the man ogling her, Tootie named his price. Tootie pocketed five hundred dollars, then said good night. Cindi put up no resistance. She was desperate to find anyone who could provide her with dope and didn't beat her. If she'd known the smooth-talking man with the jeweled cane was a pimp, she would have gone with him anyway. Tootie never missed her and Elvis Tubbs provided a steady stream of fresh girls anyway. He didn't say any of this to Beppe.

Beppe nodded. A serious look came over his face.

"Toot, I'm getting some heat over dat shipment you lost. I need to send something back east."

Tootie had been anticipating this and was a bit surprised it had taken Beppe so long to address it. "Hey, man, that's the price of doing business. Shit. Tell those mutha--"

Beppe cut him off. "That was a lot of product, and you don't tell these guys nuthin, see? They tell you."

Tootie turned off the bravado and sat silent, thinking and listening.

"It's just business, like a loan, you know? They fronted some product and don't care what ya did wit it," Beppe said unnecessarily.

Tootie knew how the mob worked and had seen what happened to anyone who crossed them. "How much, man?" he asked, looking into his coffee.

"Couple hundred was the agreement."

Tootie swallowed hard. "Two hundred thousand dollars?"

"Sure, fifty keys of coke goes for bout nine hundred yards on the street. So I'd say yer getting a deal.

The heavyset man ran a comb through his thick graying hair as he sat across the glass-topped table from Tootie. He dropped the comb into his shirt pocket, twisted a pinky ring around his finger, and studied Tootie's face. The ring was a heavy gold affair with a flat black stone in the middle and a diamond-encrusted horseshoe inlay. Tootie looked into the hoodlum's cruel, impassive eyes and willed himself to be calm and think. He had enough going on that he could put the money together but it would hurt and he hated to do it. But pissing this wise guy off would help nothing and was dangerous.

"All right, give me couple a days, man," Tootie said.

"Sure, kid, couple days is good. Say, tell me more about this guy Dimetre Walker."

"Man, I told you Dee's my boy," Tootie said.

"He sure looked good. Like to meet him an' talk business," Beppe said. "You think ya can set something up?"

Tootie smelled an opportunity. "Sure, man, I can do that."

A smile spread across Beppe's face. He stood and hiked up his tan double- knit slacks. Tootie noted the butt of a .45 auto under Beppe's matching leisure suit coat.

"Good, Toot, gimme a call when you get it set up. I gotta run... Don't take no plugged nickels, kid."

Tootie watched Beppe walk away.

What the fuck's a plugged nickel? Tootie wondered. He ordered another coffee and pondered his situation.

Ten miles east of him on Sunset Boulevard, Cindi Sykovski looked up and down the crowded street, and wondered why she had gone back to Tootie. It seemed she had made nothing but bad decisions since she met him. Now here she was standing on a street corner in Hollywood turning tricks for rock. A dirty silver Toyota stopped at the curb several feet from where she stood. Cindi walked to the open passenger window of the car. When she bent over to look at the driver, her black leather skirt hiked up, exposing her hairless crotch to a group of Japanese tourists behind her. The delighted Hollywood visitors whispered among themselves for a moment. Then, chattering and pointing, they snapped a few photographs and were on their way. From a distance Cindi was still attractive. But as she looked into the car, the man at the wheel could see that life was turning her old before her time. She licked her glossed lips and smiled seductively.

"Hi, baby. Looking for a date?"

The scooped neck of her hot pink tank top hung down, exposing her tiny breasts. The outline of her ribs stood out beneath them and her collarbone pressed against her skin. Her heavy eye makeup did not hide the dark circles beneath her eyes. The middle-aged man took notice of the two hands that gripped his car door. Remnants of red nail polish adorned nails that were chewed deep into their nail beds.

"Ah, um, yes, sure," he said.

He looked around, looked at her, and then looked down at the seat.

"Um, what do I do?" the man said.

Cindi pulled the car door open and slid onto the seat next to him. She swung her legs into the car and pulled down the zipper on one of her black vinyl boots. She flipped her dry, lifeless hair and looked at the nervous man seated next to her. She brought with her from the street the sweet odor of drugstore perfume and cigarette smoke.

"What do you want baby?"

Like the other girls had taught her, Cindi ran her hand along his waistband, then across his chest, looking for a gun. He let out a nervous laugh and looked down at his growing crotch.

"Ah, you know, but I have to get back to work in a bit. I work at the studio."

He pushed his shaggy hair out of his eyes and his eyes moved all over her.

"You a movie star, baby?" she said.

"Oh n-no, I'm just a grip," he said.

"Hmmm," she said. She looked at the child seat strapped into the backseat. Satisfied that the man was not a vice cop, she lifted her leather skirt a bit, and provided a glimpse of her moneymaker.

"You wanna grip this? It's gonna be a hundred dollars, sweetie," Cindi said.

"A hundred dollars? Um, I don't have that much," the man said.

Cindi let her skirt down.

"How much you got, baby?"

"I-I-I have fifty dollars."

"Fifty will get you head," came her answer.

"Head? You mean fifty dollars for a blow job?"

He pressed down and released the Toyota's brake pedal several times. A man half a block behind slipped his car into gear and whispered into his Rover.

"Best head you ever had." Cindi reached over and groped him.

"Um, where do we go?" he said.

"Just pull ahead and turn right at the corner."

Cindi bent over, reached into her boot top and retrieved a condom. She felt the car accelerate, and sat up straight. The man made a left turn.

"No, the other way," she said.

Then the man retrieved a badge from under his leg and flashed it at Cindi.

"Honey, you are under arrest. Just sit back and behave yourself."

"Shit!" Cindi said.

She fumbled with the door handle. "Come on, please, just let me go. I'll stay off the track. I promise you won't ever see me again. I can't go to jail."

The vice cop grabbed her by the wrist.

"Sit still and don't make this any worse than it has to be."

He spun the steering wheel and the car bounced into a liquor store parking lot. Within seconds they were behind the store, where several people were standing around a police car. Two uniformed officers approached as the Toyota came to a stop. Cindi's mind raced as tears streamed down her face. She knew there were several warrants out for her arrest and a small bag of rock cocaine was in her boot. She just couldn't go to jail.

Ninety minutes later, one of the 77th Street homicide detectives yelled across the squad room, "Dapper Davy, your public is on line two-four!"

Davy smiled at the detective and punched the flashing button on the telephone on his desk. He held the receiver to his ear. "Detective Treats."

A low raspy voice said, "What are you wearing? I have nothing on but a grass skirt and a boner."

A smile spread across Dapper Davy's face. "Pig Pen, you pervert! How the hell are you?"

Mark Morris had been christened "Pig Pen" by their senior drill instructor in Marine Corps boot camp in 1966, and the name had stuck with him ever since.

"I'm good, buddy. Working Hollywood vice these days."

Davy imagined his former partner on the other end of the line wearing a wrinkled denim shirt with his perpetual six o'clock shadow.

"Well, if you ever decide to go back to work I'm sure we can find a spot for you here. No lack of things to do," Dapper Davy said.

"No, I'll stick with my booze and broads, partner."

"Yeah? Well, if that was all you had to put up with over there I'd be banging on your door looking for a job. But you can't tell the players without a program in Hollyweird, and I don't like surprises."

"Hey, they're all God's children, buddy."

"Now you sound like the Preacher, here," Dapper Davy said. "So what's cookin', partner?"

"One of my guys brought in a hooker who wants to play *Let's Make a Deal.*"

"Oh, what's she got? " Dapper Davy said. He grabbed a pencil.

"She says she's got info on some ex-con that's been slingin' rock all over the south end. Says the guy's good for several 187s."

"Hmmm. What's this player's name?" Dapper Davy asked.

"She's not saying a lot yet, but she said the guy's name is Tootie. Says he killed some girl in a motel down there bout a month ago. Ring any bells?"

Davy waved at Preacher and pointed to the telephone. Preacher hurried to his desk, punched the line Davy was on, and held the phone to his ear.

"Yeah," Dapper Davy said. "You think she'll roll on this Tootie, or is she just blowin' smoke up yer ass?"

"This girl's a base head, but she's kind of a cherry. She's scared shitless of jail," Pig Pen said. "I think she'll roll like a circus dog if you offer the right kind of treats. She's got a couple misdemeanor warrants and we found some dope on her. Nothing I can't make go away if you think it's worth talking to her."

"Hell, yes, it's worth it! She still at Hollywood Station? What's her name?"

"Her name's Cindi Sykovski... And Davy?" Pig Pen hesitated, then said, "Sounds like she might have something else. She says this guy Tootie once flashed a big black revolver and bragged he took it off a cop."

Dapper Davy's pencil stopped moving. He looked across the room at Preacher Pruitt, who was looking back at him.

"We're on our way, brother," Dapper Davy said, and hung up the phone.

Pig Pen had been Davy's partner in RHD, and they'd worked the Danny Lugo murder together. Davy knew Pig Pen would not have called him unless he thought the girl had good information. He scribbled a few notes, grabbed his tape recorder and walked toward the doorway where Preacher was already waiting.

BENCHED

B rian glanced at his attorney. He was nervous about the Internal Affairs interview but relieved that it had finally come. For a little over a month, much of his time had been consumed sitting around his apartment, waiting for telephone calls, and running the events of the last five and a half months over in his head. He spent a lot time at the gym but mostly he walked the streets of downtown Los Angeles. He made friends with several street people and on many of his sleepless nights he'd imagined himself going to prison and, when released, joining the ranks of the lost on skid row.

A week ago, after reviewing the investigation conducted by RHD detectives on the circumstances surrounding Raymond Dubois' death, the District Attorney's office had refused to file charges against Brian. They decided that while circumstantial evidence existed, they had found no compelling evidence or witness statements to implicate him in Ray Ray's murder. Brian was off the hook criminally but not exonerated in the eyes of the department. Where the legal system required evidence beyond a reasonable doubt, LAPD discipline standards called for significantly less. Before Brian could don a police uniform again the chief of police had to believe that he had nothing to do with the crime. It remained for him to be shown blameless within the structure of a discipline system in which you were guilty until proven innocent. Once again stepping into the Parker Center elevator Brian wondered how it had come to this.

Andy Tomlinson was pleased with the DA's decision and delighted when he learned that Pap Goodings had been assigned to the personnel investigation. After talking with Pap the day before, Andy felt good about advising Brian to submit to this interview. He entered the elevator with Brian and Charlie and pushed the button for the fifth floor. The stainless steel doors closed. Andy turned to Brian.

"Pap Goodings is a solid guy, Brian. I worked with him years ago and have had dealings with him on several occasions as an IA investigator. We couldn't ask for a fairer person. He's been on the job for twenty years, and he's not a lap dog," Andy told him. "If Griefwielder or Price think they're going to control this investigation they are mistaken. This is a good thing."

The doors opened and the trio stepped out. Charlie nodded to two officers who stepped into the elevator car they had just vacated.

"Good luck," one of them said as the doors closed.

The trio walked from the foyer and turned east down a pale green corridor. An officer sat on the same wooden bench where Brian had spent several hours a little over a month before. The cop looked up and made an attempt at a smile. Charlie and Brian acknowledged him; Andy had his head in his notes.

"Sit down for a moment, Brian," Andy said. "I want to talk to Charlie."

The two men strolled back down the hall, turned the corner, and stood next to the elevators.

"You sure you're comfortable representing him, Charlie? I have league reps that I use for these types of interviews. You know the department won't allow me in there with you."

As the lawyer spoke Charlie stood with his forearms folded across his chest, staring at his combat boots. When Andy finished, Charlie met the man's eyes.

"Yeah, I know, Andy. I told Brian the same thing, but he asked me to rep him and I owe him. But I sure as heck don't feel comfortable with it."

Andy smiled and took in the vision of command presence in front of him. Charlie's uniform fit his athletic build perfectly. His trousers were sharply creased and rested lightly on the toe of his boot. Like his boots, Charlie's Sam Browne equipment belt was spit-shined. Every piece of metal on his blouse was buffed to a high gloss. He looked at the rows of military and departmental ribbons that sat above his glistening badge.

"You got the Medal of Valor twice?" Andy asked.

"Yeah, every time I turn around I step in shit," Charlie said.

"What's this one?" Andy asked. He pointed to a ribbon that sat atop all the others. It was a navy blue field with silver stars.

Charlie looked down on the ribbon and said, "I stepped in some shit in Hue City one day, too."

Andy waited a moment for further explanation but received none. "Right, well, I'm glad you took my advice and wore your ribbons. Never know who they will impress," Andy said.

"Uh huh, ya have anything else for me?" Charlie asked.

"Just keep them honest and keep Brian calm. If you see that look coming over him, just call a time out."

"That look?" Charlie said.

Andy slapped Charlie on the back as they turned toward the east corridor.

"Yes, Charlie, that look."

Soon after they rejoined Brian a stout, round-shouldered man with bags under his eyes called out, "Officer O'Callahan?"

Brian stood up. The man's large, sad eyes complimented his soft honest face and Brian liked him instantly. He stood as straight as he could then answered, "Yes, sir."

"I'm Sergeant Goodings," said the man. He extended a beefy hand. Brian took it and recalled Andy's description of Pap as a hard-charging ghetto cop in his day.

Pap turned to Andy. "Hi, Andy. How's the beach?"

"Always bitchen, Pap," Andy said, displaying a mouth full of whitened teeth.

Pap turned to Charlie and glanced at his rows of service ribbons. He stiffened then looked at Charlie's hard, scarred face, and back at the ribbon that sat atop all the others. Twenty-one years after being discharged from the Marine Corps, Pap was still conditioned to snap to attention at the sight of stars in a field of blue.

"Pap Goodings, this is Charlie Bender, Brian's Employee Representative."

"It's an honor to shake your hand, Officer Bender," Pap said.

"Name's Charlie, and that was a long time ago, in another world," Charlie said as he glanced at the gold globe and anchor pin on Pap's pocket flap.

Pap's shoulders dropped, he relaxed his potbelly, and he nodded. "Roger that," he said.

"Err--umm," Monty Price cleared his throat and stepped from behind his partner. He had followed Pap into the hall but no one seemed to notice.

"Oh, I'm sorry, you guys know Sergeant Price?" Pap said.

Charlie and Andy nodded out of civility but hands weren't extended. Brian appeared to look right through Price.

"Well, Charlie, Brian, come on in," Pap said backing through the threshold of the office where Andy had met with Sullivan, Sherman, and Price the night this had all started.

Pap pointed to a chair in the office lobby and said, "Andy, have a seat if you like, or go on downstairs and grab a cup. It could take a while."

"I'll head downstairs for a bit, Pap," Andy said.

Pap ushered Brian and Charlie into the wood-paneled room. Price squeezed past them and sat at the far end of the table in one of the six high-backed wooden chairs that were arranged around it. On the table were two yellow legal writing tablets, several sharpened pencils, and a cassette recorder. Next to the recorder was a closed brown briefcase. Price busied himself with a folder full of documents he had retrieved from the briefcase. Brian took a seat to Price's right until Charlie had him move down and then wedged himself in between Price and Brian. Pap Goodings smiled at Charlie's tactic then made himself comfortable directly across the table from Brian and Charlie. After completing the perfunctory paperwork and admonitions, Pap looked at Brian.

"Officer O'Callahan, may I call you Brian?"

Brian cleared his throat. "Yes, sir."

"We are only looking for the truth, and your honesty in this matter is critical in order for us to document that truth. Brian, do you know a man who went by the moniker of Ray-Ray?"

Brian had been instructed by Andy and Charlie to provide "yes or no" answers whenever possible.

"Yes," said Brian.

"Did you have any personal grudge against this Ray-Ray?" Pap asked.

"Yes."

"Did you kill him?" Monty Price burst in.

Brian's eyes settled on Price as he answered, "No, did you?"

Charlie stifled a laugh and Pap held up his hand.

"That's enough gentlemen," Pap said mildly. "Brian did a woman named Demi provide you information about a quantity of cocaine she had been arrested with?

"Yes, sir."

"What became of her?" Pap asked.

"Ray-Ray and someone else murdered her."

"Witnesses have stated that you became very upset when you learned of Demi's death. What did you do when you heard about her murder?"

"I don't remember exactly, sir," Brian said

"I understand that you immediately left the station. Where did you go, Brian?" Pap asked.

"I don't know, just driving," Brian said licking his lips.

"Did you go to the hospital where Ray-Ray was being treated?"

Brian glanced at Charlie then looked down. "No," he said quietly.

"Brian, I don't think you are being completely honest with us here. Do you know a nurse by the name of Mandy Green?" Pap asked.

Brian's head snapped up and a look of surprise covered his reddening face. He could hear blood rushing in his ears. Price frowned and began scribbling on the yellow paper in front of him. Both men wished Pap Goodings had not asked the question. Before Brian could answer, Price pushed his writing tablet in front of the senior sergeant. Pap read from it, then rose to his feet.

"Hang on a moment, fellas," he said to Brian and Charlie. "Excuse us." Pap reached across the table and pushed the stop button on the cassette recorder.

The two Internal Affairs investigators rose and walked from the room then closed the door. Charlie looked at Brian, who appeared to be on the verge of an explanation. Charlie held a finger to his lips, pointed to Price's briefcase on the table, then leaned toward Brian and whispered. "There's a second tape recorder in the briefcase. Jes stay quiet."

Charlie leaned toward it and put his mouth next to the brief case. "Fuck you, you little pig fucker," Charlie whispered. He sat up straight and winked at Brian.

In the outer office, the two IA investigators spoke in low tones.

"I don't think it is wise mentioning Mandy Green. We are tipping our hand to O'Callahan," Monty Price said to Pap.

"Monty, someone here is lying about what O'Callahan did the night of the murder," Pap said. "Miss Green's account of the night is contrary to O'Callahan's. I want to determine who is lying, and why."

"If it's O'Callahan, that's another allegation of misconduct," Price said.

Pap put his hand on Price's thin shoulder. "Yes, if that's the case then we will amend the charges. For now let's just concentrate on determining if Officer O'Callahan had anything to do with the death of Raymond Dubois. If it makes you feel better I won't pursue the Mandy Green questioning for now. I think I got the answer I was looking for anyway."

Pap opened the door, walked to his chair, sat, and then turned the tape recorder back on. Price followed. Pap allowed Sergeant Price to ask a few pointless questions, then asked Brian if there were anything he would like to add.

Brian said, "I went to the hospital that night to visit a friend, uh, Mandy, Miss Green."

Pap nodded.

"She works at the hospital, and I didn't want her to get involved. She just got hired and has a bunch of kids to feed. That's why I said I wasn't there." Brian looked directly into Pap Goodings' eyes.

"So you are saying you were at the hospital to visit Mandy Green that night?" Price said.

"Yes. I walked inside to let her know I was there. She was just getting off work so we hung out and talked for a while. I wanted someone to talk with, someone who wasn't a cop," Brian admitted.

"Where did you hang out, Brian?" Pap asked.

"We drove over to the 7-11 at Adams and Figueroa. Got a couple coffees and sat in my car."

Pap jotted himself a note. It read, *Check on security video from 7-11 @ Adams/ Fig on 1-7-84.*

"So, Officer O'Callahan, why did you lie to us and say you were not at the hospital?" said Price.

Charlie interrupted, "Hold on, he already answered that."

"Well, I was j-j-just..." Price began.

Charlie cut him off. "Yeah, well, he's not going to answer your question so let's move on, Sarge."

Price looked at Pap Goodings, who spun a paper clip on the table with the tip of his pencil, the corners of his mouth turned slightly up.

"So you met this woman on duty and established an off-duty relationship with her, Officer O'Callahan?" Price asked.

"Yes," said Brian.

"You realize that is against department policy, and that another allegation of misconduct will be added to this complaint?" Price demanded.

Pap rolled his eyes. Charlie bit his tongue.

"Yes, I realize that," Brian said. "But it's the truth, so I guess I'll just have to take a hit on that one, sergeant."

Brian leaned onto the table, looked toward Price and his eyes flashed, "But I did not kill Ray-Ray, and that's the truth, too."

Price leaned away from the officer as if he were hot and shuffled the papers in front of him.

"I don't have anything else," Price said.

Brian, Charlie, and Pap rose and exited the room, leaving Price behind. They walked to the door that led to the hall and lingered there several minutes.

"Brian, if we need to set up a follow-up interview I'll call, understand?"

Pap addressed Charlie. "Do you mind my asking--?" He pointed to the blue ribbon on Charlie's uniform.

"Tet Offensive," Charlie said.

Pap studied Charlie's face. "Once again, it was an honor to meet you." Pap stopped then added the universal greeting between Marines, "Semper Fi, brother."

"Semper Fi," Charlie answered.

The three men parted company. Pap returned to the conference room.

Monty Price had his back to Pap and was talking on the telephone. "Yes, and you'd think Pap was his rep, the way he mollycoddled O'Callahan, and kissed this Charlie Bender's ass like he was some kind of hero."

"Tell Chief Griefwielder I said hi," Pap said.

Price's head jerked.

"I'll talk to you later, sir, I have to go." He hung up the phone. The two men gathered up their things in silence and walked to the elevator. Pap pushed the elevator button and the doors opened immediately. He stepped in, turned, and put his hand on Price's chest, preventing him from following.

"Monty, did you see the blue ribbon with the stars on Charlie Bender's uniform?"

Monty Price didn't answer.

"Well, that is the Congressional Medal of Honor. Charlie Bender <u>is</u> a bona fide hero, son, and you couldn't carry his underwear. See you tomorrow."

The elevator doors closed. Monty Price stared at the two stainless steel doors.

The next day Brian submitted to a lie detector test. Several days later he got a call at home from Andy Tomlinson.

"Great news, Brian. With Mandy Green's statement, the tape from the 7-11, and your poly results, the Chief of Police just determined you could return to work on Monday. Lieutenant Cicotti and Captain Sullivan really went to bat for you. Good thing, too, because Deputy Chief Griefwielder and Sergeant Price lobbied the Chief of Police to keep you at home without pay. Sounds to me like Pap Goodings was the tiebreaker. So watch yourself, and I'll be talking with you soon."

OLD FASHIONED DISCIPLINE

Upon returning to work, Brian was assigned to 77th Street Station's front desk until the formal conclusion of the criminal and internal investigations. He didn't care; he was glad to be back in uniform and working. He was assigned with Charlie Bender, who had moved to pm's recently. Charlie softened the blow of being tied to the desk by providing an endless array of stories.

"Ol' Stogie, now that was a foot beat cop. He walked a beat in the projects back in the late sixties when I was a boot. I was working the desk one night and a feller comes up to me an hands me a field interview card. I take the FI an look at it. It was one a Stogie's. I ask that ol' boy, 'Whaddaya want me to do with this?' He says, 'Officer Stogie told me I had a warrant, told me to come to the station and give y'all this here card, and turn myself in,'" Charlie said.

"And he did it?" Brian asked.

"Yep, took the bus straight up Broadway to the station," Charlie said. "Stogie gave him fare."

Brian laughed; he loved Charlie's tales of the good ol' days. They reminded him of being a boy and listening to his father and his friends reminisce about the fight game. Charlie had finished a coughing jag, spit a gob into the wastebasket, and cleared his throat.

"Stogie wasn't jus feared, he was respected, and that's more important. When folks respect a cop he becomes part of the community, and people feel safe when he's around. They watch out fer him, too. Ol 'Stogie worked by hisself an that was 'fore we had portable radios. Every cop had a dime stashed somewhere on him to make that emergency telephone call. Yep, that and an extra handcuff key." The phone rang and Charlie stopped mid-story and answered it. "77th po-lice."

Charlie jotted down some information, asked a series of questions, and then put the caller on hold. He picked up the Rover assigned to the front desk and said, "12L90, citizen reports a man with a gun walking southbound San Pedro from Florence. Suspect's a male black, fifteen to seventeen years, five-ten, slight build, wearing a red baseball cap, white t-shirt, black pants, white shoes with red laces. Weapon is a blue steel handgun tucked into suspect's waistband. PR will meet at San Pedro and Florence, southwest corner at the phone booth."

Before the RTO could type in the information and rebroadcast it, 12A69 broadcast that they were in route and would be code-six in one minute.

Charlie said into the phone, "Stay where y'all are an' the po-lice are gonna be there quick as a wink. Alright, bye."

Without missing a beat Charlie dropped the phone into its cradle, flipped a cigarette into his mouth, and turned to Brian.

"Used to have police call boxes on the corners so coppers could ring in every hour or so. I worked with an ol 'timer who used to go to the call box over on Vermont and Slauson and call his ex-partner workin' the desk couple times a night. He'd say he needed to call the station an' would drive to the box. Heck, I knew he had a bottle in there. Now, once a year I would drive home to Virginia for a visit and help my daddy on the home place. When I headed back to California my daddy always made sure I had a case of Mason jars in the trunk of my car, smoothest moonshine you ever tasted. Well, one night before work I put a jar a' my daddy's stump water in that call box. Less than an hour outta roll call this feller says he needs to call the station. I drive there and he hops outta the car an' hurries over to the box. I see him duck his head behind the door. His head pops back up and he looks toward the police car, then ducks back down for a couple seconds."

Charlie took a deep drag on his cigarette and shot a string of perfect smoke rings across the station lobby. He stared ahead, lost in a moment past.

"That shine was smooth, but it wasn't fer small children or sissies, neither. When my partner come on back to the car he was sweatin' a bit. He loosened his tie and popped a piece of gum in his mouth. Within a couple minutes he got to talkin' and laughin', happiest I ever seen 'em. We drove back to that box 'bout once an hour 'til I finally had to put him ta bed in the backseat of the car. I covered him with one of those leather uniform coats we used to wear. That was 'fore the brass decided we looked too mean in 'em an' only motor cops got to wear 'em. I worked the rest of the night by myself as an L-car. He started stirrin' 'bout sunup, got in the front seat, put on his sunglasses, and never said a word about it."

Brian loved it.

While Charlie reminisced in the station, Lenny and Butch sped east. As they approached San Pedro Boulevard with their headlights off, they saw a figure wearing a white t-shirt and red cap walking southbound on San Pedro across 76th street.

"There he is," Lenny said. "Slow down, let him cross and walk down the street a little. We'll zoom him midblock."

The cruiser rolled down the street and stopped at the corner. The suspect had not seen them yet. Butch waited until the figure was halfway between 76th Street and 76th Place. The suspect was walking along a chain-link fenced yard that both officers knew contained a large pit bull dog. They figured the he would be hesitant to climb into the waiting jaws of the land shark.

"Okay, go!" Lenny said.

Lenny grabbed the microphone from the dashboard as Butch accelerated toward the figure.

"12A69, we got our suspect walking south on the west side of San Pedro from 76th Street. We're code-six."

When they were behind the suspect, Butch flipped on the headlights and high beams. The right front wheel bounced over the curb and the police car jerked to a stop about fifteen feet behind the suspect. Lenny pushed his door open and braced it with his foot.

"Freeze! Get your hands up!" Lenny shouted, looking at the suspect over the hood of the car and down the six-inch barrel of his Smith and Wesson revolver. Lil' Monster, a seventeen-year-old member of the Bloods gang, was trapped. He looked around in panic. He had few options. He was too far from 76th Place to run to it. Further south on San Pedro, he saw another police car stopped in the middle of the street with its red lights on. The dog to his right was barking, snarling, and throwing himself against the fence. He wasn't going that way. Lil' Monster couldn't even try to ditch his gun. The cops were right on him. If he reached for the revolver they would see it and shoot him. Still, if he ran right now he might be able to make the corner.

While Lenny kept the gangster in his sights, Butch removed the Ithaca shotgun from its rack. He lifted and slid the horizontally mounted .12-gauge along the driver's seat and brought it to a port arms position. His right index finger found the slide release, and his left hand gripped the wooden forearm of the slide. As he leveled the shotgun at the figure on the sidewalk Butch racked the action.

Butch yelled, "Get your fuckin' hands up, asshole, or I'm gonna cut you in half!"

Hearing the sound of the shotgun shell being chambered was all Lil' Monster needed to hear. The officers' threats were well supported, and in the seventeen-year-old's mind they were real. Monster pushed his hands into the night air and finally followed Lenny's directions. Within seconds he was face down on the sidewalk with his arms and legs spread. He lay motionless until he was handcuffed and rolled over. Lenny pulled an inexpensive .38 caliber revolver from Lil' Monster's waistband and handed it to Butch, who took the weapon with one hand while still training the shotgun on the head of the prone suspect. Once satisfied the suspect was no longer armed, Lenny grabbed a fistful of the youthful gangster's waistband and lifted him to his feet, with one hand. With the other hand he grabbed the kid's red hat from the ground. He walked the gang member to the police car, opened the back door, and put his hand on the back of the arrestee's head and directed him into the car. Before closing the door Lenny flipped lil' Monster's baseball cap onto his lap.

"Don't forget your hat, bud," Lenny said, and slammed the door.

A group of people began to gather, and it wasn't long before the catcalls began.

"We got any further on this call?" Lenny asked.

"No. I sent Mental and Oco to look for the PR up at Florence and San Pedro but nuthin. Looks like whoever called didn't want to stick around," Butch said.

"Can't say I blame 'em," Lenny said as he slid onto the backseat next to Lil' Monster. "Let's go book this sinner."

Butch put the car in drive. No sooner had they pulled into traffic than the youngster in the backseat started in on them.

After the shock of the moment wore off, Lil' Monster's ego and his youthful bravado had returned with a vengeance. "Y'all ain't shit!" Lil' Monster said. "I was fittin ta shoot yo ass! I should have, too, pig!"

He lambasted the officers with a barrage of insults, threats, and provoking challenges. He assumed that police officers, for all their faults, would not shoot a person handcuffed in the back of their police car. He didn't consider other options.

"Y'all think you safe," Lil' Monster continued. "We'll see... Y'all got families. Maybe I'll come see them when I get out. I don't play, muthafuckers!"

"That's it. Butch, stop the car," Lenny said.

"Whatchu gonna do hit me, Mr. po-lice? Lil' Monster said.

"Nope, gonna give you what you asked for, son, a shot at being a real hero in the hood," Lenny said.

Butch pulled into an unpaved, trash-strewn alley and stopped. Lenny opened the back door and climbed out. Then he reached back into the car and grabbed the now-silent youth by the arm.

"Come on, man, we're gonna see just how tough you really are."

He walked the arrestee to the front of the car and was joined by Butch.

"Partner, we got a bad actor here. He was gonna shoot us both, and now when he gets out he gonna kill our families," Lenny said. "Guess we better just settle this thing right now. Butch, go get Billy the Kid here's *pistola.*"

The defiant mask on the young man's face began to fade.

"Hey, man! Whatchu fittin to do?" Lil' Monster said.

Butch returned with the .38-caliber revolver and handed it to Lenny. Butch hooked his pickle-sized thumbs into his gun belt and leaned against the front fender of the police car with an amused look on his face. He was ready to be entertained. Lenny opened the cylinder of the pistol and ensured it was loaded. He closed the cylinder, stepped to Lil' Monster, hooked the front of the kid's pants with one finger, and pulled. A gap between the pants and the youth's white boxer shorts was created. Into that gap Lenny pushed the revolver. He took two steps back and faced the young man.

"Partner, take his cuffs off," Lenny said.

Butch looked around for witnesses. "This is getting interesting." Then he pushed his key into the keyhole of a cuff and turned it. When Lil' Monster's hands were free Lenny locked eyes with the youth and unsnapped the shiny black holster on his hip.

"Okay, killer! Go for it," Lenny said.

Lenny's right hand hovered near the custom wooden grip of his Smith and Wesson .38 Police Special. The young man's eyes were wide open. He licked his dry lips then threw his hands as high above his head as he could while staring into the face across from him. Lenny's face was shrouded in shadows and appeared maniacal.

"Come on, man, you're some kind of bad dude," Lenny said. "Here's your chance. Draw! Come on! Just like the old west. Come on, man! You were gonna kill me. Let's see you do it."

Lil' Monster looked at Butch, hoping for some sign he would help. But Butch only pulled on one of his plump red ears, scratched his whiskered chin, and then leaned against the police car with his arms folded across his chest.

"Don't look at me, shithead," Butch told him. "You're the one who threatened his family."

Standing alone in the alley awash in the lights of the police car, Lil' Monster was reduced to the seventeen-year-old boy he was. Stripped of any courage he might have had, his bluff was called.

"Momma, help! Somebody call my momma! They gonna kill me! Momma!" Lil' Monster cried out.

Many people heard his pleas, but no one came. The gangster waited to hear the gunshot. His knees buckled and he sobbed. "Please don't, please! I was jus' playin', man!" he said.

A voice whispered in his ear, "Yeah, you're a real bad customer. I ever see you near my family, I'll finish this."

Back at the station Brian put the Rover on the shelf under the front desk. "They got that guy over on San Pedro, Charlie," Brian said.

Charlie looked up from his report, smiled and nodded, then went back to work. It was Friday night, and the lobby was full of customers. Some were there to file crime reports. Others came to ask one of a hundred questions a desk officer answers each night. A few were there to post bail for friends and family members being held in the jail. Several children walked into the lobby hoping to score some of the candy that was in a bowl under the desk. Adding to the ambient noise of the police radio and the conversations in the lobby, the telephone rang constantly.

A small, wiry woman was seated on the lobby bench beneath a

row of framed black-and-white photographs of 77th Street officers killed in the line of duty. She sat on the end of the bench, close to the two glass doors that led outside. Brian saw her look with disdain at the woman seated next to her, whose vocabulary seemed limited to profanity. The small woman had reached a time in life where her age could not be determined. Deep creases in her dark skin ran vertically down her cheeks and horizontally across her forehead. Her eyes were sunken into their sockets but shone like two highly polished black jewels. She wore a round black hat with a small red flower atop her steel-gray hair. On her feet were black leather lace-up shoes. They reminded Brian of the shoes the nuns had worn when he was a boy attending Catholic school. She sat quietly, holding a black leather-bound Bible.

She was at the station to pick up her grandson who'd been arrested with several other boys in a stolen car. She'd apologized for any inconvenience the boy may have caused, and in a small voice explained that she had recently been made the boy's legal guardian. The old woman had sucked at her false teeth then said, "He's got the devil in him, officer, but not fo long."

Brian let Pistol Pete Rhodes and Speedboat Willie Washington know that their arrestee's grandmother had arrived. A few moments later Speedboat Willie appeared in the lobby.

"Mrs. Jackson?" Willie asked, addressing anyone in the lobby who might be her.

He had a boy of about thirteen years by the arm. The youth wore a blue rag on his head and his pants were sagging beneath his loose white t-shirt. When he stepped into the lobby, the boy jerked his arm loose from Willie's grasp.

His grandmother said, "Boy, where did you get those clothes? Those sho ain't the ones I sent you to school in."

"Are you Mrs. Jackson?" Willie asked again.

"Yes, sir, I am," she said, and then she addressed the boy. "Child, did you steal a car?"

"I ain't done shit," the boy said.

"Child, I'm fittin to snatch you baldheaded! Now you just hush!" Mrs. Jackson said.

"Yeah, right," he said and started toward the lobby door.

Mrs. Jackson set her dog-eared Bible on the front desk in front of

Brian. She pulled a broom out of the custodian's cart that Mr. Toby
had abandoned in the lobby at quitting time. With surprising speed
she covered the distance from the cart to the door. She held the
broom over her head and delivered a blow to top of the boy's skull.
The force of the strike snapped the broomstick in two and sent the
boy staggering backward.

"Now, boy, you pull up them pants, an' I don't want no sass!"
She turned to Willie, who stood beaming. "Officer, I am sorry fo
breakin' y'all's broom, but if it's all right I'm gonna hold onto this
here handle until I get this boy home and get a proper switch. I'll
bring y'all a new broom tomorrow."

Brian held up a black book. "Don't forget your Bible, ma'am."

"Thank you, child." Mrs. Jackson took the Bible from his hand,
gave him a demure smile, and walked towards her grandson who
was on his knees holding his head.

"I'm sorry, baby, but I told you I'm not gonna have this mess.
Now quit yo whining an' less go on home. You caused these officers
enough trouble tonight."

The boy walked through the double doors still rubbing his head.
The little grandma with a flower in her hat followed close behind,
her Bible in one hand and a stick in the other. The lobby was silent
for several seconds after the pair left the station. Then the room filled
with laughter and words of approval and praise from most of the
citizens in the waiting room.

Willie walked up to Charlie and leaned across the desk laughing.
"I'd say that young'un is in for a long night, Charlie."

"Shouldn't we do something?" Brian asked.

"About what? We didn't see anything," Willie and Charlie said
in unison.

Brian smiled and thought, *Just a little old-fashioned discipline.*

SPIDER SENSE

Dapper Davy Treats gazed at the pile of paperwork before him. He cracked his chewing gum one last time then spit it into the wastebasket next to his desk. "I hate to waste time briefing Nick."

Even so, Davy had to admit that on occasion, when laying an investigation in front of Nick Stupin, the supervisor came up with sound observations and insights. No great surprise; Nick had worked murders for over two decades and he knew his business. Preacher Pruitt just smiled. He didn't think the briefings were a waste of time at all. He felt that Davy didn't enjoy being second-guessed and was still angry at Nick's being promoted to Detective III over him. Preacher got up from his desk and walked across the room to a row of gray metal cabinets. He retrieved a key from his pocket, and unlocked one of the cabinets then swung open the side-by-side doors that secured four six-foot shelves. On each shelf was a line of blue three-ring binders.

"What cases you want, Dapper?" Preacher asked as he perused the notebooks.

The binders, known as "murder books," each contained an open 77th street homicide investigation. A book consisted of the original homicide crime report, property reports, vehicle reports, notes, logs, rescue ambulance report, witness statements, and the assigned detective's follow-up reports. Also included in the book was the coroner report, crime scene photos, and any other information that might be a factor in solving the crime and prosecuting the individual or individuals responsible. When a binder became filled to capacity another one was added to the investigation. At the time Davy and Preacher were assigned twenty-three murder investigations and, to date, that filled forty-nine blue notebooks.

"Umm, let's go with Scooby Brown, and the multi-three over on Kansas and Sixty-seventh," Davy said. "I guess we better come clean with the ballistics on this one."

"Yeah, guess it's about time, my brother," Preacher said.

Dapper looked down at a photograph lying on his desk. He sat slowly chewing a fresh piece of gum as he took in the grisly scene captured in the photo.

"Grab Demi Sanders's book, too. No doubt Nick's gonna want to hear about that one," Davy said.

The three investigations totaled eight binders. Preacher selected the appropriate books and in two trips carried them to Davys's desk.

Preacher put two under each of his arms. "Ready, partner?" he asked. "Let's go face the music."

Davy stood and picked up the remaining binders. "Yes, let's do," he responded.

Thus laden, the two detectives headed toward the open door of Nick Stupin's office, which was not much bigger than a walk-in closet. The walls were cluttered with certificates of completion and accomplishment. There were a couple of bowling trophies and rows of photographs chronicling the lives of his three sons on a small maple bookshelf against the wall. On his tan metal desk sat a telephone and a city-issued blotter that doubled as a department telephone directory. Next to the in-box on the corner of the desk was a black-and-white photograph of three young soldiers standing in front of a sandbagged, bullet- pocked wall. One of the soldiers held a mortar tube over his shoulder. Anyone who looked could see that the bare-chested youth was Nick Stupin. Davy poked his head into the small room.

"Ready, boss?"

Nick spun around in his ancient wooden swivel chair to face the door. It squeaked under his weight. "Come on in, guys. Have a seat." He pointed in the direction of three wooden chairs of the same vintage.

Preacher set his burden on Nick's desk and pulled up a chair. Dapper Davy placed his murder books on the tiled floor, then removed a handkerchief from his pocket and wiped the seat of his chair before he sat down. He crossed his legs, picked a piece of lint from his trouser leg, put his hands in his lap, and sighed.

"Thanks for taking time out to get me up to speed," Nick said. "I realize you guys are buried, so we'll make it quick. Whaddaya got for me?"

Preacher hefted a notebook. On its spine next to a file number, "Franklin + 2" was printed in black marker.

"Nick, this is that shooting back on December second, it occurred on the twelve hundred block of West Sixty-seventh Street," Preacher said. "Three victims rolled up on our suspect and another young man who were walking westbound on the sidewalk. Words and shots were exchanged. Victim one, the driver, Franklin, was mortally wounded but managed to drive about half a block. Victim two, Anthony Thomas, was seated in the front seat and took a round to the temple after it passed through Franklin's neck."

Nick raised his eyebrows and said, "Big gun."

"Lord, yes, looks to be a .357," said Preacher. "Victim three, Duwayne Jones, was seated in the back behind the driver and fired one shot from a sawed-off shotgun. Our witness says he hit the boy walking with our suspect. Suspect put four rounds in victim Jones. Hit him in the hand, shoulder, mouth, and chest. The RA transported Franklin, who was DOA. Victims Thomas and Jones were dead at the scene."

"You say you got a witness?" Nick said.

Preacher and Dapper Davy exchanged looks.

"Yeah, a little kid saw the two peds remove what he described as a big black cowboy gun from an old truck parked in the kid's backyard," Davy said. "He also says he saw the boy that was shot hide the gun there. We checked into it, and Trevon Williams was arrested inside the kid's home on the night of O'Callahan's shooting."

Nick's chair squeaked as he sat up straight. "And?"

"Well, we confirmed that Trevon Williams was treated at County for a shotgun wound to the abdomen the night of our shooting. He's out now, sporting a shit bag and living in an apartment with his mother on the 800 block of West Eighty- first Street."

"Trevon Williams. Why does that name ring a bell?" Nick said.

"His street name is Tre," Davy said. "He's the little prick that threw PCP in Manny Magana's face."

"Yes, and got his eyeball knocked out by Mental Spinner for his sins," added Preacher.

"He should change his name to Lucky," Nick mused.

All three men enjoyed a short chuckle.

"Williams hangs out with a base head named Mo-Mo, who fits our shooter's description," said Preacher.

"You got an ID on this Mo-Mo?" said Nick.

"Yes. His name's Maurice Oswald Jefferson. He just turned eighteen years old," Preacher said. He's the Eight-Tray who copped out to the painting all that "kill the po-lice" graffiti.

"So pick him up," said Nick. "Can the kid testify?"

"That's the problem. The witness won't talk to anyone but O'Callahan, and O'Callahan isn't cooperating," Dapper Davy said. "Some bullshit about protecting the kid. Kid's mother thinks if her son talks some hoodlum might smoke him."

"I'd say that was a legitimate concern, my brother," Preacher said.

Dapper Davy and Nick looked at the third detective for a long moment.

Preacher looked at his hands, then went on. "You know we can't protect our witnesses from these little criminals, Dapper. They would hit that little boy without so much as a thought. I'm sorry, guys, I understand we have to get folks to talk and all, but I'm kinda proud of O'Callahan for sticking up for the kid."

"For Christ sake, not another member of the O'Callahan fan club," said Davy. "Not you, Preach, please!"

"I'm just saying O'Callahan got the shooter identified, and we have lots to go on. Let's put a case together without using the kid if we can. I don't want to bury a witness if we can avoid it, especially a child."

"Squeeze this Tre guy and maybe sweat Mo-Mo," said Nick. "You say he's an addict? Maybe he'll talk."

"We're taking this thing slow for a couple reasons, Nick."

Dapper Davy stopped and glanced at his partner.

"Our victims were shot with the same gun Darrel Brown was killed with."

"Refresh my memory," Nick said.

"Pooh-butt dope dealer named Scooby," Davy said. "He took one between the running lights. We found him leaning against a fire hydrant back in August."

"Oh, yeah. How could I forget that one?" Nick said. "Okay, great. Looks like we might clear several killings. If we got the same gun, good chance it could be the same shooter."

"Could be." Dapper Davy drew a deep breath and inched to the edge of his chair. "The gun's a .357 mag." He hesitated, then added, "It's the same one that killed Danny Lugo."

Nick looked at Davy, then at Preacher. His face began to color.

"How long have you known this?"

"Just got the ballistics back," Dapper Davy said.

"On both shootings?" Nick said. "God damn it, Davy, the Lugo shooting is not your case anymore! How long have you been sitting on this?"

"Ballistics came back in October," Davy mumbled.

"Shit! Preacher, did you know about this?" Nick demanded.

Preacher sighed and said, "Yes, I did."

Nick leaned toward the two detectives and partially rose from his chair. "Why? Why the fuck would you guys hold back such hot information?"

Preacher stared at the photograph on Nick's desk, a little bit amused at how red some white folk's faces could get.

Davy looked at the murder book in his lap then locked eyes with those of his supervisor. "Cause *it is* my fucking case! The case that has been keeping me awake for ten damn years. It's the only one that counts.

Only reason I left RHD was to get closer to the investigation. I want that goddamn gun and whoever picked it up and ran off with it. I want to nail that son of a bitch! That's why I sat on it. So do what you gotta do boss, because I'm gonna find that gun and if I solve a couple of other homicides while I do it, fine! But I don't really give a shit, Nick. Danny comes to me in my dreams and I got a pretty good idea I'm not the only one."

Nick and Preacher were stunned. Neither of them had ever seen such an emotional outburst from the cool and collected Dapper Davy Treats. Davy felt like someone who had just vomited--weak and unsteady, but infinitely better.

"Let me think on this," Nick said. "I'll sell it to the old man. You guys need any help, let me know. How's the Demi Sanders investigation going?"

In a lower, softer voice, Dapper Davy read off a list of clues they were working.

"We got some good prints out of the hotel room and the Buick parked in the lot. The car comes back to some woman over on the eleven hundred block of West Eighty-third Street. We door-knocked the place, but no one was home. We're gonna bring the motel manager and the drag-queen in today to look at the mug book. We got some info from a working girl who got scooped up in Hollywood on an ex-con named Andre Hicks that looks good, too."

Davy dropped several photographs onto Nick's desk. Nick lifted the top photo off the pile. He examined each one while being briefed.

"When Preach and I attended the autopsy, it was pretty obvious she had been beaten and raped. The Coroner's report confirmed these guys did a number on this girl. You can see the ligature marks on her wrists, neck, and ankles in the photos, so it looks like the killers kept her tied up most of the time they were working her over."

Dapper Davy stood and tossed the typewritten report onto Nick's desk. "I can't wait to catch the other animal that did this," Davy said.

"Amen," Preacher whispered. "Be a lot easier if Ray-Ray was still around."

Nick laid the last photo on his desk. He had seen hundreds of murder victims over the years and had become hardened to the sight. But what was done to Demi sickened him. He rubbed his face, then ran his fingers through his cropped graying hair. He took a deep breath and let it out slowly through his mouth.

"You think O'Callahan killed Ray-Ray?" Nick said.

Dapper Davy was momentarily stunned by the frank question.

"No. He had motive, Officer Sontag saw him at the hospital the night of the killing," Davy answered. "There is something in him that is, I think, capable of anything. But I just don't see him doing it. Just my spider sense talking, I guess."

"Spider sense?" Nick asked.

"You know," said Dapper Davy. "It's that voice that tells you to turn left, or to stop a certain person, or to use extra caution. It's that third eye that sees what we don't consciously recognize--that thing that our training officers always told us to listen to--the voice that keeps us alive."

"It's the voice of our guardian angel," said Preacher.

Davy and Nick nodded.

"Anyway," Davy went on, "there were a couple nurses who remember seeing an orderly they didn't know walk out of the area in a big hurry… We found a set of scrubs discarded in a restroom, too, so we have some work to do on those leads."

"You guys get the scrubs over to Scientific Investigations Division yet?" Nick asked.

"Yeah, and we're going to re-interview the nurses, too," Preacher added.

Davy was still thinking of Brian. "The kid's salty for his time on the job, but he's gonna be a legend," Dapper Davy said. "If he doesn't get smoked or fired."

"Lots of people in the division think an awful lot of him, too," Preacher said. "He and Quint King are quite a team."

Davy uncrossed his legs and stood. He put both hands on the desk and leaned forward.

"You asked if we could use anything. How 'bout getting O'Callahan and King loaned to homicide for a couple Deployment Periods?"

"Are you outta your mind?" Nick said. "Brian O'Callahan is suspect in a fucking 187, Davy!"

"Was, Nick. *Was.* He's back to work. They never had anything other than the kid got mad and stormed out of the station," Davy said. "If they did, O'Callahan would still be sitting at home watching *Andy Griffith* reruns, and you know it. That prick Griefwielder and his butt-boy Price are behind this. Ray Charles could see that."

Then Preacher said, "Gee, partner, don't tell me you're a member of the O'Callahan fan club, too?"

Dapper Davy grabbed his crotch. "I got your fan club, Preach."

"Well, I don't see the Chief of Police wanting to explain to the fucking *LA Times* why he has an officer working on the same murder he was suspected of committing," Nick said. "Sorry, guys, I just don't see that happening. As it is, the Captain is going to be ripping me a new one over the Lugo gun. All right, we all have enough to do, so let's get back to work. You two have anything else I need to know before I go throw myself on the mercy of the Captain? I don't want any more surprises."

"Nope, I'm good," Dapper Davy said as he collected his murder books from the floor.

Preacher had seen them already, but as he gathered up the horrific photos of Demi Sanders's ruined body he whispered, "Oh, my dear sweet Jesus, the things we do to each other." He closed his eyes and said a short prayer for the little country girl who could drive like hell.

Several hours after the meeting with Nick, Preacher Pruitt walked into the Homicide office. Davy was back at his desk poring over an evidence report.

"Davy, news of Danny Lugo's revolver being used in four homicides didn't take long to get out. I was asked about it by three separate people as I walked from the restroom to here."

"God damn it, how did it get around so fast?" Dapper Davy bellowed.

Preacher cringed. Of the profanity so common in a police station his partner just used the only phrase that really bothered him, and Dapper Davy knew it.

"Sorry, Preach, it slipped out."

"That's all right, Davy. It's frustrating. Could have come from anywhere. You know how things are around here. Gossip spreads like wildfire on a brushy hill."

"Yeah I do, and that's why I was holding back information. Tell you what, if the Captain tries to bust my ass for it I'm going to use this as an example of why I did."

Shawndra, from records, kept her head down and typed as Dapper Davy and Preacher spoke.

"Well, we better get out there and scoop up Mo-Mo and Tre as soon as possible," Davy said. "Now that every blue suit in the division is talking about Danny's gun being out there, we need to move before word hits the street and that gun and its owner go underground. Tre is still living over on Eighty-first Street with mom, isn't he?"

"Yep, far as I know he is," Preacher said. "Quint King told me O'Callahan has seen Mo-Mo wandering around Fifth and Wall in Central Division with the rest of the base heads."

"O'Callahan works the desk. What's he doing downtown?" Davy asked.

"He lives there," Preacher said.

"O'Callahan lives on Skid Row?"

"Near it. I heard he lives above one of those little shops near Third and Broadway."

"Why the hell would he live in that shit-hole?"

"Quint says O'Callahan grew up in the inner city. Said his dad was a professional boxer, and he lived in fleabag hotels all across the country for most of his life. That's where he's comfortable"

"He's comfortable with drug fiends, winos, hypes, bums, whores and rats as big as cats? That's nuts."

"Yeah, well, Quint said O'Callahan sees Mo-Mo panhandling all the time. Brian's even talked to him a couple times."

"What, O'Callahan knows our suspect? Why the fuck would an off-duty police officer be hanging out with a base head?" Dapper Davy asked.

"Mo-Mo is the brother of this boxer Dee that O'Callahan helps train."

"A boxer?" Davy asked.

"Yeah, he's a ranked middleweight. I think he's the guy Danny Lugo took under his wing," Preacher said. "That was before you got here. I have a photo of him from the newspaper in my desk."

Preacher rummaged through the top drawer of his desk, found a clipping from the LA Times sports page, and handed it to Davy.

Dapper Davy regarded the photo then did a double take. "I've seen this guy somewhere." He studied the fighter's face, then asked, "Can I hang onto this Preach?"

"Sure man," Preacher said.

"Here ya go, Detective Pruitt," Shawndra said in a voice dripping with honey.

She dropped a pile of reports she'd proof-read and retyped on his desk, then hurried out of the office, her high heels clicking on the tile. Davy and Preacher both stopped and watched Shawndra's more than ample buttocks bounce and wiggle under her skintight skirt as she made her way out.

"Looks like two wildcats fighting in a burlap bag," Dapper Davy said.

"Um, um, um, my goodness," was all Preacher allowed himself to say.

Shawndra walked down the south hall to the records office. It was nearly five, and the other records personnel had left for dinner. She looked over a row of filing cabinets that served double duty as storage and room dividers. On the other side of the cabinets was her supervisor's empty desk. Shawndra turned and shut the door behind her, then she peeked out of a second door into the north hall. Once satisfied that no one was nearby, she picked up the phone, and dialed.

On the third ring a man picked up. "Yeah?"

"Hi, this me. Yeah, its fine, nobody's here. They're fixing to pick up a boy named Mo-Mo. I heard the homicide detectives talking about it. This Mo-Mo has a brother named Dee. He's a boxer. It's all about a Magnum gun being used in some murders. Yeah, that's it, a .357 Magnum. Uh-huh, yeah. They say this Mo- Mo is staying down on Skid Row downtown. Yeah, one of the officers he saw him there. Yes. Uh-huh, I will. Oh, and they're gonna try and sweat Tre from Hoover. Yeah. Fine, all right. Bye."

Shawndra placed the phone in the cradle then reached under her desk and pulled out a counterfeit black Gucci purse. She rummaged around in the purse until she found her makeup bag. Clutching the bag in her purple acrylic talons, she opened the door to the south hall and made her way to the ladies room.

When she looked over the filing cabinets at her boss's desk Shawndra didn't see Brian O'Callahan rifling through the bottom drawer of a cabinet on the other side of the room. He listened and waited until he was sure Shawndra had left the room, then stood. His first response was to tell someone, maybe the watch commander or Charlie. At least he should tell Quint. Then Danny Lugo spoke to Brian as clearly as if he were standing next to him. Brian froze staring and listening like a child in a dark room.

"Watch commander wants to know what's holding you up, O'Callahan. The phones are ringing off the hook out there!" Abe Palmer stood in the doorway opposite the one Shawndra had just exited.

Startled, Brian snapped out of his trance. "Oh, yes, sir. Sorry. I was just looking for a report. Sorry it took so long. I'm on my way, Sarge."

Brian pushed the drawer closed with the toe of his boot, then squeezed past Abe and hurried down the hall to the front desk. Radio Rick was taking a telephone report while his dark brown cigarette smoldered away in an ashtray next to his arm. All the public lines were ringing, and several people were standing at the desk waiting to be heard.

"Sorry Rich, got hung up. Brian reached for a ringing phone.

Rich shrugged his shoulders and held his telephone away from his ear. "No problem, man."

A few minutes later Brian glanced into the watch commander's office and saw Shawndra wiggle her way up to Leo's desk and pick up a stack of reports from his outbox. Brian felt his face become hot.

"What's up, man? You're looking at her like she owes you money," Rick said.

"Huh? No, I was just thinking I got to get out of here early. You think Leo would give me an early out?"

"Yeah, Bri, tell him we got a couple U-boats working. I'll call one in to cover you until mids come down."

Brian cleared an early departure with Leo, finished up the report he was working on, and hurried into the locker room. He changed, jogged to his VW, and then drove as fast as he could to the Hoover Street Gym.

SLINGING ROCK

Tootie dropped the phone into its cradle and stood staring out at Marina del Rey. Instinctively he touched his wrist, looking for the calming effect he always got from stroking his silver bracelet. Where the hell had he put it? It didn't matter now. Tootie had business to attend to. He walked to his bedroom and removed his 9-mm semiautomatic pistol from the nightstand drawer. He held the gun in his right hand and examined it at arm's length.

"No, muthafucker, I got somethin' for y'all," he said.

Tootie dropped the semi auto back into the drawer, reached under his mattress, and retrieved the Colt. He opened the cylinder and ensured that it was loaded. "Y'all looking fo the snake? He's looking for y'all, too."

He pushed the gun into his waistband and concealed it with the tail of his navy blue silk shirt. He pulled on a black knee-length leather jacket and dropped a box of ammunition into his coat pocket as he left the condo. He walked down the hallway and down a flight of stairs. Once outside he flipped up the jacket's hood. His face was lost in shadow. He walked into the carport without noticing Elvis Tubbs, who had just climbed out of his car.

"Hey, Toot, is that you, man? Wassup?" Tubbs asked. "You got any product bro? I'm going to a party tonight and, you know."

Tootie stared at the tall figure and tried to process what he was being asked. His mind was focused on other things. "What?" Tootie said.

Despite the men's disparity in the men's size, Tootie's tone and body language sent a tremor of fear through Tubbs.

"You know, man, I was hoping you could set me up with some coke for tonight," Tubbs said.

"Nigger, can't you see I got shit to do?" Tootie said.

Shock expressed itself on Elvis Tubbs's face. Tootie calmed.

"Sorry, homes. Whatchu need?"

295

"An O-Z be cool, man," Tubbs said, looking around.

Tootie reached into his pocket and fished for his keys. As the coat parted, Tubbs glimpsed the mahogany grips of the revolver in Tootie's waistband. Tootie removed the door key from his key ring and tossed it to Tubbs.

"Here, man, I got a couple ounces in a box of vanilla wafers in the fridge. Jus lock the apartment when y'all leave. I got to bone out, man!"

"What about your key?" Tubbs asked.

"I'll get it later. I got another in my ride." Tootie abruptly turned and walked to his BMW, coattails flapping behind him.

Tubbs watched the hoodlum and realized just how much Tootie frightened him. He recalled the stories Tootie had told him over the past months. Often the two men sipped expensive cognac, smoked hashish, and enjoyed the ocean air and harbor views together. At times, when the alcohol and THC had worked their way into the murderer's brain, Tootie recreated for Tubbs scenes of violence and retribution that had been his life. Tootie was exciting, but recently Tubbs was becoming more and more uncomfortable with the man.

Elvis Tubbs had problems of his own. His game had been rapidly declining. It felt like everyone was always on his ass. There was increased talk around the league of mandatory drug tests. It was not that Tubbs couldn't stop using drugs, he just didn't want to. A couple of lines of the white powder, it seemed, were the only thing these days that felt right. Tubbs trotted up the stairs and walked to Tootie's apartment. He slipped the key into Tootie's door lock and turned it.

Neither Tootie nor Tubbs had seen James Trask in the laundry room. Trask was cleaning the dryers' lint traps when he'd heard Tubbs greeting Tootie. Trask moved to the doorway, a couple of yards from where the two men stood talking. He paid close attention, and when he repeated the conversation to Manny that evening over dinner, it was verbatim. Manny excused himself from the table and made a couple of phone calls.

Tre sat deep in the old stuffed couch. He'd moved it to the bottom of the apartment stairs just outside the carport to allow for a head start on anyone approaching, especially the police. He sat watching the traffic roll past and chain-smoked cigarettes.

Since being shot, Tre was finally starting to feel a little better.

Sales had been good and he'd hired several neighborhood kids to do his bidding. He staged the youngsters on either end of 81st Street watching for the police. They buzzed around the street on bicycles Tre bought for them like bees around a hive. At the first sign of a police car the boys would whistle, then scatter to the four winds. Tre also hired a tough, streetwise fifteen-year-old he called "Burn Rubber," a name quickly shortened to B-Rubber by the local kids. B-Rubber did Tre's hand-to-hand sales, or "slinging," as it was called. Tre doled out small quantities of rock cocaine to the skinny youth with the long legs and bulbous eyes. B-Rubber stashed the dope nearby and kept several rocks in his mouth. When customers drove up and stopped the boy walked to the car and made the deal. Once money was produced, he spat a rock into his palm and handed it to the buyer. If there were ever a problem, "Burn Rubber" showed how he earned his name.

Tre looked up Hoover Street and saw a hooded figure walking toward him in the dusky light. He painfully pushed on the arm of the old couch and prepared to move up the stairs.

"Don't go runnin' off, fool! I'll pop a cap in yo ass right now!"

Tre recognized the voice and froze. He knew if he ran to his apartment he would be followed and caught. The police usually stopped at a closed door, but Tootie would not. At least here they were in public view and there was still a little daylight left. Tootie might be less likely to make a scene. Tre lowered himself back down and tried to play it cool.

"Sup, Tootie? Didn't know it was you, homes."

The kids on their bikes congregated in a semicircle across the street and watched. Tootie waved to B-Rubber, who peddled a new BMX bicycle over. He stopped beyond arm's reach of the hooded figure and straddled the bicycle.

"Look here, man, y'all need to go on. I'm fittin to talk with my man here," Tootie told him.

When he reached into his pocket and removed a roll of twenties and B-Rubber saw the grips of the pistol. Watching the man peel off a twenty for each boy, B-Rubber took in the frantic look on Tre's face and knew this man was someone to obey.

"Yes, sir," the boy said as Tootie held out the bills.

He grabbed the wad of bills, turned his bike around, and stood on his pedals as he rode up to the group of boys. Within a minute Tre and Tootie were the only ones on the street. Tootie turned to Tre.

"Where's your boy? I thought he was always kickin' it with y'all. I got somethin' big and I need you and what's-his-name?"

"Mo-Mo," Tre said before he could hold the words back.

"Yeah, Mo-Mo. Little crazy-ass nigger is just what I need for this job. Where he at?" Tootie asked.

"Don't know, man," Tre said, being as nonchalant as he could.

Tootie flipped the hood off his head and looked at Tre. He lifted his silk shirt a few inches.

"Now answer my question again, only tell the truth, my man."

"I really don't know, Toot. He ain't been round. He go downtown sometime to score, I heard."

Tre hoped he was convincing.

"Think Dee knows where he's at?" Tootie asked.

"Maybe. Dee usually at the gym. "You can ask him."

"No, *we* fittin' to go ask him."

Tootie drew the revolver from his waistband and put the barrel against Tre's forehead.

"Right?"

Tre stood up and followed Tootie to a black BMW parked several addresses east of Tre's apartment building; they got in and drove off.

MUSCLING IN

Brian saw Dee and Boomer in a corner of the gym. Boomer was talking in his animated manner, throwing shadow punches and weaving to and fro as he spoke, while Dee sat on the apron of the ring, a towel draped over his head like a hood and his cotton sweats soaked through around his neck and chest. He sat leaning back, his ankles crossed and his arms hanging over the ropes. Boomer stopped his schooling and broke into a wide smile when he saw Brian.

Boomer plucked the stump of a fat cigar from the corner of his mouth and said," Hey now slugger," and feigned a left hook to Brian's body.

Brian pinned his elbow to his side to block the playful blow. "Hi, guys," he said. "What's cookin'?"

Dee shrugged his shoulders, then spat into a galvanized pail on the floor. "Nuthin much, man. Wassup?" Dee asked him.

"I need to talk to you, Dee. It's kind of important. Sorry to interrupt the workout, Boomer. Won't be a second."

"That's all right, man, we jus talking now. Y'all missed a good sparring session, though. Dee here jus keeps getting stronger an' stronger."

"Hell, yes! He's gonna be champ!" Brian said and punched Dee on the shoulder.

Dee smiled, then wiped his dripping face with his towel. He hopped off the apron and walked toward the front door, dabbing at his face with the towel as Brian walked alongside him.

"Sup, Bri?" Dee asked.

"I need to find Mo-Mo.

Dee stopped and looked at Brian.

"You're the second dude who's been in here looking for him today. What he do now?"

"Who was here?" Brian shot back.

The two men stepped into the dimly lit parking lot just outside the gym's wooden screen door.

"Tre was just here, said he needed to talk to him bout something," Dee said. "'Cep …"

"What?" Brian asked. There was an urgency in his voice.

"I've known Tre all his life, and he's kinda like a little cousin an' all. Sumpthin was botherin' him. He was scared, an' I've only seen him scared once before. Something else. He wouldn't look at my face. It was like he was ashamed."

"What did you tell him?" Brian asked.

"I told him Mo's been staying up by Fifth an' Wall. Livin' in one of those cardboard boxes on the street. Unless the po-lice run them off because of the Olympics an' all. I heard they're fittin to do that."

"Yeah, I heard that, too." Brian said.

"Then he just left and jumped in a car with some dude I couldn't see. He was parked down the street," Dee said. "What'd Mo do?"

"I can't tell you, Dee. But he's got himself involved with some real bad actors," Brian said. "If you see him, tell him to come to my place. If I'm not home, tell him to go to a police station and have the police contact me."

"Whatchu mean you can't tell me, man?" Dee said.

"Dee, I can't talk about it. I just got outta trouble," Brian said. "They thought I killed Ray-Ray and… well… Just have him find me or go to a police station and wait for me."

"You didn't kill Ray-Ray, man! Everybody knows who killed Ray-Ray."

A heavy car door slammed and both men turned. A stocky, middle-aged man was walking toward them from a black El Dorado that was parked on the small paved lot in front of the gym. He was wearing silver-rimmed, rose-tinted glasses and a silk shirt unbuttoned low enough to show off a chest full of gray and black hair. His Stacy Adam's loafers crunched the loose gravel on the pavement as he walked.

"Check this Al Capone lookin guy out," Dee whispered. "Damn."

The man stopped in front of them. "Either of you know a fighter named Dimetre Walker?"

Brian stiffened. He had not seen Beppe Fazio since he was eighteen years old. Even under the poor light in the parking lot Brian recognized him.

"Whatchu need with him?" Dee asked.

Beppe looked Dee up and down. He measured him to be a middleweight, and he looked like the man he had seen fight at the Olympic.

"You Dimetre?" Beppe asked. "A mutual acquaintance said I would find you here."

"Yeah? Who's that?" Dee said.

"Tootie said you was his man. Said you guys grew up in this neighborhood together."

Dee could feel panic welling up from within. He wondered why Tootie would send this wise guy to see him.

"Yeah, I know Tootie," was all Dee could think to say.

"Good to meetcha," Beppe said, and held out his plump hand. "My name's Beppe Fazio."

Dee looked at Beppe's hand and after a second or two of silence he gave it a light shake. "Sup," Dee mumbled.

Turning to Brian, Dee said, "This here's my training partner, Brian--"

"Brian Turner," O'Callahan interjected.

Beppe glanced at Brian.

"Yeah, how ya doin'?" He turned his attention back to Dee. "Listen, Dimetre, I would like to talk some business witchu. How's 'bout we step over to my car for a minute?"

Dee looked at Brian. He did not want to get in the car with a guy who resembled a Hollywood hit man but he'd said he knew Tootie. Dee did not want any trouble with Tootie.

"Nah, I'm all sweaty, man. I don't want to mess up your ride, man. We can just talk here, or go inside the gym."

Beppe stepped toward the Cadillac, and said, "No. Let's sit in da car. Much better. I don't give a shit about da seats."

Brian said, "I'll wait right here, Dee. I still need to talk with you."

Beppe stopped to wait for Dee, who was not following. He shot Brian a hard look. Brian tried not to respond, but driven by an urge forged by years of loathing, he returned Fazio's look with a searing stare.

Brian's mind slipped into his life's most horrific memory: *Brian stood helpless as Beppe pressed the muzzle of the pistol against his head. He put his face to Brian's and hissed, "Yer ol' man cost me*

301

a lotta dough, kid." His breath reeked of tobacco and garlic. "He thinks he can pull a fast one on me? I don't think so."

An enormous man in a black suit stood in the alley with one hand on the Cadillac's door and the other holding a thick braided cotton cord that was tied around Brian's father's neck. A second, shorter, rotund man held his dad's right hand against the car's doorpost. On Beppe's signal, the man in black slammed the heavy door then pulled it open. Seamus O'Callahan grunted, then struggled like a wild animal as he attempted to break free. His tormentor jerked the rope tight and with his huge foot held Seamus down. The fat man fed Seamus's left hand into the open door. Brian closed his eyes but heard the door slam again and then his father's single cry. Rage and tears lighted Brian's eyes. He pulled against the hand that clutched a fistful of his hair, but Fazio pulled Brian's head closer to him with one hand, and kept the barrel of his revolver snuggly against his temple with the other.

"See that, Mick? That's what happens when you're told to take a fall and you don't. So, if you think about getting cute remember this."

Fazio nodded to the two thugs who stood over Seamus. The big man pulled the cord around the fighter's neck even tighter, which lifted him from the wet bricks of the alley. Brian's father's reached to his neck. His face turned blue and his tongue hung from his mouth as the warrior's eyes flickered and closed. Fatso pulled a black leather glove onto a fist the size of a brick, then reached back and let fly a blow that smashed into a face that had withstood a thousand others. The other man released the rope and Seamus dropped unconscious onto the alley. The gloved hand opened and a roll of dimes dropped next to the fighter's bleeding mouth.

"There you go, Punchy! Take a cab home," the thug said.

Beppe and the other hoodlum's laughter sounded like the grunts of hogs.

Brian opened his eyes and saw Beppe and Dee fifteen feet away, standing next to the caddy. Brian closed the distance and stood next to Dee, his eyes fixed on the mobster.

When Beppe first saw Brian he hadn't given him a thought. Now he took a closer look. Something was familiar about him. "Do I know you?" Beppe asked.

Brian slowly shook his head 'no'. He felt his two-inch revolver burning against his lower back, secured in his waistband. His chest heaved in choppy breaths.

"No, I seen you somewheres before," Beppe said.

He searched his memory as Brian felt his rage tumbling downhill and picking up speed. He took a deep breath.

"I don't think so, Sport."

Beppe eyed the young man and tried to determine what he would do about the veiled disrespect he had just been shown. He would need to be dealt with, but now was not the time. Now was the time for business.

"Hmm, I guess not," Beppe said. "Dimetre, I was saying, I seen you fight da other night an' liked what I saw. I just wanted to meet ya an' help with your training an' expenses. I see big things for you, and I can help. I know people. Ya know?"

Fazio removed a pack of matches from his pants pocket and wrote a telephone number on the inside cover. He handed the matches to Dee, and then removed a roll of bills from his other pocket. He pared off five new hundred-dollar bills.

"Gimmie a call. We'll talk business, kid."

As Fazio reached to tuck the money into the waistband of Dee's sweat pants, a hand plucked the bills from his hand. The wise guy looked up and met the glare of two green eyes. Brian pushed the bills into Fazio's shirt pocket.

"He doesn't need your money or your help, Beppe."

"What the fuck--?" Fazio stopped in mid-sentence. Those eyes. He remembered now. His mouth bent into a snarl. "Hey kid, I hear your punchy ol' man croaked?"

The El Dorado's interior dome light went on as the passenger door opened. The vehicle rocked as a large man climbed out of the car and started toward Brian.

You keep that side of beef in the cooler, Beppe. This isn't New York, and I'm not your kid," Brian said.

Brian lifted his shirt and exposed the shield clipped to his belt. "How about I call someone downtown and tell 'em about this hood that's trying to muscle into the fight game here in Los Angeles? Maybe they'll dig around and find something else, too."

"I learned your ol' man, thought I learned you, too," Fazio said.

"Shoulda left ya both walking round on Queer Street."

Fazio's bluster was tempered by the look on Brian's face. He recognized the cold finger of danger.

Headlights illuminated the scene as a police car pulled onto the lot and stopped perpendicular to the Cadillac. Fazio looked across his car then at Brian. The cruisers doors opened and Lenny and Butch exited the car. Brian was glad to see them. Lenny walked around back of the El Dorado while Butch moved quietly to the front.

"Hey, Brian, who's your pals?" a deep voice asked behind Beppe.

Fazio's head twisted around to see Lenny Custer striding toward him.

The thug who was rounding the front of the El Dorado was looking toward Lenny when he felt a hand grab the back of his neck.

"Where you goin', pal?" Butch Caldwell asked.

He tried to twist free, but Butch's hand became a vise that closed around the thug's neck with enough force to drop him to his knees. Butch removed a spring-loaded beaver tail sap from his trouser pocket and tapped the thug twice lightly on the top of his head with it.

"Easy there, tough guy, or I'm gonna splatter your skull all over this parking lot."

The 11-inch long impact weapon was comprised of a of spring steel handle with a flat piece of lead at the business end. It was bound in thick black bull hide and in the hands of Caldwell, one application of the sap could prove fatal. The department no longer authorized its use but that was no deterrent to Butch.

Beppe Fazio twisted the horseshoe ring on his pinky finger while he sized up the situation. "No problem here, officers. We was just leaving."

He stepped to the door of his car and looked at Butch and his bodyguard. Butch released his grip on the man's neck and hauled him to his feet by the collar of his brown polyester leisure suit, then shoved the man toward the car, causing him to stumble. The man regained his balance and slinked into the passenger seat of the Cadillac. Beppe Fazio glared at Brian as he opened the door of his car.

"See ya 'round, kid," he said.

Beppe slammed the door and fired the engine. The street yacht rolled through the lot then bounced out of the driveway and sailed north on Hoover. Lenny gave Brian a quizzical look, but Brian's mind was elsewhere, fixed on a face that had been battered until the mind behind it was forever ruined. His father had tried to resume fighting after his hands healed, but the damage was done. He soon became fodder for up-and-coming fighters in the cruel sport.

Dee had stepped back at the start of the conflict. He was mesmerized by the violence hanging in the air. Dee was no stranger to the aggressive behavior of men, but this was something different. It was premeditated, and moved with a gravity that threatened to suck up anyone within range. Most amazing was the change that had come over his friend. He had long ago stopped thinking of Brian as a police officer and saw him as a friend, even a brother. Brian's reputation was well known throughout the hood, and Dee had seen his friend's abilities in the ring first-hand. Still, Dee was struck by the change in him. The sweet, harsh fragrance of death seemed to ooze from Brian's pores. His person became dangerous and frightful. If the two officers had not arrived, Dee was sure Brian would have killed both of the hoodlums.

No sooner had the Cadillac pulled out of the parking lot then three sharp beeps sounded from the police radio. The beeps were a precursor, meant to get the officers' attention for a high-priority radio call. Lenny and Butch stopped in their tracks and listened. A woman's voice broadcast, *77th Street units, and any 77th Street unit to handle a shooting in progress, 74th and Figueroa Streets.* Both uniformed officers turned and jogged toward their police car. Lenny looked over his shoulder.

"Gotta run, Brian! Talk to ya later, man."

Lenny hopped into the driver's seat, dropped the car into reverse and looked over his shoulder. He backed out onto Hoover, dropped the car in drive, and took off with tires squealing. Holding the microphone to his lips Butch looked out the car window and smiled his big, river horse smile.

Dee watched the black-and-white speed north, then took a couple steps to Brian's side.

"Dee, I know you want an explanation. Just trust me. I have to find Mo-Mo. If you see him, take him to the police station. I'll fill you in later.

Dee acknowledged Brian's directions and watched him walk to his Beetle. After he got in the car, he rolled down the window. "Remember the night I told you about my father and how a local hood had tried to make him take a fall?"

Dee nodded.

"That guy Fazio who just tried to buy you... that was him. If those assholes come back, call the police and don't go anywhere with 'em. Trust me."

Dee watched the little red car ping north on Hoover Street. He turned to Boomer, who had been watching the drama from the doorway of the gym.

"Kinda cool, seeing the po-lice jack up white folks for a change, eh Boom?"

"Damn right!" Boomer said. "Now let's us finish this workout so I kin get me something to eat." The two men walked back into the gym, allowing the screen door to slam shut behind them.

LORD LORD

Preacher read from the scrap of paper in his hand, then read the numbers painted on the curb. "Seven forty-three, west Eightieth Street. This is it."

Dapper Davy parked their unmarked police car a few houses east of the address. The wooden structure needed paint and was in disrepair. A three-foot high rusted chain-link fence enclosed an overgrown, trash-strewn yard. The windows were covered with yellowed shades and wrought iron bars. As he walked Preacher held an evidence envelope in one hand and a flashlight in his other. He stopped when he got to a gate that hung off a broken hinge. Dapper Davy's hands were free and he shoved open the gate allowing Preacher to step through it and up the walk to the front porch. Davy followed behind him, looking for dog turds and water bowls among the tufts of dried grass. The front porch groaned under Preacher's weight as he put his ear against the steel-mesh door that secured the home, and listened. He could make out the voice of a popular female TV host inside the small white house. He heard nothing else. Preacher knocked on the door and listened. The sound of the television was muted, and he heard a rustling from within. Davy stood on the walkway keeping an eye out for dogs.

The porch light came on and a small voice on the other side of the door called out, "Who's that?"

"Miss Dubois, its Detective Pruitt. We talked on the phone a bit ago," Preacher said. "You said you would try to identify your grandson's things for me."

Several locks and dead bolts were heard turning within the door. Then it opened a crack and a frail face peered through the mesh. She looked him up and down then backed up, pulling the door open with her. The old woman turned the bolt on the outer security door and pushed it open.

"Come in, sir," she said.

She looked at Dapper Davy standing in the yard.

"You come on in, too, officer."

Mattie Dubois's home was tidy, but reeked of age and stale air. Her vintage furniture was well worn. Pictures and portraits adorned nearly every space on the walls of the small living room; most were school portraits of children. On the coffee table next to the recliner where the old woman had settled was an ornately framed black-and-white photograph of a young soldier and his bride. When she saw Preacher looking at the photograph, she smiled and exposed an impossibly straight row of gleaming white teeth. She lightly touched the frame, then directed her attention back to Preacher, who made himself comfortable on a lumpy sofa that was covered with a crocheted blanket. Dapper Davy had come in, and stood where he could see down the hallway leading to the bedrooms.

"Miss Dubois, thank you for allowing us to come into your home. I have some things that may belong to your grandson. I was hoping you could tell me if any of this was Raymond's," said Preacher.

"It's Mrs. Dubois, young man. However, you may call me Mattie if you like," she said.

Preacher opened the manila evidence bag he had been holding. He removed a clear plastic bag from it and poured the contents onto the coffee table.

Mrs. Dubois donned a thick pair of wire-rimmed eyeglasses, then used a bony finger with swollen knuckles to push at the small pile of gold chains, necklaces, and assorted pieces of jewelry.

"Hmmm-hmm, that's Raymond's. He did like to wear all that gold jewelry. I never thought much of it, but he was always coming home with some new necklace or something. Oh, this here, this isn't his, sir," she said.

Mrs. Dubois pushed a braided silver bracelet across the table, away from the pile.

"No, he wouldn't have worn that. Raymond didn't like silver, only gold. That's all he ever wore," she said.

"Maybe it was for his girlfriend or sister," Preacher said.

"His momma never had a girl child and Raymond didn't have nobody special that I knew of. These boys nowadays, they just stay with a girl long enough to get her pregnant, then run off to the next one. It's just sinful. That's why Raymond's mother left him and his brother with me, so she could go off like an alley cat."

She glanced up at the wall. A fading photo of a young girl in cap and gown hung next to the picture of a muscular teenage boy holding a football. "She's passed now," the old woman said.

Preacher studied the photos. "Is that your other grandson?" he asked.

The old woman sighed. "Yes, that's Thomas. He was a football star. They shot him right here in my front yard. He really was a good boy, never got caught up in this gang mess." She stared at the photo for a moment and shook her head. "Now Raymond, well, that child was always full of the devil. I know he gave as much grief as he got. The boys who shot Thomas, they were shooting at Raymond and killed the wrong boy." Mattie Dubois whispered, "Lord, Lord."

Preacher took her hands in his and they prayed in silence.

Thirty minutes later the two detectives were sitting in their pastel blue Plymouth munching on double cheeseburgers.

"Cindi Sykovski got arrested bout ten days ago. Is she out now?" Preacher asked.

"Yeah, her father came and bailed her out right away. Pig Pen worked it out so she never even went to Sybil Brand. After she talked to us he had her booked on a misdemeanor possession charge. Figure she'll get some sort of rehabilitation and probation. They got so many people in lock-up now on dope charges the courts are looking for ways not to hold people."

"Quint King says her dad's a big shot surgeon of some sort," Preacher said between bites. "We have his address?"

Dapper Davy pulled out the paper napkin he had tucked into the collar of his shirt and dabbed his lips. "Just so happens we do, partner, and as soon as you're done choking down that burger we'll be on our way."

The sun had been down for an hour when Dapper Davy exited the San Diego Freeway at Sunset Boulevard. He made a left and drove toward the exclusive West Los Angeles community of Brentwood, where million-dollar ranch-style homes overlooked meticulously manicured landscapes.

Stopped at a well-lit intersection, Preacher admired a shiny maroon and white Silverado. The truck bed was loaded with mowers and lawn tools. "Even the gardeners drive nice cars around here."

"I used to hate working capers out here," Dapper Davy said. "Everyone thinks they're special."

"Aren't they?" Preacher asked.

Davy shrugged.

Dapper Davy parked down the street from a sprawling, Mission-style home. The house sat atop a hill and had a long driveway that led from the street to the home above. Low light lantern fixtures marked the drive.

"Home sweet home, partner. Welcome to the hacienda!" Davy said.

A spotlight was trained on each of the three large Navajo White, stucco arches that comprised the front of the home, which was topped with a red tile roof. Heavy black hinges on the rustic oak front door and window shutters had been tastefully used to accent the early California look. A black Porsche sat at the top of the brick driveway next to a Mercedes-Benz.

"Well, Preach, let's work off those burgers," Dapper Davy said getting out of the car.

The two homicide detectives made their way up the long drive. As they stood on the porch, they were both a little winded, so Davy gave them a moment before he rapped on the door with the heavy black iron ring bolted to it. A short Hispanic woman in a starched uniform answered the door and showed them to the living room. The room was open and highlighted by a huge window from which Davy figured you could see the Pacific Ocean several miles to the west on a clear day. In the middle of the room, Cindi sat, hugging her knees on a snow-white rug in front of a massive stone fireplace. Her father was seated on an equally white sofa with a colorful Mexican serape thrown over the back. He sipped from an etched glass half full of amber liquid. Next to the doctor was an attractive blond woman in her forties. The elegantly dressed and groomed woman sat motionless, except for the slight tremor in her clasped hands. She stared at the coffee table in front of her through tired eyes.

Doctor Sykovski got up and shook the detectives' hands and introduced his wife. She didn't get up. Cindi stared into the fireplace with her back to them all.

"Honey, Detective Treats and Pruitt are here to speak with you," Sykovski said.

310

She turned and said, "Why are you hassling me? I've told you everything I know."

It had been nearly two weeks since she'd smoked any rock cocaine, and she was feeling very edgy. "Daddy, why did you even tell these cops they could come over here?" she sniffed.

Deep in thought, her father placed his glass on a wooden coaster on the coffee table, which appeared to have been made from a heavy wooden barn door. His hard Slavic features drew tight as he looked at the girl. "Cynthia, what did I tell you? You can answer these officer's questions, or I will call you a cab right now. As you may recall, coming home was your idea, not mine. We made an agreement, young lady. Own up to it or leave."

Cindi looked at the woman. "Mommy?" she pleaded.

Mrs. Sykovski's eyes filled and reddened, and her hands shook, but she was angry. "No," she yelled at her. "Cindi, don't try that 'Mommy's little girl' crap! You are done. You are a drug addict and a prostitute who has stolen from this house. Now you answer this officer's questions or get the hell out!" Then the woman rose from the couch with her face in her hands and walked from the room.

With a defeated look Cindi faced the detectives. "What do want to know?" she said.

Preacher walked over and sat on the floor next to her. "We just need to know a couple more things Cindi," he said softly. "You said this man Tootie's real name is Andre Hicks?"

"Uhhuh."

"And he told you he had killed a girl in a motel?"

She looked at her father then said, "Yes, one night just before I moved to Hollywood, Tootie got real drunk and told me if I ever talked to the police about him he would...," she hesitated then continued, "He said he would fuck me up so my mamma and daddy wouldn't know me, like he did to a girl in a hotel he said lost his dope and snitched."

"Did he say her name?"

"He just called her a country-ass bitch."

"Ok, Cindi you said he had a large pistol. Did you ever see it?"

"Yes. It was a Colt Python," she sniffed.

Dapper Davy was sitting on the couch and leaned toward the conversation.

"How do you know that, Cindi?" he asked.

"I saw it up close and read it on the barrel." Cindi's voice trembled. "Tootie made me suck the barrel of the gun while he told me about the things he did to that girl."

Her father gasped and she burst into tears. Sykovski got up and took his little girl into his arms.

Preacher whispered, "Sweet Jesus," under his breath.

Davy wrote it all down on a yellow tablet.

"That's enough questions," Sykovski said as he rocked Cindi in his arms.

"One more please, Doctor Sykovski," Preacher said. "Cindi, have you ever seen this?"

He held up the braided silver bracelet that had been recovered in Ray-Ray's hospital room.

She separated from her father's embrace, wiped her eyes with her forearm, and took the bracelet in her hand. "It's Tootie's. He wears it all the time. It was his dead brother's, I think."

"You sure?" Dapper Davy asked.

"Yeah, I am. If you look on the clasp you can see his brother's initial engraved on it," Cindi said as she set the bangle on the coffee table.

Dapper Davy picked up the bracelet and did just that. The letter G was engraved on it.

Preacher stood. "Look, Cindi, I know you are hurting right now," he said. "Hang in there. Do not go out on the street, no matter how bad you want to score. From what we can see, Tootie is trying to cut any loose ends from his life, and you, my dear, are one of those loose ends. We have enough evidence for an arrest warrant and we are going to pick him up as soon as possible." As an afterthought Preacher turned to the doctor. "Does Tootie know where you live?"

All eyes went to Cindi.

She shook her head. "No, I don't think so."

"Good. Just the same, I'll call over to West Los Angeles Division and request extra patrol," Preacher said.

"Thanks, but I took care of it yesterday. Two off-duty officers will be here by eight tonight."

He looked at Cindi.

"They are going to be our houseguests until I receive a phone call from one of these gentlemen telling me that Andre Hicks has been arrested, or is dead."

"Works for me," said Dapper Davy.

Soon the detectives were driving east on Sunset.

"Preach, it don't matter whether you're rich or poor. Life's gonna happen to ya." He added, "But man, I'm glad I got boys."

MET HELL HALFWAY

West Hollywood was a strange combination of refined hip and brazen debauchery. The beautiful people partied there. Perhaps that was on Elvis Tubbs's mind as he drove his bronze-colored Jaguar around the corner, off La Cienega Boulevard and onto Sunset Boulevard. Or maybe he was thinking about how Andre Hicks had scared the crap out of him earlier in the evening. Regardless of the reason, he failed to stop for a red light and now two men in khaki uniforms were following him in a black-and-white Chevrolet with red lights flashing.

About the same time Dapper and Preacher were heading home from their interview with Cindi Sykovski, Tubbs was squinting into a Los Angeles County Deputy Sheriff's flashlight.

"Good evening, sir. May I see your driver's license and registration?" the deputy asked.

"What seems to be the problem, officer?" Tubbs asked.

"You ran the red light back on La Cienega and from your breath I'd say you've been drinking. So, why don't you step from your car?"

Tubbs handed the deputy his driver's license then unfolded himself from the car. He looked at the green name patch above the lawman's right pocket and said, "Sorry about the light, Deputy Statts. I was thinking about New York. We got a game there on Monday, you know? Y'all like B-ball? I'll set y'all up with VIP boxes sometime, no problem."

Tubbs knew he was talking too much, and too fast. His dry lips were popping as he spoke and his eyes darted from one deputy to the other. He couldn't keep still, and fidgeted with the chain around his neck as he constantly shifted his weight from foot to foot. *Be cool, man. It's just a ticket,* Tubbs admonished himself.

Statts said, "Stand over on the sidewalk, sir."

As soon as Tubbs complied, the ruddy-faced deputy shined a

penlight in each of Tubbs's eyes, then up his nose. He placed his hand on Tubbs's chest. Statts nodded to his partner, obviously a weightlifter, who wore a skintight, tailored, tan, uniform shirt. The overhead streetlight glinted off the gold star on the deputy's chest as he stepped behind Tubbs and handcuffed him.

"What's going on, man? What's this bullshit? A black man can't drive a nice car down Sunset Boulevard? You muthafuckers know who I am?"

"Sure do, pal. You're the guy I just caught running a red light with booze on his breath and white powder up his nose. Also the guy who's going to jail," Statts answered.

Before placing him into the backseat of his car, Statts conducted a search for weapons or contraband. He reached into the inside pocket of Tubbs's dun- colored calfskin bomber coat and removed an intricately tooled silver box. Inside the box were a rolled-up hundred dollar bill and about a tablespoon of white powder. Statts looked up at Tubbs and smiled. Just then his partner called his name. He was leaning out of the Jaguar and with a muscular arm holding up a clear plastic sandwich bag half full of white powder.

"Looks like it's the penalty box for you, big guy. Oh, in answer to your other question, a black man can drive a nice car down Sunset anytime he wants. Just not with a bag of cocaine in the car."

"Look, deputy, can we talk, man?"

"I'm sure lots of people are gonna want to talk with you, Mr. Tubbs. Don't waste it on me," Statts answered.

"No, look here, man! I know a guy who your looking for. He's killed all sorts of dudes and he sells coke by the kilo."

"All right, you tell that to the detectives, and if it turns out to be good we'll see if we can't save your career," Statts said.

He seated Tubbs in the back of his cruiser, and just before he closed the door Deputy Statts poked his head inside the car.

"Now I know why you been playing like shit."

While Elvis Tubbs sat in the West Hollywood Sheriff's Station and told detectives everything he knew about Andre Hicks, across town on Skid Row, Tootie hunted Mo-Mo with Tre in tow. The evening had cooled off and small fires fueled by trash warmed the ragged shadows who looked into the flames. The odor of unbathed humanity mixed with the smoky, ammonia-laden air. The scene was like an abstract colony, removed from civilization and functioning at man's lowest level of existence. Unconscious figures lay willy-nilly on cardboard pallets and blocked pedestrian passage on the sidewalk. Predatory faces peered out from the darkened recesses of uninhabited storefronts as the two men walked down Wall Street.

"This place smell like piss!" Tootie grumbled.

Tre sensed an opening.

"Tootie, maybe he not here. We checked the missions and hotels. We been lookin for a couple hours."

"He's here," Tootie replied.

The two continued down the filthy sidewalk. A group of men stood huddled around a fire in the street. A pile of broken wood pallets lay behind them. The flickering light illuminated the street sign's above them: 5th Street and Wall Street.

Tootie gestured toward the group. Tre walked among the men, searching their vacant faces. Twenty feet away the flame of a butane torch outlined two human figures standing together. Tre changed direction and walked toward the men, who stood at the mouth of an alley pressed between two weathered brick buildings. He heard the sound of his childhood friend's voice.

"Get off me, muthafucker! I'll cut yo ass!" Mo-Mo said.

Mo-Mo pushed the other man away with one hand and held a glass tube to his lips with the other. He flicked his lighter and held it to the end of the tube.

The other man pressed in, drawn like a moth to the flame. "Come on, man!" he said.

Tre looked back at the hooded figure standing on the sidewalk and nodded. He could not see Tootie's face as he approached.

"There go Mo, over there," Tre whispered indicating the shorter of two men standing in the shadows of the buildings.

Mo-Mo was Tre's best friend. He felt like Judas and hoped Tootie just wanted to talk to Mo-Mo about a job. But he knew the grim reaper when he saw him.

Tootie closed on the pair near the alley, "Wassup y'all?"

Tre wanted to call out to Mo- Mo, to warn him. Instead, he quietly backed away.

Mo-Mo continued to hit his pipe while the other man eyed the hooded figure suspiciously. Tootie turned to the man.

"Here, take this and get the fuck outta here."

Tootie held out his open hand. In his palm was a waxy off-white rock the size of a thumbnail. Dirty fingers snatched the item from Tootie's hand in an instant, and the man dissolved into the darkness.

"Yo, Mo-Mo! Less talk, homes," Tootie said.

Mo-Mo raised his eyes over his pipe and looked at the faceless figure. He slowly lowered the pipe. "Who's that?"

"I got a job for you, man," Tootie said. "Looks to me like y'all could use some spendin money." Tootie fanned out a stack of twenty-dollar bills. "Interested, man?" he hissed.

Mo-Mo slipped the pipe and lighter into his pants pocket. He looked up and down the street, suspicious of the offer.

"Whatchu need, man?"

"Come on, I'll tell you."

Tootie walked into the alley. Mo-Mo trailed behind at a safe distance. The smell of rot and defecation in the alley was thick, and Tootie grimaced when a large rat darted across his foot. He continued on for a few steps then noticed Tre was not with them. He considered going back for him but decided to deal with Mo-Mo first.

Mo-Mo hung back while Tootie lit a cigarette. The lighter illuminated his face. Mo-Mo stopped cold. Tootie took a long drag on his cigarette and exhaled slowly, looking at the ground, then he looked up at the figure in front of him.

"Whatchu doing, muthafucker? Get yo simple ass over here so we can talk. Man, if I was fittin to do sumpthin it would have been done already, fool!"

Mo-Mo's mind was racing, but Tootie's words made sense. He slowly approached as his right hand gripped the knife in his pants pocket.

"I need someone to deliver a package. Someone who's not gonna fuck things up. I heard y'all been livin' down here and know wassup."

Mo-Mo relaxed a bit. He could use some money. When Mo-Mo stepped closer Tootie got his first good look at him, it occurred to him that the youth had aged since he last saw him. Mo-Mo's teeth looked like pegs and his eyes were dull and sunken.

"Thas it?" Mo-Mo said.

"No, that ain't all. Y'all gonna pick up a package, too, and bring it to me. But first you gonna make sure that package is right. I hear y'all capped those three niggas over on Sixty-seventh Street. That so?"

Mo-Mo nodded.

"Good! I need ya to do the same thing to these here muthafuckers if they start acting the fool. Think y'all can do that, man?"

Mo-Mo felt his confidence returning. He smiled a picket-fence smile and scratched his scaly scalp through his nappy, dusty hair.

"Yeah, Tootie. I can do that."

"All right then," Tootie said.

Brian parked in his usual spot and walked to skid row all the while searching the evening darkness for Mo-Mo, too. He walked the streets and alleys, looking into the faces of the homeless and the hopeless. Just with a different frame of mind than Tootie. He ducked into cardboard shelters and lifted lice infested blankets off sleeping figures. As he walked the fetid streets he checked all the nighttime hangouts where the living dead replaced the pigeons after dark. None of the faces he saw belonged to Mo-Mo. A grimy figure brushed past Brian, then stopped and turned back to him.

"You looking to score?"

"No, man, I'm not," Brian said. "I'm looking for a friend. His name is Mo-Mo. You know him?"

The man shook his oily mop of blond hair and eyed Brian up and down.

"Cause if you are, there is a guy over in the alley with this dude. He's holdin," the addict said. "He turned me on just to get me to leave him and this guy alone. You and me could wait for him and, you know. You look like you're pretty tough. I'll split anything we get."

The man held up a steak knife in his puffy red hand. Something keyed in Brian's mind.

"He gave you dope to split?" Brian said.

"Yeah. He wanted to be alone with the guy. They walked up that alley." He pointed to where Mo-Mo and Tootie had just gone. "If we go around the block we can jump him as he comes out of the alley onto Fourth Street."

"What did this guy look like?" Brian asked.

"Buffed up black dude with a black leather jacket. Looked like a con to me. Why you wanna know?" the man asked.

"I thought he might be the guy I'm looking for. What did the other guy look like?"

"Oh, he's a smoker. Young guy, always talks tough. Says he's a Crip from South Central and shit like that. He's just a punk. He won't cause us any problems."

Brian turned and headed toward the alley.

"Yeah. Wait for me, man! Wanna hit before we go?" the man called out.

"No," yelled Brian straining to see into the dark alley.

Tootie flipped his cigarette away then shook another out of his pack and held it out to Mo-Mo, who let go of the knife in his pocket and took it. He fished around in his pockets until he found a lighter, brought the filter to his lips, and struck a flame. As Mo-Mo held the lighter to the cigarette he felt something splash on his face. In an instant there was a flash, and then searing heat. Mo-Mo was engulfed in hellfire. He backed and stumbled as he frantically waved his arms shrieking, first in terror, then in agony. Tootie followed, feeding the flames with the contents of his squirt bottle. Mo-Mo fell into a pile of cardboard boxes that immediately burst into flame. He rolled and writhed until he inhaled a breath of gasoline vapor and intensely heated air. Then hell met Mo-Mo halfway. The mixture exploded in his mouth, raced down his throat, and into his lungs. He gurgled and kicked listlessly, then was silent and still. Tootie tossed the plastic bottle into the fire.

"Thas right, muthafucker! Stupid hurts!"

Brian made out two backlit figures about fifty yards into the alley as a burst of flame appeared. Seconds later the flame became a wailing wall of fire. Someone within the wall moved clumsily then fell. As Brian ran toward the blaze he thought he saw another person but wasn't sure. He got as close to the fire as he was able. He could make out a figure, but approaching it was out of the question as the flaming shape had fallen onto a pile of cardboard which immediately became an inferno. The alley filled with the odor of gasoline, burnt paper, and what reminded Brian of roast pork. He stood with clenched fists, helpless. His thoughts became fragmented and he lost track of time.

In the distance he could hear radios. A stream of water blasted into the flames in front of him. He looked for its source. Several feet from him a figure wearing a heavy jacket and yellow helmet leaned into a fire hose. A second figure quickly joined the man. Within seconds the area swarmed with firefighters. A sickening steam rose from the charred pile as two firefighters prodded the cardboard looking for hot spots while making an effort to avoid disturbing Mo-Mo's contorted remains. Strong hands pulled Brian to the side. Shouts and flashing lights penetrated his head but gained no purchase. His eyes remained fixed on the charred, wet body. Brian knew this was Dee's brother, he recognized the corpse's shoes as ones he had recently given Mo-Mo. More so, something deep within him identified the body that lay in front of him with its mouth agape and lips burnt off. His knowledge came from the same source that for months had shined light on things Brian could not have known. He thought of that source.

Why? Brian wondered. It never helped.

Once again, Brian had let someone down, with horrific results. Tom Jefferson had opened up to Brian and asked him to look out for his son. What would he tell him, or Dee? As with Demi Sanders, Brian saw Mo-Mo's death as his failure to do what he had always failed to do. He hadn't even been able to help his father.

He became aware that he was being spoken to before he understood the words. He snapped-to and looked into the weathered face next to his. The man was a caricature of a fireman of old. His thick hands held a small notebook and pencil. His salt-and-pepper moustache drooped beyond the corners of his mouth. The indirect lights shone on the crime scene and cast shadows into the deep creases of his face. Stenciled on the man's heavy turnouts was the word "Redd." The old leather lunger's watery blue eyes scrutinized Brian from under shaggy eyebrows.

"Did you see what happened here?" he asked.

"No," said Brian. "I just got here. It was too hot. I couldn't do anything."

Redd removed his white Captain's helmet. The tops of Redd's ears were covered in scar tissue. The fire captain shined his flashlight on Brian's crotch.

"Well at least you didn't piss your pants," Redd said. "You're gonna have to wait here, son. The arson investigators and PD are gonna want to talk to you."

"Huh? Oh, okay," Brian said.

His voice trailed off as his mind swirled, like the steam rising from the alley.

Several blocks away, Tre walked south on San Pedro Boulevard. He was passing the closed warehouses of the produce district when a line of fire trucks rumbled past, lights flashing and sirens wailing. He slipped into an alcove and watched. After he determined the coast was clear Tre continued walking. All the while he kept a close watch behind him for Tootie's car. Had he paid as much attention to what was ahead of him Tre may have seen the sleek BMW at the curb across the street.

Tootie watched like a cat. When his prey was about fifty feet away, he slipped his car into gear and rolled quietly, lights out, toward Tre. By the time Tre saw the car he was trapped. A solid brick warehouse was on one side and Tootie was closing on the other. Tre ran several steps before he heard the first shot. He felt an impact on his back and fell forward. He saw a car tire, and explosions filled his head then the roar of the BMW as it raced away. Tre lay half on the sidewalk, his left hand and leg in the gutter. In a moment of clarity, he thought, *"It's not so bad this time."* Tre felt tired, and allowed himself to drift away from the pain.

Tootie laid the revolver on the passenger seat, slowed down, and made his way to the Santa Monica Freeway. He would be home soon.

HUNTED

Brian stood at the mouth of the alley being interviewed by two LAFD arson investigators. "You guys think I torched my friend's brother and then just stood there and admired my handiwork? You have to be shitting me!"

Brian could feel something deep within letting loose, like an iceberg calving.

"Just settle down, man. No one said that," one investigator said.

The other glanced over Brian's shoulder and gave a slight nod. Brian heard the sound of a handcuff case open behind him. He spun.

"Oh, no. You're not cuffing me. I've been blamed for just about everything that happens in this city. Not this time, pal. Put those away, because you aren't putting them on me!"

The uniformed police officer stopped. "Come on, sir! This is just for your safety and ours. Let's not make this worse than it already is."

Brian could feel bodies closing in around him. Someone grabbed his right arm. The ice broke loose within Brian and created an enormous wave. He turned into the grasp, peeled the hand off him, and pivoted into his aggressor, driving his fist deep into his foe's abdomen. As the police officer crumpled to the ground, others rushed in. Brian felt a surge of anger and abandon. Nothing mattered now. He was not going to let these people decide his guilt and fate. Chief Griefwielder's face flashed into his mind. He saw himself on the bench, handcuffed, then in a jail cell.

He said aloud, "While the animals go free?"

Brian felt he'd crossed the line he had been walking his whole life. A force beyond his control now stifled the goodness that kept him from letting go. He shook off several hands and ran into the night.

The roar of a police car engine is as recognizable as the buzzing rumble of a police helicopter to anyone who has ever hidden with his heartbeat in his ears. Brian heard barking and peeked around the edge of a building. He pressed his cheek against the brick of an old building. The odor of mold and mortar filled his nostrils. The streetlights provided an amber hue through which Brian could see a K-9 handler and his four-legged partner searching two blocks away. His mind raced as police radios all around him relayed messages from the ground to the air and car-to-car. The airship's night sun flickered between the buildings like frames in an old silent movie. He looked up, saw the rusted bottom rung of a ladder. Brian jumped, and grabbed hold, pulled then swung his legs onto the steel grate of the fire escape. He got to his hands and knees then rose and made his way to the roof of the building.

He peered down onto Broadway, remembering Charlie Bender's teachings. *Cops never look up when searching.* Brian hoped his actions might even thwart the efforts of the police dog. Keeping an eye out for the airship as it made wide orbits over the search perimeter, Brian jumped from roof to roof until he reached the fire escape on his own building. He clambered down and dropped into the trash dumpster below. Brian listened for several moments then climbed out of the rank receptacle and ran to the stairs that led to his apartment. He hoped he was out of the police perimeter.

Brian opened the door and closed it behind him, breathing hard and thinking. He had not identified himself to anyone at the scene of Mo-Mo's death but knew it would not take long for the police to learn who he was and show up at his apartment. He hurriedly changed clothes, picked up his duty bag from the floor, laid it on his bed and stuffed some clothes and toiletries into the Cardura satchel. As an afterthought he dropped his two-inch revolver into the bag. He grabbed the two loops that comprised the handles of his bag, and walked down the stairs to the street. A feeling of impending doom lurked at the edge of his thoughts. He walked down the empty streets hoping he didn't look as conspicuous as he felt. Occasionally he looked over one shoulder or the other, expecting to see a police car behind him.

Soon he was standing on the corner of Sixth and Los Angeles Streets looking at a massive three-story building. The structure encompassed a city block and from its roof a spire rose high above the downtown streets. Impaled on its tip was the image of a greyhound. Directly beneath the running dog were four oval signs that each faced a different direction and all read, "BUS." Until recently the terminal had housed the Southern California Rapid Transit District and Greyhound Bus services. But SCRTD had moved out and only the struggling "dog" remained. Brian stepped into the brightly lit lobby. A few people slept slumped in chairs in the otherwise uninhabited waiting area. He reached into his pocket and produced a wad of bills. Counting the cash he held it close, like a man examining a poker hand, and kept a wary eye out. Then he cautiously approached the ticket counter, manned by a disinterested cashier with hair growing out of his ears.

"What time does the next bus leave?" he asked.

"To where?" the curmudgeon answered, obviously annoyed at being disturbed.

"New York."

He looked at his watch and then said, "Last bus left at nine-forty five, and there's nuthin headed that way until the morning. You're gonna have to wait."

"Why so long," Brian asked.

The surly little man set the book he had been reading down on the counter and said, "Cause lots of buses are cancelled due to the strike."

Reluctantly Brian purchased a ticket, then found a secluded bench and sat down. He reached into his duty bag, grabbed his pistol wrapped it in his blue windbreaker and laid the bundle on his lap. He settled back and watched the glass doors that led to the street.

Dapper Davy rolled over in bed, and lifted the receiver to his ear after the first ring.

"Hello?"

"Davy boy. Bruno Cicotti here."

Davy's eyes popped open. "Hey LT, what's up?" he asked.

The woman in bed next to him moaned lightly and rolled over. Davy looked at the mound of blankets and soft brown hair then slipped out of bed.

"Hang on, sir."

He laid the receiver on the nightstand and glanced at the clock. It was nearly midnight.

"Honey, hang up when I get downstairs."

Davy stumbled down to the kitchen and flipped on the light. He lifted the phone from the wall and called to his wife upstairs.

"Okay, I got it, honey!"

As he held the phone to his ear Davy heard a click on the other end.

"Alright, LT, I'm here," Davy said.

"I just got a call from LASO. A couple deputies scooped up Elvis Tubbs, the basketball player. He had about an ounce of high-grade cocaine in his car. Turns out he's buddies with some Crip named Andre Hicks, goes by Tootie. Seems Tootie's been a busy bee."

"Jeez, I talked with a girl who fingered him for several murders about five hours ago," Dapper Davy said.

"Did she tell you this guy killed Ray-Ray and might have Danny Lugo's gun?" Cicotti said.

Davy didn't respond, but now he was wide-awake.

"I heard you matched up some ballistics reports in which Danny's .357 was the murder weapon," Cicotti said.

Shit! Dapper Davy thought. Davy wanted to avoid the question, but knew that was not done with the man on the other end of the telephone.

"Yes, I did, sir. Sorry I didn't—"

Cicotti cut him off. "Don't worry about that. Good work, Davy boy! I knew you would stay with the Lugo case until the end. That's why I didn't give you any grief when you wanted to transfer to 77th. Now we got a name. All we need to do is put a case together. Can you get up to PAB in the morning, say about 0700?"

"Sure, boss," Dapper Davy said.

"Good! We are going to put everything on the table and see exactly what we have and where we go from here. Looks like we might be able to put this one to bed. I just got a call from the Chief. For some reason he wants me to roll on an arson downtown. Probably be an all-nighter. Sorry to wake you, but I knew you would want to get going on this. See you in the morning."

Davy heard a click and then hung his phone on the wall. He picked up the coffee pot and was pleased to find some left over from breakfast. He emptied the brew into a mug and poped it into the microwave oven. While the stale coffee warmed, Davy retrieved a manila folder from the nightstand in his bedroom. He dropped the folder onto the kitchen table. Rubing his eyes with one hand he opened the file labeled, Lugo, with his other. Dapper Davy Treats was done sleeping this night.

HERO

"So where ya off to, Bri?"

Charlie Bender plopped onto the bench where Brian slept. Brian's head rose slowly. The lobby was filled with people and sunlight filtered into the room.

Charlie glanced at the barrel of Brian's revolver peeking out from under his windbreaker.

"Thought you might be here," he said.

Charlie plucked the bus ticket out of Brian's shirt pocket and examined it.

"So y'all had enough. Goin on home. This all too tough for ya?" he asked. "Cause if it is, y'all ain't the man I thought you were, an' I owe you an apology for getting y'all into this mess."

"I guess you were wrong, Charlie."

Then Brian's pent-up feelings gushed out of him. "I'm sorry I let you down. I don't know what made you think I was up to this. I'm no hero like you. I look at these officers and wonder, how can they be so confident, so brave, know all the answers? I don't know anything, and it seems I'm worried about something most of the time. After my shooting I couldn't sleep. Seems like anyone who puts trust in me gets killed."

Brian could feel tears welling up in his eyes. He took a ragged breath and ran his forearm across his face.

"First, I've got sergeants and deputy chiefs wanting to chop my head off. Now they're trying to put Mo-Mo's murder on me. Did you see what that monster did to that boy? What the hell kind of place is this, Charlie?"

Brian hung his head. He was embarrassed to have shown such emotion in front of this man of stone.

Charlie leaned forward, put his elbows on his knees and laced his fingers together. He studied his hands for a bit then said, "What do you think a hero is, Brian? It's somebody who's in a bind and can't find any way out but to fight. His options er limited by duty, or anger, but usually it's jess plain fear that makes a feller fight agin somethin' that seems unbeatable. We usually don't do it fer any other reason than bein' ascaret--scaret a' bein' figgered yeller, or lettin' folks down, or not bein' able to look in the mirror if ya don't. Hell, most cops 'er more scaret a' that then dyin'."

He hung an arm around Brian's shoulders.

"Bravery ain't the absence a fear, Bri. It's bein scaret shitless and pushing on through anyways. Anyone that says he don't get frightened out here once in a while is either a fool or a dang liar. Fear keeps us on our toes, fills us with adrenaline, an' speeds up our thinkin'. They ain't no shame in it. Some fellers freeze out here, true, but that's cause they ain't got a plan. Y'all got a plan, I know. I put it in there myself. Y'all been makin' fear work for you since ya got here. Y'all er young, but experience builds confidence and gives you depth. I figger takes 'bout five years in this job an yer way ahead a' the curve on that. Anyway, too much confidence makes a feller sloppy an' dangerous. Most of the guys you think are so damn confident are just puttin' on the hog."

Charlie saw two police officers looking at them from the back door of the terminal. Charlie held up four fingers, which is the sign for Code-four, no assistance needed.

"Well, we gotta go face the fiddler on your little use of force las' night, pal. Remember, like it or not, y'all a hero to a whole gang a' folks, and you owe it to 'em to play the part. Folks need their heroes, Brian."

As an afterthought Charlie said, "Price and Griefwielder, they're weak sisters that run from fear, pal. That's why they hate ya. Cause y'all everything they ain't."

He stood and faced Brian then put his hands on his shoulders and looked into his eyes. "As fer folks dying, yep, that's the way it goes. Y'all a Los Angeles police officer, and people all around you are gonna die, maybe me, maybe you. We jes try an' keep the numbers tolerable. As fer y'all missin' yer beauty sleep, I'da been worried bout y'all if killing didn't make a ripple in yer pond."

Brian placed his pistol and windbreaker back into his bag and stood.

"Thanks, Charlie."

He rubbed Brian's head. "I got yer back, partner."

Charlie hesitated, then said, "…and so does Danny. Listen to 'im. Y'all been a pretty fair team so far."

THE VISITOR

The next day Fire Department Arson investigators completed their interview with Brian while Bruno Cicotti sat in. Andy Tomlinson also attended the interview and drove Brian home that afternoon. His muscle car rumbled to a stop in front of Brian's apartment.

Brian said, "Thanks for the ride. I love this car Andy."

Andy revved the engine and grinned at Brian. "Me, too, buddy, and with all the business I'm getting from you I can afford to get this baby painted," he said.

"Hope I can make payments 'cause I don't think I'm going to have a paycheck for a while. Even though the fire department decided I'm not some kind of pyromaniac I'm sure things aren't square with the department."

"Not to worry, Brian. I was just pulling your leg. I'm going to call Pap Goodings and find out where we stand with your 'Great Escape.' So just try and relax. I'll give you a call in the next day or two."

Brian climbed out of the bright street rod and gently closed the door. He bent and spoke through the open window.

"Andy, I don't..."

"Dude, I'd love to chat all day, but I heard there is a monster break in Malibu. I gotta get on home and pick up my stick. Later."

Andy popped the clutch and gassed the Camaro. Smoke boiled off the rear tires as he sped down Broadway. Brian could hear Andy going through the gears long after he was out of sight.

Brian trudged up the stairs to his apartment and flopped onto the Murphy bed. He hadn't slept much the night before and was soon fast asleep.

Brian awoke with a start. His darkened room was awash with red and amber lights. They flashed on his wall as a police car raced down Broadway, lights flashing and siren wailing.

Lying on his bed, vague memories of the night's dreams lingered. He recalled a boy, his face remained clear and familiar in Brian's mind for several seconds then became grainy and was gone.

After several minutes of trying to bring the image back he got out of bed and walked across the room to the antique floor lamp and pulled its chain. The yellow lampshade directed a soft light onto the small oak secretaire beneath it. Still in sleep's hold he rummaged through a drawer and found a pen and pad of paper. With eye-lids at half-staff he sat at the small wooden writing table and began to write. The words flowed from him, but he was detached from their content. He wrote of places he had never been, people he never knew, and feelings he didn't recall. After what seemed a long while he sat and stared at the pile of paper before him. Five pages were covered on both sides but Brian had no memory of what he'd written. He folded the pages and pushed them into an envelope, licked the glued edge, and sealed the words away. Then in large letters on the front he wrote "Danny."

Brian looked at the small window to his right and saw that the sun was rising. He drank coffee and watched the city wake. By the time the sun was up he felt invigorated and energetic despite his slow start. He pulled on his sweats and went for a run.

Afterward he clipped his nails, shaved, and took a shower. Then he shaved again. When he was finished he picked up a bottle of amber liquid with a wooden cap. He removed the cap, and sniffed the familiar fragrance, then splashed it liberally on his face and chest.

Brian examined himself in the mirror in a manner he never had before. He looked closely for errant nasal and ear hairs and combed his hair until everyone lay down. He spent a considerable amount of time selecting his clothing. He settled on the flowing emerald colored shirt and black double knit slacks he'd impulsively purchased several days before from a downtown clothier. He polished his black oxfords to a high gloss and slipped them on over the black argyle socks he'd gotten with the shirt and slacks. Then he stood in front of the bathroom mirror and admired his handiwork. His muscular neck disappeared into the soft material of his shirt and the slacks hugged his powerful thighs. He was ready, but for what?

Brian grabbed the envelope, jogged down the stairs, and walked briskly to his car. The little car leaned into him as he sat behind the wheel. He put his keys into the ignition and soon the engine was rattling along as only a vintage VW Bug could. He waved to the man who ran the parking lot and pulled onto Broadway, not really sure where he was headed but delighted at the prospect.

Forty minutes later Brian pulled to the curb in front of a well-cared for home in West Covina, a small community east of Los Angeles. Not sure of his next move, Brian glanced at his watch and saw it was only 7:30 am. He looked at the house he was parked in front of. It seemed he'd been to the little yellow house many times before, but couldn't remember when. Roses grew under a picture window which ran from one end of the house to the front door. On the other side of the door was a small high window with opaque glass that he knew to be a bathroom. Next to that, two bedroom windows filled in the front of the home. The wooden shake roof angled along the length of the house. A minivan sat parked in the driveway a cloud puffed from its exhaust pipe. Sprinklers sprayed overlapping circles of water onto the homes lush lawn. A great affection for the little house swelled within Brian.

Suddenly the front door flew open and a boy bounded down the front steps. He stopped and turned off the sprinklers. A shock of chestnut hair covered his forehead. The child stopped, looked directly at Brian, and smiled brilliantly. He looked back toward the front door at a woman, who stood staring at Brian. Instinctively Brian opened the car door and got out. He felt like a marionette being controlled by an invisible puppeteer as walked up the wet lawn toward the two. The boy was familiar in a way Brian could not comprehend. He felt a rush of affection and stooped down on one knee then asked, "Hi! Are you Danny?"

"Yes, sir, Danny Jr. You're a policeman, huh?"

"Yeah, how did you figure that?"

"My dad was a policeman, and I know lots of 'em. Like my Uncle Charlie. He said another policeman might come by and visit us."

Danny Jr. held out his hand. "Nice to meet you," he said.

Brian took the boy's slender hand in his and held it. The boy moved toward Brian and embraced him around the neck with his other arm. They held one another for a long moment. Then Brian put his hand on the boy's head and tousled his thick silky hair.

Danny broke free and took a step back. "Do you like the

Dodgers?"

"Ah, yeah, sure I do!" Brian answered.

"Could you and me go to Dodger stadium and see a game?"

The woman, had not moved an inch since Brian approached her son. Her dark, liquid eyes were fixed on him.

"Sure, partner, if it's okay with your mom." Brian looked up at her.

Catalina Lugo fussed with the thick black hair that flowed down her shoulders.

"First you go to school, mijo, then we'll talk about the Dodgers."

Danny Jr. hugged Brian again then started toward the minivan. He opened the side door and was greeted by a troop of children who along with the mini-van's driver had watched the entire event with interest.

He turned and yelled, "See ya later! Hey, what's your name?"

"Brian. My name's Brian."

"See ya, Brian!"

The boy pulled the sliding door shut and the woman behind the wheel backed down the drive and headed down the street. Brian watched until the van drove out of sight.

Catalina held the front door open.

"Would you like to come in, Brian?" she asked.

He moved toward the door. As he passed her he breathed in her scent, and she his. He took several steps into the hallway, drew the envelope from his back pocket, and held it out to her.

"I know it sounds crazy. I wrote this for your son but I don't know what it says."

She took it from his hand, allowing her fingers to run along his. She broke the seal on the envelope and withdrew the letter. Brian watched her eyes follow the lines as she read the first page. She walked into the living room and sat in a chair next to a coffee table. The photo of a man Brian recognized as Danny Lugo was on the table. Brian watched as she read the entire letter. When done she laid the papers next to the photograph, then turned and looked in Brian's direction. She seemed to be looking through him. Her lips parted and she moistened them with the tip of her tongue, then closed her eyes tightly and opened them. Through her tears she saw a handsome young man before her—her man. He had not changed since the day he'd walked out of Catalina's life ten years ago.

"I'm sorry. I don't even know why I'm here…"

Catalina stood and stepped toward him then placed a fingertip on his lips. He could smell her skin and breath. Brian felt another presence in the room.

"Shhh. No se nada. I want to speak with my husband."

Catalina put her fingers lightly on Brian's forehead and drew them downward. Brian's eyes closed. She slipped her arms around his neck and drew Brian to her breast.

Brian heard a whisper in his ear.

"Mi corazon."

He didn't know how much time passed before he opened his eyes. When he did he was seated on a small couch in a bedroom that smelled of flowers. Across the room in a large bed, two people made love. The depth of passion he witnessed mesmerized him. The man's hands slid over the woman's body slowly, as if he were memorizing every inch of her. Brian became aware of his voyeurism and looked away, then fell into a deep sleep.

"Wake up Brian! You have to go! My son will be home from school soon."

Brian awoke with a start. His face was pressed into a soft down pillow that smelled of lilac. He rolled onto his back in time to see a naked female form disappear into the bathroom. Brian was naked also, and covered with the same scent he'd smelled when he'd passed so close to Catalina. Frantically he donned his clothes. The bathroom door opened and Catalina appeared, radiant in a full-length dressing gown. He stood in the center of the bedroom, searching for an explanation.

She walked to Brian and kissed him lightly on the cheek.

"Thank you for the letter and for bringing Danny to me one last time."

She pushed lightly on his chest. Brian turned and showed himself to the door.

DISHEVELED

B rian answered the knock on his front door and was surprised to see Dee standing there. They had not spoken at Mo-Mo's funeral and he assumed Dee felt Brian bore some responsibility for his brother's death.

This was a day for surprises. Earlier Brian had a visit from Dapper Davy Treats. The detective had asked him a battery of questions about Dee and their relationship. He seemed especially interested in whether Dee had ever mentioned Danny Lugo. He showed Brian a photograph he had taken ten years ago at Lugo's funeral. It depicted a young man standing on a hill above the grave site. He wore a hooded jacket and the photo was of poor quality but the man with the blue rag hanging from his back pocket was clearly Dimetre Wallace. At the end of his interrogation Davy gave no explanation for his questions. The visit left Brian feeling disheveled inside and out.

Now two hours later here stood Dee. Brian took a step back bringing the door with him. Dee followed the door and stepped into the small apartment.

"Dee I..."

Dee held up his hand. "Wait Brian I have something to say. I never mentioned him before but I used to know a policeman named Danny Lugo. He was real good to me and I looked at him like a father. He was the one who taught me to box and helped me get out of gangs. You reminded me of him from when I first met you." The two men found seats and Dee continued. "Theres this dude named Tootie. We wern't tight friends we just kicked it together sometime, us both being from the hood an all."

The young man hesitated and looked at Brian for some sign of understanding. Getting none he continued. "One night Tootie and I were in Kim's Market trying to lift some beer when these dudes busted into the store waiving guns and yelling. I'm telling you these brothers were crazy… I thought they were gonna kill us all. Then the cops came in and the shooting started. I ducked down by the coolers until it got quiet; you could smell the gun smoke and blood. I walked up to the front of the store and saw it was Danny and another officer, I think his name was Bender. They're all shot up but still alive and two other guys, the robbers I guess, were dead on the floor. Then Bender whose face was all covered in blood got up and ran out of the store."

Dee stopped and reflected. Then in a solemn tone said, "Tootie was next to me and he just walked over to Danny picked up his gun and held it to Danny's face." Tears welled up in Dee's eyes. "I just stood there I wanted to run or yell but I couldn't move. Just before Dee pulled the trigger Danny looked at me." Dee wiped the tears from his face, swallowed and continued. "Then Tootie pointed the gun at Mr. Kim and told him he would kill his family if he said anything. Then we boned out the back door."

Dee met Brian's steady stare. "I let Tootie kill Danny and I think God punished me by letting him kill Mo. But I'm not letting that muthafucker kill you man." Dee hesitated then said, "Tootie's out for you Brian. He's still got Danny's gun and he's fit'in to use it on you.

About fifteen miles away, Tootie sat in his large leather chair and looked out his apartment window. The ocean breeze caused the row of palm trees that lined the walkway to the marina to sway. He didn't notice. He lit a cigarette, sucked the menthol smoke deep into his lungs, and held it for a moment. He had always been very careful not to leave a trail to his door. Now it seemed that all roads led to him. He forced his thoughts to slow as he sipped a glass of cognac and smoked. First the call from Cindi's pimp; telling him she'd been pinched on Sunset Boulevard and had not been seen since. Then last night he'd seen on television that Elvis Tubbs had been arrested. Tootie stood and paced the room and wondered. Now that damn wise guy Fazio was pressing him to pay up the money he owed.

"Shit!" he said, to no one in particular.

Tootie's thoughts were interrupted by a knock on the door. He picked up the revolver from the coffee table and returned to the window. No police cars, so he moved to the door and looked through the peephole. He couldn't make out who was on the other side of the door, but there was more than one person, and they were white men. Standing away from the door, Tootie brought the long barrel of the pistol up.

"Uh huh?"

"Toot? Dat you?" came the familiar voice.

Tootie almost wished it were the police. He tucked the gun into his waistband and opened the door. Beppe Fazio stepped into the room, followed by his bodyguard, Tony. Beppe took the measure of Tootie while Tony moved to the other side of the room and stood with his arms folded across his chest.

"What's going on, man? You look like hell," Beppe said.

"I'm all right, man."

"Sit, Toot. We gotta talk. You got the dough?"

He sat on the couch, and Tootie sat in the chair near the window where he could best watch both men.

"Nah, man. I did, but right now I'm short," Tootie said. "I got some shit goin' on and need to keep some bread handy."

"You're not planning on goin' on da lam, are you?" Beppe asked. He smiled and glanced at Tony who didn't smile.

"Please, man. You know me better than that," Tootie said trying to sound convincing.

"Maybe we can work something out," Beppe said. "You ever hear of a cop named Brian O'Callahan?"

Tootie's heart skipped a beat. "Yeah. He work Seventy-seventh."

"Yeah, and he's pals with your homeboy," Beppe said. "That boxer Dimetre Walker. Me and O'Callahan had business back east, and now he's trying to get cute wit me."

Tootie didn't say a word; he just listened.

"You take care of O'Callahan for me an' I'll get you some more time." Beppe twisted his pinky ring.

This was too good, just another reason Officer O'Callahan had to die.

NOT PLANNING ON ARRESTING ANYONE

"This guy Tootie Hicks is a damn crime wave," Nick Stupin said.

Dapper Davy, Preacher Pruitt, and Nick were sitting around Captain Sullivan's desk rehashing what Brian had reported minutes after Dee left his apartment. Abe Palmer was perched behind the men on a chair rocked back on two legs against the dark paneled wall. A toothpick twitched up and down between his teeth as he listened. Captain Sullivan was behind his desk with arms folded across his chest.

Consulting his notes, Preacher said, "Let's see. Andre "Tootie" Hicks, twenty-eight years old. Did time for robbery, got arrests for just about anything you can imagine. Guy's got a twenty page rap sheet and he's been in jail or prison for most of his adult life."

Dapper Davy shook his head and clucked. "It's nice to see the system works, Preach."

Davy Treats scooted closer to Captain Sullivan's desk and opened a manila folder. "Looks like he's good for the Demi Sanders, Raymond Dubois, and Maurice Jefferson murders for sure. Culver City looking at him for a murder that took place on the West Side. Some dope dealer named Vernell 'V-Roc' White got his brains blown out with a .357-mag in the parking lot of some fried chicken joint off Sepulveda. Turns out he was Demi Sanders' boyfriend."

"Dinah's Fried Chicken? That's some good yard bird there," Preacher said.

The conversation digressed as Davy, Preacher, and Nick each made their pitch for the best fried chicken in the city. Abe abstained.

"Gentlemen, if we can move on," Captain Sullivan said.

The room quieted down.

"And let's not forget according to O'Callahan he killed Danny Lugo," Dapper Davy said.

No one responded directly but a choirs of murmurs rolled through the room.

"The question is, which caper do we arrest him for?" Davy asked. "I don't want to lose anything on statute once we pick him up."

"Well, I'd say our strongest case is the Jefferson arson-murder and the Trevon Williams shooting," Nick Stupin said. "What did Bruno say, Davy?"

"He felt the Trevon Williams shooting would be the one to hang on him initially. That case is solid, and I have enough to file today on that one."

"Yeah, a positive identification by the victim. I can't believe that youngster lived through three .357 rounds to the back," Preacher said.

"Have we got a detail on Williams?" Sullivan asked.

"Yes, sir," Abe piped in. "My guys guarded Tre at California Hospital but since he's been moved to the county medical center, the sheriffs have a man with him twenty-four seven."

"Good, we don't want another fucking Ray-Ray on our hands," Sullivan said.

"What did Cicotti say about the Lugo case?" Nick Stupin said.

"Cicotti's guys are going to blow the dust off the Lugo case and do some legwork on it. He said until we get the gun we really don't have anything but hearsay and circumstantial evidence."

"And an eye witness." Davy said.

"What about these other shootings where Danny's gun was used?" Captain Sullivan asked.

"Well, I hear Deputy Chief Griefwielder would like to put those on Brian O'Callahan," Dapper Davy said.

The room broke out in laughter.

"Any word on O'Callahan, boss?" Davy said.

The smile melted from his face and Captain Sullivan said, "It's a damn mess, Davy boy."

Everyone sat quietly in thought for a moment. Despite the talk of recent shootings and murders, all eyes were on the prize-closure on the murder of one of their own. Brian O'Callahan played a big part in that.

"Let's just pick up this Andre Hicks, or Tootie, or whatever he's callin' himself," Sullivan said. "Then we can worry about

O'Callahan. Davy, you and Abraham get together and figure out a game plan with Abe's crew."

Dapper Davy and Abe Palmer exchanged looks.

"Speaking of your unit, Abe," Davy said to him, "good job by Magana on that Elvis Tubbs clue. How the hell did he get the skinny on that one?"

Abe Palmer said, "Well, it seems Manny worked up a pretty good source of information in the manager of the apartment building where Tubbs and Hicks live. The manager overheard a conversation between these two jokers and called Manny, who called his contact at West Hollywood Sheriff's station."

"Damn fine police work there, Abraham," Sullivan said. "Make sure Magana gets a commendation when this thing is over."

"Your boy have a lot of contacts over in West Hollywood, Abe?" Dapper Davy asked.

Abe raised his eyebrows and hunched his shoulders. "Don't know what to tell ya, Davy. It's a new world, and Manny's one top cop."

"Speaking of O'Callahan," Captain Sullivan glanced at his watch, "I have a five o'clock meeting with him, fellas, so if that's all... Fine job, let's keep it up. Oh, Abraham, since Scooter Kellerman has transferred to Air Support Division, go ahead and find a replacement for him."

The men stood and as they trooped through the door of his office Sullivan shouted, "Lads, the best fried chicken is Popeye's."

Amid the laughter coming from the outer office, Preacher stuck his head back into Sullivan's workroom.

"And so it was written," he said.

Dapper Davy stepped into the hallway looked and saw Brian talking with Leo and Charlie

"Hello, Brian! You here to punch out the skipper? I got a list o' guys I need knocked out if you're takin' reservations."

"Nah, he's here ta punch y'all out, asshole," Charlie said. "But we're gonna wait. Abe says they got a gal in his unit that don't mind handling the light work."

Abe Palmer walked in and joined the group. "That would be Diane Erickson. I'll bet she could, too," Abe said. "She's coming back soon; I'll send her over to your office Davy."

Davy smoothed his gray wool coat. "Whoever gets the mission, tell them not in the face. I'm just too damn pretty."

Abe scoffed and said, "Yeah, pretty fuckin' ugly."

"You know, Abe, I would kick your ass, but lucky for you I got on a new tie."

Dapper Davy adjusted the knot on his steel-blue neckwear.

Palmer shook his head in mock disgust as everyone else had a good laugh.

Davy's face became serious. "Charlie, you got a minute?" he said.

"Bri, tell the boss I'll be right in." Charlie said. "I gotta see what Numbnuts wants."

He followed Dapper Davy through the doorway.

Leo turned to Brian. "How ya doin, kid? Don't let this shit get you down. Like they say, it's all in twenty, and twenty years is a long time."

"I'm doing good sir, but if my first two years on the department are any indication of the next eighteen maybe it's a good idea for them to just go ahead and fire me." Brian managed a forlorn smile and looked at the clock on the wall above Leo's head. "I better get over to the Captain's office. Guess he's gonna want my badge and gun. Excuse me, sarge."

The two veteran sergeants watched Brian walk through the door and across the hall to the commanding officer's office.

"Figure he's gonna get relieved of duty because he popped that Central cop one? Hell, in the ol' days that's how we settled things. Coupla guys got in a beef, they went out into the parking lot and punched it out," Abe said.

"Yeah, well, it ain't the ol' days, Abe," Leo said. "Buddy, those days are long gone."

Brian stood in front of Rita Jones's desk, waiting for her to finish her personal phone call. She glanced up at him, then pointed a bright red acrylic fingernail at a chair against the wall. Brian sat. Several minutes later Rita's squawk-box buzzed.

She said into the phone, "Oh, no, you didn't! Mmm-huh... Hold on, girl."

Rita punched the hold button with the eraser end of her pencil, then the intercom button. "Yes, sir?" Yes, he is. Yes, sir."

She looked at Brian solemnly, and then indicated that the captain was ready for him with a jerk of her head toward the door of his office. He felt her eyes on him and headed to the door like a condemned man to his executioner.

"Good luck."

Brian said, "Everybody seems to be saying that to me." He knocked on the door.

"Come on in, Brian," said the familiar voice.

Brian walked in and sat without being asked, head up, back straight, hands resting in his lap. His eyes focused on his commanding officer's face. Captain Sullivan rustled several papers on the desk in front of him. He looked at Brian then let his eyes fall back onto his paperwork.

"Are you well, son?" he asked.

Out of nowhere Brian felt a calm come over him. He became focused and was ready for whatever occurred. He was glad to be getting things settled, regardless of the circumstances. His father had often told him, *You only worry about a fight until the first punch is thrown.* Sullivan was getting ready to throw the first punch, and Brian looked forward to it.

"I'm well, sir. Thank you," he said.

Sullivan looked up and said, "Are you, now? Well, I think if I found myself in the fix you're in I would not be feeling so fit. What were you thinking punching a police officer?"

"My guess is he was thinking the world was falling down around 'im, and he ain't got no backup."

Captain Sullivan spun in his chair to see a scarred and fierce face. Charlie took two strides into the room.

"I'll tell you something else, sir. I think I first heard this from y'all. 'Either write a guy a ticket or chew him out. Never do both.' Ain't we here for you to take Bri's badge, gun, and ID, skipper?"

Sullivan averted his eyes.

"Well then, why're ya yanking his tail, too? You know this here's pure bullshit. Do what the department says you have to do. But keep in mind what this here boy's been through, sir." He glanced at Brian then added, "An I just heard he provided some real important information on my old partners murder."

Brian stiffened.

"You should be lick'n his boots instead of takin his gun."

"You're out of line, Officer Bender!" Sullivan said.

He took a moment and regained his composure. Sullivan wasn't sure why he had scolded O'Callahan. What Charlie said was true. More importantly, Sullivan had witnessed that look on Charlie Bender's face before. He had no wish to be downrange of it.

"Um, would you... Charlie, please sit down. Let's get this damned thing over with," he said.

Charlie pulled a wooden chair next to Brian's and sat. He reminded Sullivan of a German shepherd watchdog. The captain pushed a document in front of Brian.

"Officer O'Callahan, I'm relieving you of duty. I'm ordering you to surrender your department-issue firearm, badge, and identification at this time. I'm sorry, son, but my hands are tied. I'll do whatever I can for you."

Brian picked up a pen and signed the document, set it down, and locked eyes with his captain. "Sir, I appreciate your kind words. This was my own doing and I'm willing to pay the piper. I screwed up and let down you and all the people backing me up. For that I am sorry."

He stood, removed his badge from his belt and his police identification from his wallet, and set them on the document. He drew his revolver, opened the cylinder and showed the Captain the gun was unloaded. He laid the pistol directly in front of Sullivan.

"I have to remind you now that you have no police powers of arrest and are not licensed to carry a concealed firearm, until such time that you are reinstated."

The young man's face was stone. "I don't plan on arresting anyone tonight, sir."

Kevin Sullivan's memory was jogged. Brian O'Callahan had the same look on his face that Sullivan had seen as a boy on the faces of IRA members who shared meals with his family during visits to Ireland. Those faces showed not fear but resolve, and a numbed sense of right and wrong.

"Don't be going off like you're armed with the sword of righteousness now: Let this thing lay, Brian. It will work out, it always does," Sullivan said.

Brian's face was a mask of innocence. "Sword of righteousness sir?"

Charlie stood next to his protégé. "That it, sir?" Charlie said.

"That will be all, gentlemen."

Charlie and Brian filed out of the room as Sullivan watched, overcome with a vision of the past. Ten years ago, when Kevin Sullivan was watch commander, Charlie Bender and Danny Lugo had stood in front of his desk.

Guys, we're being waylaid by these liquor store bandits. Show your car unavailable for calls and find these hooligans, Sullivan remembered saying.

Danny Lugo smiled broadly. Charlie stood at his side.

We'll find them, but we don't plan on arresting anyone tonight, sir, Danny said.

WASSUP

It was six pm when Tootie pulled his BMW into the old one-car garage, then closed and padlocked the door. He would not be driving that car for a while. He walked up the stairs to the back porch. A stout woman in her early fifties held the iron mesh security door open for him. Tootie turned sideways in order to get both his suitcases through the doorway.

"Thanks, Momma," he said.

"You welcome, baby. Take those bags back into yo old bedroom now. I got the room all made up. I'm so pleased you gonna be home fo a while. I'll cook up a real nice meal to celebrate."

Tootie could smell the ham and green beans as soon as he walked in the door. He knew that would come with red-eye gravy and mashed potatoes, too. The odor took him back to his childhood.

"Smells good! You didn't have to go through all this trouble," Tootie called from the back bedroom.

He looked around the room. It had not changed much since he was a boy. The bed he and his brother slept in was in the same corner. Even the same pictures were on the walls. The room had long been Tootie's base of operations. Now it was again. It seemed much smaller than when he was a boy, but he had no plans to stay there for long.

He heard his mother's call, "Andre, come on and eat now."

Forty minutes later Tootie pushed himself away from the dinner table. He could not remember eating so satisfying a meal.

"That was good, Momma," he said. "I'm fittin to go see some people, so don't wait up for me."

"Thank you, baby. We gonna have lotsa nice meals now that you home," Miss Hicks said as she cleared the table. In the kitchen she wiped her hands on her apron and watched her son walk to his bedroom. A moment later he reappeared, adjusting the wooden grips of the revolver in his waistband. Lucille Hicks was long past telling her son what to do, but her heart ached when she saw him carrying a gun. She closed her eyes and said a short prayer. Just as she finished she heard the steel security door slam shut. She stared at the door, trying not to imagine what her last son was up to.

Tootie stuck to side streets as he made his way to the old neighborhood. In doing so he was less likely to run into the police or a carload of gangsters wearing red. He jogged across Vermont Ave at 79th Street and turned into the nearest east-west alley. At Hoover Street he saw several young men standing around a large portable radio known as a ghetto blaster. He watched the group for a moment, then whistled.

Someone said, "There go Tootie now."

The men were really not much more than boys. They ranged in age from thirteen to twenty-four. One was tall, one was short, and the rest fit in between. What they all had in common was that they wore dark clothes and each had a blue bandana prominently displayed on his person. In a manner they were all brothers in uniform. One of the group broke off and approached Tootie.

"Wassup, Toot?"

Tootie shook hands with the light-skinned youngster. His brown hair was braided in rows that ran from the front to the back of his head. At the end of each "corn row" was a small blue clip. The right side of the boy's face was slightly swollen and his eye drooped above a fresh scar that ran in the depression where his cheekbone should have been. He was of average height and solidly built, but carried himself in a manner that indicated he was top dog in the group.

"Sup, Tip? Who these muthafuckers?" Tootie nodded toward the others.

"Oh, man, those my boys," Q-Tip said with his teeth clenched.

He pointed at a youngster who looked vaguely familiar to Tootie.

"That there my little cousin, called Burn Rubber," he said.

As the two spoke, an old Chevrolet Impala cruised north on Hoover with three male occupants. Conversation stopped, and all attention focused on the car. The group began to spread out. The passenger in the front seat held his arm out the window. His fingers were contorted into a gang sign. Two of the group standing near Tootie held up their hands and "threw up" the same sign. The car sped off and a round of bravado circulated through the group, each member asserting what he would have done had the car been full of Bloods, or "Slobs," as Crips referred to them. Tootie watched the car turn onto 80th Street, then directed his attention back to Q-Tip.

"How's where O'Callahan socked you up?" Tootie asked.

Q-Tip gingerly touched his cheek. "It's all right, my jaws still wired shut."

"Wassup wif y'alls case?" Tootie asked.

Oh, man, I got a D.A. reject on the shooting and time served on the strap, they didn't have shit on me," Q-Tip answered.

"I want y'all to find out everything you can about O'Callahan," Tootie said. "What he drive, what time he work, who he kicks it with, when he's in da hood. Anything you find out is good. Page this number as soon as you got sumpthin for me. An' nigger, stay by the phone and don't even mention my name in any of this shit."

"Sure, it's cool, man. You know me."

"All right then," Tootie said.

They performed an intricate handshake or "dap," then separated. Q-Tip walked back to the band and was immediately handed a bottle wrapped in a brown paper bag. He took a long draw on it, then looked behind him. Tootie was gone.

Tootie walked along the alley until he came to 81st Street, then stepped onto the sidewalk and entered Mr. Kim's liquor store. A small bell rang above the door and Kim looked up from behind the counter. His eyes followed Tootie as he walked around the store looking at his various snack options. Soon Tootie approached the register and dropped a handful of Slim Jims on the counter and set a quart bottle of red soda down next to them.

"Gimme two packs of Newports and a pint of vodka, man," said Tootie.

Mr. Kim glanced at his mother, who immediately stood and slipped behind a curtain that led to a small storeroom. He kept his eyes down while he gathered and bagged Tootie's purchases. Tootie had not been in the store for years, but they remembered one another. After completing his purchase Tootie meandered to the doorway, then stopped and turned around. As he expected, Kim's eyes were on him. A fierce expression overtook Tootie's face as he stood in the doorway. In a show of ghetto swagger, he held his arms

347

at a forty-five degree angle from his body. Clutching the paper sack in one hand and making a gang sign with the other, he challenged the storekeeper. "Wassup, fool?" he challenged. "Don't you be looking at me like I owe you money, muthafucker!"

Kim lowered his eyes.

"Thas right, punk ass bitch!" Tootie snarled. He kicked the partially open screen door so hard it slammed against the building, and walked in the dim light to the adjacent parking lot. He strolled up to a stripped car that was sitting on blocks and set his brown paper sack on the roof of what once was an automobile, took out the red soda, and poured a third of it onto the gravel and broken asphalt. Then he emptied the vodka into the soda bottle and took a drink of his concoction. The pager in his pocket began to vibrate; he retrieved it and read the phone number. Tootie gulped from his bottle as he walked to the public phone in front of the store, dropped in a coin and dialed the number and waited. On the second ring a young woman's voice answered.

"This Shawndra? Hey girl, whatchu got for me? Uh huh, I'm at Kim's liquor store on Hoover. Yeah, all right then."

MUZZLE FLASHES

Charlie held the door open and looked into the dimly lit station parking lot. Many of the lights had burned out some years ago. He smiled at the mass of plumbing situated just outside the station's back door. Nothing ever changed here, except that more pipes and valves were added onto the archaic air-conditioning system that was only able to cool the air in the winter. He thought of what Dapper Davy had just shared with him and whispered under his breath, "We're getting there, Danny."

"You need anything, Bri?" he asked as Brian followed him out the door.

"No thanks, I'm good Charlie and thanks for standing up for me with the captain. I hope it doesn't cause you any grief."

"Nah. Kevin an I go way back. I got too much on 'im. He's a street copper at heart, jes got a little excited, so I poured some spring water in his britches, thas all. You woulda done the same for me."

Brian took a deep breath, "Charlie I'm sorry I didn't tell you about...um the shooting with you and Danny. I didn't know how to tell you."

"Bri you know there always was a hole in my memory that night. You don't know how much y'all have done to fill it. Don't fret about it."

Inside the station Shawndra walked to her desk, opened the top drawer, grabbed a beaded pouch and pulled a cigarette from it. She placed the smoke between her lips as she walked to the back door and squeezed past Charlie, leaving a flowery trail of perfume behind.

"Excuse me, Shawndra," he said.

She ignored his remark and continued out the door. As she passed Brian he scrutinized her, then looked back at Charlie.

"I gotta get going, Charlie." Brian patted the bulge under his shirt in the small of his back. "And thanks for this."

Brian turned on his heel, jogged down the walk after Shawndra and caught up with her as she stood next to her Corolla, lighting a cigarette.

Charlie watched Brian and rubbed the scar on the side of his face.

"Can you spare a minute?" Brian asked.

"Yeah, but hurry up," she snapped, holding the smoke between her bright red lips.

"Can we sit?" he asked, indicating her little red Toyota.

Shawndra studied his face and decided he looked different but she couldn't put her finger on how. It seemed his features had softened and his eyes possessed a depth that drew her gaze. She had always found Brian handsome but now she felt a strong attraction to him as he stood smiling at her. She felt giddy when she said, "Alright," then opened the driver's side door and wiggled into the seat. She reached across the car and unlocked the other door.

As soon as he was seated in her car the scent of Brian's cologne became pleasantly noticeable. Without thinking, she inhaled the fragrance deeply and felt a stirring between her legs.

Brian's face was filtered by shadow as he turned in the seat and leaned slightly toward her. "I don't know how to say this, but I've been watching you and, lately, you've been on my mind a lot."

She placed her cigarette in the ashtray. "Oh?" was all she could manage. She looked away and felt herself blush.

"Yes," he breathed into her ear.

Shawndra could feel his whisper on her cheek. She turned toward him, his lips were inches from hers. She parted her lips, closed her eyes and leaned toward him. At the touching of their skin a slight moan escaped from within her. The soft borders of his mouth moved with hers and the moment hung in time. Her tongue moved to his lips and slipped into his mouth.

Suddenly his lips hardened and became dry. She pulled away and looked at Brian. His handsome face slowly collapsed into itself. The luminosity of his eyes dulled. His right eyeball deflated and oozed bloody liquid, which ran down his cheek. A gaping hole opened above the eye and caused the other to peer out at an unnatural angle. Bones cracked and his face lost symmetry. His jaw dropped slightly agape and pieces of scalp slipped from the jagged hole that was once the back of his head. A gag caught in Shawndra's throat as she inhaled the stench of putrefied flesh and stared into the ruined face inches from her own.

"Like I said, Ive been watching you and I know about Tootie," he murmured.

Shawndra closed her eyes in absolute terror and flattened her back against the car door. Unable to help herself, she stole a peek at the frightening creature he seemed to have become but, to her amazement, it was gone and Brian O'Callahan was once again gazing at her.

"What's wrong?" he asked.

"You changed. You were a monster," she said.

"We all change, Shawndra, and sometimes we do monstrous things that get others killed. People can betray our trust, then rationalize their behavior in order to live with themselves. If they are found out, the cost can be dear." He stopped and lightly touched her cheek. "And you are found out."

As Brian spoke she wasn't sure who he was. She glimpsed the demon along the contours of his face. The horrific image never showed itself again but she knew it lingered just beneath his skin.

"I don't know why you've been helping him, but as of right now you are going to stop. Otherwise, I'll expose you. Now, where's Tootie?"

Her heart was pounding. "He's over at Kim's store waiting for me. Please don't tell him," she groaned.

"No, I won't tell anyone anything. You just be a good girl, okay?"

Her nod was nearly imperceptible. Brian got out of the car, slammed the door and strode across the parking lot toward 76th Street, leaving Shawndra with mascara tracks running down her cheeks.

Brian crossed Broadway and headed west on 76th Street. He passed Burn Rubber, who was talking on the payphone at the corner.

"He jes walk past me, Tootie. He goin' toward Figueroa. No, he by his self."

About nine blocks away from Brian, Tootie hung up the phone then dropped another dime into the slot and punched in Q-Tip's telephone number. He answered on the second ring.

Tootie didn't waste any time with niceties. "This you, Tip? Look here, man, get yo ass down here to Kim's and bring yer shit. It's fittin to go down, cuz, so hurry yo ass."

Tootie dropped the handset and let it dangle, then returned to the south side of Kim's, drinking from the red soda bottle as he walked. *Thas right, O'Callahan. Make this easy for me,* he thought.

He put the bottle to his lips and lifted it until it poured straight down his throat. It popped as he broke the vacuum caused by sucking out the last drop. He tossed the empty into the parking lot and waited.

Q-Tip arrived a few minutes later, dressed in dark clothing and a stocking cap. His eyes searched Tootie's for a measure of the situation. Tootie lit a marijuana cigarette and handed it to Q-Tip. The two stood in the shadow of Kim's liquor store, sharing the joint.

"You strapped?" Tootie said.

Q-Tip lifted his jacket and revealed the stock of a semi-automatic pistol. Tootie nodded and looked up Hoover. He could make out Burn Rubber several blocks north of him on a bicycle, weaving slowly down the street toward Kim's. At the same distance he saw another person walking toward him on the west sidewalk. Tootie knew it was O'Callahan.

"Here he come, man," Tootie said. "Get round behind 'em and stitch his ass up when he get past the field. Ima be on this side so when he runs it's gonna run right into this." Tootie pulled the Python from his waistband and held it in front of him at eye level. "This here Colt's fittin' to kill another po-lice man."

Q-Tip gazed at the gleaming piece of blued steel. A chill ran down his spine, and then settled in his gut as dread. For a moment he considered trying to dissuade Tootie from his plan.

Tootie saw a shadow cross over the teens face. He took a step toward Q-Tip and locked eyes with him.

"You ain't thinking bout punkin out on me are ya?" Tootie snarled.

The boy's doubt succumed to the more immediate threat standing before him. Q-Tip summoned all the bravado he could muster, pulled the pistol from his waist band, and said, "Don't worry about me."

Q-Tip turned, and jogged off. Tootie's eyes followed the dark figure until it faded into the shadows. Satisfied, Tootie set a course toward a tree that loomed over the sidewalk two blocks south of his intended victim.

As he trudged past the Hoover Street Gym the burning in Brian's stomach was accompanied by an ache in his lower back. He considered stopping, but an invisible hand on his back urged him forward.

Up to this point Brian had tracked Burn Rubber's pace by the squeak emitted with each rotation of his bike's peddles. Once past the gym, Brian glanced over his left shoulder to affirm that the kid was still across the street and following at a car's length.

As he crossed the mouth of an alley Brian saw movement in the corner of his eye. His head spun toward the alley while his hand crept to the small of his back. Brian was relieved to see a mongrel dog, a grease-stained fast-food bag in his mouth, trot out of the shadows. A troupe of mismatched mutts followed the dog at a safe distance, each with his eyes on the prize. As quick as they appeared the caravan of "ghetto elk" crossed the street and vanished into the dark.

In an attempt to settle himself Brian stopped, closed his eyes, and took a deep breath. He heard the bike squeal to a stop behind him as he exhaled. Brian opened his eyes then continued down the sidewalk as fast as he could without changing gait. Passing a vacant lot he became aware of another presence. Someone stood smoking a cigarette in the field about thirty yards to Brian's right.

Q-Tip's eyes followed Brian as he passed. The teen took another drag from his cigarette; in doing so his mending bones produced a wave of pain that radiated across his face. He grimaced as he exhaled a stream of smoke. Q-Tip let the semi-automatic hang at his side and summoned his courage. "O'Callahan, now it's my turn, muthafucker," he murmured.

Brian's pulse pounded in his ears as he considered his options. *I can run and take cover across the street, or just turn back and confront these guys.* He stole a look back and saw Burn Rubber had fallen off but the figure he now recognized as Q-Tip was on the sidewalk and closing. Brian's sense of danger was raging while his eyes scanned his surroundings for cover or concealment. A car was parked at the curb several hundred feet down the street; *too far.* He caught sight of a slightly askew wooden fence that ran perpendicular to the sidewalk, several yards ahead on his right; it was all he had. He looked back in time to see Q-Tip with his pistol raised and pointed at him. Brian broke into a run but only took two strides before he heard the report of Q-Tip's pistol and felt a searing pain in his back. Brian stopped and spun while drawing Charlie's .45-caliber pistol from his rear waistband. Brian found Q-Tip in his front sight and pressed the trigger; just as his opponent did the same. Both combatants were momentarily illuminated in yellow and orange. A fraction of a second hung suspended in time as the two men looked into each others eyes. Brian turned, covered the remaining distance to the fence, and threw himself behind it. Q-Tip ran toward him hoping to get lucky by shooting into the fence. Wood splinters rained down on Brian, who lay flat on the ground. His adrenalin-charged senses amplified Q-Tip's footfalls which ceased just north of the fence. Brian rolled onto his back and waited.

Brian heard shuffling on the other side of the fence then saw the muzzle of Q-Tip's pistol emerge. Brian sat up raised the .45 and took aim where he believed Q-Tip's head would follow. Just as he peeked around the fence, the gangster was backlit by the lights of a passing automobile, Brian pressed off two shots in rapid succession. The first round tore through Q-Tip's neck, pierced his carotid artery and left a fist-sized exit hole. The second went through his second cervical vertebra, splintered it, and severed his spinal cord. Q-Tip dropped to the sidewalk like a trash bag full of Jell-O. He gurgled for a moment, and then lay wide-eyed, his lips opening and closing. Still on the ground, Brian looked at the dying youngster and was reminded of a fish he'd once seen gasping for oxygen on a dock.

Just before Brian and Q-Tip engaged, Tootie took cover behind the shady contour of the avocado tree next to the wooden fence where Brian lay. From there he witnessed Q-Tip's demise and Brian's position. Tootie aimed then jerked the trigger twice. Both shots missed.

After Tootie fired, Brian rolled onto his stomach and faced his adversary. He saw a shadowy figure next to the tree and triggered his pistol three times. The bullets slammed harmlessly into the tree. Tootie remained motionless until Brian stopped firing, then stepped out from cover, and fired two quick shots. Tootie got lucky; his second round smashed into Brian's pistol and ripped it from his grasp. Distant sirens could be heard while Brian scrambled on hands and knees in search of his gun.

Tootie seized the opportunity and charged forward, shooting and shouting, "O'Callahan! Wassup?"

After several steps Tootie stood over Brian who looked up into the barrel of the Colt. *It's enormous,* he thought. Then Brian heard a voice deep within him say, *don't just sit there and be executed.* Brian coiled and lunged as Tootie pulled the Python's trigger. Brian sensed heat and saw the flash but heard and felt nothing. A thousand thoughts, images, and emotions raced through his brain as he fell at Tootie's feet. Tootie took careful aim and pulled the trigger but the hammer fell on a spent case.

Don't much matter, Tootie thought, looking at the bloody pulp of Brian's head and face.

The sirens were closer. Tootie took a last look at Brian, then ran south on Hoover. He loaded the revolver from his pants pocket as he went.

Gradually, a flicker of light returned to Brian's mind. Not enough to create conscious thought but sufficient to illuminate a dim, place between life and death. Sirens filled his head but gained no purchase in his thoughts. The sidewalk embraced him as gravity increased its pull. Suspended between up and down, Brian felt a profound sadness as the light and sirens began to fade.

Don't lay down, lad! Fight!" his father called from the depths of his slowly spinning mind.

A second voice spoke to him.

You've got this, Brian! Hang on!" Danny whispered in his ear.

Brian felt his father's hand on his chest and Danny Lugo's breath in his ear. His eyes fluttered and opened.

At 77th station Quint King was working mid-pm watch with Charlie Bender. They had cleared roll call and were deciding where to get a cup of coffee when the first call was broadcast.

77th Street units, a shooting in progress, Hoover and 79th Streets. PR reports numerous shots being fired. One man down... Any 77th units to handle code 3, identify.

Charlie and Quint ran to their police car. Charlie jumped into the driver's seat, fired the engine up, threw the vehicle into gear and mashed the gas pedal as Quint pulled his door closed with one hand and keyed the mike with his other.

"12X45 is in route," Quint said over the scream of the siren.

12X45, roger. Additional on your call, suspects are a male black in dark clothing and a male white. Both suspects are armed with handguns.

"Shit, that's Brian!" Quint said.

He keyed the mike again and broadcast, "X45, advise units the male white is possibly an off-duty police officer. Can we get an airship on it?"

Officers throughout the division interrupted everything and raced in the direction of 79th and Hoover. A line of police cars roared from the station parking lot. They careened down 76th Street toward the call, all with emergency lights whirling and sirens wailing. At Figueroa and 76th Street each police car bottomed out into a dip in the roadway. Quint and Charlie's car hit the dip, slammed into the pavement then recoiled into the air, leaving behind a spray of sparks and exhaust parts. Charlie's foot never left the accelerator. The engine screamed until the drive tires grabbed the asphalt again. Charlie held the pedal to the floor until just before reaching Hoover. He braked hard, then powered into a left turn onto Hoover. Goodyear Eagles smoking and screeching, they drifted through the intersection and sped toward the call. The vibrating but recognizable voice of Scooter Kellerman broadcast from the cabin of the helicopter that streaked nose-down across the night sky.

Air Ten is in route to Hoover and 79th. ETA 30 seconds.

Charlie screeched to a stop behind Q-Tip's body, which was sprawled on the sidewalk. The headlights and rotating red and blue lights of the cop car cast a macabre light on the scene.

Quint detected the telltale sulfurous odor of gun smoke hanging in the night air as he approached the dead gangster. "This guy's done," Quint said.

Charlie scanned his surroundings and saw a bicycle disappear around the corner a block away. He separated from Quint and watched for a layoff man.

Charlie spoke into the night, *Y'all not getting me, again.*

Quint kicked away the pistol that lay near Q-Tip's hand and moved toward the fence which he leaned around and shined his flashlight behind. First, he saw a .45-caliber Colt pistol on the ground, then something else. He stepped closer and stopped. His heart rose into his throat.

"Brian," Quint whispered. He stood staring at a bloody hunk of flesh that resembled an ear. It had a flap of skin covered with matted, blood-drenched hair attached to it. Blood was splattered on the fence and puddled on the cracked and dirty sidewalk. Quint looked frantically for Brian, but he was nowhere to be seen. Charlie stepped next to Quint and looked down. He immediately wanted a cigarette. They heard police cars arrive and the airship overhead but didn't look up.

"Look!" Quint said. His light picked up a line of red splatters on the sidewalk leading south.

A shot cracked down the street and the two cops took off running, following the bloody trail.

When gunshots sounded outside, all boxing activities in the Hoover Street Gym ceased. Everyone, including Dee, directed his attention toward the front door, except Boomer, who ran to the pay phone on the wall and dialed 911. A group of people gathered around the door and watched a flood of emergency vehicles streak past the gym. A premonition overcame Dee, *"Brian."* He felt weak in the knees and slightly nauseated as he shouldered his way outside and walked across the parking lot to Hoover. A block down the street he saw two officers looking at a figure on the sidewalk and Dee started walking toward them, slowly at first, and then he began to pick up speed. As he neared the scene the report of a single shot sounded farther down the street. Dee broke into a run and followed in the steps of the two police officers ahead of him.

Tootie had covered the two blocks to 81st Street then looked back. Hoover Street was filled with flashing lights. He sprinted to Kim's liquor store and jerked the screen door open. Mr. Kim's grandson squatted near the door, stocking shelves from a cardboard box. Hearing gunshots, followed soon after by the slam of the screen door, Kim rushed from the back room just as Tootie grabbed a handful of his grandson's thick black hair. Tootie jerked the slip of a boy to his feet and jammed the muzzle of the revolver into the side of the boy's head.

"You gonna hide me or I'm gonna kill this little punk!"

Kim's face steeled. "Let go, I hide," he approached Tootie, talking constantly as he moved toward him. "No problem. Let grandson go," Kim said.

Tootie brought the gun up toward Mr. Kim. "You better get back, Kim I'll kill all y'all!" he yelled.

Seeing his chance, the boy grabbed the hand that had him by the hair. He peeled Tootie's thumb away from his grip and bent it back. He twisted, and a distinct "pop" emitted from Tootie's hand. The move broke Tootie's grasp on the boy's hair and diverted the killer's attention at a critical moment. Kim let the military knife drop from his coat sleeve into his hand. Tootie's finger jerked the trigger but the gun didn't fire. Puzzled, he looked at it and saw the web of a bloody hand smashed between the hammer and cylinder.

His face a mask of blood, Brian reached around Tootie, grabbed the pistol with both hands, drew it to his chest and dropped to the floor, pulling Tootie with him. He brought his knees to his chest, curled his body around the pistol, closed his eyes and held onto the Python tightly; he had finally found Danny's gun and resolved never to release it. In an attempt to free the revolver from his grip Brian sank his teeth into Tootie's arm until they touched. Tootie bellowed and pulled on the gun. He kicked at the bloody figure that was wrapped around his hand like a snake with its fangs buried into his flesh. As they rolled on the floor, Tootie reached into his jacket pocket with his left hand and retrieved his 9-mm pistol. He pressed the muzzle against Brian's bloody, matted hair and his finger went to the trigger.

A moment before Tootie pulled the trigger a hand cupped his chin and twisted it sharply to the left. The gun discharged harmlessly, sending a bullet through a bottle of Jim Beam on a shelf. Mr. Kim was behind him, his legs wrapped around Tootie's torso and holding the murderer's head to the side. The former ROK marine rammed the seven-inch blade of his combat knife into the space between Tootie's neck, clavicle, and trapezoid muscle, severing the subclavian artery. Kim's knife made a wet sucking sound as he pulled it straight up and out of the wound. Then, with a fluid backhanded slash, Kim drew the razor-sharp blade across Tootie's throat. Gore spurted from the cut. A tug of Tootie's chin toward the ceiling caused the wound to open like a ghastly smile. Finally, Kim reached down and drove the blade to its hilt into the struggling man's lower abdomen and jerked it upwards to the killer's sternum. Gutted like a fish, Tootie's entrails spilled onto the floor. The storekeeper held him tightly until his death throes subsided, then let him slip to the floor.

Brian was losing consciousness. In a dream state he heard voices, heavy footfalls, and the thwapping of helicopter blades. He fought to stay awake and hold on to the pistol until he felt arms close around him and lift him from the floor. Brian looked up into Danny Lugo's face. He released the gun to its rightful owner and then drifted off.

HOW THE BOY ATE CABBAGE

At 81st street, a police officer stepped in front of Dee and would allow him to go no further. So Dee stood with a rapidly growing group of bystanders outside Kim's Market. Over the next few minutes, cops, firefighters and paramedics ran in and out of the well-lit portal of Kim's store. Word began to circulate through the crowd that Officer O'Callahan was inside and had been killed. A line of cops approached the crowd and ordered them to move back. The police helicopter that had been hovering over the scene began its descent. The night sky above turned to day and the roar of the ghetto bird overwhelmed all other sounds. To the crowd's surprise and delight, Air Ten landed in the intersection of Hoover and 82nd. The helicopter's blades kicked up clouds of dust and trash as its skids settled onto the asphalt. As soon as it landed two firefighters emerged from the store with Brian suspended between them. Their arms were joined beneath his thighs and behind his back, forming a chair for the injured cop. As they scurried toward the aircraft and carefully deposited him into the rear seat his bandaged head hung forward, his chin resting on his chest. Immediately behind the firefighters was a paramedic who climbed into the bird next to the officer. Just before the helicopter hatch was closed Dee saw Charlie Bender run, bent at the waist, to the airship and hand the paramedic something wrapped in a bloody handkerchief. The flashing emergency lights coupled with the airship's navigational lights and spinning rotors created a strobe effect over the chaotic scene. The door slammed shut, the engine revved and the blades sliced the air, once again kicking up debris and blowing blue baseball caps from the heads of several youngsters in the crowd. Sitting in the front passenger seat the observer, Scooter Kellerman, gave Charlie the thumbs up as Air Ten rose into the night.

Charlie lit a cigarette and watched the helicopter's lights as they became indiscernible from the lights of downtown LA. Dee managed to catch Charlie's eye and waved him over to the yellow crime scene tape he was standing behind.

"Officer Bender, was it Brian?" Dee asked.

Charlie walked up, silently lifted the tape and motioned for Dee to follow him. The two men walked to the far side of the store and stood in the parking lot while Charlie shared what little he knew with the boxer.

"Thanks for telling me, sir. I know it doesn't seem natural, but Brian's kinda like a brother to me. I know he felt somehow Mo-Mo's death was his fault and it isn't," Dee said. "I also have to tell you something else and you might hate me for it and I understand, but I've gotta say it."

Charlie held up his hand, "I know. I ain't sorted the thing out in my head jes yet. But I sure don't hold you no grudge, son."

"Thank you, sir, I've been carrying that around with me for a long time now." Then almost as an afterthought Dee said, "Officer Bender, did Brian ever talk about his daddy and some gangster named Beppe Fazio?"

"No, why?" Charlie answered.

Dee told Charlie about Fazio showing up at the gym and then he shared what Fazio had done to Brian's father. Charlie listened intently and at times even jotted notes into the small notebook he pulled from his shirt pocket.

"Y'all have this feller's phone number, huh? I want ya to give 'em a call and set up a meet. Tell 'em y'all decided to accept his offer of help. Then let me know when and where. Figure you kin do that Dee?"

"Sure, but what…"

Charlie cut him off. "Don't fret on it, I'll show this Fazio feller how the boy ate cabbage."

Two days after the shoot-out, Brian lay in a coma at USC Medical Center. Across town, Charlie Bender had taken a string of days off and was sitting at a bistro in Westwood Village sipping the first two-dollar cup of coffee he had ever purchased. Two tables from Charlie sat Beppe Fazio, munching on a bagel and waiting for Dee Wallace to show up.

In the days following the Brian O'Callahan shooting, Dapper Davy Treats completed the follow-up reports that closed the investigation into the murder of Police Officer Danny Lugo. His report included two eyewitness accounts of the event. Mr. Kim corroborated Dee's story. The last line of Detective Davy Treat's report read. *All suspects deceased, murder weapon recovered, case closed.*

WELDED SHUT

The night Brian was shot, Doctor Stanley Sykovski had been watching the news when a bleached blond newscaster recounted with a scowl on her face how a suspended Los Angeles police officer had engaged in a running gun battle in South Central Los Angeles. She shook her head as she added that the shooting had resulted in the deaths of "two youthful residents." When Brian's Academy photo flashed onto the television screen, Sykovski jumped to his feet and picked up the telephone. Within thirty minutes Air Ten had landed on the practice field at UCLA, picked the doctor up, and delivered him to USCMC. An hour later, Dr. Sykovski performed the first of several delicate procedures on Brian. Afterward, he'd assembled a renowned team of physicians to help him provide the follow-up care the young officer would need. Once stabilized, he had Brian transferred to Cedars Sinai Hospital and oversaw his treatment.

After his initial surgery, Brian was kept in an induced coma to allow the swelling of his brain to subside. Two weeks later his doctors began weaning him off the drugs that kept him unconscious. For two more months he remained heavily sedated and semi-comatose. In early June he was taken off all sedation and doctors, nurses, and friends maintained a bedside vigil in anticipation of Brian waking.

Mandy Green spent as much time at Brian's bedside as her schedule allowed and the walls of Brian's hospital room were covered with drawings and letters from her children. Her son Donavan had overseen a get-well card campaign at his school in which his entire class had participated.

On a sunny morning three months after being shot, Brian slowly opened an eye. The other was hidden under the gauze wrapping on his head. Charlie Bender was sleeping in a chair next to his bed, a black marker dangling from his fingers. Brian had difficulty focusing and blinked several times. Before slipping back to an insentient state he saw the hazy image of Danny Lugo standing behind Charlie. Danny put his hands on Charlie's shoulders and the slumbering man stirred. Brian struggled to say something but was unable to keep from falling back to sleep. In his dreams, he heard the indestructible Charlie Bender at his bedside, whispering for him to awaken. Brian slowly came around. Quint sat slouched in the chair where Charlie had been. A white straw cowboy hat was pushed back on his head, his arms were crossed on his plaid, pearl-buttoned shirt, and his blue-jeaned legs were kicked out in front of him.

When he saw Brian's eye open Quint uncrossed his cowboy boots and sat upright. "Hey pard, you hear me?" he said louder than intended.

Brian nodded slightly and cleared his throat.

Quint picked up the handset attached to Brian's bed, pushed the intercom button, and spoke into the device. "Would ya let Doctor Sykovski know that Brian O'Callahan is conscious, please?"

A pleasant female voice came from the handset. "The doctor is doing his rounds on the floor. I'll let him know."

Within moments the room was full of nurses and doctors. The crowd parted as a beaming Dr. Sykovski stepped into the room.

"I do good work," he announced.

"Yes, sir," came Brian's raspy reply. He managed a crooked smile.

Sykovski glanced at his wristwatch and said, "Brian, I'm due in surgery in a bit. You rest, I'll check on you later." At the door, the doctor turned and added, "Welcome back son."

Several nurses and technicians lingered in the room, while Brian noticed something on the bed sheet that had been neatly folded back at his waist. Attached to a 3X4 inch index card pinned to the sheet was the Congressional Medal of Honor.

Written in thick black letters on the card were the words, *Our Hero.*

Brian gently touched the deep blue ribbon that was affixed to the medal. "Quint, where's Charlie?" he croaked.

Quint adjusted his seat in the chair and took a drink of water from the pink plastic cup on the nightstand before he spoke.

"After you were shot ol' Charlie disappeared for a couple days. When he came back he sat in this here chair day and night just watching you. Did that til the doc said you were gonna make it. Next day he turned in his papers and retired. No party, nothing, just headed home to those mountains he come from. But before he left, he came in here and pinned his medal to yer sheet. He also left the card." Quint set a yellow cigar box on Brian's chest, "An this."

Brian fumbled with the box until he was able to open it. It held Charlie's braided copper bracelet and Beppe Fazio's gold ring with the diamond-encrusted horseshoe. Brian gingerly lifted the bracelet and slipped it around his wrist. He then plucked the ring from the box and squeezed it in the palm of his hand. At the bottom of the box was a slip of paper that had been folded in half. Brian unfolded the note which had a single line printed on it. It read: *Bri, you ever meet a feller who really needs killin', be patient, somebody's likely to do it for ya.*

Brian folded the note and returned it to the box. "But I woke up earlier and Charlie was here, sitting in that chair where you were," he asserted.

Quint clasped his hands together and looked at the floor and said, "Bri, Charlie had cancer, had er bad. Doctors figure he knew long before it was diagnosed. He refused treatment an jes went on back to Virginia."

"No! I saw him," Brian insisted. "Maybe he's back in town."

Quint shook his head slowly. "Ain't possible, partner. Ah got a phone call a few minutes ago from Charlie's brother. He said Charlie died bout an hour ago. Said he was sitting in a rocker on the front porch of his home place an' jes slipped away."

Brian turned his head and closed his eyes. Soon he was asleep, dreaming. *He saw his father in his prime, bouncing on the balls of his feet. A referee dressed in a white, long-sleeved shirt and a bow tie held Seamus O'Callahan's gloved hand above his head. Afterward, he and Brian walked together into the locker room and stood in front of Locker 32. Brian tried to open it but found the locker had been welded shut. He looked back at his father, but Charlie Bender stood in his place. Charlie snapped his lighter open, lit a cigarette, took a drag and blew a series of smoke rings, which floated toward the locker. Brian watched the rings glide past him then vanish into the vents at the top of the gray locker door. He whirled around to face Charlie. Only the fragrance of English*

Leather cologne remained.

Brian slept easily that night and many nights to follow. He dreamed of his father and Charlie often...and never dreamed of Danny Lugo again.

END

Made in the USA
Middletown, DE
13 June 2018